I hope Tempest's story lifts your spirits

John Lack
11/30/2018

Tempest's Arc

JOHN LACK

Printed by CreateSpace

ISBN: 1519714335
ISBN-13: 978-1519714336

For Ditha, Christy, Nadya and Dhea

"Philosophy is written in this grand book - I mean the universe - which stands continually open to our gaze, but it cannot be understood unless one first learns to comprehend the language and interpret the characters in which it is written. It is written in the language of mathematics, and its characters are triangles, circles and other geometrical figures, without which it is humanly impossible to understand a single word of it; without these, one is wandering about in a dark labyrinth."   *Galileo Galilei*

CONTENTS

	Acknowledgments	ix
1	Tempest	10
2	Tempest's Friends	16
3	School Days	22
4	A Little Tickle	30
5	Repeating Decimals	35
6	Laid Up	42
7	Treating Tempest	45
8	Our Little Girl Gets Help	50
9	First Impressions	57
10	Fast Friends	62
11	The Dirty Little Secret	69
12	The Final Session	81
13	Tuber Something	88
14	A Surprise Exit	93
15	Seeking Help	101

16   The Stars Prepare to Align   106

17   Return to Averton   112

18   Orientation   121

19   First Week of the New Year   127

20   Fast Forward to Seventh Grade   133

21   School Days and Nights   143

22   Zurck is Not a Jerk   153

23   A Family Affair   159

24   The Written Hypothesis   167

25   An Old Friend Returns   176

26   Christmas Presents   185

27   Zurck Returns   195

28   Thank You Sensei   204

29   Wedding Bells   210

30   Leather Books and Red Flags   218

31   My Test Tube Baby   227

32   Junior Prom   237

33   A Working Girl   248

34	First Night	257
35	Read Any Good Books Lately?	263
36	The News Gets Out	272
37	Senior Year Begins	275
38	Good News and Bad News	284
39	The Unthinkable	290
40	A Frosty Thanksgiving	297
41	Everything is Not OK	303
42	Life Without Caleb	306
43	A New Start	311
44	The Revelation	316
45	A Measured Start	326
46	Same Day Different Year	331
47	A Surprise Visit	338
48	The Day in the Spotlight	347
49	Popping Something	356
50	Home for Christmas	362

51	Christmas Present	372
52	A Trip to Europe	379
53	Change in Plans	386
54	The Days Before	393
55	A Lifetime of Regret	397
56	Words from Beyond	406
57	Where Did the Dollar Go?	414
	About the Author	419

John Lack

ACKNOWLEDGMENTS

To my math teachers. Collectively my favorite educators, despite their regularly succumbing to the understandable impulse to launch an arsenal of blackboard erasers and colored chalk in reaction to my repeated classroom disrupting comments. Being an attentive and wiry lad, I deftly dodged the heatedly thrown projectiles and grew to love "The Math". With the exception of one stick of yellow chalk, a direct hit to the forehead, they never laid a glove on me. The potentially lethal round was provoked by an unnecessary remark regarding a fellow classmate's mention of her newly made acquaintance Phillip Sill. "Phil Sill, Ah yes, I know his brother window." Who could ever forget that magical little gem? Hurling the "attention getter" in response was indeed more than warranted and entirely excusable.

Special thanks to our niece Nadya for the cover artwork.

Special appreciation to Dan of Bedford, New York for his tremendous help and ongoing support.

CHAPTER ONE:

Tempest

In an average sized small town, near the center of a loosely defined region referred to as upstate New York, there once lived an unusual girl. At age nine she fell within the routine measurements to be considered of regular size for a girl of her years. Despite her red hair, she was often lost in a crowd of other youngsters since she was fairly commonplace in appearance and had not yet acquired the ravishing beauty that would one day turn the head of many an Avertonian. In the early stages of what was considered the conventional schooling for an adolescent, she performed modestly above what was generally considered slightly above standard. Upon first look there was really nothing special about her. A closer assessment would reveal two very significant exceptions that separated her from the typical child. First, she often did relatively remarkable things in what normal people would describe to be a most particular style. In addition there was her very distinctive name. She was known to all as Tempest Arrck.

To many in Averton, Tempest's most noteworthy exploits were linked to a love for her favorite school subject. Her mathematical deeds spotlighted a certain brightness not often found in the average child. The capability was revealed in a variety of ways. A casual inquiry into her family makeup was a surefire means to draw this cleverness to the surface. When asked about the Arrcks, Tempest would playfully provide two pieces of information, indicating that she was the third of four children and that she had one older brother. She omitted the fact that she had an older sister and a younger brother. A query into her family structure was never met with a complete answer. For Tempest, the composition of the Arrck household was a ready-made word problem.

In what would one day be acknowledged as her well above average mind, she was intent on determining if the inquiring party could calculate the existence and order of her missing siblings based on the specified knowns. Although Tempest might have found it very intriguing, she was regularly chastised for administering the mathematical quiz. Despite continual rebuke, the young girl never failed to take the opportunity to introduce the riddle whenever the conditions were presented. Tempest determined early on that the most bitter disapproval came from those least mathematically inclined.

Tempest's parents were very usual people who fit into the normal mold and went about life with little fanfare. Both parents were natives of their upstate New York community. Each had graduated from the local high school, ranking squarely in the middle of the academic center of their respective classes. They grew up in average family dwellings and made a home together after becoming joined in marriage. Tempest's father played high school baseball. His rate of success with the bat was slightly above average for the team that had eleven wins and ten losses in his senior year. His divergence from the norm was on the football field, once leading Averton to a memorable well above average season. Tempest's mother had a passing interest in music and was sometimes second, sometimes third chair flutist for the high school orchestra. In the school yearbook, she was also recognized as having been an alternate on the archery team.

Although this story is more about Tempest than her family, it is instructive in understanding the relatively mediocre world in which she was raised to be aware of the circumstances surrounding the naming of her nearest kin. The given names of the Arrck family may in fact be the most distinctive aspect of Tempest's very average to moderately above average family. One source of the interesting labels could be traced back to the impact of strong, family based naming traditions provided by Tempest's maternal grandparents. Tempest's mother's maiden name was Mann. In the Mann family the given male names needed to rhyme. The Mann brothers were Stan, Dan and Francis, aka Fran. This was considered by some to have been the main reason Tempest's mother found a comforting attraction to Mark Arrck. The rhyming convention in the Mann family did not however completely extend to the women. Although Tempest's mother was named Diane.

Tempest's older brother was named Noah. For those who needed it spelled out, Tempest, who was well-known for being a master of the obvious, would readily refer to her brother as Noah's Arrck. This name was unplanned. The agreed upon appellation was Tarkington. Day to day he would be called Tark. The change came about when Tempest's very young parents were providing biological information to the local hospital administrator. In that fateful meeting her father stammered when providing the answer to the question regarding the newborn's given name and "No, Ah" was recorded by the staffer. When the hospital employee made mention of how creative a name they had chosen, Noah's youthful parents were so delighted to have done anything that anyone would consider remotely creative, they proudly took credit for the selection.

The name of Tempest's older sister was the product of a game of distraction designed on the fly by Mark and Diane to take the soon to be mother's mind off of the quickening contractions while on route to the hospital. Diane closed her eyes in an uncharacteristic effort to bring some pure randomness to name selection. The first name she saw upon opening them was agreed to become the identity of their first daughter. As chance would have it, their car was passing the local beauty salon. Based on the neon logo that graced Joan's nail emporium, Tempest's sister would go through life as Joan. As Tempest was quick to point out her sister was Joan of Arrck's. The wave of creativity was later attributed to a spike in cognitive ability brought on by the pain of childbirth. In many ways it could have been worse. There was also a parking garage in sight at the time. If a boy had been delivered, he would have been christened Carpark Arrck.

To further illuminate the foundation of the one of a kind branding possessed by the Arrck clan, there was also a clear and sound basis for the naming of Tempest's youngest sibling.

In a moment of nostalgia, after the untimely death of her brother Francis, Diane decided that their second son should carry with him through life a rhyming name. This commemorative motivation led to Tempest's younger brother being named Clark. To provide a complete accounting to all the limbs of the family tree it should be noted that Tempest was born during what was generally referred to as hurricane season.

All four of the Arrck children attended the local public school system and each was an average to slightly above average student. They ranged across a six year age span and as a result attended grades from second through seventh. All but Noah attended classes in the same building. The four lived close enough to walk to any Averton school. On rainy days, Mark would drive the three elementary school students to class and continue on to work opening up the shoe store, in which he was a part owner, a few minutes earlier than usual. Just about everyone in town knew that on rainy days you could purchase footwear at "Two by Two Shoes" any time after eight thirty. When the weather was bad, Diane would drive Noah to the junior high school on the way to her job at the nearby library.

There was really nothing very special about the Arrcks. In fact, the only aspect of the Arrck family that really stood out was their names. But even here there were limits to the renown. Since most people were unaware of the unorthodox spelling of their last name, the family was rarely bothered with unimaginative pirate humor or frivolous buccaneer references. Although Joan and Noah had quite recognizable handles, if not tied to their last name they would barely raise an eyebrow. Neither would the names Mark or Clark without the rhyming surname in tow. But the name Tempest was different. No one else in their average sized small town shared the same title. When anyone simply uttered the name Tempest, everyone knew who you were talking about.

Although the nine-year-old girl lived in a slightly above average sized small town and was herself considered fairly average in most ways that anyone might be interested in measuring, she was anything but ordinary. Tempest was very different from every other person in her town. Although the world around her was average, or slightly above average, normal or usual, Tempest's love for numbers and math-centric view grew from an obsession that everything around her needed to be precise. She detested middling comparisons and mediocre terms to describe her world. She abhorred close enough assessments and reviled estimated answers.

In Tempest's domain she was nine years and three hundred and thirty four days old when she entered the fifth grade. The prior year she was a C+ student, but earned an A in math. The exactness that numbers brought to her run-of-the-mill existence was a haven of precision and an oasis from the "close enough". She found it comforting. Two plus two wasn't sometimes four, it was always four. Seven times nine wasn't about sixty three, it was sixty three. Exactitude and truth mattered to Tempest. This unrelenting quest to seek out truth, precision and accuracy would ultimately serve to define her life, as she shaped the world of all those around her.

Chapter Two: Tempest's Friends

Like most young girls who grew up in the same town as their parents, went to the same school for their entire lives and lived in the same house since birth, Tempest had a number of close friends. If you were to ask Tempest who was her very best girlfriend, her answer would no doubt be Arlene Sharp. The Sharps were one of the few families that had recently moved to Averton, arriving weeks after the birth of their only daughter. This made Arlene as close to being a lifelong resident as possible without actually being one. She would never be considered a dyed-in-the-wool Avertonian. Given Arlene's official resident status as it pertained to Averton, she would often be heard to say that she was a girl without a town. Arlene's relationship with Tempest was such a defining aspect of the newcomer's being that whenever anyone would ask Arlene to say something about herself she would immediately answer without a hint of hesitation, "I am Tempest Arrck's best friend."

There were a handful of other young women who considered themselves best friends with Tempest. She was for that matter a very likeable girl. The only other female confidant Tempest might agree was on her short list of best buddies was Carla Blount. The Blounts had lived in Averton since before this piece of upstate New York was even called Averton. Their family had a long history of leading the faithful opposition to whatever political machine dominated Averton politics at the time. Whenever there was a local election, you could count on there being at least one Blount on the ballot. It was rare however, that there was a celebration at Blount headquarters the evening of the vote count. Over the years the immediate and extended family had grown so large they were often accused of attempting to dominate local politics through the birthing process. Because of the failure to regularly gain public office however, the Blounts needed to rely on other sources of income to support their rather large family. Many Blounts earned a living running the local mushroom plant. It did not go unnoticed by pundits that in both of these pursuits the Blounts were well-practiced in shoveling the crap.

There was also a young man who Tempest considered a very close acquaintance. He was more a brother than a friend. His name was Caleb Baxter. The Baxters lived in the house next to the Arrck's slightly above average home on Lincoln Avenue. Young Caleb Baxter shared the same date of birth as Tempest. Early in their young lives there had been mild speculation around certain quarters that died out quickly that Caleb and Tempest had actually been switched at birth. The basis of the theory was that Tempest's physical appearance was much better aligned with Paul Baxter. Some of the locals would even say that Tempest had signs of the "Baxter nose", leading to other more nefarious forms of speculation. Additionally, her love for mathematics was much better in synch with that of Mr. Baxter, a math professor at the local community college.

This was fairly scant evidence however and over time the gossip became barely a whisper. Tempest was an Arrck and lived in her home with the rest of the Arrcks and had a bedroom, that if she opened her window, she would be able to speak with her friend Caleb any time day or night.

Both the Baxters and the Arrcks had already completed dinner on that Tuesday evening in early September and Tempest went to her room, as she usually would on a warm school night and opened that window. Caleb had not yet arrived but moments later she heard the familiar sound of his window raising through its rather snug frame. Just as though she was continuing a conversation that had stretched for years on end Tempest began, "Did you get a chance to look at the homework that old "Tomato Head" Hessing gave us for tomorrow? I can't believe he would load us down on the first day of school." "Not only did I look at it, I showed it to my dad. He was surprised that we were jumping right into this material in fifth grade math," was Caleb's answer. Tempest then said, "Well, I haven't had a chance to look at it that closely but this repeating decimal idea he was speaking about in class has made me a little uneasy."

Tempest took her math studies seriously; some might say a little too seriously. When she first confronted fractions back in the third grade, she was so shaken by the notion that a whole number could be broken into pieces that she hardly ate for four and a half days. It took Mr. Baxter to finally talk her down from that intellectual ledge. Her third grade arithmetic teacher had thrown up her hands days earlier when Tempest refused to accept the idea of adding and subtracting partial numbers using a least common denominator. "Why is it my decision as to what this number is to be called? I understand that one half is also four eights, but why am I allowed to just change its value on my own," she was heard to say.

It was only after Mr. Baxter came to the rescue that Tempest reluctantly accepted the concept. Once he was able to get the distraught student to listen he carefully provided a simple example for her to contemplate. While sitting at the Baxter family kitchen table he patiently took an apple and cut it in half. He asked Tempest, "Do you agree these are the same?" Tempest studied the two halves and said, "They are not exactly the same." Knowing Tempest's penchant for exactitude Mr. Baxter replied, "If I had more precision in my cut and had selected a more perfect apple would you agree these are the same?" Tempest's response was, "Well, I guess I can imagine that they are the same." Mr. Baxter said, "Good, now watch this." He proceeded to cut one half of the apple into four pieces and then asked, "Tempest, do you agree these are the same?" She responded, "No they are not the same, there are four pieces on this side and one piece on that side." "But Tempest, would you agree there is just as much apple on both sides assuming the apple was perfect and my initial cut was proper?" he asked. After a few minutes of consideration Tempest reluctantly agreed but still had some reservations about the methodology.

Caleb's father then asked for her attention and cut the other half of the apple into quarters, leaving eight total pieces and said, "The reason we do this is because sometimes you need to add fractions." Taking three pieces from one side of the apple and placing it next to the four pieces from the other half he said, "This is how you get seven eights of an apple or of anything else you are looking to add. You have to be able to add fractions of a whole for business purposes or recipes and the like and this is how we do it."

Tempest once again pondered the process and the underlying concepts and reluctantly agreed to the basic logic behind the example. After a few more moments of consideration Tempest finally rose from her chair, thanked her teacher with a hug and left to play in the yard with Caleb. Once the door had closed behind her, Mr. Baxter remarked, "For a little kid she asks some tough questions."

Caleb was well aware of the apple incident and many of Tempest's other prior harangues and diatribes regarding the need for precision and upon hearing her concern knew where it could all lead if left unaddressed. Not wanting to relive those trying days, he attempted to ease her objections about repeating decimals by making light of her previous antics. "What are you going to do this time, lock yourself in your room until you croak?" Tempest responded mimicking some comments she had heard one of the Blounts use when referencing pranks employed by his political opposition. "Don't make light of this. You know when the hooey people toss around willy-nilly to make their case doesn't add up it can drive me up a wall." Caleb knew his companion all too well and apologized for his careless remark. Being such good friends, his neighbor thanked him for his understanding.

John Lack

Chapter Three: School Days

The next morning was clear and bright and the two young scholars, equipped with light jackets to guard against the late summer morning chill, walked together to the Averton Elementary School, which was well within walking distance of their homes. Joan and Clark walked along not far behind and within earshot of Tempest and her friend. Somewhere around halfway through the journey Caleb summoned the nerve to ask, "Did you do the math homework?" Tempest answered, "I couldn't get passed the first question." Caleb's cautious reply was, "What do you mean? It was easy." Tempest stopped and took out her work. The first question on the paper read, "Express four divided by six as a decimal." Tempest had written .6666 with sixes continuing until she reached the bottom of the page. There must have been three hundred sixes behind the initial decimal point. She paused saying, "Wait a second," took out a pencil and squeezed two more sixes at the very end of the page. Then looking up at Caleb she said, "I don't get it. This still isn't right."

Joan, who had been witness to the least common denominator affair, rolled her eyes and said to Clark, "Well little brother, here we go again." Clark being very young and unaware of what might be coming next and unfamiliar with the context of Joan's remark said, "Where are we going? I thought we were walking to school." Joan, who was average to slightly above average in most categories, had a better than ordinary comedic sense and commented back to her youngest sibling, "We are going to school all right. The one where any sense of flexible thinking gets left at the front door." The truth was that Joan was just being overly critical of her only sister. Tempest could be flexible and did allow for leeway in some areas. She didn't obsess about her looks or the condition of her room, she just provided no quarter for inaccuracy when it came to the one subject that she truly cared about. She needed precision when it came to the numbers.

Caleb looked at Tempest's homework. He had a feeling where all this might be headed and said, "Why don't we wait until math class this afternoon and see what Mr. Hessey has to say about this. There must be some math trick we haven't learned yet." Tempest responded, "There is a trick, but it is nonsense. Didn't you read the book where it explained rounding to the nearest decimal? This is just a nice way of saying close is good enough." When Tempest uttered those words her body gave a slight tremble as she had nearly combined the two words that could trigger her most well-known trademark reaction. Everyone who knew Tempest was aware to never use the phrase "close enough" in her presence. Those who were unaware of the consequences or mistakenly spoke the words were treated to a taste of why she was appropriately named Tempest.

Caleb was a responsible young lad. Keeping focused on the task at hand he knew the four needed to continue their trek to school or risk being late. He convinced his friend that she should wait until math class that afternoon before going off half-cocked, using a slang firearms related term that was common amongst the people in this section of upstate New York. Tempest being highly principled but not unreasonable, agreed to move on and the group from Lincoln Avenue arrived at the Averton Elementary School with time to spare before class was to begin.

Upon entering the school, Tempest said good-bye to her sister and hugged her little brother before they all moved off to their respective classrooms. Caleb and Tempest proceeded to room five with the other thirty five or so fifth graders that attended Averton Elementary. Years before they would have been entering room eleven but when Tempest was in second grade she made the suggestion that first graders should be in room one, second graders in room two and so on up the line. Prior to that, the rooms were arranged in a hodgepodge of numbers that made little sense. The administrator agreed that this was a worthy request and over one summer the change was made. Even at that very young age, those around her were treated to the orderly precision of Tempest's mind.

Tempest and Caleb made their way across the front of the classroom, towards the window, where the alphabetical arranging of the students dictated that most of the As, Bs and Cs be located. There were two As, one being Tempest, but more than a fair representation of Bs as the various scions of the Blount family tree accounted for nearly half of an entire row. Tempest hugged Carla Blount. Carla missed the first day of school due to a nagging cough. Tempest had not seen her close friend in nearly a month as contrasting summer plans had kept them apart. Now, for the remainder of the school year, they would once again see each other on a daily basis.

As the clock approached eight, the children were dutifully finding their assigned seats when Mr. Hessey made his way into the classroom. He had clearly been at his previously occupied desk earlier and gone out of the room, maybe to the teacher's lounge, to grab some coffee or cop a quick kiss and a hug from Miss Hankins, the second grade teacher. Their relationship was one of the worst kept secrets in Averton. Seeing that Mr. Hessey was a bachelor and Miss Hankins was a Miss, the only direction that the administration gave to both of them was to keep it low key. They had done a fairly good job of staying under the radar with the exception of one incident during graduation two years prior. Mr. Hessey did not realize the microphone was on when he made his now famous on stage comment to Miss Hankins, suggesting that he wanted to see her naked. It brought a gasp from the adults, giggles from the graduating sixth graders, a reprimand for Mr. Hessey and some embarrassment for Miss Hankins.

When the classroom was finally settled, Caleb was seated immediately behind Tempest. Carla was directly to her right. Arlene Sharp's desk was three quarters of the way across the room. Tempest did not get a chance to say anything to Arlene that morning as she arrived promptly before the bell rang, which was her standard practice. When Arlene settled into her seat she gave Tempest an exaggerated wave. That bell would ring eighteen times during the school day. Half would signal an all clear for movement between classes. The other half would define the time to start the next lesson. Although the students in grade five only left room five for their lunch break and gym class, the repetitious signal was necessary to accommodate other between class passages required by the other seven classrooms full of students.

Mr. Robert Hessey was a jack-of-all-trades. It was his job to remain with the students from eight in the morning until sixteen minutes past two in the afternoon and provide instruction for every subject from history to math. He was considered a good teacher. The thirty something native of Averton was known by most of the students as "Tomato Head" Hessey. He had been "Tomato Head" since his high school days. No one remembered why he was given his nickname and no one really cared. But everyone knew the name and used it.

The first subject for that Wednesday, the second day of school that year was history. In the fifth grade, the students in the Averton School District moved beyond accounts of America's past to a more international backdrop with a course curriculum titled European Studies. The lesson plan spanned the beginning of the Dark Ages through the Renaissance and ended with the time just prior to the First World War. Mr. Hessey always looked forward to a class, which if he was on schedule, would happen to take place the week of Thanksgiving. The material included a hasty recollection of the Protestant Reformation. One of the highlights of his semester was the student's reaction to the term, "Diet of Worms". The faces and the comments made by past pupils were standard fare at the Hessey family Thanksgiving table, which in recent years was attended by his love interest as she was not born and raised in Averton. Her family was faraway on the west coast. Today the subject would be a more mundane chapter titled, "Roman Influence on the Emerging Societies." The material would whisk "Tomato Head" back to memories of a vacation in Southern France that he and Miss Hawkins enjoyed over the summer four years earlier.

The teaching style employed by Mr. Hessey and most of the educators at Averton Elementary was a combination of textbook reading and daily lecture. Typically students were asked to read a chapter or a portion of a chapter the prior evening and the lecture would focus on key topics related to the material. To ensure class participation, Mr. Hessey would ask the students questions about the prior night's reading. Being a very orderly and systematic man, Robert would not randomly select the targets for his inquiries. He started with the first child in row one and continued through the classroom until the end of that day and began the ensuing day where his questioning left off.

From time to time he would work backwards and rather than starting with the next student he would begin the succeeding day with the last student in class and work back to the middle. When you were the alphabetically final student in "Tomato Head's" classroom you needed to be constantly on your toes. The historical grade distribution brought on by his not so

27

random dispersal of questions would indicate that his approach served to ensure more than a fair share of the Zubert children rose to the level of High School Valedictorian, while the Mainer boys, who could always see the questions coming, were barely C students.

Since it was the second day of class and it was the first day he had assigned work, Kelly Ackerly was the target for Mr. Hessey's first inquiry of the new school year. "Tomato Head" considered himself rather worldly and drew a parallel between the predictive powers of the first question of the day with that of a Buddhist shopkeeper's first morning customer. A good initial experience would portend the day's success. Seeing that this was the first question of the year, the outcome would cast a long shadow. He asked the children to open their books to Chapter One, page one and he proceeded to throw Kelly a softball. "Kelly, can you tell me what part of the world we will be studying this year?" Kelly, being a precocious little girl, replied after standing, "Yes Mr. Hessey, we will be studying Western Europe from the 1200's to the early 1900's." The year was starting off well.

Mr. Hessey had prepared the second question to be just as easy seeing that the answer was part of the title of the textbook. But Kelley had expanded her response to include the time period the students would be exploring and he had to move on to question three. A slightly more difficult question that would have required the student to have read the material. Tempest Arrck was in the crosshairs for his next inquiry.

Mr. Hessey began, "Tempest, tell me one country that we know of today which would emerge from the area in Europe we will be studying." Hessey considered this a relative softball as the map of Europe was also easily seen on the cover of the text. Tempest rose from her seat and said in a rather sure voice for a girl of nearly ten years, "To tell you the truth Mr. Hessey, I wasn't able to get to read the history material last night." There was some audible mumbling and reactive mooching from the remainder of her classmates. Mr. Hessey calmly asked, "Why were you unable to read the material Tempest?" She replied, "I was so thrown off by the first math question that I never made it that far."

Knowing Tempest's record when it came to math, Mr. Hessey patiently said, "We will get to the math this afternoon Tempest. Can you look at the map on the cover of the book and tell me one country we will be studying?" She looked down at the book, raised her head and answered, "India?" Mr. Hessey remaining tolerant said, "No Tempest, not India. Caleb, can you answer the question?" Caleb rose and answered, "France will be one of the countries we will be studying." "Tomato Head" said, "That is correct Caleb." With Caleb's answer they both took their seats. Tempest did have one excuse. The cover of the book indicated that the publisher was The Northeast India Press. She would later tell Caleb that this threw her off. As Robert was preparing to ask his third question, he knew it was going to be a long year.

Chapter Four: A Little Tickle

The size of the school building and a limited amount of space for the cafeteria meant there were three separate lunch periods scheduled daily at Averton Elementary. As far as the students were concerned, one was considered too early, one was considered too late and one was considered just right. As a fifth grader Tempest, along with members of the sixth grade, would be faced with the later timeframe. The lunchroom was a good place to meet friends and the dining period on the second day of school was a great time to find out what the rest of the fifth graders had done over the summer. Since Tempest did not have the necessary gabbing interval with Carla on day one of the semester, they made sure they sat together and were joined by Tempest's usual dining mates, Arlene and Caleb. Rounding out the table of six were the Nubbler twins, Anne and Wilma. The Nubblers had lived next to the Arrcks in the house on the side opposite of the Baxters but moved a few years ago seeking a more rural setting than midtown Averton. Tempest made her feelings about the move known by remarking, "I am not sure what your parents were thinking when they moved you two girls so far out into the sticks."

Anne and Wilma were starved for company and looked forward to the beginning of school. During the summer period they spent most of the time assisting their father tending the livestock and performing other more routine chores you tend to find on a farm. Arlene asked if there were laws to protect against exploitation of children that should prevent them from having to perform such duties. The girls responded that they didn't mind the work, in fact without it there was little else to keep them busy. Nonetheless Arlene commented, "It just doesn't seem right to have you two out slopping the hogs at your age."

Wilma and Anne were less interested in reviewing their circumstances. They knew this all too well. They were drawn to what the townies had been up to that summer. Tempest was also interested in what Arlene had been doing that August and she became the focus of attention.

Arlene Sharp's family was considered to be well off. Her father was a lawyer. Arlene's mother was a nurse practitioner for the only urologist within twenty miles. If someone in Averton had bladder or prostate issues, Mrs. Sharp had a hand in it. Although her classmate was relatively new to Averton, Arlene's mom had descended from the Mann family tree and as a result she and Tempest were second or third cousins. Being related to another classmate was not a rare occurrence for the children of Averton.

Arlene and her family usually had at least one noteworthy week of summer vacation and this year was no different. The Sharps had enjoyed seven days in Washington D.C. and during their visit were not only treated to the monuments and museums but were also lucky enough to catch a glimpse of first year President William Jefferson Clinton. The President was on one of his famous jogs and the Sharps just happened to be walking past the rear of the White House and caught the most powerful man in the world scampering through the rose garden. "Wow," said Wilma, "You have to be kidding us. Did you really see the President?" Arlene replied, "Honestly, I was a little late turning around and all I caught was his butt. My mom and dad had a much better view and said they were witness to the full spectacle of him running away in his grey sweat pants being followed by Secret Service agents." Anne remarked, "Wow, that is so cool. I have never seen a President before." Tempest also thought it was pretty amazing and commented that she would give anything to be that close to a sitting President. Since her remark had little to do with precision related to numbers, the quasi close enough reference did not rattle her in the least.

Arlene then indicated that she and her family also visited Arlington National Cemetery and prayed at the graves of the four Mann brothers who had given their lives for freedom during the Second World War. It was yet another example of three young boys serving under the same unfortunate command, with a fourth encountering an unrelated faulty parachute. That day in 1945 was a sad one in Averton and memorialized every year with the laying of a wreath by members of the VFW. Whatever the weather, on July eighth there was a solemn ceremony of remembrance. After a moment of reflection Caleb asked respectfully, "Did you see the eternal flame at President Kennedy's grave?" Arlene said, "Of course we did. You know my mother is a big JFK fan."

Tempest said to Arlene, "Sounds like you and your family had a great trip." Arlene responded, "It was good. There was a lot to see and remember. It was a little like being on a school field trip. It would have been a lot more fun if my oldest brother wasn't being such a pain. But what can you expect from an idiot." Wilma, who had a huge crush on Arlene's Brother Bill, nearly jumped across the table, which would have been an interesting feat for the young woman who usually beat her sister to the dinner table. "What did he do? What did he do?" The words came flying out of Wilma's mouth accompanied by fragments of the snack cake she was in the process of devouring. Arlene replied, "Oh nothing specific, just the usual nonsense I can expect from that immature moron." Wilma knew that her next two years at Averton Elementary would go by slowly with Billy attending the Junior High School along with Tempest's older sibling Noah. But Arlene's brother couldn't care less about being separated from Wilma.

On the other hand, Anne Nubbler had a thing for Noah. She was devastated when the Nubblers moved from Lincoln Avenue to their rural habitat. In this case however, Noah was also slightly disappointed. He had well-hidden feelings for Anne, who was measurably trimmer than her larger twin. She also exhibited early hints of growing up to possess the "Nubbler face" which was considered a coveted attribute for any young Avertonian lass. Anne was cooler and did not spray any portion of her lunch when inquiring about Noah.

Tempest answered her nonchalant request by saying, "Noah is Noah. He spent his summer figuring out how to make his bike go faster." She reported that he and Charlie Dennis built a tree fort that her brother's friend spent all summer trying to get her to inspect. As with many local boys, Charlie had hidden feelings for Tempest.

The six friends gabbed away for what seemed like only a few moments in time. Before long the bell was ringing signaling the end of the sixth period. Tempest made a comment heard by her friends, "Good, in a little while we can get to the bottom of this repeating decimal nonsense." After she made the remark she paused to cover her mouth in response to a dry cough. She announced to the group that she had a tickle in her throat. Caleb gave her some water for the tickle and rolled his eyes about the math.

Chapter Five: Repeating Decimals

The six refreshed students made their way back to room number five, arriving just about the same time as Mr. Hessey, who had run a couple of errands during his lunch period. He was finishing a banana as he walked into the classroom. Some of the students speculated that he had slipped away to have some "naked time" with Miss Hankins. The idea caused a few red faces amongst the young scholars. Tempest was growing somewhat pensive as she knew that once she made it through the next forty two minutes she would seek her clarity when it came to dividing the number four into sixths.

The next subject that would be tackled that day was English. Of all the subjects that were taught in the Averton Elementary curriculum, English and language related class material was Miss Arrck's least favorite. She often speculated that the nobles of early England made the language more difficult than it needed to be in order to ensure that the common people would not have the mental capacity to comprehend and use the language effectively. It was the Duke's and the Earl's dirty little secret for keeping the peasants dumb and controllable. She would often be heard to say, "Now we all have to pay with stupid words like knight and night so the monarchs could hold on to their lifestyle." Tempest often demonstrated deeper insight than she was generally credited with possessing.

Although not her strongest subject, there were also memorable moments when it came to Tempest's bouts with English. Once while she was trying to be genuinely enthusiastic about a language related subject, she attempted to psyche herself up for phonics by stating out loud, "Goody, goody, time for phonics." Her teacher, knowing Tempest's aversion to all things language related, assumed she was interjecting a heavy dose of sarcasm into the proceedings. Seeing that cynicism was a less than desirable trait in any young woman, the teacher punished her with a hefty penalty. The delinquent young girl was required to write, "Goody, goody, time for phonics," one hundred times and deliver the transcribed punishment the next day prior to class. The sentence did little to diminish Tempest's penchant for sarcasm and did even less to instill a joy for phonics. She recalled this incident with greater clarity than she would ever remember phonics and continued to gripe about the reprimand years later.

Today's English class built on material discussed the prior day and delved deeper into the discipline of sentence structure, more specifically the diagraming of a sentence. Tempest assessed the entire process as being nothing more than paying homage to the first known utilization of decryption. This system was no doubt used by the smartest peasant in the field to untangle the web of verbs, adverbs and nouns that the royals had placed in the serf's path to literacy. Once he or she knew the building blocks of the complex communication medium, the basics could be taught to the other commoners leading to the eventual downfall of the king. Aside from this tedious process being revealed hundreds of years later, Tempest was chagrined by a more practical consideration. "When would I ever use this garbage in real life," was all her precise mind could contemplate. The subject matter also did not seem to excite Wilma. When asked a question about the attributes of a particular adverb, although next in order, she was entirely caught off guard by "Tomato Head's" inquiry. The fact that she had recently slipped a jaw breaker into her mouth did little to assist in her response. The candy did however provide some relief for the growing tickle in her throat, which was becoming more than a mild annoyance.

After what Tempest would refer to as the most painful forty two minutes of the day it was time for math. She would consider this to be the best forty two minutes of the day. Today however, would not go down in anyone's book as one of the best days on record for math class. It all started innocently enough when by Freudian slip, sheer lack of attention, or a severe lapse in judgment, Robert diverted from his usual script and threw some red meat to a patiently waiting Tempest. Mr. Hessey began math class by saying, "Let's take out our math books. Did anyone have any difficulty with last night's assignment?" No sooner did the words leave his mouth when Tempest's hand shot straight up. He immediately realized that he had inadvertently activated the launch sequence.

Seeing that the second student in row one was the only student with her hand raised it was not easy for "Tomato

Head" to avoid her. He tried for a moment but Caleb had been right, the material was fairly easy. Tempest turned to scan the rest of the class. Her hand was the only one raised. She squirmed slightly in her seat, cleared her throat, which may have been to address the escalating tickle or to get attention and proceeded to raise her hand higher. The reluctant educator had no other choice than to utter the words he knew invited calamity, "Tell me Tempest, what difficulty did you have with the assignment?"

The average sized young pupil rose from her chair and said, "Mr. Hessey, it is unclear to me how a repeating decimal of .666 and how many more sixes you chose to add would ever make a precise substitute for the fraction four sixths. Isn't this just watering down the correct answer every time it gets used to make a calculation?" Tempest had done it again. Robert knew she was right, but he also knew this was the method that was in vogue for Averton students, for the New York State Board of Education curriculum and for the global mathematics community writ large. He realized he had to tread lightly or risk duplicating the dreadful result of the well-documented and high profile "least common denominator incident".

Although Mr. Baxter had been able to quell Tempest's concerns regarding the least common denominator with his apple example, the events leading up to that were somewhat legendary at Averton Elementary. The oft told story chronicled the actions that resulted in the resignation of the former third grade teacher on grounds related to a suspected nervous breakdown. On that fateful day, Mrs. Grady chose to engage in a debate with young Tempest. After the ninth or tenth time having to hear Tempest say, "One third is not the same as three ninths, otherwise why wouldn't we call it three ninths," Alice Grady marched to the principal's office, said, "I really don't need to take this crap," and resigned.

Today's discussion had all the earmarks of being much more difficult. As opposed to her previous now fabled objection to common denominators, in this instance Tempest was dead on correct. But right or not Robert had a class to teach. A bold Mr. Hessey waded into dangerous waters. In an effort to ameliorate Tempest, he suggested that depending on the level of precision required you could determine the number of decimals to round your answer. For example, rounding to thousandths, which he claimed was very precise, would be expressed as .667. Tempest who was beginning to see "close enough" plastered all over this logic asked, "But who decides how correct is correct? If I have two apples and cut those apples into thirds I get six pieces. If I then divided that by three I would be left with two pieces or two thirds of an apple. Not .6666 no matter how many sixes you decide to use." The dissected apple example, which had proven so helpful in comforting Tempest years ago, had come home to roost and like a cheap loaded cigar, it blew up in "Tomato Head's" face.

Mr. Hessey was struggling with the realization he had just been outflanked by a nine-year-old fifth grader and launched a full array of diversionary tactics. His first move was to ask the class, "Who can tell Tempest why what she is suggesting is not correct and that rounding decimals is a very appropriate mathematical method?" After asking the question you could have heard crickets, if there were any crickets squirming about the corners of room five. None of the students was brave enough or dumb enough to step in front of that train. "Tomato Head" who began to find himself on the slippery slope then said, "Have any of you ever actually seen one one thousandths of an apple?" Tempest fired back, "What about a pumpkin. One of those great big specially grown pumpkins. Certainly you could see one one thousandths of a big pumpkin." The other children began to murmur agreement with Tempest and she drew strength from their support.

Tempest then said, "Mr. Hessey, multiplying and dividing decimals is just bad math. Why do we teach it in our schools?" Robert, who felt as though he was defending the entire New York Board of Education against the modern day equivalent of a miniature female Visigoth replied with the least logical but most compelling reason he could muster, "Because that is what we teach here at Averton and in the rest of the civilized world and that is what you need to learn." Tempest, who had never exhibited any level of pragmatism before and was in no frame of mind to exhibit the attribute now, dug in and decided she was going to bear down to make her point. As she prepared a more logical response than had been offered by her teacher she began to cough. When she went to speak she coughed again. It turned out that she couldn't stop coughing and had to be helped to the nurse's office by a concerned Caleb and a relieved "Tomato Head". When Mr. Hessey arrived back in room five, after taking the distressed student to the nurse's office, he regained his composure and said, "Ok, now where were we?"

Chapter Six: Laid Up

At one thirty nine on that Wednesday afternoon the Averton Elementary School nurse's office was a veritable beehive of activity. It was buzzing with students from grades K through six all of whom shared a similar cough. Tempest was the most recent member to join the ailing chorus as Miss Mary Blount, famed Averton spinster and great aunt of Carla Blount, attempted to keep a lid on the boiling cauldron that had become of her generally placid medical facility. Miss Mary's status as the most famous unmarried woman in town was connected to the long ago tragic loss of her third cousin on that fateful day when his parachute failed to open in the skies over Northern France. The town, often to her chagrin, took the time to remind her annually of her loss and she was never truly allowed to get over it. Although third cousins, they were often described as "torrid teenage lovers who were unable to keep their hands off of each other." The army enlistment of Cranford "Cran" Mann came as a relief to some, but the relief did not last.

The night before he was to ship out to Europe, Mary and Cran decided to consummate their relationship with a final frenzied climax. Nine months later Mary had a little boy to carry on her lost partner's legacy. Out of grief and in memory of her lover the young man was named Gregory. She could not bear a rhyming name. Gregory Blount was his name and around town he became known as "G.B.".

It was never clear whether it was the emotional environment in which the young man was raised, the mating of close cousins or the tragic, "dropping the kid" incident that occurred during the town's St Patrick's Day parade shortly after the child's third birthday. As Gregory matured however, he rounded into what some quite uncharitably and rather unfairly described as the "Village Idiot". Every village needs one and Gregory served Averton well. As a result of his impaired learning ability, sullen nature and stunted maturity, Gregory still lived with Mary in a little house on the outskirts of town. He did many of the jobs that few Avertonians wanted to do, among them throwing out the trash at the various schools. The job description included the nurse's office. In 1993 there was no thought of protection from biohazard, and none was needed. They had Gregory. On this day he would be fully occupied with brimming pails of contaminated tissues from coughing kids.

Mary's first job was to comfort the children. She then assessed the situation. If first aid was required the school nurse administered it. In rare cases she had to call the local sheriff or summon the ambulance service to drive a child to the nearby community hospital. Today she was chief comforter and operator, passing out tissues and punching out telephone numbers from her emergency contact list. As Tempest was getting comfortable in her seat, the first of the parents arrived to pick up their hacking charges. Soon the staff at the local library would be operating without the Head Librarian.

Once all the children had been retrieved and the school day had ended Mary had time to collect her thoughts. She recalled some guidance that had come from the State regarding incidents of this nature. She found the proper tab in the up to date administrative binder and flipped to the notifications section. Under the tab were a number of sub-topics from poisons to nuclear waste but she focused on the heading titled "outbreaks". The instructions included a hot-line number that was to be called if more than the lesser of three percent or ten students in the school population reported the same illness.

Mary pondered the poorly worded instruction. There were approximately two hundred and eighty children enrolled at the school and she had treated nine students that day. Mary being a better nurse than she was a mathematician decided that since nine was less than ten no notification was required. If she had made the call the State might have advised her to close the school for a few days to prevent the further spreading of the illness. Had Tempest still been in the clinic and learned of the faulty calculation she would have left with a cough and a headache. If Mary asked Tempest for assistance the call would have been made.

Chapter Seven: Treating Tempest

Had Mary been a little better at math and made the call to the State hot-line, she might have been instructed to close the school to avoid the near epidemic consequences that followed. Over the coming days just about every person at Averton Elementary, Middle and High School succumbed to what became known that year as "the cough". Anyone with a connection to a student or had contact with a person who frequented the schools was also infected. What seemed to begin rather unassumingly with patient alpha, Carla Blount, who came back to school a little too early, had now stricken the entire town.

Most people had symptoms ranging from a mild tickle to a dry cough that ran a couple of days. It also appeared that once healed you were safe from relapsing and no longer contagious. This feature of the unknown malady allowed for school to continue unabated albeit with a host of substitute teachers and an abundance of empty chairs. Tempest's confrontation was considered to be a particularly bad case and although a generally healthy girl she struggled to free herself from "the cough's" grip.

The Arrcks were becoming uneasy as Tempest began the fourth day of unguarded quarantine in her bedroom. The ailing girl did not appear to be getting the upper hand on the yet unclassified disease. Tempest did her best to stay abreast of school work. Because she thought the Math textbook could best be described as, "Pablum meant for lesser minds," there was a fear that she would fall behind in her favorite field of study. Her mother, who had completely avoided the infection, would accompany Tempest and prepare the ailing girls meals as the library was closed out of an abundance of caution. After returning to the doctor for the second time in three days, only to be told again the illness had to run its course, Diane Arrck decided she needed to step in or Tempest would fall woefully behind and not be able to catch up with her studies. She recalled Mary Blount one time ascribing similar circumstances to G.B.'s early upbringing and did not want to tempt fate with that outcome.

Returning home from the doctor's office late that Saturday morning Diane saw Paul Baxter outside painting his white mailbox. Mrs. Arrck decided that she would see if he could provide some advice regarding the schooling of her sick child. She knew that Paul had already been afflicted with "the cough" and was no longer at risk of infection by the still ailing Tempest. Mrs. Arrck walked from her front door and greeted Paul, who she had known for the many years that she and Mark had owned their home. Paul laid his paint brush down and said, "Good morning Diane, it is a beautiful day. How is our little Tempest fairing on this fine morning?" Diane replied, "Funny you should mention Tempest. I am worried that she was falling terribly behind in her studies and was hoping you might be able to help."

Paul certainly had the capability to help the young girl and was also interested in providing assistance. He said to Diane, "Maybe once I finish this paint job it will be time to take a break. I will go speak with her to see how far along she has moved on her own." Diane replied, "That would be wonderful Paul. She really likes you and will open up to your questions. Don't be surprised however, if you find that she considers the fifth grade math textbook to be one step above witchcraft." Paul replied, "Well, I know our favorite student has a way of forming opinions. Let me see what I can do." Diane thanked Paul for his help and returned to the Arrck's house to prepare Tempest for a visitor.

An hour later the doorbell rang. Paul Baxter was standing on the porch having washed clean any remnants of the white paint he had been applying. Diane welcomed him in and Paul asked, "Is she ready for me?" Diane responded, "Yes, she knows you are coming and is looking forward to your visit. Her cough seems to be getting better today, but we also thought that yesterday and she still had a tough night." Paul said, "Well, I will go easy on her and see what we can do to keep her current with the rest of her class." When Paul arrived at the top of the stairs Tempest's door was closed and he knocked lightly. From behind the door came a small voice, "Who is it?" "It's Mr. Baxter. I understand you are expecting me." Tempest coughed lightly and said, "Just a minute" and she answered the door dressed in her usual play clothes except today they were covered by a pink robe.

Mr. Baxter stood in the doorway and asked if it was safe to come in. Tempest replied that since he already had "the cough" and gotten over it he would be fine. Tempest then said, "I hear my mother has asked if you can help me keep up with my math work. You know I have actually already read the entire book. It gets better as you go through it. But this whole rounding of decimals reminds me of voodoo mathematics." She was paraphrasing a term that she had heard a year earlier on television during a Presidential debate her father was watching. Mr. Baxter replied, "You might think it is voodoo and it is clearly not as precise as other forms of math but that is the way the world does it. I recommend you understand the shortcomings of the process, stay true to your principals but keep your objections to yourself. Most importantly try not to be threatening to people who don't want to be out classed by a soon to be ten-year-old girl."

Tempest understood exactly what Mr. Baxter was saying. He had offered similar advice during the least common denominator tribulations. She did not give up easily, again objecting to the fact that this time it was worse because at least the common denominator provides an accurate answer. Mr. Baxter said, "Tempest, I haven't steered you wrong yet, have I?" She replied in a meeker tone, "No sir, you have not."

Paul asked Tempest if he could see her math textbook and she handed it to him. He began flipping through the pages and found notes and comments that Tempest had made in the margins. Some were not very flattering to the author. Many were pretty funny. Tempest laid her head on the pillow as her

48

adult neighbor continued to work his way through the text. She had not slept well the night before and overcome with drowsiness was soon sound asleep. Paul Baxter continued his journey through the text and marveled at the concepts that Tempest had grasped without the benefit of "Tomato Head's" accompanying lectures. After a while he saw that the young girl had fallen asleep and so not to wake her, put the book down and prepared to leave the room. Before leaving he leaned down and kissed her lightly on the forehead saying, "Get well soon my child."

Chapter Eight: Our Little Girl Gets Help

Monday afternoon came and Tempest was still not healthy enough to attend class. Her trusted friend and companion Caleb made an after class visit to bring Tempest up to speed on the assignments and the material that had been covered. Caleb shook "the cough" earlier the prior week and was no longer at risk of re-contracting the illness. The boy knew Tempest would quickly catch up on her return but was still troubled by the amount of school she was missing this early in the semester. Her mother was also growing ever more worried and wanted to follow up with her adult neighbor on any thoughts he had from the visit made the prior Saturday. The library had reopened and Tempest for the most part was home alone, although various family friends and cousins would stop during the day to check in on her. Diane's visit to the Baxter house needed to wait until after dinner that evening.

The sun was still lighting her way at seven o'clock that Monday night. She knew the Baxters had completed their dinner as Caleb had already taken the garbage can to the curb for Tuesday morning pick-up. When Diane rang the bell Caleb answered and she said, "Hi sweetheart, how are you this evening?" Caleb answered, "Fine Mrs. Arrck, how are you?" She replied, "I am doing well but I am here to ask your father a question about Tempest." The boy showed Diane into their home and they found Mrs. Ruth Baxter on the living room couch reading the garden section of the local paper. Ruth was a Nubbler, but of somewhat below standard appearance for your customary Nubbler, not being totally blessed with the well-known features of the trademark face.

Upon seeing her neighbor enter the living room she said, "Diane welcome, how is our little Tempest doing? Has she begun to get over the cough?" Mrs. Arrck replied, "Hello Ruth, good to see you. Funny you are so close and we never seem to get together. The reason I am here concerns Tempest. She is still missing school and I wanted to ask Paul if there might be a student at the college we could hire as a tutor until she improves?" Ruth remarked, "That is a wonderful idea. There is always some enterprising young student looking to use their skills to earn a few extra dollars." Diane replied, "That is what I am hoping for." Caleb added, "I will go find my dad," and left the room. Ruth then asked, "How are your other children. Have they all gotten over their illness?" Diane said, "Yes, for the most part it was mild, but in Tempest's case it just won't go away. Mark was affected for a couple days, and I never got it." Ruth then commented proudly, "You know I never got it either. Not even a tickle in my throat. Some things are just funny that way." As she finished her comment Paul entered the room.

Paul had been in the basement fixing the lawn mower and smelled a little bit of gasoline as he wiped his hands on an oily light brown cloth. "Hi Diane," he began, "Caleb tells me you think it might be a good idea to hire a tutor to get Tempest over the next few days until she improves. I have been thinking about the overall curriculum the kids have this year and might have just the fellow for you." Diane said, "That is wonderful Paul. Is there any way we can get in touch with him to learn more?" Paul answered, "There certainly is, I will call him when I am done downstairs and ask him to give you a call. How's that?" Diane gratefully replied, "Again that would be fantastic." Paul said, "The fellow's name is Charles Farley. He is an international student from England. He is one of my brightest and can be helpful with much more than just math. One thing though, don't call him Charlie. His parents never anticipated that their son would come to America and face being called Charlie Farley." Diane appreciated Paul's gesture and went home to await Charles' call, all the while missing the point of why he did not like being referred to as Charlie.

When Mark arrived home from a long day at the shoe store Diane let him know of her plan to ensure Tempest did not fall too far behind in her studies. Mark had always been a strong supporter of the kid's education and was in favor of keeping "his little girl" on track with the rest of her class. This was the third busiest time in the shoe business. With the exception of Christmas and Easter the post back to school period, when all the kids saw what other kids were wearing, meant late hours at "Two by Two Shoes". Because Tempest spent most of Sunday sleeping, he had not seen much of his daughter since "the cough" intervened in their lives and tonight was no exception. Mark asked how Tempest was doing and Diane indicated she had maintained her weight, was fairly energetic and was still interested in her studies but she just couldn't shake the infernal cough. Mark said, "If it doesn't get better soon we will have to take her to Albany to see a specialist." Diane was in complete agreement.

Noah, who joined the dinner conversation with his parents after doing his own homework, was asked what was new at the junior high school. Noah reported that nearly every child had returned from their sicknesses and classes were getting back to normal. This information served to create additional edginess in the nervous father. His father then asked, "How are your lessons going so far this year son?" Noah indicated that he was enjoying his classes and his teachers were easy to understand. The biggest plus about being in junior high was that he was no longer stalked by Anne Nubbler. Noah chose not to divulge this to his father. Being a typical young male any discussion about what was happening on the girl front was beyond sharing with his parents.

Clark was already in bed as was Tempest. When Joan arrived the potential attendees to join their father for his late night meal was complete. Diane mentioned to the two oldest Arrck children that there was a chance that she would be hiring a tutor for Tempest until she became well enough to return to school. She did not know much about the young man with the exception that he was an international student at the community college and Mr. Baxter thought highly of him. Diane also mentioned that his name was Charles Farley. Then added in a quizzical manner her surprise that for some reason he preferred not to be called Charlie. The four Arrcks shared a look of puzzlement and the discussion quickly moved on to other more mundane family matters.

Mark was finishing his dinner and Joan was clearing the table when the phone rang. Diane picked up the receiver. The caller was a young man with a British accent. He began in a very polite manner, "Good evening, I hope I am not disturbing you at this late hour. My name is Charles Farley and Professor Baxter asked that I give you a call this evening regarding tutoring your daughter." Diane was immediately taken by the sound of Charles' accent and thanked him for calling. Mrs. Arrck spent a few moments explaining the situation to Charles and when done she finished with the question, "Have you already had the cough?" Charles responded that he had already been visited by the malady and had completed the unpleasant duty of allowing the illness to run its course. Diane was pleased to hear the answer. Given what she had already heard the potential tutor was imminently suited but a wrong answer to this question would have immediately disqualified him for the position.

The purpose of Mrs. Arrck's supplementing of Tempest's studies was underpinned by a desire to get started quickly. Diane focused her attention to how rapidly Charles could begin in his role. The young Brit indicated that he could be available as early as the next afternoon at three o'clock. Diane was thrilled at the prospect of getting started so fast. Charles made the request that Tempest have her texts available for his review so that he could tailor the sessions to the school curriculum. Diane replied she would make arrangements for the books to be available. With that there were respectful farewells spoken as the wheels of keeping Tempest on par with the balance of "Tomato Head's" pupils had been set into motion. Diane considered it too late to call Paul Baxter to thank him but made a mental note to ensure she did so the following day.

The next afternoon Diane left her post at the library early in order to pick up Caleb, Joan and Clark at school. Caleb had collected Tempest's books as requested by Charles and would not have been able to carry the excessive load, even though the Arrck's home was well within walking distance of the Averton Elementary School. As long as she was there, it made sense to transport her remaining children as the afternoon had turned into a drizzly affair not totally consistent with a lovely stroll through the town's streets. When Diane pulled her modest four door sedan into the driveway she saw a lone figure shielded by an umbrella, standing in front of the house. It was the first time she would make the acquaintance of Charles Farley but far from the last time he would play a role in the lives of the Arrck family.

Charles was a rather tall young man. He was a little pale for the generally sun-drenched days that had been experienced across upstate New York that summer but his appearance fit perfectly into the rather dreary day that had unfolded on that September afternoon. He had dark hair and dark eyes and made a rather cheerless appearance standing in the light rain with his black umbrella and dark overcoat. Diane's initial assessment of Charles being a little bleak was shattered when she engaged him in their second short conversation. Diane approached Charles, who had unassumingly remained on the sidewalk despite the arrival of the Arrck vehicle. She asked the stranger, "Excuse me sir, are you Charles Farley?" Charles responded, "Yes that would be me. Charles Farley is my name. And you my lady must no doubt be Diane Arrck. The day has certainly turned into a bit of gloomy one has it not?" With that brief exchange Charles followed Diane up the walkway to the Arrck home. As they headed towards the door the curtain moved slightly and if you listened hard enough you would have heard the sound of light footsteps running up the stairs.

Chapter Nine: First Impressions

Charles closed his umbrella and left it on the porch as they entered the front hallway. After hanging his topcoat he was invited by Diane to join her at the dining room table to discuss the specifics of his employment. The lady of the house described the reason for a tutor and that the engagement could end as soon as "the cough" had run its course. Diane indicated that Charles would be responsible for keeping Tempest current in all subjects. This would require at least two hours of study time daily during his period of service. They negotiated a reasonable price for his help, indicating payment be made daily at the conclusion of his duties. It was an amicable arrangement. Charles could use the money and he could count the experience towards tutoring hours to satisfy a requirement for a course he was enrolled in at the community college. Charles was utilizing his attendance in a two year program as a stepping stone to a four year degree at another yet to be named university.

Once most of the specifics had been ironed out, Diane went to Tempest's room to bring her down to meet Charles. The plan was for the duo to do their work at the dining room table. Caleb had already left a stack of books on the corner of the table with bookmarks indicating the point to where Mr. Hessey's class had advanced in Tempest's absence. When

Tempest entered the room dressed in her school clothes Charles had his head down scanning the material in Tempest's European Civilizations textbook. He raised his head and with a smile in his eyes said, "Hello, you must be Tempest. My name is Charles Farley."

The young student had not been advised of Charles' aspersion to the nickname Charlie and without a moment's delay said, "So you must be Charlie Farley." Her mother readily admonished her saying, "Tempest, you must address Mr. Farley appropriately." Charles was enjoying a bit of a chuckle in response to Tempest's spontaneity and replied, "You can call me anything you want young lady, on two conditions. First is that you focus on your studies and do the work I give you. Second, you need to promise to get better as quickly as possible." Charles felt a purpose in Tempest that he rarely felt in other people. He had the premonition that this girl was destined to do something special in her life and he was going to play whatever small role was required of him to help her achieve it. Primarily he felt an immediate fondness for the young girl.

Once the introductions were complete Diane said, "There is no time like the present. Why don't you two get started?" Young Master Farley said, "I am ready, how about you Tempest?" His student replied, "I am ready. Let's start with math." Charles had been briefed by Mr. Baxter and was aware of Tempest's special talents in the field of math and suggested, "Why don't we work through these other subjects first and once done we can get to math? Professor Baxter has told me that you have thus far consumed the entire semester of math already without any support from tutorial assistance." Tempest felt as though she had been ratted on and regretted sharing with her neighbor that she had for the most part completed the entire math syllabus during the time she was out of commission. In an effort to comply with her new educator's request and not display too high a level of rigidity she acquiesced to his desires. After a few moderate coughs the new team began to work their way through European history. Tempest would wait until later to exhibit her fabled stubbornness.

The teacher and student hit it off. The two hours were flying by with Charles leading Tempest through the appropriate texts, touching on key points and focusing on areas where he thought she might have issues of comprehension without some additional context. Soon Tempest was completely caught up in history and English. She was pleased with Charles' informed assessment that diagramming a sentence was pure rubbish. But he indicated that sometimes you have to comply with the standards or risk being labelled a malcontent. He then explained to Tempest the definition of a malcontent.

There were twenty minutes left in their class time and Charles suggested that they take a bite out of the science work. The subject matter for year five Averton students was an eclectic compilation of disparate subjects wrapped under the heading of General Science. The course work included everything from magnets and electricity to the study of molecules and atoms. After they browsed the science book together Charles said, "Tell you what, tomorrow I will bring you something that will explain the way magnets work and we can conduct experiments that would be much better than just reading about it in a book." Tempest became excited saying, "That would be great." After giving out a slight cough she then asked Charles, "Do you think there would be time for a little math?" Charles replied in a somewhat capitulating manner, "Yes, if we get done with the rest of our work we will spend some time on math. But you need to read the material I am going to give you as homework." Tempest said, "That seems fair. Just don't load me down." Charles smiled inwardly at the maturity of his young charge. He considered himself fortunate that Paul had given him this opportunity.

After a little more than two hours Diane came into the room and asked how it all went and Tempest said, "This was great, I may never go back to class with "Tomato Head". Mr. Farley makes this seem so simple." Charles was pleased at his student's assessment and gave a smile to Diane suggesting, "She is a quick learner. It is also good to know I compare favorably to "Tomato Head"." Diane responded, "She is a surprising little girl that's for sure." With that Charles checked his watch and indicated he needed to leave to catch his bus back to the college and after Diane compensated him for his work Charles left for the evening. On his way out the door he said, "Remember, no homework no math." As Charles walked out the door he was proud of himself for finding an incentive that would induce his pupil to be compliant with his desires.

Little did he realize that it was not Tempest who was yielding to his requests but that description was more applicable to him.

Chapter Ten: Fast Friends

When Tempest awoke on that Wednesday "the cough" had not yet run its course and once again she was required to stay home from school. This was day five of her absence and if not for Charles Farley the Arrcks would be growing more anxious about their daughter's ability to catch up with her schooling once she became healthy. When everyone had left the house for their daily duties, Tempest curled up on the couch and began to read the homework she had been assigned by her new teacher. Although she missed the day to day contact with all of her friends, being able to stay home and focus on the aspects of her education that suited her was something she could find appealing if it were to last.

Today she was assigned two chapters of history to read and a chapter of English, which included answering some questions at the end. She was also instructed to study the first chapter in her science book. In addition to the homework Charles had given her, today she would be prepared to initiate a discussion around math, which would hopefully move her favorite subject higher in the order of educational priorities.

No one came to visit Tempest today as her self-sufficiency was becoming apparent. When midday arrived and pangs of hunger stirred she went to the kitchen and prepared herself some oatmeal. She cut up an apple to add to her hot cereal in order to create a more balanced meal. She liked apples and was actually more interested with the taste of her lunch than its nutritional content. While cutting the apple she thought back to the example that Mr. Baxter had used to explain the now famous addition of fractions conundrum. Maybe she could introduce the subject of math by contrasting the precision of that prior outcome with what she had now concluded to be the "fuzzy math" related to repeating decimals.

While seated at the kitchen table, Tempest heard a car door close in the backyard of the Baxter house. Mrs. Baxter must have been to the large grocery store in Barretown as she had a number of bags to unload. It may have been her third or fourth trip to the car but when Tempest heard her walking back into the house she caught the sound of her neighbor coughing. It was a familiar cough. Although Mrs. Baxter had proudly boasted a few days earlier that she had completely avoided "the cough", it would appear she had either been concealing her condition or it had recently been contracted. It was then that Tempest realized that up until that point in the day she herself had not coughed. There could have been a slight clearing of her throat but nothing akin to the symptoms she had been previously experiencing. It might have been the power of suggestion or sympathy for her neighbor but just before she ate her first spoonful of oatmeal she was once again treated to a mild revisiting of her own illness.

Tempest was fully prepared for her afternoon studies when the door opened at around two thirty and Noah arrived back home from middle school. Joan and Clark would not be arriving until three thirty as Mr. Potter had put the elementary school on extended days for the rest of the week in order to get everyone caught up with their work. Noah asked Tempest how she was feeling. She replied, "Much better, I have coughed fewer times in the past six and one half hours than I have in over a week." His sister added to her own surprise, "I am healthy enough to go back to school soon." Noah was happy to hear that the patient was finally on the mend. Although he knew that her illness had not been life threatening, the length of her recovery was beginning to elevate his concern. Noah replied, "Mom and Dad will be glad to hear that. They were really beginning to worry about you."

Noah offered half of the doughnut that he had stopped to pick up at the shop he now passed daily on his way to and from Averton Junior High School. Tempest thanked him for sharing as they sat together. While enjoying the sugary pastry Tempest asked her older brother what he thought of his new school. He said he liked it, but being with the eighth and ninth graders put him back at the bottom of the food chain. Noah made particular mention of the seventh grade math teacher Mr. Zurck. The teacher made a wry comment about Noah's name on day one and now, in very obvious fashion, every question that had the answer two he would direct towards her older brother. Noah said, "It is easy to understand why his nickname is, "Zurck the Jerk"."

A few minutes later there was a knock on the door which Noah went to answer. Standing there minus umbrella and overcoat was Charles Farley. Devoid of his rainy day wear you could see the young man had an athletic build and was not nearly as dour as he appeared the prior day. He carried with him a thin flat board which was about one and a half by two feet in size. He smiled when Noah opened the door. Charles was slightly preoccupied saying, "Thanks Caleb," as he entered. Noah politely corrected him saying, "I am not Caleb. I am Noah. Tempest's older brother." The tutor replied, "Sorry I thought you were your younger brother." Noah again politely corrected Charles saying, "Caleb is not my brother, he is our neighbor and a classmate of Tempest's. My brother Clark is in second grade and I am not sure you met him."

Charles apologized to Noah. His sharp mind was wrestling with two competing thoughts. With a name like Clark Arrck he now understood why the Arrcks had little appreciation for why he might not like to be called Charlie. He was also bothered with the lack of attention he had paid the day before. He needed to be more mindful of detail if he was to have any chance in the medical profession which he one day aspired to join. He completely glossed over the fact that Tempest's brother shared a name with a major character straight from the Bible.

Charles entered the dining room with Noah who announced his arrival saying to Tempest, "Your teacher is here. I will leave you two alone." Tempest welcomed Charles and asked him if he would like some tea, which the tutor gracefully declined realizing the preparation would cut into the short two hours they had for study. Charles then inquired, "So how did you do with the homework we agreed to?" Tempest said to the relief of Charles, "I completed it all and am ready to discuss it with you." Charles was hoping she had done the work as assigned. He had no desire to include any aspect of disciplinarian in his temporary job description. Although he had not been briefed on the complete circumstances of the high profile "Mrs. Grady Affair", Charles had a sense that Tempest could be a handful on certain occasions.

Charles placed the smooth board on the table and said to Tempest, "So what subject would you like to tackle first?" Tempest's response was, "What is the board for if you don't mind me asking?" Charles pulled a vial and a small case from his pocket and said, "The board is for a demonstration regarding magnets and magnetic fields. How about we start with science?" Tempest agreed that science would be first, although she would have preferred math be the opening topic.

Her tutor took two equal size metal bars from the case he had previously produced. Each was about the size of an ordinary stick of gum, although dark metallic gray and about five times thicker. Charles placed the two bars on the board and then opened the vial. From the vial he poured two nearly equal gray piles of material which turned out to be metal shavings. He placed the magnets on the table, away from the shavings and began to demonstrate to Tempest the attracting and repelling properties of the two bar magnets. He encouraged Tempest to handle each magnet to get a feel for the force being exerted by the unseen fields. Charles said, "In nature Tempest, there are forces that govern the physical world that you cannot see but they are there if you know where to find them."

Charles spent the next thirty minutes or so rearranging the magnets to display various properties. He re-created certain diagrams that had been illustrated in the science text and encouraged Tempest to move the magnets around on the smooth surface of the board. She was surprised at the near perfect distribution of the metal shavings when she placed them between the magnets and watched as they moved magically to form an arc between the two poles. Charles skipped ahead a few chapters and related to Tempest that the earth is like a big magnet. He said, "Visualize one of these bars passing right through the poles and forming a huge magnetic field that looks just like those metal shavings." Tempest was amazed at the power of the magnets and was pleased that Charles had made what had just been an idea in a textbook come alive for her.

The two young minds probably spent a little too much time contemplating the unseen forces. Neither wanted to move on to the much drier subject of history but that is just what they did at about quarter to four. After an hour plowing through the rest of the subjects, with ten minutes left in the session there was barely enough time to get into math. Charles was comfortable that Tempest was able to handle the math and that any roadblock to her learning was likely something that she put up as an obstruction, not a limit to her ability to comprehend on her own. With such little time to discuss her favorite subject she took the opportunity to draw a parallel between the visual illustration regarding the magnets and the apple example that Mr. Baxter had used years earlier. She made the point, "Precision is the natural order of things not estimation. Shouldn't we try to make our conclusions as precise as possible?" Charles didn't need to spend months with his young pupil to recognize her gift. But he also realized that in a world full of "close enough" she would be challenged on a daily basis.

Chapter Eleven: The Dirty Little Secret

The next day Tempest jumped from bed and ran downstairs announcing that she was ready to return to school. Her cough had run its course. Diane was relieved but questioned Tempest whether she was sure that she no longer had "the cough" and Tempest convinced her mother that she was certain. It was a warm bright morning on one of the last days of the summer season. Diane and Mark thought the fresh air would do Tempest good and the three elementary school students left home in time to arrive at their respective classrooms with time to spare. Caleb, who was never late for the morning walk, was not ready when they left the house, so they made the journey without him.

When Tempest arrived at room five she was swamped by her frenzied classmates welcoming her back. Even "Tomato Head" was surprised at his pleasure that she had returned. Tempest let her friends know she was happy to be back and glad to be done with "the cough". She approached Mr. Hessey to let him know that her absence would not be a burden on the other students as she had kept up with the material with the help of Caleb and her tutor Charlie Farley, a student at the county community college. Hessey was glad to hear this and advised Tempest of the extended days which were planned to continue for that Thursday and Friday. Tempest once reminded of the supplemental class time thought maybe it would have been better if she held out and managed to have a little cough until the end of the week.

Just before the bell rang Arlene made her appearance and prior to taking her seat slipped across the front of the room to grab a quick hug from the returnee. Caleb followed Arlene through the door. He was more disheveled for a school day than Tempest had ever seen him previously. His unkempt appearance raised a questioning eyebrow from the other students in classroom number five but it was a real source of uneasiness for Tempest. Caleb was always well-groomed and fully prepared for his day of school. Today his hair was not properly combed, his shirt had not been pressed and he was late. Something was surely amiss in the Baxter house.

Later that morning Diane Arrck backed her car out of the driveway on her way to the library. As she was nearing the road Ruth Baxter opened the door to retrieve her newspaper. It was not unusual for Diane's exit to coincide with Ruth's appearance which would happen on a more than slightly regular basis. Mrs. Baxter was usually dressed for her average day of attending garden club meetings or drinking coffee with some of the higher brows of Averton who Ruth would count amongst her closest friends.

Diane would sometimes toot the horn and wave but today it did not appear as though Ruth wanted to be noticed. Bending down to retrieve the local paper she was still in her robe with a towel wrapped around her neck, hair undone and holding a rumpled tissue. Ruth appeared to be sick. She may have even been visited by "the cough".

Diane was mildly shocked as Ruth had only a few days before suggested that she had up until then avoided the illness. Mrs. Arrck further mulled the idea that the rest of the town had already weathered the sickness as it had nearly completely run its course. Diane who had studied nursing in college before deciding to become a librarian also knew that there was something more that needed to be factored into the calculus to truly assess the current health of her neighbor. But it was a piece of information only three people knew and a circumstance that had been agreed to remain a secret never to be spoken of again.

Ten years earlier Ruth Baxter had a plan. It was a plan concocted to ensure she would make her husband happy. The plot was hatched in her slightly deranged mind one fine spring afternoon while she and Diane sat chatting on the back porch of the Baxter home. Until that day Ruth had not been aware of Diane's due date but while discussing it over a friendly cup of tea, she realized they were both on track to give birth the very same day. Less surprisingly, they had also arranged to deliver their children in the very same local hospital.

In order to improve the odds that the infants would arrive in the maternity ward concurrently, Mrs. Baxter arranged for a cesarean birth to be conducted on the very same day Diane was planning her trip to the hospital. In her previous two pregnancies the Arrck children had arrived like clockwork and

Ruth was counting on her dependable neighbor's biology to be just as reliable on this occasion.

During their entire relationship from high school until today Ruth Nubbler, although not the possessor of the prototypical "Nubbler face", held a mystical spell over Paul Baxter. If Ruth asked Paul to jump the only question he would ask was, "How high?" There was one exception to this manipulating influence that Ruth held over Paul. It was an area where her husband refused to compromise. As a couple they must have a son to carry on the family name. Paul was the last in a long line of distinguished Baxter men. Without a son, when he was done with life, both his name and the original male version of the "Baxter nose" would go with him.

A few weeks before the neonatal double header, Ruth sought to secure Paul's involvement with the incomplete plan that would provide a twofold increase in their chances of ensuring they left the hospital with a boy. First, she made Paul aware that her doctor had informed her that it was very likely she would be able to carry only one child in her life. This would be her only safe pregnancy. Given the lone opportunity to have a boy they needed to improve the odds. She then advised Paul of her scheme to deliver at the same time as their neighbors. An accomplice was required to swap children if necessary in order to ensure there was a Baxter boy. The baby would not be a true Baxter, complete with the most critical Baxter feature, but the name would live on. Perhaps one day the child could marry someone with Baxter genes to reset the time-honored genetic profile. Paul found himself on the horns of an ethical dilemma. He was compelled to be compliant due to the spell he had lived under for so many years and supportive because his one line in the sand was the reason underlying the deception. As is the case with many bad decisions, he knew it was wrong but he agreed to go along.

Nature continued to take its course and soon the day of the deliveries arrived. As was anticipated, Diane's water broke at nine fifteen that morning. Ruth was scheduled to deliver at eleven. The babies made their entries into the world at precisely the same moment. One was a boy and one was a girl. Diane Arrck required a sedative that knocked her out just prior to her delivery. Ruth was also in a quasi-comatose state when the babies were born. Neither knew the result of their childbirth.

Paul had set up camp at the maternity ward and was ready when the babies wrapped tightly in small blankets appeared on the scene. He took the child wrapped in blue, who he knew was the Arrck's child and said to the nurse, "Can I please hold my son?" The nurse who had been in the delivery rooms and being brighter than Paul had hoped said, "Oh Mr. Baxter, this child over here is the Baxter baby," and she went to pick up the girl. Paul said, "Oh, you must be mistaken," handing the nurse a large wad of one hundred dollar bills saying, "This child is indeed the Baxter baby don't you agree?" The dumbstruck nurse, who had financial issues to care for, made a poor decision that she would come to regret. She knew it was wrong but agreed to go along. The nurse took the money and renamed the two newborns. Paul never shared with Ruth that he needed to bribe the nurse to achieve the swap.

In theory the only two that truly knew the details of the kidnapping were Paul and the nurse. At least initially Ruth thought the boy was hers but a few evenings after returning young Caleb home his fabricated father could no longer keep the dark secret and he shared it with the unsuspecting new mother. Caleb was the neighbor's boy and the girl the Arrcks had named Tempest was their child.

The combination of pangs of guilt and the realization early on that Tempest was likely to grow into the "Baxter nose", which she was already exhibiting, initially caused Paul to consider a plan to put the babies back with their proper parents. He could not however bring himself to do it. So the status quo was set. Ruth quickly grew to love young Caleb as her own and nurtured him through his infancy. Paul kept a watchful eye on Tempest, paying a little more than the average level of attention you would expect from a neighbor. It was this above average attention that one day was the root cause for another name to be entered onto the unholy slate of those aware of the dirty little secret.

When Caleb and Tempest were three years old they were scheduled to receive a raft of vaccinations. The parents were notified of the requirement by a letter that arrived at residences across town sent from the Averton School District. Ruth was prepared to take Caleb for the shots but when Paul looked at the list of injections he turned ghostly white. The inoculations included a particular immunization that thirty years earlier was blamed for taking the life of his older and only brother. If Tempest was going to receive these same shots she could be in danger. Paul needed to act, but he needed a plan to do it.

The Arrcks were busy people and had their hands full with work and the introduction of young Clark Arrck into the family. The backdrop provided the perfect cover for Paul to create yet another purposeful deception. The Baxters would offer to take Tempest along with Caleb to receive the inoculations. While with the medical staff they would decline the lethal injection for Tempest and no one would be the wiser. The plot was set into motion. The Arrcks were happy to let the Baxters take Tempest to the local doctor. When the Baxters refused the particularly deadly shot on the Arrck's behalf the nurse made note of it but didn't object and the rest of the procedure went off without a hitch.

There was only one small unforeseen problem with the plan. The nurse who administered the vaccinations was a former nursing school colleague of Mrs. Arrck. When Diane bumped into her friend on the street mention was made of her daughter's allergics. Tempest's mother did not overreact to the information provided by her friend and continued the conversation as though nothing newsworthy was reported. Her mind was however spinning like a top.

When Diane returned home she immediately raced next door to the residence of Ruth and Paul Baxter. When Ruth answered the door she knew by Diane's facial expression that the three year fraud had been exposed. She invited Diane in and asked her to calm down and said that she would explain, which she attempted to do. Ruth didn't try to make a case for the shot being sidestepped on general safety grounds. In what was likely an effort to clear her long troubled conscience she spilled her guts regarding the baby swap. Diane was livid and was ready to call the police to report the ruse when Paul entered the room and in a very comforting and calm voice said, "Diane, I know this is wrong. But think of the impact it might have on the kids if we let them know."

Diane was initially unmoved by Paul's comment and at this moment reviled both of her neighbors to the core for putting her in this position. She ran from the Baxter's home and returned to her house to pick up the phone. Then she paused to consider the ramifications of the story being circulated in this above average sized small town and how the label would hound the two children for their entire lives. Agonized she returned the phone to the cradle.

Caleb's birth mother was torn. She had been separated from her little boy, but she had come to love Tempest with all her heart. She realized her prime consideration needed to rest with what was best for the children. She did an about-face and returned to the Baxter house. Paul answered the door and Diane flew inside. She roasted her neighbors with a well-deserved hail of blistering words. The Baxters accepted the admonishment without offering a verbal defense. When Diane's offensive onslaught fell flat due to a lack of response to buttress her ire she dropped to the floor and broke down. She whimpered repeatedly, "This isn't done, it just isn't done." Paul waited for Diane to compose herself and said calmly, "We can't be sorrier and have no excuse for our actions." Diane replied viciously, "You aren't sorry you did it. You are sorry you were caught!" Paul knew she was right and waited before making his next comment, "Before you tell anyone else realize that matters fall further and further out of your control once you do. We are obligated to do exactly what you want. Not everyone you involve might agree with your solution."

Diane was sickened both mentally and physically with what the Baxters had done. But she put the future happiness of the children at the top of her list. Any stigma of this nature in Averton would put them on the same road as poor G.B. Blount. She did not want to be the sole instigator of what would become known as the mental equivalent of the tragic "dropping the kid" incident. The wronged woman was still shaken but elevated herself to a moment of flawless pragmatism saying, "I will be back before the end of the week to tell you what we are going to do about this," and then she left.

There was no counsel available to Mrs. Atick as she pondered the remedy for what she considered an unspeakable act on the part of her selfish neighbors. After days of thoughtful consideration, that included everything from committing felonies of her own to forgiving and forgetting, she came up with what she considered to be the best way forward. She would let the status quo stand. But there would be a letter written, to be signed by the Baxters, outlining the entire sordid affair. It would also define a set of conditions to which the Baxters must abide.

Tempest's adopted mother called the Baxters Thursday evening to arrange to see them in private the next day at four o'clock to present her solution for the scurrilous act. When Diane arrived at the front door of the uncharged felons she was carrying two pieces of paper. Diane was invited into the living room. They were alone as Caleb and Tempest were outside playing prior to dinnertime. Diane presented one copy of the letter to Ruth. She kept a copy for herself. Ruth was asked to read it in silence with her husband.

Diane had crafted a well-considered correspondence that would serve as a binding agreement between the parties. The terms were clear. The letter required that all three sign the document. It spelled out what the Baxters had done. Diane wanted this in writing in the event that someday there was a question of Tempest's paternity and she did not want rampant speculation that she and Paul had conceived her in sin. Second there was agreement that none of the parties would ever speak of the occurrences of that fateful day at the county hospital. The third requirement was for the two families to continue to live as neighbors and do nothing that might raise suspicion or cause any inquiry into the current state. The fourth requirement was that the Baxters could not move from their current residence until Caleb had reached the age of twenty one. Finally the parties were charged with secreting their copy of the letter so it would never be seen again. Diane could produce the letter at her discretion in the event she alone felt it was necessary to protect the children from harm.

After reading the document the Baxters retired to the kitchen to discuss the contents. Ruth, being a little bit proud, was reluctant to be told what to do by her neighbor and registered an objection with her husband. She did not want to sign the letter. Paul, who realized immediately that they were getting off easy and that Diane's demands were more than reasonable said, "Sign the letter. If it wasn't for your cockamamie idea in the first place, we wouldn't be in this mess." Apparently the long running spell that Ruth had over Paul was finally broken.

The Baxters returned to the living room with the letter signed by both of them in a signature that Diane accepted to be what others would recognize to be theirs. She checked the letter to ensure no alterations had been made and signed it herself. Then in her presence, she asked that the Baxters sign the letter that was never out of her sight. They signed and returned it. Before signing the copy that would become hers to keep forever she said, "May my loving husband, our beautiful children and God forgive me for this travesty that you have compelled me to carry out here today." She then put pen to paper.

In keeping with the third term and condition of what Diane would always just think of as "the letter", life between the two families was little changed after the revelation. As time marched on there were days when Diane nearly forgot that her loving daughter was not her own flesh and blood. But she would always consider Caleb to be her son. When she saw Ruth's physical condition that morning and recalled Tempest's struggle with "the cough" her nurse's intuition cried out that there was something going on at a genetic level. It could endanger Ruth unless somehow two and two could be put together without revealing the dirty little secret.

Chapter Twelve: The Final Session

When Tempest and the other two children returned from school late that afternoon they were surprised to find Charles Farley sitting on the doorstep waiting for someone to arrive at the Arrck household. Being such a close neighborhood, with alert fellow citizens, Charles had needed to explain his loitering to the local sheriff fifteen minutes prior to the children's arrival. When the young girl saw her tutor his presence did not require an explanation. Tempest had been healthy enough to go to school that day and her parents were so thrilled at the prospect of her well-being that they forgot to advise Charles that his services were no longer needed. He was there as bargained to continue in his role as interim teacher.

Tempest's immediate reaction was to say, "Sorry Charlie Farley, we forgot to let you know that I was well enough to attend school today. Please come in. I am sure there is something we can discuss between now and five o'clock. Maybe we can finally get to that math you have been avoiding." Joan, Clark, Tempest and her teacher entered the home and the tutor and his pupil settled in the dining room. Clark went to his small room upstairs. Joan picked up the phone to call her mother at the library to let her know that Charles had arrived to tutor Tempest.

Tempest asked Charles, "Would you like some tea?" Although it had been a warm day, Charles' bones had become chilled resting on the shady steps of the Arrck's porch and he took Tempest up on her offer. While Tempest retreated to the kitchen to make tea you could hear Joan speaking with her mother on the phone. She told her mom that Tempest had engaged Charles in discussion and he would more than likely be there upon her return home from work. Diane instructed Joan to let Charles know she would be home just before five and was sorry she forgot to advise him of Tempest's recovery. In Diane's defense, she did have a few other things on her mind that morning.

Tempest returned to the dining room and convinced Charles that she was entirely up to speed with her other subjects and as she put it, "Would like to get his views on a few math concepts." Charles had been notified by Mr. Baxter to approach this subject with care but dropped his guard quite uncharacteristically and spontaneously throwing caution to the wind said, "I would be delighted to discuss some math concepts with you." This reply, with the full benefit of clear twenty-twenty hindsight, might later have been rightly put in the "Goody, goody time for phonics" genre of responses. Tempest sensed that she had caught Charlie with his guard down. Perhaps he had been more focused on the soothing cup of Earl Grey and his chilled bones. Tempest replied, "I am glad you agree." As the kettle whistled she returned to the kitchen to prepare the hot drink.

Tempest returned later with a small tray holding a cup and saucer. The tea bag and the hot water were already in the steaming cup. She had arranged a small pitcher of milk, the sugar bowl and a spoon for Charles' convenience. "I am not sure how you take your tea," Tempest said. Charles replied, "How could you be? This is just perfect, a little milk and sugar just like my Irish great grandmother and I am fine."

He prepared his tea as Tempest watched attentively asking, "You have an Irish great grandmother. I thought you were from England?" Charles replied, "My roots are in England. My great grandfather married an Irish girl he met on his travels through the islands." Tempest replied, "Around here people don't travel all that much. No one has married anyone from the islands. With the exception of Margie Rosenberg, who is from Long Island, I don't even know anyone from an island." Charles considered that this fact might explain why there were such common characteristics seen in the features of many Avertonians, but became much less judgmental when considering the trace of common ancestry visible in many an Englander's teeth.

Charles sipped his tea, pronounced it perfectly done and again with a frightful head strong giddiness asked Tempest what math concepts she would like to discuss. Tempest was struck silly by Charles' open desire to take a crack at any of her wildest math dreams and decided to revisit the old chestnut with which she had not yet fully come to grips. The young mathematician thought about how to word her question and finally decided to phrase it as follows; "If two thirds times three is two, why is .667 times three a number other than two? Wouldn't that mean .667 is a very imprecise estimate for two thirds?"

Charles thought for a moment and said, "Whoa, slow down a second there governor. Run that by me again?" Tempest restated the question slightly differently, "If I take two thirds of something three times I get two of that thing. Professor Baxter once showed me slices of apple to visually prove something similar." Charles said, "I am following you." Tempest went on to say "So two thirds of something taken three times equals two, right?" Charles said, "Ok, sounds right." Then Tempest said, "The decimal lovers tell me that .667 is two divided by three or two thirds." Charles said, "Ok, keep going." Tempest concluded, "So why if I multiple .667 by three do I get a number larger than two?"

Charles was just about to step on the "close enough" landmine when Joan who had been listening at the door came in to rescue him asking, "Charles, would you like one of these cookies that I baked?" Tempest was a little miffed at the interruption but not being completely aware of her sister's purpose grabbed a cookie as well. Joan was hoping that the disruption might derail Tempest but as the slightly distracted interrogator started inspecting her cookie, counting the chips she asked, "So seriously Charles, why the difference?" "Well there is a difference," he replied. "But the convenience of calculating fractions that are far more complex than one third or one half is the trade-off. Tell me Tempest how you would multiply 127 thousandths times 6435 ten thousandths using your method? You would need to be pretty skilled at slicing apples and have an awfully sharp knife to pull that off."

In a tribute to her intellectual honesty she paused to consider the point. She then said in her predictably stubborn way, "Yes but it is still not accurate." Then Charles who had danced around the hat without planting a wayward foot on it said the magic words. "Tempest, a number rounded to the thousandths is close enough." "Close enough, close enough, who decides what is close enough Charlie. We are talking about math here! If everyone in the United States decided to send me one thousandths of a dollar, I would have two hundred and fifty thousand dollars. The difference between zero and two hundred and fifty thousand dollars is close enough for you? I think not." Tempest's new example was better thought through and far less ambiguous than the previous massive pumpkin rationale that she had offered "Tomato Head".

Charles was a very mature twenty plus year old. He did not mind getting into an intelligent debate with the girl who was about to be ten even though any casual observer might conclude that at this point he was getting bested. He again attempted to make his case on the basis of complex financial calculations, industrial applications, chemical combinations and other more complex numbers than the simple fractions that Tempest chose to use in her narrow examples. In an equally mature manner, because she liked Charlie, the young pupil made a comment she had heard made by adults numerous times in the past, "Charles, I think we are just going to have to agree to disagree." Her teacher replied, "I guess that pretty much sums it up doesn't it." Tempest concluded, "Yes, it most certainly does."

As the two well-mannered combatants returned to their respective corners Diane Arrck came through the front door. She immediately went to the dining room to apologize to Charles for not promptly informing him of Tempest's improved health. Charles was very courteous in return indicating that the opening in the study schedule afforded them the opportunity for a spirited discussion on the topic of math. Diane said, "Oh really, well I know how much Tempest loves her math, it must have been very stimulating indeed." Joan piped up indicating that the conversation was so animated you could even hear Tempest from outside. Diane Arrck gave Tempest a look and she lowered her head slightly and said, "Sorry mom."

Charles sensed that it was getting late and taking a glance at his watch said, "I need to excuse myself. If I don't leave soon I will miss the last bus out to the college this evening." Diane said, "Yes Charles, please don't let us keep you." Charles rose from the table and told them all that it was a pleasure to meet them. He made a specific point of telling Tempest that he had truly enjoyed making her acquaintance and he looked forward to seeing her again someday. Tempest was equally happy to have met Charles and was sad that their time together had come to an end. Diane walked with Charles to the door and compensated him for his work, giving him twice the normal agreed upon amount for the previously identified math confrontation. She considered it combat pay.

Charles did not count the cash but simply put it in his pocket and thanked Mrs. Arrck. As he headed up the walk towards the street Charles pondered the tenacity Tempest had exhibited when challenging the status quo related to repeating decimals. He applauded her desire for precision. Charles admired Tempest's passion for the numbers. She stood her ground and made some very compelling arguments. He thought for a moment, if she has issues with repeating decimals her head is going to explode when she gets to geometry and has to deal with pi. As it turned out, Charles exhibited the same storied predictive power as Nostradamus as when the time came for Tempest to tackle the area and circumference of a circle, her head as well as those around her nearly did explode.

Chapter Thirteen: Tuber Something

After Charles made his exit Mrs. Arrck headed for the kitchen. The concerned mother asked Tempest how she felt which produced a response that she was feeling fine. Diane then made a general inquiry into her school day. Tempest indicated that the session at school was normal but the extended hours had made it a little more than an average day. She said, "I am glad tomorrow will be the last day for additional hours." Joan responded, "You should try doing it for a week. It isn't much fun." Their mother countered the mild griping by saying, "Now girls, this is a small price to pay for the town to finally put the issues of "the cough" behind all of us." Upon saying this Diane was reminded of her encounter with Ruth that morning and asked Tempest, "Was Caleb at school today?"

Tempest rose to begin to clear the tea cup and accessories that had been provided for Charles and in the process replied that Caleb had come to school but there was something different about him. "It looked like he may had woken up late and I know for sure he didn't have his usual breakfast. He told me that by the time sixth period lunch rolled around he was ready to eat one of his books. I am pretty sure his tummy rumbled. I could hear it clear across at my seat in class." "Did he say why his morning routine was disrupted?" her mother asked. Tempest replied, "He said that his mother wasn't feeling well and that she was going to see a specialist over in Barretown this afternoon." Diane pondered why Ruth felt the need to go all the way to Barretown which was over thirty miles away. There were more than enough capable doctors much nearer to Averton. She worried that the illness her neighbor was dealing with might be much more complex than a simple tickle of the throat.

All the talk of Caleb made Tempest curious. Seeing that dinner would be a little late that evening, because her father always made it home for the Thursday night family meal, she left the rear door of the house and went over to the Baxter's. She knocked on the door and waited on the step as the back entrance was locked. Her customary practice was to knock, turn the knob, open and enter in a rapid four step process that might generally be reserved for family members but today she needed to wait. Paul had told Tempest repeatedly, "There is no need to knock, you can just come in. You are just like family." But Tempest was a polite little girl and always felt knocking, albeit perfunctory, was still what good manners dictated.

While standing on the back steps she could hear Caleb walking across the kitchen floor on a path to open the door. Had they both been a little taller she would be visible through the window. When he arrived he asked, "Who is it?", as his parents had always instructed him to do when he was home alone. Tempest replied, "It's me. The door is locked. Please let me in." Caleb opened the door and said, "It is Ok for you to come in because you are just like family. But my mother told me no one else was allowed in until she came home." Before he closed the door Caleb emphatically looked both ways as though he was running a speakeasy or a gambling den. Then he closed the door quickly.

Tempest stood in the kitchen and said to her friend, "What is going on? Why the need for all the secrecy?" Caleb shifted from side to side while standing in front of Tempest and said, "I don't really know. I think my mother might be really sick. My father cancelled his classes this afternoon and took her to see a special doctor. To tell you the truth Tempest, I am a little scared." Tempest asked, "What is wrong with her?" Caleb said, "I am really not sure and neither is she. I heard her talking with my father. She is tired and has no appetite. There is also a heavy feeling in her chest. Today when my mom woke up, she was so dizzy she nearly fell down."

Tempest asked, "When are they supposed to be back?" Caleb said, "My father called from the hospital before they left. They should be home soon." Tempest noticed Caleb's books on the kitchen table. The history text was open to the reading assignment they had been given by "Tomato Head". She said, "I haven't cracked a book yet. Charles was at our house when we arrived home this afternoon. We had a chance to talk about some math concepts. It was good." Then Tempest remembered that her young friend did not make the walk back from school with her. She asked, "Where did you run off to when class ended? Don't you want to walk home with me anymore?" Caleb confided in his neighbor that he had been told to go to the nurse's office and once there they stuck a funny pin in him. He lifted the bandage to show a small circle of tiny holes in his left arm. In slightly more than a whisper Caleb said, "The nurse told me to come see her in three days or see a doctor immediately if the spot gets red."

Tempest took a close look at Caleb's arm and then asked, "Did she tell you what this is for?" Caleb replied, "She said it was a test for an illness called tuber something or other. The doctor from Barretown called the school and asked that I be tested. Nurse Blount said they are just being careful and doing this out of what she called an abundance of caution. By the way, I am not going to school tomorrow. I have to stay home until they get the results of the test." Tempest answered, "I will take good notes and share them with you like you did when I missed class." Caleb said, "Who knows, if I am out long enough maybe I can see if Charles can tutor me?" Tempest commented, "You should be so lucky. Charlie is a good teacher although not as precise as he should be."

The Baxter's car made the usual sounds as it came into the driveway and entered the detached garage in the rear of the yard. Caleb said, "You better go. It is best you leave through the front so my parents don't see you. Tempest, please don't let anyone know what is going on with my mother. She told me that she wanted to keep it in the family until she knows more." His best friend said she wouldn't share their conversation with anyone and made her way to the front door, slipping out just as Mr. and Mrs. Baxter entered the kitchen. They were not speaking much. Caleb noticed the familiar small round bandage on both of their left arms. It was the same one he was wearing.

That night Tempest did her homework in her room. Since she had moved slightly ahead of the class under Charles' tutelage, she was able to go lights out at nine thirty. It would be good to get a little extra sleep. She was feeling well enough to go to school but she was still a little listless and could use the additional rest. As she laid on her side in bed she saw the light go on in Caleb's bedroom. Her lifelong friend had finally decided it was time to turn in for the evening. She was able to see him moving around. She was sad that he was dealing with anxiety over his mother's health. Just before she drifted off to sleep she saw Caleb standing in front of the mirror over his dresser lifting the edge of the bandage. He was checking on the recently administered pin holes in his left arm.

Chapter Fourteen: A Surprise Exit

Mrs. Baxter woke the next day refreshed from a good sound sleep feeling better than she had in a number of mornings. She rose at the usual time to wake her son. When Caleb rolled over he reminded his mother he would not be attending Averton Elementary that morning. Ruth felt so good she had forgotten most of the events of the prior day. When reminded, the bounce in her step was significantly reduced.

Ruth made her way to the kitchen and found Paul already engaged in reading a day old newspaper with his morning coffee. He asked his wife how she felt and she said, "I felt a lot better before being reminded that I was supposed to be sick." Paul replied, "You know I have been thinking. There are two people in this town who seemed to be the most affected by the recent epidemic. That would be you and Tempest. Tempest had to fight "the cough" for a longer time than most but she got better. If the illness was something spectacularly troublesome it would not have just run its course." Paul chose his words purposely substituting the term "spectacularly troublesome" for the more commonly used phrase "life threatening".

The observation that both she and Tempest had the most severe reactions had crossed Ruth's mind previously but she did not dwell on the diagnostic implications of her natural daughter's bout with what was more than likely the same germ. It would be wise however to keep an eye on Tempest as she continued her convalescence in order to gain any additional insight into what might be in store. After some additional time at the kitchen table the Baxters heard the Arrck children leaving for school. Ruth peeked out the window and observed Tempest. She looked happy and healthy, holding Clark's hand, walking just ahead of Joan, as they hiked up Lincoln Avenue towards Averton Elementary. While she was watching, Noah bounded from the porch and proceeded in the opposite direction, towards Averton Junior High.

Fifteen minutes later, the sound of the Averton Daily hitting the front door occurred nearly simultaneously to the sound of Diane starting her car to begin her short commute to the Averton library. This morning as she backed out of the driveway, she saw Paul in his weekend clothes bending over to pick up today's edition of the local news. When he saw Diane reversing out of the driveway he waved. Then he made an awkward move to return inside the house realizing that it might have been better had he been a little stealthier in the retrieval of his reading material.

Tempest had dutifully kept the secret about Caleb's tuber something test and the fact that he would not be attending school on doctor's orders. But Paul's lack of awareness as to Diane's normal schedule had served to let the proverbial cat out of the bag. Having studied to be a medical professional as well as being the third bow on the Averton Women's Archery team, she also spotted what appeared to be a round plaster bull's-eye on the inside of Paul's left forearm. There were only a few reasons for the need for such a bandage. Paul may have just randomly injured himself performing one of his usual household chores. A more ominous cause might be the administering of a Tine test, the most current tool available to the medical profession for assessing the existence of tuberculosis. Diane considered that it would be routine for any good physician to check for just about anything when the symptoms didn't point in a particular direction. Tuberculosis was likely just a shot in the dark, but the fact that it was even being considered made her wonder just how sick her neighbor might be.

The question of the condition of the mother of her daughter slipped in and out of her mind during what proved to be a busy morning at the library. Some local women had a book club meeting that had been moved from the town hall due to emergency renovations and figured what better place to hold their gathering than the library. The answer to Diane's gnawing questions regarding Ruth Baxter came sooner than she expected. It came before she could warn her family to steer clear of the Baxter residence for the time being. It came sooner than she had the chance to offer any assistance in the more mundane shopping activities that they were likely told not to partake in.

When the phone rang at the library at eleven twenty two Diane heard Paul Baxter's voice. He was in a mild state of panic. "Diane, I know it is a lot to ask, but can you come home to keep an eye on Caleb? Ruth just had what the ambulance service thinks might have been a stroke and I need to go with her to the hospital." Diane immediately said, "I am on my way. Go with Ruth and I will be there in no time." Diane spouted some orders to her part-time assistant as she grabbed her keys and bolted for the door. She ran to her car and was on her way home in a flash.

When Diane arrived she found Caleb sobbing in the living room of the Baxter home in dire need of some emotional attention. Despite the significant risk of infection, if he was indeed positive for tuberculosis, she held her natural son in a loving embrace in an effort to comfort him. It was the first time she had ever done so. Caleb had just been witness to a disturbing event that would more than likely haunt him at some level for the remainder of his life.

Mrs. Arrck was ready to do whatever she could do to protect Caleb and bring any possible relief to her young son. Through the tears Caleb asked Diane, "Is my mother going to be alright?" Diane held him closely and put her hand on the back of his shaking head and said, "I am sure your father will let us know something as soon as he knows. For now she is in good hands." Caleb sobbed, "I hope so. I need my mother!" Diane resisted with all her heart the desire to say, "I am here." She merely held Caleb even closer and rocked him gently until he calmed down.

It was a long afternoon with little news and when the phone rang in the Baxter house around two o'clock that afternoon it was Mark Arrck who had gone to the hospital to be with his neighbor. The news was devastating. Ruth had succumbed to what was described as a massive heart attack. Mark indicated that she never regained consciousness at the hospital after slipping into a coma on the floor of the Baxter kitchen. Ruth was alone with Caleb at the time she took that last waking breath. Paul was on the phone calling nine one one.

When Diane heard the news she sat quietly on the couch in the Baxter's living room. She did not know what she should say to Caleb. Based on her reaction no words were necessary as the young man already knew the verdict. His mother had passed away at the hospital and he would never again have her in his life. He did not yell or scream or shout out loud. He was surprisingly resigned and walked into the kitchen to sit at the table where his mother usually sat when having her morning coffee. He looked at Diane with eyes verging on bursting with tears and said, "What am I to do now?" Diane looked at the ten-year-old boy sitting before her and saw him less as a child and more as a young man facing one of the most difficult moments in anyone's life and said simply, "Carry on son, that's all we can do."

The next days were very difficult for Paul, Caleb and most of the Arrck family. The untimely death and wake of Ruth Baxter was the biggest thing to happen in Averton in quite some time. Those close to the family battled to ensure the ceremonies maintained an appropriate level of solemn decorum. The day of the funeral half of the town was invited back to the Baxter house in the time-honored tradition designed to raise the spirits of the burdened family. The overt attention by the close and distant relatives did help lessen the sorrow and some of Orville Blount's recollections of the late Ruth Nubbler Baxter's antics from her days at Averton Elementary School actually brought a fleeting smile to Paul's face. Caleb was another story however. He would need to grieve on his own and hopefully time would heal his wounds. Throughout the entire affair Diane watched Caleb from afar. She was trying to be sure her natural son received the support he needed. When the last of the relatives finally exited the Baxter home, it was Caleb, Paul and Diane left alone.

Diane said to Paul, "Don't bother worrying about cleaning up all this food and these dishes. I will be over early with the girls tomorrow and we will fix this place up for you." Paul was thankful to have such good neighbors. He told Diane he needed to lay down and get some rest and went upstairs to the room he had shared with Ruth since they moved to this house many years earlier. Diane found herself again with the abandoned Caleb. He was still alone staring at a pepper shaker that was always sitting on the kitchen table just as it had been the prior week before all this started. He was lost in his thoughts.

Diane joined him and said nothing for the longest time. It was Caleb that broke the silence saying, "Mrs. Arrck, I really don't understand why my mother said to me what she did right before she went into that coma. I was panicked and upset and might not have actually understood what she told me." Diane tensed up thinking that Ruth had broken her vow to talk of things that were never to be spoken of again. She did not want to seem overly apprehensive and did not want to intrude upon the emotions of her natural son but said gently, "What did she say to you?" Caleb replied slowly, "It was a little weird what she said. I am not sure why she said it." Again Diane made an effort to encourage Caleb to speak, taking every precaution not to badger the young boy. "She must have had good reason. She wanted you to know something important." Caleb said, "I know that's the case. But with everything she could have told me, why would her last words be about her engagement ring and in her final conscious breath whisper, Caleb, make sure you take care of Tempest."

Diane had no response for Caleb. She acted as though she was just as puzzled with Ruth's final words to her son but Diane knew what she said and why she said it. Out of respect for the dead, Mrs. Arrck did not judge her former neighbor and actually gave her credit for not revealing more to her fraudulently acquired son. She had left a rather huge clue that if pursued by Caleb might have unraveled the tangled web that for nearly ten years had grown wider and deeper. In an effort to comfort her true son Diane simply said, "Well who knows why she said it. Maybe she just knew Tempest was important to you and she made you happy." Once she had made the comment she looked down at the young boy's forearm. The pins that had been pressed into his skin the week before had not turned red and were no longer visible.

Soon Caleb went off to bed and Diane left the Baxter house to join her own family, most of whom had already gone to sleep on that stressful Saturday evening in their still slightly above average sized small town. Saturdays came and Saturdays went, most without any notable event to distinguish them in her memory. But this Saturday would be different for Diane.

She realized that although the world would never officially count her as Caleb's mother, in the absence of Ruth she had the opportunity to reclaim the role. It excited her and scared her at the same time. Ruth's untimely death might have moved her peculiar situation back into a more normal balance. She had always dreamed it could be this way. At this point it was all she could hope for in making something positive from Caleb's sorrow. The events of the coming months would however alter the calculus of the situation unfolding as she initially wished it might.

Chapter Fifteen: Seeking Help

It took a few weeks but the healing power of time began to have its effect and life, although changed forever, began to take on a new sense of normalcy for the Baxters and the Arrcks. Caleb was required to be more self-sufficient than previously in recognition of the increased duties his father had now undertaken. He needed to wake himself, prepare himself for school and be ready to go to meet Tempest and the rest of the Arrck clan as they headed off daily. He would join the three Arrck children as their brother made his trademark bolt from the door and trekked in the opposite direction. The new arrangement seemed workable but it was putting a great deal of unseen pressure on Paul. Prior to this he would spend additional hours at the college in order to make financial ends meet. With the added responsibilities of caring for a son, who had recently turned ten, this was no longer the case.

The Arrcks were more than willing to chip in and do their part in support of Caleb's care. Paul could see Diane had settled into a more nurturing relationship with his son. He was happy for the emotional support Caleb was getting while at the same time uneasy that her maternal instinct might push her actions beyond reason. Caleb, although not in possession of the "Baxter nose", was still his son after all. The lone surviving true Baxter male had just lost his wife. Paul was feeling somewhat vulnerable and was considering ways to protect the relationship he enjoyed with the young man.

Should the real truth of the matter be known, it wasn't Diane who was spearheading the additional care bestowed upon the sad youngster. The river of emotional support he was receiving was flowing from Tempest. She had taken her injured friend under her wing and was making certain that he didn't drift into a bad place due to the loss of his mother. Of all the people in Averton she was closest to Caleb and felt it was up to her to help her best friend through these difficult times. When Paul returned from work a little late that Tuesday because of slick roadways he walked through the layer of snow on his yet unshoveled walkway to collect his son. He would no doubt find Caleb at his usual station with Tempest, sharing the Arrck's dining room table, while they both conquered the homework doled out generously by "Tomato Head".

Paul knocked on the door and it was answered by Joan Arrck. She welcomed him in and asked if he would like something hot to drink. Paul thanked her and indicated he needed to bring Caleb home and get dinner started. His son had begun to know the drill by this point so when his father arrived he collected his books and prepared for the short walk back to his home. He told Tempest he would see her in the morning and left with his father.

Fifteen minutes later as Tempest was setting the table for dinner she heard the sound of a snow shovel on the sidewalk outside of the Baxter's house. When she looked out the window, she saw the lonely figure of her ten-year-old friend removing the three inches of snow that had already accumulated on the walkway passing his house. She cried out to her older brother, "Noah, can you clear our walkway the snow is getting deeper?" Noah knew that being the oldest son and now in junior high school this was his job and rose from in front of the television. Soon he was on the street working side by side with Caleb to clear the two sidewalks.

The snow was supposed to have stopped by late evening. The front had stalled off of the coast and when the denizens of Averton awoke that morning they were either confronted with or treated to, depending on your point of reference, nearly a foot of new snow. Caleb sat at his kitchen table listening in anticipation to the school closings being announced over the Barretown radio station. He and the Arrcks would be able to trudge to school, but it was the kids who lived further out in the rural areas, like the Nubbler twins, who would have the most difficult time getting to school in these conditions. Just as the clock was beginning to dictate that Caleb begin preparing for his usual day, the announcement came on the radio that the Averton Central Schools would be closed. If you listened closely enough you could have heard a hoot come from the Arrck residence. The announcement went on to say that classes at the community college would start at eleven. What would have previously caused little concern, now created another dilemma for Paul, the newly minted single parent.

A foot of snow meant there were special jobs that needed to be cared for in addition to the regular duties. Paul took his snow shovel and began to clear two tracks in the driveway for his car to escape to the town streets. He would never just clear two paths but would always shovel the entire egress. Just opening the tracks would lead to an ice build-up he would be forced to deal with the entirety of the long winter. But he no longer had the luxury of time to perform the task completely.

Once done with the snow removal he checked out the fridge to be sure his son had adequate stores for the day. He was lucky that the food he had purchased that weekend was still sufficient to get Caleb through the coming hours. Paul knew the Arrcks would care for Caleb in his absence but he was unsettled in having to rely on their good nature. He didn't like leaving so much to chance and felt the urge to change the trajectory of his situation before more unforeseen events made his life even more complex. What if he became ill? Even for a few days. He realized the current arrangement wasn't going to work in the long or even medium term and he needed to take swift and decisive action.

Paul's younger sister Marley lived in Barretown. She had been divorced for a little over a year. She had a son who was the same age as Noah. His sister was an artist who made a decent living selling paintings and pottery to a well-heeled clientele she had cultivated over the years. Between the money her art brought in and child support she was able to live a relatively stable life while managing the random pitfalls with the same sense of impending doom that now confronted her brother.

The library was also closed that day. When Paul knocked on the door of the Arrck residence to ask Diane if she would be so kind as to keep an eye on Caleb, he knew it was not even necessary. But he did so anyway and it made him feel bad. While he was standing in the doorway speaking to Diane, Tempest squeezed past him all dressed for winter fun saying, "I am going to get Caleb and we are going to build a snow fort." Paul knew his son was in good hands but it distressed him nonetheless. While driving to the college that morning he decided he was going to pay Marley a visit.

The following Sunday was warmer than most December days and the snow that had fallen the prior week was melting quickly. Paul woke early and took the opportunity to clear the entire driveway of snow. He would be ready for the next snowfall and not have to worry about a freezing mess for the remaining four months of an upstate New York winter. After they had a chance to have breakfast, Paul and Caleb took a ride to Barretown.

Chapter Sixteen: The Stars Prepare to Align

Due to wet roads and holiday traffic it took a little over an hour for the two travelers to reach Barretown. When they arrived in the center of town it was a few quick turns before finding themselves on the street where his sister lived. Marley Baxter and her twelve-year-old son, Edward Jacobs, now resided alone in the tidy pale yellow three bedroom home with the lovely green shuttered windows and open porch. Her former husband of fifteen years, a local attorney with a family law practice, had cited irreconcilable differences as the reason for the divorce he sought, but it was more than likely his desire to be with the beverage cart girl from the local golf course that drove his behavior. Marley was shocked at first but then realized that her husband had been no more than an accommodation for her to maintain the life that she pursued. She was wed more to her artwork and her son than to her husband. She was not sad to be single.

The Avertonians pulled into the driveway. When the car came to a stop Caleb stepped out and his foot found a puddle as it touched the ground outside. He quickly jumped to a dry spot in the driveway. Then he and his father proceeded to the porch where Marley had opened the door and was waiting. Although they lived fairly close, Paul had not been to visit Marley since the divorce. Paul did see Marley and Edward when Ruth passed away but that hadn't afforded much of an opportunity to catch up on the other important events in their lives. This meeting would give them some brother and sister time. It would also allow Paul the chance to deliver an offer to his remaining sibling.

Marley invited Paul and Caleb in. Caleb left his shoes by the door since one was soaking wet. They walked to the kitchen table. Seated at the table was Marley's son Edward. He was reading a physics textbook. It was not for school. Edward did this sort of thing for fun. When the company came the book was put away and they all sat down to discuss the kind of light topics that families discuss when they haven't seen one another for a while. Both Marley and Paul knew there was something more important on the agenda. Paul because he knew the subject. Marley because she knew her brother. After a half an hour of idle chat, Marley suggested to the boys that they might enjoy going to the basement to play with Edward's model race car set. When Caleb heard there was such an assembly hiding in the cellar he could hardly wait to descend the stairs and begin playing. When the boys were gone, Paul came to the purpose of his visit.

"Marley, you no doubt realize that our visit here today is not entirely a random social call," he began. She replied, "I know you well brother. Tell me what is on your mind." Paul opened by describing the circumstances that he had been managing since Ruth's death, thinking that Marley likely had similar issues to manage since her divorce. He made it clear that whatever she decided he would accept as an answer. Then he popped the question. "Why don't you and Edward come to live with us over in Averton? It would sure help both of us deal with our current situations."

His sister had been dealing with numerous issues but since she worked at home did not have as many of the same problems with which Paul was now wrestling. She liked Barretown because there was more to do and it kept her close to her clients. Averton was quiet and a little backward for her liking. She was not immediately taken by her brother's offer. It was within the range of the kind of request she might expect from Paul but definitely far on the outer edge of the spectrum.

She was struck by the amount of pressure that must be on her brother for him to even make such a suggestion. Then she thought of how to craft a response. As she considered her options the boys came running up from the basement. They had clearly been having a good time. Edward said, "Boy, it is fun having Caleb around. They should visit more often!" Marley, knowing how hard it was for her son to make friends began to look at her brother's proposition as more of a potential opportunity than a burden. She told her brother, "Let me think about it a few days and I will let you know."

The visit stretched towards the noon hour and Paul suggested that they go for lunch. He would be glad to buy. Marley had to decline as she was to meet a client at her house at one o'clock. She said, "If you want to take the boys somewhere that would be fine with me." The two gave up a cheer confirming their assent to the motion and Paul and the two boys were soon deciding the venue for a midday meal. Marley thanked Paul for taking Edward off of her hands for a few hours. After the threesome made their way to Paul's car, they waved good-bye and the hunter-gatherers were off in search of food.

Marley had a fair-sized array of glazed pottery to go along with the handful of paintings available for sale. She tried to balance inventory with production as she wanted to maintain some level of scarcity and not flood the market with her artwork. Today a regular customer was bringing along a friend. The newcomer was apparently very interested in Marley's work. A few minutes after the appointed time two well-dressed women appeared on Marley's porch. Before they rang the doorbell, the homeowner heard them coming across the wooden entryway and opened the front door.

Connie Plank had met Marley seventeen years ago when she first moved from Averton to make a name for herself in the thriving municipality of Barretown. Connie purchased the first item Marley put on sale and had been a fan ever since. Connie's husband's law partner was named Steve Parker and Steve's wife was named Ashley. Ashley Parker was a younger woman with a capacity for making money and an ability to spot talent. Ashley was in the process of opening two stores dedicated to the works of local artists. One was to be in Barretown and one was planned for what she called the posh quaint town of Averton. Ashley was on the hunt for some strong anchor talent to feature in her boutiques.

Marley invited the two women into to her well-kempt, spacious home. The light was streaming through the south facing windows on that mid-December day and the pieces that Marley had moved into the sunroom were just crying out to Ashley. The truth was that Marley was a more than above average artist. Connie could see that Ashley was pleased with her prior assessment as the entrepreneur moved amongst the paintings only to be distracted from time to time by what she called, "the delightful ceramic pieces", which Marley had put on display. After Ashley had surveyed the room, making at least two passes, she said to Connie and Marley, "This is a wonderful surprise. Not that I should be surprised that someone from Barretown or Averton would have such talent but this is mind numbing." Marley modestly thanked Ashley for her kind words.

The artist was feeling very good about herself when she asked Ashley and Connie if they would like some tea. The businesswoman replied, "Oh, thank you so much for your offer, but we have to be going. Time is money you know." At that point Marley came back to earth assuming all she was going to get was the lonely compliment without a sale to keep it company. The ladies exchanged niceties as they walked to the door. As the two were nearing the exit Ashley said, "So Marley let me ask you, how much do you want?" Marley was a little surprised and said, "How much do I want for what?" Ashley then said, "For everything, of course."

It turned out Ashley was indeed delighted with Marley's work and purchased everything in the house. She even called back later to make an offer on the house, which was not even on the market. She also put Marley on a retained basis for twenty more pieces to be completed prior to the end of June the following year.

When Paul returned with the boys at three o'clock, Caleb still had a half full milk shake in his possession and Edward was wearing some sort of branded fast food chain paper hat. They were laughing and having a grand old time. Paul said, "Well I hope you had as good an afternoon as we did?" Marley was still in a mild form of shock and said, "You might say it was also a good afternoon. In fact, brother, you might even say it has been one hell of a day." Paul was hoping the positive response from his sister was a reflection on her state of mind regarding the offer to come to Averton. The truth was this was only part of the reason for her elation.

Chapter Seventeen: Return to Averton

When Paul and Caleb arrived home they found Tempest and Clark playing in the snow in the Arrck's front yard. The two were trying to roll together a snowman. They had made three decent-sized snowballs but the weight of the heavy snow prevented them for stacking the components into recognizable form. Caleb said to his father, "I want to go play with Tempest and Clark before dinner." His father said, "That would be fine, but you need to change into some play clothes or you will ruin the ones you have on." Caleb bounced from the stopped car, ran up the driveway and yelled to Tempest that he would be right out and then entered the rear door of the house with his dad. The boy ran upstairs. Paul went into the kitchen noticing a flashing light on the answering machine. He pressed the button and the machine whirred to life announcing in a very robotic voice, "One new message."

After a beep that signaled the start of the recording Marley's voice began, "Hi Paul, it's your sister. I have given some thought to our discussion and actually getting out of Barretown right now seems like a good idea. I will call you later tonight. We can talk more about it then." Caleb had left his door open and heard the message while changing in the private spot that you could not see from the Arrck's upstairs windows. He heard his aunt mention leaving Barretown. Being a smart boy he put two and two together and made an assumption about what it might mean.

Caleb changed quickly and was soon helping Clark and Tempest lift the heavy balls of snow to construct a somewhat squat snowman. Tempest was not happy with the precise roundness of the balls and after looking at their creation kicked it over in disgust. They had some additional random snow day fun including making snow angels and throwing snowballs at some now neurotic squirrels. Once they were played out they sat on the porch of the Arrck home. Tempest asked Caleb, "Where did you guys go today?" Caleb answered, "We went to Barretown to see my aunt and my cousin. He has a model car set in his basement which is very cool and we played with it." "That sounds like fun, but why did you go all the way up there?" Tempest asked. Caleb said, "You know I am not one hundred percent sure, but I think my father asked Aunt Marley if she would move to Averton and live with us."

The kids played for a while longer and soon it turned dark, as it usually did before five o'clock in that part of upstate New York with winter approaching. The kids said their good-byes and Tempest and Clark retired to the Arrck home. Diane was there instructing the snow bunnies to take off the wet clothes before they dripped water all over the wooden floors. The two complied, leaving two piles of fluffy winter wear in the foyer along with two red-skinned children, complaining that they couldn't feel their toes.

Tempest and Clark were warmed, raising their body temperature to the requisite level to avoid hypothermia with the help of hot chocolate. A piping hot, hot chocolate was the best thing there was about winter according to Tempest. As she and Clark sipped the steaming drinks from their favorite mugs Diane asked, "When did Caleb come over? I heard him and his father going out rather early this morning." Tempest replied, "He came by about four. They had just come home from visiting his Aunt Marley and his Cousin Edward in Barretown. According to Caleb he thinks they might be moving here to stay with him and his father." Tempest's mother asked, "Oh really, did he say that for sure?" "He wasn't sure. He was putting two and two together. Maybe he came up with three, right mom," Tempest quipped with a slight laugh. Diane gazed off through the kitchen window towards the Baxter house saying, "Maybe he did, but Caleb is a much smarter boy than that."

Later that evening when the children and Mark had all gone to bed, Diane pulled out a very used copy of her high school year book. The spine of the text read *The Avertonian* Class of 1974. Diane flipped through the pages until she reached the section of the annual dedicated to the graduating class. There amongst a flurry of handwritten comments was a photograph of a girl named Marley Baxter. Marley had a rather long list of accomplishments to accompany her photo but it was not the list of achievements that interested Diane. It was the photo. Marley Baxter of the "Baxter nose", the traces of what might have been a distantly related Nubbler face and the flowing unbranded recessive flaming red hair, was what anyone with any sense of the aging process would surmise to be a dead ringer for Tempest. Since Marley had a fairly attractive shape at least Diane could presume to someday lay claim to certain genes that might have easily come from the Mann clan. But the true source of what would soon become Tempest's ravishing good looks, although a dirty little secret, would be entirely from Baxter-Nubbler stock.

Diane flipped through the rest of the pages and found her own photo. At that age there was little if any resemblance to Tempest, although Joan was well on her way to being a spitting image of her mother. Diane chucked to herself, "Well, I can always say one out of two isn't bad." But after the short laugh the protective mother became immediately more sullen when thinking that one day, a teenage Tempest, would be standing next to Marley and only a blind man would not be able to see the connection between the two. Marley accepting an invitation to live with Paul and Caleb might seem like a real positive result for the widower. It was looking more like a "Goody, goody time for phonics" moment, for those with even an ounce of foresight.

When Paul and Marley had the chance to speak that evening there seemed to be very few reasons for her to remain in Barretown. She relayed the goings on from the afternoon and saw no better time than the present to cut the cord with her current community. She had no painting or pottery inventory that would get damaged in the move. She had landed what sounded like a steady source of income. Ashley was locating

John Lack

one of the stores in Averton and was looking to give the town a makeover. The boys enjoyed each other's company. Lastly, she wouldn't have to worry about selling her house because it had just sold itself for a handsome price. There were all these positive reasons and none even touched upon the real motive for Paul's very rational suggestion in the first place. Based upon all that had happened that day it was hard not to assume that the stars had just aligned in support of the move.

Seeing that it was the week before Christmas, the plan was for Edward to begin seventh grade in Averton right after the Christmas holiday break. Given the somewhat consistent curriculum taught between districts the young man should not have too difficult a time acclimating to a new school. Besides, Edward Jacobs was described by most people who knew him as a brainiac. He would have little trouble adapting because of the course material.

The plan was taking shape. To provide flexibility in the event of delays in closing on the property or any issues with the move, Marley could stay behind and join her son in Averton when any hurdles were cleared. The important thing for her was a place to paint and a place for her kiln. Paul had promised her these accommodations. Marley knew the Baxter house had five good-sized bedrooms. Two would be for her and Edward and another, with the best light, would be for a studio to empower her now rocketing career.

There were a few title issues with the house in Barretown that delayed the closing and Edward arrived to take up residence

116

before the planned appearance of his mother. Paul went to retrieve the boy a couple days before the end of the holiday period in order to allow time for Edward to acclimatize to his new surroundings. The Baxter mobile, as Tempest called it, returned back in Averton from its roundtrip mission to Barretown at around three o'clock that afternoon. The car was weighed down with clothes and books and other sundry items that Edward felt he could not live without in the interim period between his arrival and the formal movement of the balance of his belongings. The newcomer would be sleeping in a bed meant for visitors, in a partially sun-drenched room, that was next to Caleb's bedroom. In a few weeks Caleb's room would become Marley's studio.

The next morning Caleb woke before the rest of the inhabitants and turned on the television, keeping the volume low so not to interrupt the sleep of the other residents. It was Friday but the college was closed for the holidays and Caleb's father was enjoying a little extra rest. The hosts of the morning talk show he was watching were in winter attire, outside the normal confines of their broadcast booth, mingling with their viewers on the street. They were referencing the end of another twelve months and that 1993 had been one hell of a year. Caleb reflected that it had indeed been a hell of a year and remembered the loss of his mother. It was terrible to have lost his mom but he had people around him who loved him. Probably no one more than his friend from next door. Maybe he should start thinking about her a little differently as they entered the New Year.

It wasn't long after that Caleb filled the kettle and put it on the stove. The steam from the hot water sent a whistle through the house that woke Paul to a new day. It was the last new day of the year. You would also not get much of an argument from him that it had indeed been one hell of a year. Father and son were seated at the kitchen table, each reading something of their choosing, when Edward joined them for breakfast. It was difficult to put a finger on but the Baxter men noticed something different about Edward this morning than they had observed in the past. Nothing was good, even the boiled water was not to his liking. The best way either would have described his attitude, using the vernacular of the day was bitchy. Edward was a little bitchy in the morning. Paul and Caleb were not well-acquainted with bitchiness. They were at a loss regarding how to handle Edward's morning behavior. In an effort to save their own sanity the Baxter men instinctively reverted to an age old method for riding out bitchiness. They ignored him.

After breakfast and while Edward Jacobs was taking a morning shower, Paul took the opportunity to call Marley. He was interested in whether this was Edward's morning baseline or whether they could ascribe his moodiness to the new surroundings and the recent volume of upheaval in his life. Marley was candid with Paul saying, "Yes there are times when Edward can get moody. It generally doesn't last more than a few hours and he is back to being himself. The doctors have told me it is a function of an overactive mind and there is little that can be done about it. And believe me, I have tried everything." Her words were comforting while at the same time foreboding. The Baxters didn't need a temperamental addition to their home. As far as trying everything, Paul considered that if it became any worse there were a few tried and true tricks up his sleeve that might serve to temper the young man's grumpiness.

Edward returned to the kitchen after his shower. He was like a different boy. He apologized for his shortness and said he would try not to be such a self-assessed pain but there were times when he could not control himself. The two members of the home team accepted his apology and Paul said he also needed to provide better support for the transition. Paul then asked, "Caleb what do you think would be a good agenda for Edward's first day here in Averton?" Caleb was still digesting his father's comment about not providing adequate support and as of yet had not considered a plan for Edward's orientation. He had clearly been caught off guard and when he was about to suggest a walk into town, on what was a brisk but clear day, there was a knock on the rear door. The best laid plans would not have mattered. Tempest was about to set the agenda.

At the arrival of his biological daughter Paul internalized the thought, "Now this ought to get interesting." As Caleb walked to the door he turned and said to Edward, "This is part of your orientation to Averton. Please let me introduce Tempest Arrck." With that he unlocked and opened the door. Tempest had great ears and the Baxter's door was not sound proof. Listening to the buildup she could tell there was some great

anticipation to her arrival. To play along she came through the
door in the style of a vaudevillian entertainer and with knit hat
in hand shouted, "Ta Da!" Paul was taken by the young
entertainer and applauded with great vigor. Caleb bowed at
the waist and slowly turned his hand in her direction to
accentuate her arrival. Edward stared as though he had never
seen anything quite as beautiful in his entire life.

At the sight of Tempest, the transplant from Barretown
realized that to have any chance of impressing this young girl
he needed to be continually on his best behavior. Being a
moody little boy would not put him in good stead with her or
his new extended family. Just the sight of his new neighbor
had a positive impact on Edward. She made him mindful of
the need to clean up his act. When she offered her hand in a
hearty welcome saying, "Pleased to meet you Eddie," the
touch of her skin sent chills up his spine. It was certainly not
the usual reaction one should expect when meeting a first
cousin.

Chapter Eighteen: Orientation

Caleb spent New Year's Eve preparing to watch the Times Square festivities on television. But as with most years once again he fell asleep before the moment of truth. This year he had a companion to share the evening as the boy who now preferred to be called "Eddie" was sprawled out on the floor just beneath the couch where his cousin laid as they welcomed in 1994. For the boy formerly known as Edward, it would be a new year, in a new town, at a new school and for the first time a girl to drive him crazy.

The lion's share of the holiday weekend was spent by Caleb showing Eddie around the environs. Some of the time they were joined by Tempest, some of the time it was just the two boys. When Caleb wanted to show Eddie the way to his new school on that New Year's Day, he enlisted the help of Noah. Noah and Eddie would be attending the junior high school together.

As the three boys walked side by side to the school, Eddie, who was always interested in comparisons and relationships asked, "Noah if you are in the seventh grade and Joan is in the sixth grade and Tempest is in the fifth grade, when did your mother have time to rest?" Noah chuckled to himself at the question and replied, "Well it isn't that simple. You see, I am just one day shy of being too old to be in seventh grade.

Tempest and Caleb are both just one day too old to be in fourth. Joan happens to land right in the middle. So although we appear to be three children spread over three years, we are actually three children that are two days short of being spread over five years. Now, if you were to ask that question to the McCarthy's, they would give an exact opposite answer. Those three kids are rolling sets of Irish twins."

Eddie had been looking for a clever way to find out Tempest's true age but instead was actually treated to a more interesting data point. Eddie asked Caleb, "So you and Tempest must be pretty close in age to one another?" Caleb replied to the boy he thought was his cousin, "Tempest and I were born on the same day, in the same hospital and arrived home within the same hour."

The three boys approached the school building. Since it was his style to repeat certain acts or become subject to bad juju Noah needed to pull on the handle of the school door even though he knew it would be locked. Much to their collective surprise however the door was open. Caleb said, "Why is the door open. Shouldn't it be locked over the holidays?" Noah said, "You would think so but maybe someone is here. A teacher or a maintenance person might be working today. Maybe they have to turn up the heat a couple days early so the building warms up for the start of classes?" Eddie said, "Why don't we go in? What harm could it be? You can show me my new classroom." Caleb was reluctant but Noah being more the adventurous sort and more likely to act first and think later gave a sideways glance at the other two boys, opened the door and went inside.

The school was warmer than the outside but not the usual temperature for a school day. The lights were off but the sunshine streaming in through the open classroom doors was sufficient to light the long hallway of the first floor. Noah said, "Come on, I will show you the location of my homeroom and the principal's office. You and your mother will have to report to the principal's office first thing on Monday. My guess is that you will be in the same homeroom as me but you might get placed in the second seventh grade group since your last name begins with J. Plus there are fewer kids in that homeroom now. The room is right next to mine anyway and I can show it to you. My locker is also right there." The boys went up the hall enjoying the freedom to run and jump and the general frolicking that they would not normally experience traversing these halls during a regular school day.

Edward began to get loud, becoming a little overcome by the freedom. Noah had to ask him to be quieter since there might be someone in the school and he didn't want it to appear that the boys were intent on mischief. They walked past the administrative offices on the first floor. This tiny headquarters complex housed the work space of the principal Ms. Carter. She had been the principal here for as long as anyone could remember. The admin center was dark but the rear office of the principal looked as though there might have been a light on. For some reason Edward tried the door and it was unlocked. Noah was peering through the glass trying to determine whether someone was in the office when the new boy pushed the door open. Noah said in a harsh whispering voice, "What are you doing? What if she is in there?" Edward had not considered that outcome, he was motivated by the headlong purpose of an adventurer. Thinking was not on the top of his list.

Edward began to close the door gently when Caleb, who was standing next to him held the door saying, "Wait, I smell something funny. I smelled it when we entered the building but I really smell it now." Noah put his nose to air and the aroma was unmistakable. It was an odor he had encountered in the Arrck attic when inadvertently leaving a mouse in a closed trap for a few extra days a couple of summers ago. It was the pungent stench of death. Edward wanted to run. Noah wanted to exit quietly. Caleb said, "Stop, don't you want to find out what's happened? Maybe Ms. Carter died at her desk or something." Noah said, "If she did someone else will find her." Edward appearing somewhat the coward added, "Let's leave and call the cops." Caleb stood his ground with the older boys and said, "You guys can leave. I am going to see what's happened."

Caleb entered the small suite of offices and cubicles as the others reluctantly followed. When they came to the open door of the lit room, Caleb peered slowly around the corner. No one was seated in the chair behind Ms. Carter's desk. In fact, no one was visible in the room. The boys entered the office less worried about the chances of a surprise encounter than they were moments earlier.

There was no obvious source of the foul scent and Edward continued into the office. After advancing behind Ms. Carter's desk, he let out a rather feminine shriek and scurried back around the table. Noah grabbed Edward as he ran for the door and asked, "What is it? What did you see?" Edward said in a nervous voice, "It looks to me like one rat eating another rat." When Noah made his way around the desk he was just as disgusted with the visual as he absorbed the horror of the carcass of a decaying rat being nibbled on by a now much more attentive cannibal. The surviving rat attempted to run but was stuck to the same trap as the previously expired rodent and only served to minutely shift the large sticky plate when it struggled to escape.

Noah exclaimed, "Oh, you have to be kidding me." Edward said, "I have seen enough thank you. Let's get out of here. What kind of school is this?" Caleb however, wanted to see and he came around the principal's desk to observe the gross image with his own eyes. Caleb stood firm and said, "This is amazing. Your school is infested with rats and the principal must know about it or there wouldn't be a trap in her office." Just as Caleb was closing in to get a really good look, the boys heard someone moving a chair or table on the floor above them. They looked at each other and at the same time said something that was the equivalent of, "We need to get out of here!"

The three dashed quickly and quietly back through the office door and retraced their path to the exit. When they were finally outside the school building they each took a deep breath and gave a sigh of relief. On the walk home agreement was reached to keep the discovery a secret since any knowledge of the rat in the principal's office would invite questions into how they knew. About a half hour after the boys had exited the school, G.B. Blount entered the principal's office carrying a small club. When he saw the live rat caught in the trap he quietly and humanely clubbed it to death.

Chapter Nineteen: First Week of the New Year

Sunday came and after the families made their religious observances the above average temperature of the January afternoon was a magnet for the children of Averton to spend time outside. There were no formal activities to engage in that day. The warm weather had softened the ice on the local creek making it unsafe for group skating and previous warm days had created bare spots on the sledding hill. The major activity of the day appeared to be an organically developing mud and snow football game that sprang from nothing on the lawn of the elementary school. Tempest, Caleb and Eddie had wandered in the direction of the school and came upon the game which included high school boys and a few ninth graders. No elementary school children engaged in the game. Tempest noticed the age of the contestants early on and suggested that the game might be fun to watch. She selected a spot near the improvised sidelines to view the proceedings.

Neither of the teams had fielded a complete squad. When certain players saw Edward and Caleb they invited them to join. Tempest said, "I don't know boys. Those guys look a lot bigger than you two." Edward said, "I think you are right Tempest. Looks like I will wait this one out." Caleb on the other hand said, "I am going to play." Before they knew it he was running to join the team that was currently playing defense.

Caleb was noticeably smaller than the other boys and the unofficial captain of the red team told the newcomer to play defensive back. There he would be less likely to get run over by one of the bigger kids. When the makeshift blue team's quarterback observed the smaller boy's defensive post, he immediately called a play that sent the ball flying into Caleb's zone of responsibility. Much to the blue team signal caller's dismay however, Caleb jumped the route, intercepted the ball and ran for a touchdown. A star was born. Not since crazy legs Mark Arrck, back in the early seventies, had Averton fans seen such well above average raw talent on the football field.

The game progressed until one of the red team players was seriously hurt and the combatants realized tackle football without equipment, even on a partially snow covered field, was still dangerous. Before the game broke up, a few of the older boys asked Caleb his name and invited him to play again. They requested his telephone number so that he could be notified of future games. Caleb complied providing his number feeling a pride that he had accomplished a great feat by measuring up to the more mature competitors. Tempest was proud of him but not star struck as she chastised her longtime friend for putting himself in harm's way. He said to Tempest, "Your father was a high school football hero back in his day. You would think that football would be in your blood." Tempest said, "Maybe it is, but I am still smart enough to know you can get seriously hurt with this sort of unsupervised activity." Caleb realized that Tempest sounded like his mother and went from adrenalin high to momentary funk as he began thinking about his recently deceased mom.

During the time Caleb was playing football, Eddie had already spilled his guts to Tempest about the rat sighting in the junior high school. He took personal credit for uncovering the situation. So much for keeping it a secret, although he did tell Tempest not to share the information. Tempest was mildly impressed with Eddie's heroics but cared little about rats and was more interested in watching Caleb. It was not Tempest who would spread the news however. In his first week at Averton Junior High School, in an effort to be the cool new kid, Eddie shared his secret with no fewer than ten new acquaintances. By Thursday of that week, the School Board was holding an emergency meeting on the subject. The two key witnesses were Ms. Carter and G.B. Blount.

Neither G.B. nor the principal had any idea how the news of their holiday remediation program, that the two well intentioned conspirators nicknamed "Operation Rat Roundup Weekend", had become common knowledge. They confidently assured the Board that the situation had been dealt with over the holiday break and based on careful monitoring there were no longer any rats on the premises. At least none of the four legged variety.

When Friday arrived signaling the end of the first week of the new calendar school year the kids were ready for a two day break. Noah and Edward were walking home from school to close out his first week. They arrived home about the same time that the four students from the elementary school arrived from the opposite direction. All six were witness to a half-sized moving van parked in front of the Baxter house.

The three burly moving men had nearly finished delivering the new items from Barretown and were going to take away some excess unneeded articles that collected in the Baxter residence over the years. Caleb had already consented to their removal. When Tempest and Caleb walked near the truck the men said, "Heads up kids, this thing is really heavy and we don't want to have an accident." The three men carried Marley's kiln out of the truck and the portable incline stressed at the combined weight of the men and the oven. Upon reaching the sidewalk they put it down and rested. The youngest member of the group said to the man who appeared to be the boss, "We had the old coal chute to pull this monster up from the cellar in Barretown, but there is no way the basement stairs of this house will support the weight."

Raising an eyebrow the man in charge leaned on the unit, thought for a moment and had to admit his employee made a good point. The wooden stairs would likely not hold the weight and may not even have been wide enough to fit the ancient kiln. Armed with this discouraging news, the lead man entered the house to deliver the update. Moments later a woman with flaming red hair walked purposefully towards the pottery cooker with the contrite moving man following sheepishly behind. She arrived at the kiln, stopped, turned and showed the experienced but perplexed mover how to disassemble sizable pieces of the oven. Once complete she looked at the head man and said, "You should have said something before you had to struggle with this monstrosity. All you had to do was ask." The moving men were relieved although somewhat upset and embarrassed that their lack of knowledge had nearly caused an across the board trifecta of hernias.

Marley had saved the day for the moving crew and was exceedingly pleased that they could locate the kiln in the basement as planned. If it had to go upstairs or worse yet in the garage, she was not sure what she would have done. Feeling good about her accomplishment she was getting ready to walk back into the house and she turned to call Edward. That is when she first saw Tempest. For a time that could be considered a little more than an above average moment she was dumbstruck. Marley thought she must be looking into a strange mirror equipped with time lapse capabilities that had carried her back to the fifth grade at Averton Elementary School. She was looking at her own "Baxter nose", the familiar trace of a "Nubbler face" and her flowing fiery red hair.

Marley regained her composure and walked over to Edward and Tempest. The other four children were nearby either playing in the truck or busy engaging in general horseplay. Marley asked Edward, "Who is your young friend?" In a feeble effort to replicate Caleb's glorious introduction of the prior week, Edward took a deep bow, pretended to remove his non-existent carnival barker hat and said, "Please let me introduce to you our neighbor Tempest Arrck, Ta Da." Marley looked at her son and said, "Really Edward, you don't have to be so grand in your introductions." She then leaned down, put out her hand and said to her new neighbor, "Hi Tempest, I am Edward's mother, Marley Baxter."

Later that night when Tempest and her siblings were preparing for their evening meal, the young girl asked her mother why Eddie was Edward Jacobs and his mother was named Marley Baxter. First Diane said, "That is Ms. Marley Baxter to you. Why do you ask?" Tempest said, "When I met her this afternoon that is how she introduced herself." Diane became immediately interested and asked Tempest, "Where did you meet her?" Tempest's response was, "She saw me when she came out to show something to the movers and came over to me." Diane asked, "Did she introduce herself to the other children?" Tempest replied with a slight laugh, "Well mom, she didn't have to introduce herself to Eddie. No, she just spoke to me."

Tempest was too young to understand the reason for Marley's interest, all the better it be that way. The meeting had to happen sooner or later. It was a spark in a room full of flammable lies that threatened to expose the dirty little secret. A secret that would become harder and harder to keep as Tempest became older. All Diane could pray for was that more recessive genes would intervene. As Mrs. Arrck was once again pondering what the three conspirators had done, the oven timer rang signifying dinner was ready. Tempest never did get her answer as to why Eddie was Edward Jacobs.

Chapter Twenty: Fast Forward to Seventh Grade

Life went on and the next two years flew by with no major changes. Marley and Edward became more ingrained in the Averton Way. The other children continued to be slightly above average students. Caleb began to demonstrate some well above average capability in organized sports. Paul Baxter persisted in the life of a bachelor and although some women at the college vied for his attention, he was still suffering from the unexpected and tragic loss of his wife. Mark Arrck opened the doors of "Two by Two Shoes" six out of seven days a week. Diane Arrck was the librarian and now had five assistants. Due to school budget consolidation the town had become responsible for the school libraries and she was now required from time to time to visit these facilities.

The dirty little secret remained a secret held by the two living conspiratorial parents. The secret about the dirty little secret was still closely held by Paul and the compromised nurse. Tempest continued to expect a precise world and would go off the rails when she was asked to accept an answer of "close enough" to a question where more was expected. She was entering the seventh grade at Averton Junior High School. It had come to be known by some as "Rat Central", even though nary a rat had been seen since January first 1994. Her studies included the standard math curriculum for anxious seventh graders. Each day began with Mr. Zurck. The subject was geometry.

Tempest's shift from elementary to junior high school meant that there were now three Arrck children headed in that direction on the first morning of the new school year. She and Joan were joining Noah, who still bounded off the porch and sometimes slowed to walk with Edward and sometimes just kept going. Clark Arrck was the remaining child attending fourth grade at the elementary school. At least initially he would be getting a ride with Marley Baxter, who had taken a job as the sixth grade art teacher. She held this post in addition to her business pursuits as she continued to provide exquisite pieces to Ashley Parker's growing number of boutiques. Diane didn't count on Marley's help for the long haul but was hoping Clark could make some nearby friends to walk to school with once the school year matured.

One morning, a year or so prior, Edward asked Noah why he usually bounded from the porch. He shared the rationale with his acquaintance, who he really couldn't quite count as a friend. The exit ritual originated before the Nubblers moved out of the center of town to "the sticks". Anne Nubbler would often hide in a bush near the porch and stalk the oldest Arrck child on the walk to school. At first, Anne was subtle and did everything she could to discreetly get Noah's attention. After a few weeks of being ignored she became more overt. Finally one day, she badgered Noah the entire walk. He realized that Anne was intercepting him immediately upon exit from the house, hiding in what he referred to secretly as the "Nubbler bush". Noah could no longer cope and got into the habit of running from his house in order to leave Anne behind. He just couldn't stand knowing that she was stalking him. Although Anne and her family had moved from the neighborhood years earlier, he was so traumatized by the treatment, he regularly leaped just for old times' sake.

The teens and preteens made the walk together to the junior high school. The first day of the semester always brought with it a certain amount of apprehension and today was no different. For Tempest and Caleb their daily routine would change. Although in the sixth grade they became familiar with the concept of multiple teachers depending on the subject, junior high would be far different. The students would begin the day in homeroom then move from class to class between specified time periods.

The alphabetical distribution still called for Tempest, Caleb and the Blounts to share a homeroom. But during the day they would come and go to different classes as there were now two full classes for seventh graders in Averton. Ashley Parker had been right. The quaint little town was more posh than originally thought and was becoming a haven for many escaping the city grind for a more relaxed lifestyle. Although Tempest and Caleb were still together in homeroom, they were separated by the Attman twins, Mary and Cary, who had recently moved to what was now becoming a much more than slightly average sized small town.

135

Tempest had never met the Attman twins before today and when she arrived at class was surprised that she and Caleb would no longer be seated in tandem. The Averton veteran did not allow this to affect her as she introduced herself to the girls, who being identical twins, were the near spitting image of one another. When Tempest shared her name with the Attmans they both found it to be interesting. Cary, who was two hours older than her sister remarked, "We have never known anyone named Tempest but we did know a girl named Storm." Mary added, "I guess that is close enough to Tempest." You only get one chance to make a first impression and Mary Attman had just made it for both of them.

The Blounts were for the most part lined up in the next row. Carla was no longer seated directly across from Tempest. She was over Tempest's right shoulder a couple desks back. When her friend came into the room, Tempest went to her seat and administered a welcoming hug. This year there was no germ to transmit as Carla had come to class in good health. Arlene Sharp was in another classroom altogether and probably still showed up just as the bell was about to ring. For the remainder of her Averton school career, Arlene would report to homeroom beyond the watchful eye of Tempest.

Kelly Ackerly the know it all, who had become even more of a know it all, still sat directly in front of Tempest. She was no longer the first student in class as Richard Abeles, who had joined them in sixth grade, was also in attendance. The facility at Averton Junior High was truly close to bursting at the seams. It was a good thing there had been spare rooms left from when this building had housed both the high school and junior high school. The added good news is that the structure no longer provided secluded sanctuary for four legged rats to reside.

Classes were bigger. There were more students. The teachers who had lived a much more comfortable life over the years had become more stressed. Receiving new students from other districts, where the discipline may have been maintained at a different level than the Averton Way, also put a strain on the system. Ms. Carter had made it a point of emphasis that in this school year the teachers would exercise more of what she called "muscle" in restoring the decorum of the Averton classroom standard. She herself was under pressure from the Board because the students she was sending to the high school seemed to be, "a little loose in the discipline department" as her superiors put it. She had also lost a few points with the leadership, that she never quite regained, over the "Operation Rat Roundup Weekend" affair.

It may have been by design or maybe dumb luck but Tempest's homeroom teacher was the seventh grade math instructor Mr. Zurck. As the clock approached ten minutes to eight on day one, Mr. Zurck enthusiastically strode into the room to welcome the students and to get them excited about a new year of learning. Although many students had given the middle-aged, well-groomed, eligible single man the easy nickname "Zurck the Jerk", he was actually a very dedicated teacher who liked kids. It was just that these same kids weren't crazy about math. Seeing that her first period class was also with Mr. Zurck and that Richard Abeles and Kelly shared the same schedule, Tempest was not required to move between classes when the short stay in homeroom was over. After Mr. Zurck provided the necessary orientation information, that had been agreed to by the entire teaching staff, the bell rang and most of the members of her homeroom were out the door and on to other challenges.

The majority of the children in Mr. Zurck's homeroom were on the move but Richard, Kelly and Tempest remained in place. Mr. Zurck, whose first name was Harold, took the opportunity to speak with his captive audience as he truly did like to talk with young people. He had been briefed on Tempest's strong feelings when it came to math. Unlike most of his colleagues, he saw it as a huge positive that any child would have such a great passion for the subject he had dedicated his life to teaching. Harold walked over to the three patiently waiting pupils and said with a broad smile, "So Tempest, are you ready to give the wonderful world of geometry a spin?" Tempest could feel that he was trying to be a good sport and gave a positive and upbeat response. It was upbeat but luckily fell far short of the "Goody, goody time for phonics" level of enthusiasm.

There were two significant changes in Tempest that had occurred over the past eighteen months. She had begun to have a better feel for the impact she had on others and she began to get a sense of how to get her way in a diplomatic manner. She became aware of the impact she was having on

Tempest's Arc

others by observing Edward and how his actions were viewed. She had become more of a diplomat by watching Marley.

Once the rest of the class arrived and the bell rang starting the first period, Mr. Zurck began by saying, "Welcome to seventh grade math. I am Mr. Zurck." He passed out folded pieces of four by ten inch white cardboard. The stationary had a crease along its length and was meant to be folded in half. He gave the proper number to the head of each row and asked the students to take one and pass the rest back. After each pupil had a piece of the cardboard he said, "Now write your first and last name bold and clear so I can see it. This way I will get to know your names. Bring these tent cards with you to class every day and place them on your desk. Also carry the card with you to your next class."

The random nature in which the directions were followed always gave him his first snicker of the year. He tried not to single anyone out for scrutiny realizing that the attention and potential embarrassment might be too much for a young person to easily handle. There were some real beauties in this class however. Over the years he had drawn a statistically valid mathematical relationship between the students who brought their cards through at least Christmas and the ones who forgot them by Halloween. Those that remembered did at least ten points better in his class. The other teachers would share similar results. Mr. Zurck then repeating some of his prior message saying, "Keep this card with you and take it to each class you go to. Also try to sit in the same seat each day. My analysis shows that students who bring the cards and tend to sit in the same seats learn the most and get the best grades."

After Mr. Zurck had finished there was a hand raised by a student Tempest did not know yet. She was unable to see the girl's tent card from her position. The question was, "Can we move to a seat of our liking if we plan on staying there all semester?" Mr. Zurck said, "Ok, here is our deal. I will let you move. But once settled you all agree to stay there for the rest of the year, agreed?" The students agreed and with that there was a mad scramble in the classroom. Tempest kept her seat realizing that she would never have to deal with a seat robber. Plus she liked her location. Close to the second story window for boring days and close to the front for interesting days. When Tempest looked next to her she found herself surrounded by Arlene Sharp and Anne Nubbler, of the "Nubbler face". Caleb had math class later in the day. After homeroom, Tempest did not see Caleb until lunch and only again at the day's conclusion.

Once the kids were in place Mr. Zurck said, "OK this is it. Are you all settled?" The children replied with a resounding "Yes!" Harold produced an instant flash camera and said, "Say cheese." The kids smiled and with that the seating was henceforth locked in for the year. He placed the photo on his desk and said to the class, "Now again, welcome to seventh grade math. This year we are studying geometry. Think of it as the math of shapes and angles. Now take a look at the textbook on your desk. Who can tell me the name for one of the shapes on the cover?" Kelly Ackerly nearly jumped out of her chair in the process of raising her hand.

Harold's style was much different than "Tomato Head's". If you chose not to participate it was up to you, but if you were not engaged you did so at your own peril. Kelly said, "The figure in the lower left corner is a rectangle. The one directly in the center is a rectangle too." Mr. Zurck replied, "That is good Kelly. How about someone else taking a shot?" Tempest muttered in a low voice, "The one at the top left is a right triangle." Mr. Zurck said, "Tempest in this class we raise our hands, get recognized and shout out our answers." Tempest said, "Sorry Mr. Zurck" and she raised her hand.

Harold had a little fun with Tempest and when she raised her hand he pretended for a moment not to see her and then turned saying, "Tempest, please identify another shape for us." Tempest replied, "The shape in the top left looks like a right triangle. That lower left angle might be ninety degrees, although I don't have a protractor handy to measure it properly." Mr. Zurck said, "It looks like a right triangle to me too. Class, Tempest has pointed out that a right triangle is a special triangle. One of its angles is ninety degrees. We will learn all about the total sum of the degrees of the angles for each of these shapes. But first, we will learn what a degree is. These degrees have nothing to do with the temperature."

Mr. Zurck thanked Tempest and said, "There is another triangle on the cover that is a special triangle; can anyone name it for us?" Zurck was trying to get other students to engage, but he knew this was his jumping off point to begin to lead the class. When he didn't get an answer he turned to the chalk board and said, "The triangle in the lower right is an isosceles triangle. Does anyone know what is special about it?" The class stared back at him. He then answered his own question, "An isosceles triangle has two sides of the same length. We are going to learn a lot about this triangle. It will help us understand much more as we make our journey through geometry. Now let's open those books on your desk to the page after the table of contents. The one that says Chapter One and we will get started." Tempest took an immediate shine to her teacher. She liked Zurck's style. He seemed to really care about the learning. She knew they would have disagreements during the year but he would be a good teacher for her. If you asked Mr. Zurck the feeling was mutual.

Chapter Twenty One: Schools Days and Nights

After math Tempest needed to make it through three more classes before she would see Caleb at fifth period lunch. Some of the young man's sports buddies wanted to eat with him but he chose to sit with Tempest. The Arrcks were well represented as Joan and Noah also ate during fifth period but lunched separately, choosing to gravitate to their own friends. When Caleb joined Tempest she was already sharing the table with Arlene Sharp and Anne Nubbler. She held the remaining seat for her neighbor. Wilma and Anne had been broken up by the schedulers. Wilma had a much preferred fourth period lunch. A fifth or sixth period lunch would have severely tested her above average appetite.

The students were gabbing in all directions comparing morning experiences. Each shared positive and negative comments. Tempest appeared the most satisfied with her morning. Caleb was wondering aloud why he needed to take typing. It was his first class of the day. He said, "My fingers aren't awake that early." This drew a light chuckle from his lunch companions. Tempest said, "I have typing next. At least it will keep me awake." Anne commented, "I go from here to Home Ec. I hope they don't ask me to cook and eat anything." Anne had been successful with the ongoing struggled she fought with her weight. Over the summer the legendary aspects of the "Nubbler face" had begun to blossom on young Anne. A development that did not go unnoticed by Noah. Prior to this he instinctively avoided Anne like the plague. Now he wasn't sure he wanted to run any more.

Arlene rounded out the table's comments saying, "Mr. Zurck seems like a nice man. I hope he stays that way. That textbook is about as dry as an old chicken bone." Caleb hadn't been treated to math yet and he asked Tempest what she thought of Zurck. Tempest replied, "Well from what I can tell he certainly isn't a jerk. He seems to be interested in his subject and willing to try to make the material tolerable." Anne chimed in, "Ooh, that's a big word, tolerable. Have you had English already?" Tempest smiled and said jokingly, "Can't you tell? I am a junior high school girl now." The bell rang concluding the lunch period. The refreshed students had three more classes before the day ended. Caleb had math as his final subject in what was agreed by all to be a brutal schedule.

When classes ended Tempest waited just outside the main doors of the school and Caleb arrived first. Eddie came along shortly thereafter. They had agreed to meet at the end of the day for the walk home. Diane also preferred that Joan join the threesome but Joan had other things to do and did not want to get tethered to her little sister's comings and goings. The five block walk to Lincoln Avenue through the even now more vibrant town was still very low risk, especially for a young girl who had begun to study martial arts and take kick boxing classes the prior year.

When Caleb had a chance to give Tempest an update he reported with a sense of inevitability, "You had to see this one coming. Butchy Wagner already lost his tent card. Zurck felt so sorry for him he gave him another one." Tempest shook her head, "Why doesn't it surprise me? Butchy would misplace his head if it wasn't attached." Unknown to the students at Averton Junior High School, Mr. Zurck had won the pool that most of the teachers participated in at the beginning of the day. He was the sole educator that predicted that this year only one seventh grade student would lose his or her card before the end of the first session. The record was nine. The average was five. Harold went for an outlier selection sensing a more responsible tone to these seventh graders than those he had encountered in prior years.

During the walk from school Tempest inquired, "So Eddie, how was your first day? What did you think of your new teachers?" Edward still slipped in and out of bitchiness, although he fought it mightily in the presence of Tempest. He wanted to complain about ninth grade science. Edward had a love for the subject but it could never come close to the devotion Tempest had for math. He was disappointed that the ninth grade science curriculum was biology. What he referred to as the analytical sciences, like chemistry or physics, were more to his liking. He believed these were better taught to students because the concepts could be easily embraced in the classroom. He said, "Biology has a lot of memorization and unless you were going to roll dead body after dead body into the lab the concepts were difficult to really bring to life, so to speak." Specifically he complained that it appeared as though they were going to spend two weeks on cell structure. To this Eddie said, "Who gives a crap about cell structure? The only time anyone remotely cares is when you are a contestant on a game show."

After Edward's mini-tirade they walked in silence until reaching their respective domiciles and Tempest indicated that she wanted to spend some time with her math text and would be staying in that afternoon. Caleb said, "Ok Tempest, see you in the morning." Eddie was obvious in showing his displeasure. He said, "Come on Tempest, why don't you come out on this beautiful afternoon and we can take a stroll down to see the new stores they are building? My mother has placed a number of her pieces in The Parker Boutique and I know she would love it if you checked them out." Edward knew Tempest had grown to respect Marley and in some ways chose to emulate her. He was counting on that wedge to change the priorities of the girl who had already become his clandestine self-appointed heartthrob. Unwavering Tempest stuck to her guns saying, "Sorry Eddie, your offer sounds nice. Maybe some other time. I have to see what is coming down the pike with this year's math text." Her love for math was unshakable.

Edward had already seen his mother's works many times and had no intention of revisiting them if he couldn't go with Tempest. When she left him high and dry, Edward had no other choice than to go inside the Baxter house and make himself busy. Despite being a near two year resident of the

Averton community, Edward had not made any close friends. It was a circumstance that really didn't bother him.

Edward walked up the stairs to the second floor leaving Caleb in the kitchen making a peanut butter and jelly sandwich. He made a planned stop in his mother's studio. Her work space occupied the quarters formerly belonging to Caleb. The younger Baxter was not troubled giving up his perfect lighting for substitute arrangements on the other side of the house. The replacement was much darker and better for sleeping-in on weekends. It was the same reason that Tempest would give as to why she loved her dark room that once faced Caleb's. The only downside registered by either of the lifelong companions was that they could no longer talk at any hour by just raising their windows and their voices.

Tempest retired to her room with a glass of milk. Puffing her pillow, she laid on the bed ready to spend a few hours flipping through the geometry text, scanning the pages to see what was ahead that semester. In order to be able to properly read she turned on the light in the darker than average room that would not have made a very good art studio. She had gone through this ritual with every math text she had ever been handed. Tempest wanted to know what to expect and be ready to deal with anything that might threaten her belief that math was a precise science.

The young scholar skimmed the first few chapters. She could see the basics of geometry being logically laid out before her. She consumed the naming, measurement and determination of angles and how to calculate different measures of various shapes with certain formulas. The term parallelogram stuck in her head and she repeated it over and over as she went into her private bathroom to pee. Tempest's room was dark, but it had its own small toilet and sink, a nice feature for a young woman growing up. It was an odd characteristic of the Arrck house but she was not complaining about its rarity. It was however necessary for Tempest to use one of the two common family bathrooms when bathing but this small porcelain haven offered her space that she greatly coveted.

Privacy was important to Tempest, as it is to any young person and had she known that her privacy was being violated at that very moment she would be livid. With nothing to do, Edward decided to retire to his mother's studio, find one of the less sunny corners and spy on the target of his desire as she conducted her math book assessment. Edward's peeping was not intended to descend into degenerate ogling of a scantily clothed Tempest. He was just mesmerized by his neighbor and would do anything to be within her orbit. Even if he was orbiting in secret.

Knowing that his behavior was not consistent with good moral norms, when Caleb finally decided to come up to his room, Edward made it appear as though he had been in his mother's studio searching for a magic marker in an effort to make duplicate tent cards. It was a quickly created and credible excuse that left Caleb without any suspicion regarding Edward's actions. The fact that Tempest was in her private water closet at the time, chanting about parallelograms, supported Edward's quickly invented narrative. He was now locked into creating duplicate name tags and would find himself scouring the two local stationary stores for the next week looking to purchase spare supplies. At least it served to keep the peeping boy busy for a few days with less inappropriate conduct.

By the time Tempest returned to her bed both boys had vacated the studio. She was about a third of the way into the book when the subject matter moved on to circles. The text defined line segments called the radius and diameter of a circle. It also defined something referred to as the circumference. When she examined the formulas she noticed a notation that looked like a small slanted tooth. She was required to slow down and read the book to learn more about the definition of what she initially deemed to be a variable. In the course of her reading she determined that the mathematical term was not a variable but was indeed a constant, referred to as pi. She found it interesting that a constant was necessary to calculate the circumference and area of a circle as well as the volume of a cylinder or a sphere. Before she had a chance to give it more thought however, Joan called up to ask if she wanted some freshly baked cookies to go along with her milk. It had been a long time since fifth period lunch and Tempest took her up on the offer.

Tempest became engaged in other non-academic activities and before she knew it the afternoon and evening had both slipped away. It was time for bed. She didn't have a chance to advance through the entire math book but a significant dent was made. Maybe there would be time later in the week to finish her annual ritual. As she drifted off to dreamland with the term parallelogram still on her lips she was soon under the spell of a sound sleep. Her ability to rest so easily was a testament to the validity of the phrase "ignorance is bliss".

The next morning when the Arrck family rose they each kicked into their morning routines and in a well-practiced synchronized manner were all ready to depart the house in time to meet the day's commitments. Like clockwork, at twenty minutes to eight, the Arrck children exited the house. Today Noah bounded from the porch and kept going, showing no intention to wait for Edward. When Eddie saw Tempest and Joan he politely asked them how they were and after replying that they were fine the three began to walk towards school.

Caleb would be coming to school a few minutes late today. According to Eddie, he had caught his finger in the door and opened a small wound that wouldn't stop bleeding. He was making every effort to stop the flow or risk bleeding all over the keys of one of the school's ancient typewriters. As Edward was explaining the details of Caleb's situation Marley backed out of the driveway with Clark in the back seat. She opened the window and said "good morning" to Tempest and Joan as she prepared to enter the street and drive off.

Joan increased her stride, creating some separation to walk on her own as they made their way up Lincoln Avenue. Eddie seeing the opportunity, made an effort to engage the target of his affections asking her, "How did you make out with your math text last night?" Tempest was reminded of her new favorite shape and said, "I learned a new word, parallelogram." Then she repeated it three times. Eddie found this to be exceedingly cute. He then asked, "Did you learn anything else?" Tempest then said, "Yes, I learned about this little tooth-like constant named pi." Eddie replied, "Yes, our good friend pi." He began to rattle off a series of numbers beginning, three point one four and on and on. Tempest said, "Why are you just saying that stream of numbers?" Eddie stopped his enumerating saying, "Because you can't calculate pi. It is an irrational number that never rounds to a repeating decimal." Tempest stopped dead in her tracks, looked at Eddie and stated incredulously, "Irrational, irrational, you have to be kidding me!" Ignorance had indeed been bliss and now, as predicted years earlier by a prescient Charlie Farley, her head was getting ready to explode.

Eddie had not been aware of the specifics of Tempest's previous math oriented tirades and did not know just how close he came to experiencing the legendary frontal assault. Tempest had become somewhat more mature as she grew older however and knew there would be a right time to deal with what she called "the pi issue". No immediate explosion was forthcoming. It would be weeks before math class would be engaged in the complexities of circles. The newly alerted guardian of mathematical precision had time to prepare.

She made an effort to put her new concern onto the back burner. When they arrived at school she said good-bye to

Eddie and walked into Mr. Zurck's homeroom. No sooner did she sit down at her desk however, than she pulled out her math textbook and turned to the index to find the definition of pi and the section where she could read more about it. The index pointed her directly back to the pages that she had ended with the prior night. Mr. Zurck caught sight of Tempest pouring through her book with a zeal he had rarely seen in all his years of teaching. She stayed fixated on the hardcover volume throughout the entire homeroom period, soaking in the knowledge like a sponge, not raising her head once. When the bell rang ending homeroom and the other children scattered towards their appropriate destinations, Mr. Zurck approached Tempest saying to her, "You are getting a little ahead of yourself aren't you?"

Tempest was mildly embarrassed wondering who else had seen her focusing so intently on the book. She couldn't even remember saying hello to Carla that morning. Tempest said, "Sorry Mr. Zurck. It is just that I heard something troubling about pi this morning and needed to confirm it." Harold replied, "Pi is still a long way off. What was so troubling to you?" Tempest realizing she was being listened to by none other than "Know it all Ackerly" and Richard Abeles tactfully said, "Can I come by at the end of the day and discuss it with you?" Mr. Zurck replied, "Let me check my schedule." After returning to his desk and flipping open a ledger that contained his day plan he said, "That would be fine Tempest. I will see you after classes end."

Chapter Twenty Two: Zurck is not a Jerk

When lunchtime rolled around Tempest tried to save the same table as the day before but other kids had already landed there. She ended up at a larger table that accommodated six students. The four regulars from the prior day were seated together. Two eighth grade girls grabbed the other two seats. One of the two was a Blount and the other was unknown to the four colleagues. When Tempest settled into her seat she couldn't help but notice Caleb's hand. It had a very large, bulky bandage holding together his left index and middle fingers. Anne saw it at about the same time and asked, "What happened to you?" Caleb said, "Edward handed me scissors this morning, pointy end first and I was dumb enough to grab them." He looked down at the bandaged hand and said, "You would think it would get me out of typing class. But that is the wild part. We haven't even begun typing. We are only studying the keys." Tempest did not comment on the differing story told by Edward related to Caleb's injury but she was more likely to believe her longtime friend than the newcomer. It was puzzling that Edward felt it necessary to fabricate a lie.

Both Arlene and Anne were fawning over Caleb, giving him a little too much attention and Tempest said, "You don't need to baby him. He's a big boy." Caleb said, "I don't know Tempest, a little babying might be just what the doctor ordered. Maybe I should show up on crutches tomorrow. Who knows what kind of attention I will get?" Tempest replied to Caleb, "Be careful what you wish for. You never know what might happen. Being on crutches doesn't look like much fun." Caleb ribbed his close friend saying, "But at least I might be able to get you to carry my books."

The other two attendees gave out a polite laugh. They knew Caleb and Tempest were as close as any young people in town but had also begun to notice what a hunk Caleb was becoming. If Tempest was going to treat him like a brother maybe they could move in on the young catch. After all, Anne had come to the conclusion that Noah was a lost cause and besides she could no longer fit behind the "Nubbler bush".

As the period grew long in the tooth, once again like clockwork the bell ended the recess and it was back to class. While the students were dispersing, the eighth grade Blount girl asked Tempest, "If you see Carla this afternoon would you please let her know we have to take the bus home?" That reminded Tempest to tell Caleb not to wait for her as she had a meeting with Mr. Zurck that afternoon.

Caleb ended his day in Mr. Zurck's classroom. Because he had a little more difficulty than usual getting his things together to prepare for the walk home, he was still present when Tempest arrived for her meeting with the math teacher. Tempest took the opportunity to ask him, "How did you really cut your hand?" Caleb said, "I asked Edward for the scissors he had been using. He was a being a little moody, became annoyed and the scissors were kind of thrown at me. He can be a pain in the butt sometimes Tempest." The young girl was surprised that Edward had behaved that way and more than a little bothered that he chose to volunteer a lie about the mishap. She had never known a liar before and didn't consider it a very positive attribute.

Caleb asked Tempest why she needed to meet Mr. Zurck. His friend's response was that she had requested the meeting. The troubled student wanted to discuss a math concept that had come to her attention. Before it became a federal case, as she called it, "The air needed clearing." Caleb asked, "Do you mind if I stick around? When you are done we can walk home together." Tempest replied, "Sure, I would be glad to have you join us. Mr. Zurck seems like a good teacher and we both might learn something new."

The math instructor had taken a break at the end of his eighth period class to have coffee in the teacher's lounge. It was a dangerous errand as a few of the unmarried young woman teachers would lie in wait and try to pigeonhole him during these short diversions. But for the time being Harold enjoyed the life of the bachelor and managed to avoid their strategically timed advances. After a short respite he returned to his classroom refreshed to find his scheduled guest and her colleague ready to discuss the troubling nuances of seventh grade geometry.

Mr. Zurck welcomed Tempest and said to Caleb, "Just can't get enough can you?" Caleb smiled and rolled his eyes looking towards his shoes in response to his approachable teacher's friendly teasing. Harold Zurck continued, "So Tempest, you seemed pretty intense this morning when you were plowing ahead in our textbook. What seems to be troubling you?" She was deliberate in defining her position. "Mr. Zurck, I am a true believer that math should be precise. I had a tough time accepting rounding to the nearest decimal. Now I have come across this constant named pi. The book says it doesn't even repeat as a decimal. It is just a random series of numbers that never ends. How can that be?"

Zurck was impressed with how Tempest's mind worked and replied, "It is one of the mysteries of math. If you take the circumference of a circle and divide it by two times the radius you get a number that never repeats as a decimal. It is a calculation that never ends." Tempest thought back to the apple example and responded, "But how can that be? The circumference of a circle and the length of the radius can be physically measured. How can we take two things that can be physically measured, divide them and come up with a number that can't be measured?"

Mr. Zurck thought for a moment and considered the position that Tempest had taken and how she approached her concern. He replied, "It is a stretch to say that the resultant of the division can't be measured. It can be measured." Tempest clarified her stance, "Yes it can be measured, but it can't be measured precisely." Then almost offhandedly she made the additional comment. "What makes everyone so sure the rest of the numbers are right if this simple one can't be expressed using the same numbering system?"

Zurck was surprised to hear such and interesting premise from a seventh grade math student. Caleb was equally impressed and waited on Harold's response. Harold was a very confident fellow. Unfazed with the specter of being bested by a precocious student in the pursuit of knowledge, he replied, "You make a great point Tempest. My job to help you understand this better. Maybe we can both learn something in the process." Tempest was not entirely done and to drive home her position said, "What if the Egyptian who first calculated pi considered its value to be a whole number? Then all the rest of the whole numbers would be affected by it. How would we count anything as easy as one, two or three? That would be a real mess." Mr. Zurck deliberated on her assertion for a moment and after silent reflection it was his head that was about to explode.

Her math teacher did not have the answers she was seeking and did not pretend to be able to come up with anything to placate her. He made a commitment that they would work on the issues together. When the time came for the rest of the class to learn about pi, they would share some of the ideas they were pondering. Harold said, "It will be good for the rest of the students to expand their thinking and to question the conventional baseline we teach every day. It might help the others to open their minds and consider new and inventive alternatives." Tempest liked the idea, but did not want to gain any additional notoriety as a math crank. She said, "Let's give it our best shot and see what we can come up with." Mr. Zurck said to her, "I would like you to frame your concern as a hypothesis that can be explored analytically. That is the best way forward." Tempest agreed to Mr. Zurck's suggestion. Caleb was proud of his friend, thinking she had certainly come a long way from her encounter with Mrs. Grady. No one was quitting or having a nervous breakdown as a result of this meeting.

Caleb and Tempest left Mr. Zurck's classroom together. Caleb said, "Wow Tempest, you really do have a knack for getting underneath what is happening with math. It really is your thing." She replied, "It isn't always just about the math. It is about the need for things that are supposed to be precise to be precise and accurate. That is what forces me to think this way." They exited the building and Edward was waiting for them. He was speaking to Carla Blount, who had not received the message that she needed to take the bus home. She was waiting for her mother. She would be waiting a long time.

Tempest felt bad and invited Carla to join them so she could wait at the Arrck house instead of standing in front of the school until nearly five o'clock. Edward had an immediate interest in Carla but it melted like ice cream in summer when Tempest entered the scene. Tempest had little interest in the advances of Edward Jacobs. After today's fibbing incident, she wasn't even sure she wanted to count him as a friend.

158

Chapter Twenty Three: A Family Affair

Carla and Tempest shared a lively conversation catching up on the topics they would have talked about if they enjoyed any classes together that semester. But this was not the case. They did pass each other at least three times a day in the hallway and had a few seconds to chat in homeroom, but that was the sum total of their opportunity for interaction. The next two hours would be put to good use. Carla had heard that Mr. Baxter's sister had joined him in the Baxter house after his wife died and was interested in any details that Tempest could supply. Nineteen ninety six would be another election year and the Blounts were always on the lookout for new voters to help with the traditional November run. Recently they had been very busy due to the influx of new people into Averton. The recruitment effort was top of mind for Carla. Tempest gave some details about Marley, indicating that she was indeed a Baxter and had graduated from Averton High School. Tempest was not sure of her political affiliation. Once those details had been provided, Carla's questions turned to Edward.

Tempest was careful in giving her friend an assessment of the boy she called Eddie. She knew that any dirt provided would more than likely find its way into the gossip mill and Tempest didn't want to make the ninth grader's life any more difficult than it had been already. She did sense that Carla might have an interest in her neighbor that went beyond the voting booth. Struggling to provide a balanced view she described the young man as an interesting boy who was a good student. He enjoyed science, especially chemistry and physics. He was a bit of a loner, who would rather read a textbook than watch a sporting event. She avoided the particulars with regards to his bouts with bitchiness that apparently could advance into aggressive behavior. When she thought she had provided enough color she inquired, "Why do you ask? Is there someone interested in him? You do realize he can't vote yet Carla?" Carla smiled and said, "Come on Tempest, you know how it is. It is always good to keep track of what's out there." Up until this point in her life, Tempest had never really given much thought to "what was out there".

That weekend was a big event for Marley. It was also a major happening for the town of Averton as the new stores that had been recently built in the community center were going to be officially opened for business. Although The Parker Boutique at Averton had been doing business under the guise of a "soft opening", this weekend was the well-advertised grand opening of the center and the six stores that would help bring additional shoppers into town. Luckily for Mark Arrck, none of the new retail locations dealt in footwear. Unfortunately for the Blounts, the current mayor who was not a Blount, was taking credit for bringing new growth to their fine municipality. The willingness for businesses to invest should give people faith in the community and its leadership, was how the current mayor positioned it with the local press.

Tempest had been invited by Edward to attend the event and she accepted his invitation. Caleb was going to attend as well despite the fact that he had not received an official invite from his cousin. Eddie calculated that at two o'clock on Saturday he and his love interest would make the walk up to the new stores and be in attendance as Marley's art played a central role in the opening of the boutique. Tempest and Caleb both planned for there to be three attendees walking to the festivities.

At around one thirty that Saturday the doorbell rang at the Arrck home. When Tempest answered it, a near formally attired Eddie was standing on the porch. His hair was slicked back with the help of some overused styling product. The overdressed boy said ceremoniously, "Tempest I am here to escort you to the opening." Tempest curtsied in a half-joking way and then called in a loud voice, "Come on Caleb, we are going!" Caleb who had been playing with Clark came out of the dining room in his school clothes saying, "Isn't it still a little early to be heading to the show?"

Eddie was visibly taken aback but could say nothing about the fact that Tempest had invited Caleb to join. After all why wouldn't she ask Caleb to come? It wasn't a date or anything and Marley was Caleb's Aunt. The thought that this might have grinded Eddie the wrong way was the furthest thing from both of their minds. The fact was however, that it did seriously irk Edward and if either of them had been observant enough they would have glimpsed his displeasure in the bitchy facial expression that flashed across the perturbed youth's face.

Leaving Lincoln Avenue the teen and two preteens strolled towards what they would find to be a beehive of activity. As they neared the stores it was becoming clearer and clearer that Ashley Parker's skill as a promoter was in full evidence that Saturday afternoon. There were balloons, streamers and a raft of eye grabbing delights to motivate both invitees and passersby alike to enjoy their participation in the day's events, return often to the locale and of course part company with their well-earned dollars.

The Parker Boutique was all abuzz when the three entered the door. Edward had two tickets which entitled him and Tempest to a goody bag. The woman at the entrance also provided one to Caleb because of his close relationship with Marley. This again grinded Eddie just a little bit more. The final rub against the day not evolving as Edward had envisioned came in the form of Tempest's attentiveness to the artwork of another local artist. Before even saying hello to her neighbor and genetic aunt, her mind was immediately captivated by the spinning concentric metallic circles of the mobiles Holly Dane had created. While Tempest stared at the moving artwork, Connie Plank, who recognized Edward from her visits to the house in Barretown, said to Edward while they both observed Tempest, "Is that young beauty your cousin? She looks just like your mother."

Edward didn't know what to say and became overtly flustered when considering Mrs. Plank's inference. In answer to her question his fight or flight instinct kicked in and rather than focusing on the "or" in that phrase, he decided to substitute the word "and". Edward chose first to fight, which came in the form of pushing an unaware Caleb, who could have honestly made the case, "I wasn't bothering anyone and had no idea what that short tempered lunatic was thinking." Caleb was propelled directly into the path of the beverage cart that was plying the spacious aisles of the well-designed retail establishment. The beverage cart happened to be in the vicinity of the artsy obligatory clothing section that featured wearable pieces, including among other things, beautifully handmade white woolen sweaters perfect for the coming chilly months. The plush wool was so welcoming you could feel the coziness and warmth with your eyes.

It was more than a stroke of luck that Eddie had chosen to take his ire out on the boy who would one day exhibit his athletic prowess on the Averton gridiron, much to the delight of the adoring local fans. Caleb deftly skirted the cart and although bumping into a small child in the process, caught the lad's chocolate treat and handed it to the child's mother just as his freshly gained momentum launched him into the stock room. Caleb disappeared from sight in a hail of empty cardboard boxes. He emerged moments later completely unscathed. Tempest, still being in a trance watching the revolving circles, had missed the entire kerfuffle.

The flight aspect of Edward's reaction followed on the heels of his aggressive act and he immediately ran from the store. When Tempest regained her focus on the present, returning from the world of equations and geometric relationships to which she had momentarily retreated, she asked Caleb, "Where did Eddie go?" Caleb who was himself just getting refocused after limiting the potential negative effects of Edward's horrid behavior said, "I think Eddie decided he didn't want to see anymore art." Tempest replied, "That is too bad. I really like these mobiles that Ms. Dane has created. They speak to me." Caleb responded with a hint of satiric flair, "Really, I didn't notice."

With Edward out of the picture the best friends had the opportunity to tour the shop in peace. The last exhibit they arrived at was the work of Marley Baxter. As Tempest was admiring her look-alike's talent, a local woman of some distinction watched intently as Marley was describing the glazing process to Tempest. The stranger said to Marley, "Your art is beautiful. But this little gem here is clearly your finest work." Marley had to think for a moment, then realized she was referring to Tempest and said, "Oh, this lovely girl is not my daughter. She is my neighbor's child."

The woman seemed a little surprised by the discovery that she had inaccurately made the connection between the two females. She was not alone however. Just after the mildly shaken woman left Tempest and Marley to continue their glazing discussion, the pair were interrupted by a local photographer. Ashley Parker was once again at work correctly identifying the pictorial value of the moment and directed the expert shutterbug to capture the interaction between Marley and Tempest for the local newspaper. The photo would run in the following Monday's edition in the section covering the weekend gala opening. The picture's caption would begin with the phrase, "Retail is a family affair in Averton". To make matters worse for Diane Arrck the shot was to be resurrected that coming December and rated as one of the ten best photographs of the year. It was requiring less and less imagination for even the most casual observer to see the growing likeness between the two neighbors.

Edward's flight returned him all the way back to the Baxter house. Along the way he knew he had overreacted but could not bring himself to return to the scene of his negative conduct. If he had circled back, only Caleb would have been able to recollect his ridiculous actions. Tempest would have been oblivious based on her distracted state. When the young redhead arrived home Eddie was outside the Baxter house and Tempest asked him, "Where did you go?" Eddie was amazed that she was even speaking to him. Caleb knew Edward was being a petulant ill-behaved twit but had not chosen to throw his cousin under the metaphorical bus.

The result was that Eddie never received adequate feedback or punishment for his bad behavior. He was never called to answer for it. He wasn't sure whether his actions were acceptable to Tempest, if she didn't care enough about him to comment or that she just didn't know what had occurred. All Eddie was really sure of was that he dodged a bullet. His growing list of offenses was not lost on Caleb. Tempest's best friend was becoming extremely worried about the serial antisocial deeds of his first cousin.

Chapter Twenty Four: The Written Hypothesis

Three weeks before Christmas Diane Arrck opened the Sunday paper upon returning home from her usual religious services. The paper had already begun to run a special segment that over the next four weeks would look back at the year in review. The first few stories recounted items of a national interest that shaped the entire country. When she looked further down in the article under the heading "local interest" she found the recurrence of the disquieting photo taken of Marley and Tempest at the boutique opening. Despite her numerous prior objections, the editors had not even taken the time to change the errant caption. She was angry and a little scared but resolved not to fall into the "she protests too much trap". When finished with that particular section she tossed it in the trash.

Tempest had performed well above average thus far in her seventh grade academics. She was doing particularly well in math, a testament to her relationship with Mr. Zurck. She could tell however that the time was beginning to close in on the subject of circles and she decided that she would use the lull in the storm to begin drafting her hypothesis related to the pesky mathematical constant pi. To her credit, she had not been obsessed with the existence of the imprecise factor. It was only something that would fill her head during moments when more pressing issues were not at the top of her mind. Given the antics displayed on a near regular basis by Eddie, especially his jealousy for Caleb, her mind had been pretty busy with other issues for the past couple of months.

One day the friction actually caused the relationship to come to blows with Caleb punching Edward right in the face because he was being extremely difficult. Eddie tattled and Caleb got in trouble but in Tempest's book the boy who she was losing respect for on a near daily basis deserved the punch. She did take the time to counsel Caleb on being more able to control his emotions and that violence was never the best decision when confronting his frustration.

The next Tuesday morning in Averton the residents of the upstate New York community awoke to anywhere from an inch to three inches of new snow. The snowfall had not been forecasted and was a function of extreme lake effect snows which generally plagued regions further to the west of the state. Tempest's first reaction was to turn her ear to the radio listening for potential school cancelations or delays. She knew that a mere inch or two was not enough of what she often called "the fluffy white stuff" to create sufficient angst for local officials to alter the usual schedule. It turned out her feelings proved to be accurate and the school day was neither postponed nor delayed and the students left home that morning a few minutes early to ensure they made it to school on time. Noah had to alter his normal schedule in order to get out and run the snow shovel across the sidewalk to clear what was more than a dusting prior to carefully bounding from the porch on his way to class.

When Joan and Tempest walked towards the school they found Caleb finishing up the Baxter walkway ready to join them on their journey. Tempest said to Caleb, "Too bad we didn't get an inch or two more; we would have had our first snow day of the year." Caleb replied, "Just as well. I would have had that much more to clear." His young friend then asked, "Where is Eddie? Doesn't he get to help with the snow removal chores?" Caleb shook his head in mild disgust answering, "No, Edward is feeling a little under the weather today and is going to be staying home."

As they were getting ready to continue, Marley backed out of the driveway with Clark in the rear seat of her car. He had once again scored a ride to school because of the inclement conditions. Tempest asked Caleb, "What is wrong with Eddie?" His response was, "Don't get me started. You don't have enough time between here and school." She said, "Don't be like that. You know what I mean. What is bothering him this morning?" Caleb said, "He would probably prefer I didn't tell you. But he has to sit down more than usual."

The three junior high pupils stayed closer than normal on their morning walk. Joan chose not to break ranks, remaining close due to the potential for an icy surprise created by the weather. They entered the school hallway to the sound of stomping feet from the herd of arriving students. The goal was to remove the remnants of any snow that once melted might seep inside their protective footwear. Some kids just stomped because it seemed like fun.

Tempest made her way to Mr. Zurck's homeroom. He was looking out the window when she arrived a little earlier than most of the other homeroom attendees. Her teacher said to Tempest in the style you would reserve more for a friend, "The ski areas received a lot more snow than we did. With what they have been making at night and this covering they plan to open this weekend. I can't wait for the season to begin." Tempest said, "I have never gone skiing. We prefer sledding. There is not enough snow yet for that." Then she said, "I am beginning to work on my hypothesis and hope to be able to get you a draft by the end of next week. Is that good timing?" Mr. Zurck had taught this course for a number of years. Knowing that he would be introducing circles just before the Christmas break he replied, 'That would be great timing. I am glad you remembered."

Christmas was coming quickly and Tempest had a lot on her mind. She wanted to get everyone she cared about a nice present. This usually meant making a small gift she could share with them. She thought about her options. The meager savings from excess allowance money did not provide much of a cushion for retail extravagance. Tempest was relieved when her father suggested that the family join forces and present a shared gift for their mother. Mark Arrck agreed to fund the purchase. Her mother made a similar secret offer the following day. That meant she now had just five items to procure. While lying in bed Saturday morning thinking about her hypothesis, she had a brainstorm of creative inspiration that provided her absolute conviction in the gifts she would give. She had enough money to buy some colored construction paper and there was string and tape already available for her use. Sticks of various sizes and lengths could be obtained for free from the nearby trees. Her decision was to create mobiles that resembled the artwork of Holly Dane that had so captivated her earlier that year.

Around noontime that Saturday she left her house and met Caleb in the front yard. She asked if he wanted to walk with her to the stationary store that was about halfway to the elementary school in the opposite direction from their current morning walk. Caleb said he had until one o'clock when he had to be back home. Tempest considered this more than enough time and off they went to purchase the raw materials for her Christmas creations. Seeing that she did not mention the purpose for the purchases, there was no concern that running the errand together might ruin Caleb's surprise.

The two made it back to the Baxter house in time to meet Caleb's schedule and when they arrived Tempest asked why he needed to be home by one. Caleb told her that Edward's father was coming to pick him up for a visit. Edward hadn't seen his father in a number of years and he wanted his cousin to meet him. As they stood in front of the Baxter house Marley backed out of the driveway in a rather hurried fashion. Apparently she had no interest whatsoever in reacquainting herself with her ex-husband.

The newly equipped artist had her supplies and needed to get to work so she thanked her friend for being good company and walked towards home. As she arrived at the front door and turned to wave to Caleb a car pulled up in front of the Baxter house. She paused to see who emerged and after a longer than expected wait a tall, handsome, well-groomed man made his way to the Baxter's front door. He knocked on the door and was met with a hug by Edward. The door closed behind them. After a moment of reflection, Tempest decided she needed to get to work.

There was a secretive nature to her labor and Tempest retired to her room with the materials available to construct five mobiles of different colors, dimensions and character. The finished pieces would be placed in small boxes so they were not ripped along with the wrapping paper when opened. She would place three of them under the tree in her home and two in the house next door. The industrious girl laid out each creation in her head and then made a sketch of each piece prior to cutting the heavy construction paper. As she fell deeper and deeper into concentrating on her task, she became one with the circles she was drawing and the shapes she was cutting out of the paper.

Tempest strove for the utmost precision and soon decided a scissor would not be adequate and opted for her father's sheetrock knife to do the cutting. The concentration she delivered in her desire to cut each circle perfectly protected her from harm as her attention to how the blade met the paper was laser like. When she was done she had twenty five circles of various sizes in assorted colors that she would use to build her presents. With the assortment of circles scattered across her bed she selected two different sized purple disks. She gazed upon their simple forms wondering how something as finite in dimensions could require a number that had so far eluded ancient and modern mathematician's ability to calculate in order to measure the circumference and area in an accurate manner. With that she grabbed her math notebook and a pencil and began to record her hypothesis.

Tempest was fully engaged in multi-tasking between artwork and schoolwork when she heard the Baxter's front door shut and the sound of two voices moving up the walk towards the road reached her ears. Remembering her neighbor's visitor she leaped to the window in time to see Eddie's father speaking with his son on the sidewalk. They were having a serious conversation and Eddie appeared intent on listening. Then the man embraced his son. With a final pat on his shoulder Mr. Jacobs circled around the car leaving the young man standing on the sidewalk alone with his long late afternoon shadow. Eddie stayed motionless, watching as his father's car sped down Lincoln Avenue and disappeared from sight.

Tempest knew Eddie could be tough to deal with but felt sorry as the solitary product of a broken home was once again deserted. Who was she to judge him for what the Jacobs' family turmoil had done to alter his young development? How had that trauma affected his personality? For a moment she paused to consider whether or not she had been unfair in judging his behavior. In the future she may need to cut him

173

some additional slack. If Caleb had shared the entire list of Edward's transgressions with Tempest however, she may have thought otherwise.

That Monday Caleb was now sitting a little more than he might usually be expected to do and would not be attending class. Apparently there was a little something making its way around the Baxter household. The source of the serial discomfort touching the population may have been diet related but more than likely it was stress. When Tempest mentioned to Edward that she had been told that his father had made a visit that Saturday and asked how it went the response was a mixture of happiness and sadness.

Edward said, "My father said he wanted to see me because it had been a long time since visiting and he missed me. It was good to see him because it had really been a long time since his last visit." Tempest said, "It must be hard not seeing him regularly." Edward replied in a defensive manner, "It isn't that hard. He is busy and I have gotten used to it. Even when he was home I didn't see him that much." Edward went on, "He wanted to tell me that he was getting remarried. The woman was someone my mother was friends with in Barretown. When she found out, the news didn't set well with her."

They walked a little further and Edward said, "When I heard my uncle and my father talking, my dad said something that my mom will have to deal with the fact that since he is getting remarried he would be looking to regain custody of his son." After a couple seconds of not getting the implications of

Eddie's comment, Tempest realized that the son he was seeking custody of was standing next to her. As Marley pulled out of the driveway that morning she was going a little too fast and scraped the bottom of her car against the slight rise in the walkway. It sent an untethered Clark flying around the backseat of the car in a pinball-like fashion.

The two walkers continued down Lincoln Avenue without comment. Joan was in front of them and although the walkways were clear, her sister chose to stay within earshot and not put her usual distance between the pair. Tempest could tell that Eddie was leading up to something when he asked, "Their wedding will be in the spring. My father wants me to attend. He said I could bring someone if I chose to. Would you give some thought to joining me?"

Chapter Twenty Five: An Old Friend Returns

There were only five days left before the long Christmas break. The first three plus months of the school year were now behind them and students were all looking forward to an extended holiday to recuperate. When Tempest stepped into homeroom that Monday she was expecting much of the same that she had come to know from the first fifteen weeks of school. What she found instead that morning was the school librarian sitting in Mr. Zurck's chair. Tempest placed her books down in the nearly empty classroom and asked the young woman, who actually reported to her mother, "Good morning, where is Mr. Zurck?"

The librarian answered in a rather ominous tone, "I will make an announcement when the class begins. Please take your seat for now." Tempest's mind began spinning as to what might be happening with her math teacher. In a short period of time she considered everything from kidnapping to serious illness. She liked Mr. Zurck and hoped nothing bad had befallen him. When the bell rang the substitute asked the students to please display their name cards so she could take attendance. At this point only fifty percent were still produced. Tempest placed her card before her and when the librarian checked her name the substitute raised an eyebrow. Once the sub completed the task, which required resorting to a roll call, she told the class,

"Mr. Zurck will not be coming in today," and did not offer any specifics as to his condition despite the fact that some in the class asked the question.

Tempest waited in her seat and when the bell rang and the rest of the students scattered she proceeded to the front of the room and asked the young woman privately, "I have been working on a special assignment for Mr. Zurck. If he is not coming back soon it will affect my work. Can you share more with me about his situation?" The librarian looked at Tempest and said in a low voice, "I am really not supposed to give specifics because I don't have any. But from what I heard Mr. Zurck broke his leg skiing and he won't return until after the Christmas recess."

The news was not great but Tempest was relieved that something worse had not happened to her favorite teacher. She thanked the librarian for sharing and said she would not blab the news of Mr. Zurck's accident. The librarian thanked her. A couple minutes before the class started, one of the boys came rolling into the room saying loudly, "Hey, I hear the jerk busted his femur on the slopes Saturday." The cat was apparently already out of the bag.

When the scheduled math class started the substitute asked the students to remain in their seats and read the next chapter. She acted as more of a babysitter than a teacher. It was unfair to expect anything more. She had been thrown into the breech on short notice until Ms. Carter could find a replacement to teach the class for the next four days. Thus far the principal had come up empty but was hoping to have better luck now that the work week had begun. The rest of the day went by fairly uneventfully. Tempest circled past her homeroom before leaving school and found that the librarian was still in charge. Relief for the substitute had not arrived on the scene. Tempest wondered how they would find someone on such short notice and confronted the prospect that she might be without her favorite subject and her favorite teacher until the start of the New Year.

The next morning when Tempest arrived at her homeroom the lights were on but no one was home. There was no librarian and of course no Mr. Zurck in sight. The students filed into class and without adult oversight were more animated than usual. Tempest sat at her desk in her normal way wondering what was going to happen next. The bell to begin homeroom rang and there was still no news. Some students retired to their seats while others remained standing, taking advantage of the unsupervised atmosphere. Those who were not seated scurried to find them quickly when much to their surprise Ms. Carter entered the room. Much to Tempest's delight she was followed by a familiar figure. Once again, Charlie Farley was being pressed into service to fill an unforeseen gap in Tempest's educational landscape.

Ms. Carter addressed the students, "Class let's all get back into our seats. This isn't a high school dance we are running here." The Principal was not being paid to come up with snappy analogies but she was a good school administrator. She stood before the class and said, "As you all know by now Mr. Zurck had a mishap on the ski slopes the other day. He is doing fine, sends his best and is hoping to return after the holiday recess. In his absence we are lucky to have Mr. Farley to teach in his place. Mr. Farley is a State Qualified math teacher and will continue where Mr. Zurck left off. You should not lose any ground due to his injury." Most of the kids made a slight moan. They thought their math holiday had already begun. Now they would have four more days of their least favorite subject. In Tempest's case, she was happy as a clam and nearly belted out, "Goody, goody time for phonics".

Ms. Carter had previously explained the homeroom duties to Charles. When she left he introduced himself in a mellow British accent, "I am Mr. Farley, please display your tent cards so we can take attendance." Upon hearing the tenor of his voice some of the girls began to swoon. He quickly realized roll call was in order. When he came to the third name on his list, he looked up and without calling her name said, "Ok, Tempest you are here." This left the other students, who had been carefully sizing up Charles, wondering how he had previously come to know their classmate.

When the bell rang and the other students flew out to the room Tempest walked to the front to reacquaint herself with her former tutor. She stood next to his desk and said, 'Hello Mr. Farley, it is a pleasure to see you again. How have you been?" It had been two years since Charles Farley had seen or thought of Tempest Arrck. As she stood before him he could not help to think how she had changed in that time. Being a mathematician by schooling he immediately connected the two data points he had regarding Tempest's appearance and calculated a trajectory to her future looks. He could only imagine how beautiful this young woman would someday become.

Charles's consideration of the direction of her appearance ended with his intellectual curiosity and he said, "Good morning Tempest, it is nice to see you. How has the math been treating you?" It was a short period between classes, leaving little time to catch up on the past two years. Tempest did have an opportunity to tell Charlie about the hypothesis she was working on. Charles responded that he thought that made a world of sense and congratulated her and Mr. Zurck for their approach. While they were reacquainting, know it all Ackerly was visually displeased by their comradery.

After math class was over, Tempest continued with her day now mentally lifted by the return of her former teacher. She thought to herself it would be helpful to get Charlie's input on the hypothesis she was preparing for Mr. Zurck. Soon it was lunchtime and when Tempest joined the regular Nubbler and Arlene Sharp for recess Anne asked Tempest, "How do you know the substitute math teacher? He is really dreamy." Tempest brought her friends up to speed, telling them she had been introduced to Mr. Farley two years earlier when she had been visited by "the cough" and was waiting for it to run its course. The redheaded girl gave some dated information regarding Zurck's replacement but indicated that she was not totally familiar with his current situation. Anne, who continued to grow into the "Nubbler face" made the comment, "I would like to get familiar with his current situation." Both Anne and Arlene found the comment worthy of a satirical laugh.

Soon lunch ended and the day rolled on. Before long Tempest was sitting in her last class watching the clock tick towards the final bell. She would not have Caleb to give her any news about how Charles had faired with his ultimate class of the day. Her friend was still at home and probably still getting too much sitting time. She would be walking home with Eddie today. She anticipated the potential of him asking if she had considered his invitation to attend the wedding and prepared herself for the question. Tempest would love to go and see all the people dressed up in their finery but knew a potential trap when she saw one and was uneasy with providing an answer. Her best bet was to indicate that she needed to speak with her parents. She could also fall back on the, "June is so far away, how does anyone know what they would be doing in June," strategic defense.

Tempest walked out of the school passing the usual spot where Caleb would normally be waiting and there was no Caleb as expected. When she passed the spot Eddie would be waiting, there was no Eddie. She waited for Eddie and while standing there Joan came by. Rather than risk having to walk home alone, she joined Joan and the two sisters walked home together for the first time in ages. It may have even been the very first time it was just the two of them making the trip.

The two sisters were silent for the first block but when they were crossing the road onto their side of the Main Street divided town Joan asked Tempest, "I saw Mr. Farley in the hall today. Do you know what he was doing here?" Tempest reported that he was filling in for the injured Mr. Zurck and she was lucky enough to have him for her teacher. Joan Arrck had noticed Charles when he tutored her younger sister and found him to be much more interesting than any of the boys at Averton Junior High School. The older sister was now fourteen but reflected optimistically that they were only plus or minus ten years different in age.

Joan held no jealousy towards her younger sister but would have to be blind and deaf not to know that any comparison of physical beauty between them always favored her redheaded sibling. She was also well aware that the nearly two year head start she had on Tempest was her only differential advantage and it was not sustainable. While holding no ill will towards her sister, she had long ago determined that to have a fair shot at a man she would need to lock one in while Tempest was still too young to be an alternative target. Joan asked Tempest some additional questions but since her sister had not been able to spend any quality time with Charles, due to the need to fulfill his duties, her questions went mostly unanswered.

When Tempest arrived home she picked up the phone to call Caleb. She asked her ailing friend how he was doing. Having no desire to get too detailed he indicated only that it was likely he would be at school the next day. Tempest was pleased with the prognosis and broke the news to her sick friend about the reemergence of Charlie Farley. Caleb did not have much of a remembrance of the tutor and realizing that math wasn't going to be an empty subject for the next three days, saw his arrival as a net negative. Tempest asked, "Did Eddie come home yet? He wasn't outside the school when Joan and I left this afternoon." Before Caleb could answer, Marley's car pulled into the driveway. When it stopped the passenger side door opened. Tempest expected to see Clark slip from the car, but instead it was Eddie who had been riding with his mother.

The next morning the threesome plus Joan in the lead made their way towards school. Noah bounded ahead in his usual manner. Tempest asked innocently, "Eddie, where did you go yesterday after school? My sister and I walked home by ourselves." Caleb cringed at the posing of the question. He had hoped to advise Tempest to avoid the subject but had not yet been afforded the opportunity. Much to Caleb's relief, Edward responded calmly to Tempest's inquiry indicating that he and his mother had an appointment with an attorney in town the prior afternoon. There was no elaboration on the subject of the meeting, although had he not wanted to raise some level of interest he could just have easily said that they merely had an appointment. Tempest, being less of a busy body than most, did not follow up with a question and chose to shift gears and further advise Caleb of the events from the prior day. Before long they had arrived at school.

In an effort to make a stronger case for retaining custody of Edward, Marley's first move was to seek a legal name change for her son. She kicked herself for not changing his name to

Baxter sooner. Although he did not possess the "Baxter nose" and was more recognizable for the "Jacobs chin", her plan was to provide another legal hurdle to support her effort for Edward to remain in her charge. In the process of the legal maneuver, she would by extension fabricate another Baxter male worthy of carrying on the Baxter name in Averton. In this case at least he would possess the requisite genetic code to support the label.

The news broken by Eddie was the Arrck's introduction to what would become a simmering battle with the potential to suck in everyone on or near the periphery at one time or another. Both Tempest and Caleb would find themselves shifted between the eye and the eye wall of the gale often without any reasonable warning. Edward Jacobs, Marley Baxter and Mr. David Jacobs could best be described as the storm itself. A storm with a mind of its own having little regard for ripping apart anything in its path.

Chapter Twenty Six: Christmas Presents

The next day in the time reserved for students to relocate between homeroom and their first class, Tempest had the chance to share some general thoughts about her hypothesis with Charlie Farley. Charles was impressed with the level of maturity his former and now once again current pupil was demonstrating with her analysis. He came to the conclusion that Tempest's head actually did not explode with the exposure to the incalculable constant pi. The hypothesis that she was formulating had thus far exclusively approached the problem from the perspective that it did not make sense that pi should defy calculation. Charles, who had dropped his goal of becoming a doctor, was now both a graduate math student and working towards a minor in philosophy, suggested that she balance the approach and also expound upon why the constant being incalculable was perfectly logical.

While Tempest was processing Charlie's contribution to the effort she proclaimed, "Why would anything that can't be calculated precisely ever be logical?" This observation caused an internal chuckle that the tutor kept to himself. He was hoping that seeing both sides of the conundrum would help expedite the expansion of Tempest's mind that Mr. Zurck had attempted to put into motion. Charles was entertained by just how large an obstacle bringing some balance to her thinking would be for his student. He was bothered however that the stubbornness might hinder her success in blossoming into her full potential. For a girl of above average intellect, she was truly set in her young ways.

Tempest returned to her seat and pondered Charlie's recommendation. She fought off the urge to put the input into terms that resembled, "Just who's side is he on?" To her credit she instead asked herself, "Why would he suggest such a methodology for finding the truth?" This was much deeper thinking than could be done in the short time before class and she tucked the chain of thought away as the bell rang for math class to start. When she opened her book she judged that with a few days to go before the holiday and the number of pages before the chapters pertaining to circles, cylinders and spheres, there was little chance for a pre-holiday confrontation with pi. This would give her the needed time to construct her theory.

The rest of the week flew by, as weeks before holidays tended to do. Tempest had not heard anything more from Edward or Caleb regarding the legal maneuvers underway that were negatively influencing the holiday cheer at the Baxter's house. Even if she had been updated, Tempest's thoughts turned inward and away from her neighbors. The Arrck family always came a little closer at Christmas. For some reason, without any formal announcement or unusual effort, the family ties tightened at this time of year. The moods in the two neighboring homes could not have been more disparate as Tempest went her way that Friday after class and Caleb and Eddie went theirs.

The community college ended classes at noon the final day before the holidays and Mr. Baxter was already home when the boys arrived. He did not hear them come into the house as he was pre-occupied with the phone call he was on. The one side of the conversation that the new arrivals could hear was not pleasant and if Paul had known the boys were there he would have certainly either toned it down or terminated the call. From what they could surmise he was speaking with David Jacobs or his proxy and the subject had to do with Mr. Baxter's suitability to act as parental oversight for Edward. The last line of the conversation that the boys were treated to, prior to Paul Baxter forcibly returning the receiver to the cradle of the phone was, "If you try to make any health problem I am having impact my sister's ability to keep custody of her son, it will be a sad day for the legal profession." When he was done putting the receiver back he made a comment meant for himself but heard by the boys, "Merry Christmas you horse's ass."

Up until that point the two young men had been sheltered from the fact, that although only barely noticeable, Paul Baxter had begun to exhibit the most early stages of Alzheimer's. A doctor in Barretown had actually been so bold to diagnosis the condition, although from Paul's perspective it was way too early to project a few forgotten errands and misplaced items to the potential for this disturbing conclusion. There had been no one in his family ever diagnosed or to have suffered from the illness. To him the physician had just been watching too many medical dramas on television. To David Jacobs, looking for anything to make his case, it was a wedge issue. A wedge that Paul Baxter was fighting hard to keep from producing the intended leverage.

Before Paul realized that the boys had returned home and heard the conversation, he went to the backyard in order to retrieve a bag he had left on the seat of his car. When he reentered the home he met the boys and assumed they had just arrived. Earlier that day Paul was putting the finishing touches on the Christmas tree that had been assembled piece by piece over the prior week. In happier times, when Ruth was alive, the Baxters would reserve the second Saturday in December for cutting a tree at a local tree farm and decorating it as a family. Those days had slipped away but Paul still wanted to have an evergreen in the house for the holiday. When placing the star atop the spruce, it had fallen from his hand and was damaged. The bag he brought into the kitchen held the replacement.

Caleb saw the broken star on the kitchen table. He was saddened. Although the focus and attention of family strife had shifted front and center to the issues Marley and Edward were facing, the young man was still struggling with his own feelings related to the passing of his mother. The loss of the symbol that had joyfully topped the tree was just one more blow to his world that had changed forever a few years earlier. But that was in the rear view mirror for the rest of the Baxter clan. He had to deal with his sorrow and watch as others were caught up in their own concerns. He told himself, "Handling adversity will make me stronger." The path that Caleb chose, without the need for overly emotional hand holding, would help shape the character that the young man would demonstrate as his life unfolded. He took the star from the kitchen table, brought it to his room and placed it in the bottom drawer of his dresser. He wasn't sure why he kept the broken ornament but felt better for not just throwing it away.

Tempest had retired to her room and was busy preparing her Christmas gifts. She was on schedule to have the presents ready to be placed under the Arrck family tree the following day and to deliver two wrapped boxes to Caleb and Edward. Having prepared the circles, she was now in the process of cutting various lengths of string that she was affixing to some interestingly shaped small branches that had been gathered and stripped of their bark.

Edward also enjoyed positive Christmas memories. As he stood in his mother's studio watching Tempest, thoughts of the morning he and his father assembled the model race car track years earlier ran through his head. In the time before his parent's divorce Christmas was a day of joy and happiness. Now the best use of the time he had available was spent watching his neighbor from the window of his mother's studio. His life had certainly changed.

Tempest finished the first mobile. It was the one she was going to give to Clark Arrck. Her little brother would open it on Christmas morning. As she inspected the finished product, she decided on a radical design change. Rather than keeping the round circular shapes in native form she decided that she would fold one along the diameter. The young woman was satisfied with the look. She then found the center of another circle by intersecting two diameters and cut a radius with her scissors. When she was done cutting, she folded a quarter of the circle's area over at a right angle to the rest of the shape. She went on modifying each of the five hanging pieces in different ways, leaving one complete circle to contrast the others. When she was done, she stood on her bed and looped the hanging hook of the mobile over the lamp on the ceiling of her room. Tempest observed how it looked and moved in the circulating air. She was happy with her work and even happier when she thought of the surprise Clark Arrck would have when receiving it.

With Caleb in his room ruminating on the direction of his life Edward had the uninterrupted opportunity to watch his neighbor that entire afternoon. The next day when Tempest brought the boxes over to the Baxter home to place under the tree, Edward already knew what was in it. While thanking his neighbor he realized he had nothing to give Tempest for Christmas. Once she left, he hurriedly went to his room to check on his financial situation. With the recent supplementing of his cash hoard by his manipulative father, Eddie had amassed a small fortune.

The boy grabbed what he thought was necessary to purchase a gift for the target of his desire and dashed directly to The Parker Boutique. Upon arrival at the store he found a line of people making last minute purchases. Purposefully he strode to the rear of the shop and found the last of Holly Dane's mobiles spinning ever so slowly in a deliberate repeating arc. He checked the price and found it was well within his budget. Without waiting for assistance he removed the mobile from its hook. Edward would surprise Tempest with the gift. He fantasized that the gesture would demonstrate a linking of their creative souls that would serve to forever cement their relationship.

When Christmas morning came, the Arrcks opened presents as a family and were all pleased with the thoughts that had gone into the gifts that had been given. It was another family Christmas to remember. The domestic warmth always was a touch subdued for Diane Arrck. She knew her son was in the house next door. She was furnished with a stark reminder as Tempest opened her gift from Caleb. In the wrapped box she found a calculator with room for ten characters. She would be able to bring much more precision to her calculations. She knew what Caleb was thinking as soon as she saw the math machine and loved him for it.

The Arrcks were enjoying Christmas morning when there was a knock on the door. No one had ever interrupted the Arrck Christmas festivities before and they were all still dressed in their sleeping attire. Noah was the most presentable to the outside world and was nominated to answer the door. When the door opened there stood Edward dressed in his church clothes holding a beautifully wrapped box. He said, "Merry Christmas Noah, I have a present for Tempest. Is it Ok if I leave it for her?" Edward really wanted to invite himself in but was smart enough to realize that he had interrupted the family

John Lack

morning and quickly adopted a fallback position. He wanted to see the expression of Tempest's face when she opened the gift. Now he knew that part of his dream would go unrealized. Noah took the gift from Edward, wished him Merry Christmas and said he would make sure Tempest received it. Then he shut the door before surrendering to the urge to bound from the porch, which was his usual next move from this position.

Noah carried the extravagant looking gift into the living room and made a royal presentation to Tempest, embarrassing her as much as might be possible in front of her family. The rest of the presents had already been opened and when the box was placed before her the entire family waited to see the contents. She hesitated before opening the gift, then ripped the paper off with a flourish. Inside was a box bearing a small logo identifying it as being from The Parker Boutique. The distinctive signage was yet another example of Ashley Parker's skillful branding.

When Tempest opened the box and saw Holly Dane's mobile she did not know what to make of it. Tempest remembered seeing Ms. Dane's assortment of artwork when visiting the shop months earlier but she did not think she had copied the idea. In fact, she had seen similar mobiles many times before. The piece did however cheapen her opinion of her own gifts. She tried not to let her disappointment show and took the present from the box displaying it to her family. They didn't quite know what to make of it either. Joan, who exhibited an above average penchant for lateral thinking knew the selection troubled her but had yet to conclude why it left her so unsettled. Although she was not definitive in her conclusion, her thoughts were not very flattering towards Edward on any number of fronts.

Later that day Tempest called upon Caleb and Eddie. She wanted to thank them both for their gifts. When she knocked on the door of the Baxter home Paul Baxter answered. He invited Tempest in. The tree was decorated as it had always been but the house was nowhere near as cheerful as in the past. The environment was not overtly hostile but the dreariness was gnawing on poor Caleb. Her best friend was in the living room watching a college football game and Eddie was in the basement. Caleb had given him a new race car. Eddie had given his cousin a football jersey. With the sound of the television Edward was not aware that they had a visitor, affording Caleb and Tempest a moment alone.

Caleb welcomed Tempest to join him on the couch and thanked her for the thoughtful and considerate gift. He said he knew exactly what she was thinking while assembling the artwork. Tempest thanked Caleb for the calculator saying to him, "You know Caleb, you really get me." It was at that moment that Caleb had finally endured enough stress in his life and said to Tempest with a slight watering of his eyes, "Really Tempest, I don't know what I would do without you." Tempest felt her lifelong friend's pain and without an instant of hesitation, put her lips on the boy's cheek close to his lips. Caleb accepted her touch without negative or positive reaction as though the act was meant to be. Her kiss had the most fortunate timing because ten seconds later Edward came into the room saying, "Tempest, I didn't hear you arrive. Had I known you were here I would have come up immediately." It was one of those critical moments in any lifetime. If he had come up earlier the trajectory of their collective futures would have been forever changed.

Edward thanked Tempest for the gift she had given him, hoping that it would lead to her praising him for his excellent choice. Before giving his love interest the chance to respond he couldn't contain himself and remarked that it was amazing that they both arrived at similar gifts when thinking of one another. He was hoping to seal a stronger bond between them. If the truth be known, he may have helped forge a stronger connection between Tempest and Holly Dane. As for his attempt at swaying other emotions, the young woman was left with a stranger assessment of Edward than before. If it was even possible it was the attachment between Tempest and Caleb that tightened that Christmas.

Chapter Twenty Seven: Zurck Returns

The holidays sailed by for some and dragged on for others. Caleb couldn't wait until he could get out of the house and back to school for seven hours a day. The cold wet rainy weather that dominated the vacation period was neither conducive to winter activities, nor warm enough to chance the flu by running around like it was early spring. It had just been sufficiently nasty that the order of the day was to wait for tomorrow but before the weather broke a nice tomorrow never came. In a testament to truly terrible timing, Monday morning brought with it a beautiful day that solicited nearly the same comment from every single student and teacher in the Averton School District, "Where was this sunshine when we were off?"

The poor conditions afforded Tempest the opportunity to spend quality time developing her hypothesis but it had been easier to ponder than actually put to paper. She grappled so many times over the ten day span that at one point Edward watched her through the window for ten minutes jumping up and down on her bed literally pulling her hair out. Not only was he observing the girl of his dreams, he was trying to see where she had hung the mobile but the Christmas gift never came into view. The fact was Tempest hung it where she considered it most appropriate, in her private bathroom, a place where she could ruminate upon the moving shapes in relative solitude.

Tempest wanted to be ready for Mr. Zurck's return and the final day of the holiday period she just began throwing ideas against paper hoping something would stick. She tried to articulate reasons why it doesn't make any sense for pi to be an incalculable constant, but came up empty. Following the advice of Charlie Farley, the heading "Why does it make perfect sense for pi to be an incalculable constant" also drew a blank. She then contemplated that she had framed the question improperly and reworded the hypothesis, "Why should it require a number that can't be calculated to determine the value of the circumference and area of a circle." There were no simple answers. The bottom line was she could not articulate the problem but knew it made no sense whatsoever. In the end she yanked her hair one more time and said, "It is almost as though someone out there is trying to tell us something."

After lying on her floor looking at the ceiling she got an idea. She also became very much aware of something more practical than her struggles with pi. From her resting place on her carpet while leaning back against the dresser she could see into her tilted mirror. Squarely in the reflection was the image of Eddie peering into the window. Apparently he thought Tempest was out of her room and decided to leave his usual secluded viewing location. Tempest watched him for a couple of minutes, then slowly slid across the floor and gently pulled the shades down. It left her feeling violated. How long did he watch her? Is this how he came up with the idea for the Christmas gift? What really angered her is that he had broken her train of thought. She was beginning to lose patience with her high maintenance and now creepy neighbor. The young woman never went into her room again without the benefit of her blinds being fully drawn.

After dinner a more relaxed student revisited the evolving premise that had morphed into, "What is it about pi that bugs me so much?" The first entry on her sheet was, "It is odd that you would encounter something as rare as an incalculable constant when determining the dimensions of something as common as a circle." Her second observation was, "If the physical properties of a circle can be measured with a string and a ruler, why is the simple mathematical calculation that determines the circumference and area not precisely measurable?" She was happy to have something on paper. In her estimation it was a good start. Before falling to sleep, for the first time behind the pulled down blinds of her windows, she grabbed her pencil and jotted down an additional observation. "What if someone is trying to send us a message? Maybe we missed an integer in our numbering system." Then feeling satisfied she drifted off to sleep.

Edward had a rough holiday. His home situation was miserable and now he had a new problem. The advent of the sinking shades was a sure indication that his spying had been detected. He was torn and actually wished the dreadful vacation period was not ending. The next morning he had to face Tempest. What might she be thinking? She had never lowered her blinds. He was pretty sure she must have seen him. Edward tried to get some sleep but had a restless night. His brain was busy considering the options available to him. Playing it cool was one thought. Would he wait until he was asked and casually brush off any assertion of malfeasance? Then again he might launch a pre-emptive strike, making up a story in a matter of fact way. He could offer an excuse that he needed to spend time in the studio. Maybe his mother asked him to rearrange some of her art supplies or clean the windows? Maybe he was starting a painting; an oil portrait of Tempest perhaps? He racked his brain for answers and around two thirty in the morning finally dropped off to sleep.

The walk to school the next morning was more than a little weird. Eddie was happy he had the fine weather as a distraction. He must have commented on it ten times during the walk. When he wasn't gabbing about the blue sky he was walking on egg shells. With a more skittish than usual approach to the regular company he overreacted to any comment that one of them made. The blinds were on the top of Edward's mind but Tempest was focused on Mr. Zurck's return and couldn't care less about the unprincipled eavesdropper. Joan did notice Tempest's blinds had been lowered when she passed her sister's room that morning. The older Arrck thought something might be up but as of yet hadn't put two and two together. Caleb had no idea that his fictional cousin was a peeping Tom.

When Tempest entered homeroom she was surprised to see that Charlie Farley was still behind the desk. She immediately went over to him and inquired as to the whereabouts of Mr. Zurck. Charles told Tempest Mr. Zurck needed to visit a specialist early that morning but would be arriving around ten o'clock. She was relieved at hearing this news and asked Charlie how his holiday was spent. He said, "It is still difficult being away from family and friends but it was not terrible. The weather reminded me of home." Tempest considered whether sometimes being with family and friends was all it took to ensure a happy holiday. It certainly didn't work for Caleb. Charles asked his former and current student about her short vacation. Tempest responded that it had been an enjoyable break and although the climate might have been better, she had a nice Christmas with her family. The Arrcks always seemed to have a good Christmas. As they were conversing Kelly Ackerly came into the room. She had a new book case and needed everyone to know it by the way she was slinging it around. She said, "Good morning Mr. Farley", and then added, "Hello Tempest", as she took her seat in what also appeared to be a new dress.

Tempest told Charlie that she had put together her thoughts on pi but it was difficult to come up with clear reasons why the constant was giving her trouble. He countered with the assertion that this is exactly why it is necessary to take the time to truly understand what you are looking to solve. She asked him if he would take a quick look at her work and she handed it to him. He slowly read the document that Tempest had prepared and once finished handed it back to her. He didn't want to deter the young scholar from her academic pursuits but was a little disappointed in the basis for her hypothesis. He cut her some slack when reminding himself that she was only in seventh grade. Charles told his student, "This looks more like a list of what bugs you so much about the existence of pi." Tempest responded, "Yes, that is exactly what I was trying to capture."

The bell rang before the exchange had more time to develop. In the process of taking the roll the class discovered that a number of mishaps had occurred over the holiday break. There was nothing serious but the adversities could have been much worse. Richard Abeles was amongst the missing. His parents had bought him a sixteen-gauge shotgun for Christmas. He was so excited that he loaded the gun while in his room and the firearm went off when he placed it in his closet. Richard needed to visit a hearing specialist in Barretown that morning. For the next few years it looked as though his clothes had been attacked by a hoard of ravenous moths. One of the more distant Blount cousins was also amongst the missing. She had received a sled for Christmas and impatiently needed to try it out. The regular sledding hill she chose was pock marked with bare spots and now her face was also pocked marked with bare spots. She would be out for the better part of a week.

Between the homeroom period and the beginning of class Tempest returned to have one more run at Charlie. She went with what she felt was the most solid reason for her anxiety about pi. Her question was, "Seriously Mr. Farley, if I can measure the physical length of the curved line segment accurately how can it be the result of two times a whole number and a third incalculable number?" Charlie corrected Tempest saying it is not the result it is the product. Then he considered the girl's point and found it a little troubling himself when considering it in that light. Charles could sense Tempest was warming to a full-scale offensive and smartly deferred to the fact that Mr. Zurck would be back that afternoon and she should take it up with him.

At the end of the day Tempest made her way to Mr. Zurck's classroom. She ran into Caleb on his way out and asked him if Zurck had returned and he replied in the affirmative. She asked her friend if he would wait as she had something to discuss with their math teacher and of course Caleb was glad to do it. When Tempest entered the room Mr. Zurck was speaking with Ms. Carter and she moved to the rear to give them the privacy they needed. To occupy her time she gazed out the second story window as the students streamed from the school in various directions. She was surprised to see Edward directly in her field of view. He was getting into a car with his father. Apparently Mr. Jacobs had come to pick her neighbor up at school. Eddie had said nothing about it that morning but then again he was completely occupied rattling off weather related trivia for most of the walk. When Ms. Carter left Tempest approached Mr. Zurck.

She was cordial and familiar beginning her conversation saying, "Welcome back. We missed you. Are you feeling better?" Zurck had his crutches leaning against the desk and said he was doing better but wouldn't lose the crutches for another six weeks. It was a bad break. He was more than ready to move on to another subject and said that Charles had commented about her extra work. He was surprised Tempest knew Charles and made the comment that it was a small world. Tempest said, "It is a small world and one that today you can't calculate the circumference of without the use of that pesky constant pi." He found her comment charming in a math-centric sort of way and asked her how she was doing with her hypothesis. She said it had evolved into more of a statement that could be titled, "What is it about pi that bugs me so much?" Zurck also found this funny. Even though he had not been the one circulating the false narrative about the cause of his broken leg, he did little to correct this misconception. He had not fallen on the ski slopes. He had actually slipped in his kitchen on some apple pie filling he had dropped by accident. He could also write a statement about what bugs him about pie. The odd symmetry struck his mathematics oriented mind as hilarious.

Harold realized he had a special role to play in his student's thirst for knowledge. Students like Tempest, with the desire to find the truth about math, did not come along every day. He encouraged her to keep trying to get to the root of her concern. The class would soon be tackling circles and spheres together. Perhaps something would come up in the normal course of events that would trigger clearer thoughts. Tempest considered this the best that she could expect at this point. The ball was still in her court but she had her teacher's support in the endeavor. She left the room saying, "See you tomorrow. Hope you are feeling better." Zurck smiled as his ace student exited the room.

Caleb was waiting patiently in the hallway and together they walked out of the school towards home. She asked him about his day. He made some general comments suggesting that they had just seen each other less than two hours ago and not much had changed. This triggered the recollection about Edward leaving with his father. Upon hearing the news, Caleb found this more distressing than she expected he would. Although her friend did not share the reason for his upset, Caleb had witnessed Marley Baxter giving strict orders to her son to avoid his father. Apparently Edward was not interested in following that dictate and in the process, if it was even possible, he was going to create even more tension in the Baxter house. Caleb had been treated to the constant haranguing for the past week. His father didn't seem to be troubled quite as much. Very often it would appear as though he was hearing the bickering for the first time.

Chapter Twenty Eight: Thank You Sensei

David Jacobs was on a mission. He was going to recover his son from the clutches of Marley Baxter. He would do so without regard for the collateral damage he might inflict on the innocent. In many ways he and Edward were like oak and acorn. Clearly no one had organized a successful swap of his son at the hospital. Not wanting to raise too much suspicion, after spending an hour with his flesh and blood, Mr. Jacobs dropped his child off on the adjacent street allowing Edward to walk home as though he was returning from school. The father had already coached his son regarding the string of lies he was to use about his whereabouts in case any suspicion arose about his late return. David Jacobs was quite the role model.

Edward walked into the Baxter house an hour later than expected and no one inquired about the delayed arrival since the only one home at that time was Caleb. He already knew why his purported cousin was tardy in his appearance. The list of secrets that Edward was managing was beginning to grow on a near daily basis. He retired to the basement and his model race cars so not to run the risk of complicating his life with a slip of the tongue. He stayed there until it was time for dinner. He said little while at the dinner table which suited Caleb. A meal without overt tension was just fine with him, although no one could avoid the simmering pressure that had become a constant source of stress and stomach ailments in the Baxter home.

Dinner conversation consisted of Mr. Baxter twice commenting on the size of his recently assembled classes. He was getting ready to say it a third time as the phone rang. When the tape began to accept the message a voice could be heard coming from the study. The message went as follows, "Good evening, my name is Beth Gasser and I am the wedding planner for the Harper-Jacobs nuptials that are planned for this coming June. In order to care for his tuxedo rental, I was hoping you could contact me with Edward's measurements or make arrangements to have him fitted. David said he spoke with your son today and he was going to inform you of my call." She gave her number and spelled her name, making clear it was properly pronounced like bazaar. When the call ended the menacing simmer transformed into a full boil.

Marley was a rank amateur when it came to dealing with the likes of David Jacobs. His professional training made him well aware of the legal levers that could be pulled in attaining his goal of custody and he was playing his cards like a pro. Marley needed Edward's help in fending off the assault but her son was being a less than supportive ally. Point blank from across the dinner table Marley pressed him, "When was the last time you spoke to your father?" The compulsive liar replied, "I haven't seen my father since meeting him here prior to Christmas." Caleb winced when he watched his cousin fire off the bald faced lie with such little effort. Caleb figured Edward had not only seen his father today but had probably also made additional contacts. He was beginning to wonder just whose side Edward was on.

Marley was not accepting Edward's version of events and again asked whether he had seen his father as suggested by the wedding planner. The teenager shouted "No" and vacated the dinner table. This left Caleb alone with Paul Baxter and his distraught sister. She said to her brother, who unconsciously rubbed his hand on the inside of his knee, "What am I going to do if he won't help me maintain custody?" In a moment of clarity Paul responded to his sister, "Maybe he doesn't want you to have complete custody. Based on some of the behaviors he has been exhibiting, the boy needs a father." Then without skipping a beat he looked over at Caleb and said, "Let me tell you about my class this semester."

Marley could understand why her son might need a strong male influence in his life but she did not think the kind of guidance that came from her ex-husband was in his best interest. She knew advice on the subject would not be acquired from her nephew or her brother, who seemed to grow less attentive with each passing day. She needed to have the ear of another woman and thought the best place to seek help was in the company of Diane Arrck. That night after dinner Marley called her former classmate and asked if she would have some time that coming Saturday for them to have coffee or lunch. Ms. Baxter said she probably should have called sooner to make her re-acquaintance on a more friendly level and would be less than truthful if she didn't tell Diane she would be seeking her advice. Diane was more than willing to spend time with Marley and they agreed that lunch the next Saturday would be a great idea. After hanging up the phone Diane also thought that reacquainting with Marley was a positive move in furtherance of maintaining the dirty little secret.

Saturday came and Marley stopped by to pick up Diane for their lunch discussion. They made a plan to go to a nice restaurant just outside of town about three quarters of the way to "the sticks". The place had a nice view of the mountains and would provide an excellent location for a quiet conversation. The discussion started with some shop talk focusing on school related items. They shared common ground that made the rest of the conversation easier to handle. When Marley laid out her concern for losing custody of Edward the issue struck a nerve with Diane. Marley thought having an outsider's perspective would be helpful in framing the subject but was surprised to find her neighbor seemed to be too close to the topic of custody to be able to give pragmatic advice. The conversation spiraled into two women with common troubles as Diane showed an uncanny understanding of the emotions related to the issue.

It was a great lunch but provided little help to the distressed woman. After thanking her neighbor for her time and dropping Diane off in front of the Arrck house, Marley parked the car in the driveway and was getting ready leave her vehicle. She looked into the back seat and saw Diane's doggy bag was still there. The chicken parmigiana her lunch partner had ordered was way too big for anyone to finish in one sitting. Marley decided to take the leftovers to the Arrck home and in the process found Joan sitting on the back porch.

Marley said hello to the young woman. The older Arrck girl asked in return, "How are you Ms. Baxter? We live next to each other and I see you all the time but we never talk." Marley was surprised at Joan's openness and agreed with her neighbor saying, "You are right, we should speak more often." Joan said, "Well, I am here most weekends and after school. We could talk about what is bothering you." Marley was even more intrigued by Joan's direct comment and said, "What have you heard about what is bothering me?" Joan replied, "Kids talk you know and I am more of a listener. I have heard you are having trouble with Edward's father and that he wants to gain custody of him."

Marley was still looking for help and figuring she had nothing to lose took a shot with the young woman asking, "Tell me Joan, what do you think I should do?" Joan did not hesitate and replied, "In martial arts we learn not to be too rigid. If you are stiff you will snap. If you are flexible you can find the right moment to use the weight of your opponent against them and beat a much larger, more powerful adversary."

Marley's jaw dropped. She could have saved herself the price of lunch, had she just run into Joan earlier. What was with these Arrck girls? They all seemed to be wrapped a lot tighter than most kids their age. Both Caleb and Edward were crazy about Tempest and now Joan comes up with the wisest advice she had heard yet. Marley could definitely build a plan around Joan's strategic framework. The fact that she hadn't already confronted David directly meant there would not be a lot of backtracking necessary. There was no bell that needed to be unrung. He would be more likely to accept her faux attitude until she could use her opponent's strength against him.

Marley knew she had to treat Edward as a bit of an unknowing double agent and did not want to give him any information he could inadvertently share with his father. At the same time, there was certain information she wanted her ex-husband to know. She needed to shift gears quietly, demonstrating a position of accepting the reentry of David Jacobs into her son's life. She would play her own cards close to the vest and once her ex-husband let his guard down she would cut the man's legs clear out from under him.

If she could find her own levers to pull, Edward's father wouldn't know what hit him. To ensure her former husband was not a vindictive loser, she swore to herself that there would be no gloating if she was victorious. For now it was necessary to bide her time and be patient. The short game might mean having to swallow hard at David's intervention in Edward's life. But the former Mrs. Jacobs was now playing the long game and had her eye on the ultimate prize, sole custody of her son.

Chapter Twenty Nine: Wedding Bells

The next few months rolled along with few major events to change the direction of life in Averton. As late May approached Noah was excited that next year he would be attending high school. The rest of the kids were happy the school year was beginning to wind down. Tempest had survived her encounter with pi but the intellectual duel was far from over as she continued to be fascinated by and still not accepting of the concepts regarding incalculable numbers.

The wedding was getting closer and Marley had done a masterful job of shifting gears to play the role of the reluctantly supportive ex-wife. Her plaint nature was the product of, "Doing it for Edward". Several weeks prior to the wedding David resurrected the question of Edward bringing a date to what was becoming the social event of the Barretown spring season. His fiancée Emily Harper was really pulling out all the stops and the guest list had continued to expand even at this late date.

Edward received the news one evening after speaking with his father by phone. He was giddy when he thought he was going to be able to invite Tempest to his father's wedding. The boy had not followed up on his previous discussion regarding the topic. It would be a chance for restoration to her good graces and put him head and shoulders above Caleb, who Edward always considered his unnamed competitor for their neighbor's affection and attention. The next day Edward would ask Tempest if she would accompany him.

The anxious young man did not sleep well that night. During the walk to school he did not have the opportunity to capture his target's full attention so the query would need to wait until the afternoon. With Caleb's participation on the baseball team the walk home would make for a better opportunity to pop the question. When Joan created some distance between the couple, Edward asked Tempest if she would consider honoring him by being his date at his father's wedding. Tempest had never been asked on a date and a different choice of words would have aided his cause. The result however, would have been the same. Tempest said she was flattered and would like to go but must ask her parents first.

That night was Thursday. Mark Arrck was in attendance at dinner and when the meal was complete Tempest raised the question, "Edward wants me to be his date for his father's wedding. Is it Ok for me to go?" The question did require some thought. They were both still kids and there would be adult supervision but it still looked like a date. Diane immediately realized that her daughter would be escorted by her cousin. Since Edward's mother had more skin in this game, Tempest's mom decided to call her friend Marley to ask what she thought.

In keeping with the flexibility theme Marley judged it would be fine for Tempest to attend. Diane and Mark Arrck talked it over seriously as they did with all decisions but one that could affect their children's well-being and came to the same conclusion as Ms. Baxter. Tempest could go. Diane knew she needed to keep a watchful eye on this budding relationship so it was not the first step in a road that would threaten to unveil acts that were to remain unspoken.

The next morning Tempest announced to Edward that she would be allowed to attend the wedding. It was news to Caleb that Edward had even invited Tempest. He took the bulletin in stride as he wanted little if anything to do with Edward at this point and certainly was not going to be attending the wedding. Edward's head was in the clouds for the rest of the week. He was going to be attending the wedding of the year with the girl who was quickly becoming the most beautiful girl in school and far and away the most desired object of his affection.

Beth Gasser, the creative wedding planner, had requested photographs of all the attendees. Slides would be arranged in an artsy montage projected for everyone to see near the end of the reception. Emily was getting excited about the event and wanted to review the guest list with Beth. Two weeks before the ceremony they enjoyed a working dinner and were flipping through photo after photo when they came upon Edward's picture. Emily said proudly, "That is David's boy. I think he has his father's dashing good looks and very little of his mother's facial features. That is quite fortunate. When David gets custody I wouldn't want to be looking at Marley Baxter's face all day long." Beth then said to Emily, "Ok, next is

Edward's date. This should be cute to see them together."
When the coordinator flipped over the photograph Emily saw
Tempest. She let out a scream as though she had just seen a
ghost saying, "What kind of a bad joke is putting Marley's
junior high photo in the stack?" Beth said, "That is not
Marley's photograph." She picked up the snapshot to read the
name written on the back. "This girl's name is Tempest
Arrck."

Emily was adamant that the girl in the photo would not be
attending her wedding. She picked up the phone and called
her fiancé. When David answered the call she was very
deliberate in hiding her anger. She said, "David my dear have
you seen the photograph of the girl Edward is bringing to our
wedding?" David said, "No, but I bet she's a cutie. Edward
can't stop talking about her." "Well David I think you need to
look at the girl's picture and decide whether you should ask
Edward to change his choice of dates," she responded. David
answered, "I should be there in about thirty minutes and we
can talk about it then. But Emily I really don't want to
disappoint him. He needs to be a good witness if we ever get
to a custody hearing." Emily had not given the photograph all
the consideration she really should have given it. If she had
she would have wondered how any girl could look so much
like someone else. The odds of her living right next door were
nearly incalculable.

When David arrived at Emily's home the lone photograph of
Tempest sat on her dining room table. His future bride
directed him to sit and slid the photo across to him like a

detective in an interrogation room asking, "Who do you think she looks like?" Tempest was donning the now developing "Baxter nose", traces of the "Nubbler face" and ravishing red hair bought on by some recessive genes from the deep reaches of her heritage. David said laughing, "This has to be someone's idea of a bad joke. Once I figure out who did it I will kill them." Beth interrupted him saying, "It isn't a joke. This is the photograph taken by my man in Averton." Emily looked at her future husband and said pointedly, "Custody or no custody, there is no way that girl is coming to my wedding!"

David wished it didn't have to be this way but neither did he want a Marley look-alike at the wedding. There were two questions running through the man's mind. First, how do I break the news to Edward without producing profound disappointment? Second, how could it be that this girl was the spitting image of his ex-wife? She had not given birth to another child. He would have noticed. The chances of her being the neighbor's kid bordered on bizarre.

Luckily for the preservation of the dirty little secret, the crap storm created by the blackballing of Edward's date shifted the focus from the second question. David was playing serious damage control as the boy was beside himself with grief. When his father finally made the trip to discuss it face to face Edward said, "How can I live without Tempest? I love her. If you marry Emily, she will never be a part of my life." The older redhead from Lincoln Avenue could not have spun a stickier web if she had tried.

The week prior to the wedding the issue had not yet been resolved. Edward had not said anything to Tempest as he had not agreed to the change. Before the other regulars showed up at the lunch table Caleb broke the news to her. He had been privy to all of the discussions that had taken place in his presence and knew the whole story. Caleb knew about Emily's flat rejection and the short and long term implications for Edward. Tempest was beginning to get an appreciation for just how attached Edward had become and was not comfortable. She would take matters into her own hands and find a way to bow out of the affair. This might not have been the best outcome for Marley, but neither was Tempest aware nor did she care about the end game she was playing.

With the father-son stalemate still in effect days before the wedding, Tempest took the opportunity to speak with Edward one evening after dinner while they lingered in the backyard before sunset. "I have been thinking, getting all dressed up for a wedding is not for me. I am changing my mind about going. I like you Eddie but hope this doesn't cause you any difficulty." All Edward actually heard was, "I like you Eddie." He couldn't care less about the rest. Based on a prior conversation with her sister, Tempest offered Joan as a replacement. She was more Eddie's age anyway. Edward accepted the substitution which left Marley somewhat satisfied. Her son would be happy, although without some additional intervention, it would not leave him despising his father's new wife. Diane was delighted because the whole affair might slip into the recesses of people's memory and serve to save the dirty little secret. The bride, groom and wedding planner were relieved for clear reasons of their own.

The day of the wedding a black sedan was sent to pick up the attendees. Joan looked delightful with styled hair, wrapped in a lovely blue gown, wearing perfect shoes for the occasion. It did not go unnoticed by a formally attired Edward that Tempest was not the only beauty in the Arrck family. Based on some premeditation between Joan and her best older friend from next door, that night Joan of the Arrcks would act more as a Trojan horse than merely a date. She was carrying specific instructions to plant the hidden seed that would ultimately flatten the more powerful.

Two hours into the reception Edward had finally gotten up the nerve to ask his date to dance. It was finally time for Joan to launch her covert action. The young man had his ear next to Joan's mouth as she pressed her body lightly against his and said, "You should know my friend, Emily single handedly torpedoed Tempest's attendance here tonight. Not only didn't she want her here, she wants nothing to do with my sister ever." Edward realized that any affiliation with his father was the death knell for winning his true love. He inwardly swore never to speak to Emily again. The mighty had fallen.

The true highlight for Emily's detractors occurred when Beth presented her artsy montage. Her poor administrative skills were in full evidence as directly after Edward's photo, for all the crowd to see, was a larger than life rendering of a smiling Tempest Arrck. The picture of the young lady who looked like

Marley Jacobs was met with a collective gasp from the crowd, a spilled drink from the new bride and a fainting spell by the wedding planner. Unlike the young woman in the photograph, whose logic seeking mind was never satisfied with uncertain conditions, the lingering question as to why there was such an unexplained likeness to the two women avoided any follow up scrutiny from the collected partygoers. As a result the dirty little secret dodged another very significant bullet and survived once more right under everyone's nose.

Chapter Thirty: Leather Books and Red Flags

It wasn't lost on Caleb Baxter that his father's mental strength was waxing and waning, but mostly waning, on a near daily basis. Although the doctor in Barretown had made a shot in the dark diagnosis, the realities were lining up that Paul Baxter was suffering from some sort of debilitating brain condition. Caleb was now a teenager and he and Tempest were both attending high school. Not only was Caleb a teenager, but he was a responsible adolescent and one day while alone with his father said, "Dad, I think it is time we admit you have a problem and begin to take the necessary steps to ensure you are cared for if this condition worsens."

Paul loved the young man who the world had been fooled into thinking was his only son. He appreciated Caleb's maturity in confronting the inevitable despite the fact that he was now only sixteen years old. Paul knew there were certain measures required to preserve the fiction he had made of the children's lives. The remaining Baxter plotter became keenly aware of the need to take those necessary steps in the lucid moments that were afforded him on a now more sporadic basis.

A year ago the college had also seen the worsening of Paul's mental health and gracefully and respectfully gave the professor an exit ramp from his day to day teaching responsibilities. His mentee and protégé Charles Farley had now completed his four year studies and returned to the community college that he loved to help the educator who had given him his start. Charles was now teaching classes on a regular basis. His forte was math and science although from time to time he would find himself exercising his other skill, participating in fierce philosophical debate. Although considered to be a young professor, Charles Farley was becoming a sought after teacher amongst the ranks of the community college students.

One afternoon when Paul was feeling particularly clear headed he decided it was necessary to provide a trail of crumbs to his copy of the letter that laid bare to the world the details of the dirty little secret. He wanted to create a contingency plan. If there was ever a question as to Caleb's or Tempest's paternity the letter could be found to set the record straight. Currently his copy did not reside in a safe deposit box or similar secure location. The letter was in his nightstand, folded between the last page and the back cover of the Baxter family Bible. The truth revealing document had been left undisturbed since the day that he and his deceased wife Ruth signed it in the presence of Diane Arrck. Diane's copy was in a much more secure place. She had created her trail of crumbs years earlier.

Paul removed the letter from its hiding place and unfolded it slowly. He took care not to damage the document. As he began reading the contents of the time capsule it was almost as though he was hoping the words would say something different. The dreadful record endured. Tempest with her "Baxter nose" and now near identical appearance to his only sister was indeed his child. Caleb who had grown up to be a responsible young man belonged to the Arrcks. For a moment he considered disclosing the entire secret but was halted when considering the negative impact this would have on the now young adults. He folded the letter and rested it on top of the Bible that now sat on his bedside table. The ailing husband's thoughts turned to his long departed wife. He knew memories of her would soon fade. In this clearheaded moment, he wanted to recollect his lost love at least one more time.

Paul's meditative state was interrupted by the doorbell. He was quickly brought out of his trance and hurriedly returned the letter to the last page of the Bible. He went downstairs, failing to return the good book to the rear of the drawer where it was previously secreted. After a conversation with the newspaper deliverer, who he had forgotten to pay for three weeks, Paul decided to make himself a cup of tea.

It was about this time that freshman Edward Jacobs arrived home from his day at Barretown State University. The young man was commuting nearly an hour each way. Between his father's financial support, which may or may not have been done with Emily's knowledge, and the money that Marley had saved over the years from her very active art business, Edward was able to attend the four year school. He had chosen a course of study that focused mostly on a liberal arts education with an initial weighting on business. As with many inexperienced scholars, the young man had not chosen a lifetime career path but felt the range of classes was broad enough that he would have options once he settled on a more specific target. When his uncle asked him why he didn't start his academic journey at the community college and transfer the credits, as many successful people had done in the past, Edward replied, "I wanted to go to a real college from the beginning." Clearly his people skills and caring for others had not improved with his added years.

As Edward was heading to his room to put his books away, just about the worst possible thing that could have happened nearly happened. He noticed that his uncle's bed had been disturbed. This was nothing new as Paul Baxter had taken to afternoon naps in recent months. The book on the bedside table caught Edward's eye. After dropping his own texts in his room, the young man returned to his uncle's sleeping quarters to check out the book sitting on his nightstand. Edward lifted the large leather covered volume and realized immediately that it was a Bible. Given his uncle's advancing condition, perhaps he was feeling the need to get closer to God.

The nephew was hoping for something more interesting and he returned the book to the table in the proximate location where he had found it. He knew his uncle would not remember exactly how it was situated given the fact that, as Edward callously referred to it, "He was losing his marbles." Had Diane Arrck been aware of how close Paul's carelessness nearly brought the dirty little secret out into the open she would have been horrified. Unknown to each of the plotters, the fact that Edward was now knowledgeable of where he could locate a Bible was just a forestallment of the inevitable.

While Paul was engaged in an effort to safeguard the history that documented the children's sordid beginnings, the young couple was looking towards their futures and to making their way in the world. Tempest had not only made a name for herself with her unrelenting desire for math to be a more exact science, she had also honed her ability when it came to making and keeping friends. With the influx of new families arriving in Averton this skill was particularly helpful in assisting in the assimilation of the newcomers. There were more than a few fresh faces in the halls of Averton High School who would say, "Tempest Arrck is the first girl I met in town. She continues to this day to be one of my best friends." She also found time for family and remained a positive influence on her brothers and sisters. She was maturing into what everyone who came into contact with her would agree to be a lovely young woman. She had not changed so much however, to have lost her ability to run a dagger through anyone who uttered the phrase "close enough".

The person who was most numb to the impact that Tempest was having on the young people of Averton was Edward. He still harbored visions of making a difference in the life of his neighbor. Had he witnessed the attention that was being regularly heaped upon her, he would not need that "Logic in Philosophy" course he was taking to deduce he had a similar chance to a snowball in hell in gaining her affection. Most of the boys figured Caleb had Tempest locked up as they were constant companions and had been so since birth. Some girls were not as willing to succumb to this thinking as the young sports star still garnered more than his fair share of notice from the young women in the school. One Kelly Ackerly in particular carried a torch for Caleb. She along with others that shared the same thoughts knew they had a steep climb to overcome in securing his affections.

Although fame was not their intention, the two friends were clearly making a positive name for themselves in Averton. Caleb Baxter was becoming synonymous with sports. Tempest was becoming well-known for the impact her surprising behavior could have on others. Most recently at a Saturday afternoon football game, their collective trademark behaviors collided in one of the most noteworthy and inspiring events of the year in Averton or for that matter anywhere in the entire upstate area.

The Mid-Region Football League title game against the dreaded cross county rival had gone into the final quarter. Averton was losing by four points but was moving smartly down the field with adequate time to score the winning touchdown. Since the game was for the league crown, additional scrutiny was afforded the proceedings and instant replay was introduced for the first time that year at the high school level in New York for games with title implications. The rules were simple. Each coach had one challenge per half, no more, no less, regardless of the outcome of the dispute. The opposing coach from Birchwood had already used his second half challenge. The Averton coach had not.

The Averton squad was facing a short third down try and the coach called a play making Caleb the target of a quick pass from his position in the backfield. Tempest and Arlene Sharp were on the sidelines watching the game, anxiously rooting for the home team. The nervous crowd was much bigger than normal. Averton had not been a serious threat to win the league title in any of the years since Mark Arrck led the locals. The third down play took place within yards of Tempest's position behind the sideline barrier. It was clear to her that Caleb was not able to secure the low pass. The closest official's view was blocked however and called it a good catch.

There was a bit of outrage from the opposing players but the most surprising comment came from Tempest. She yelled towards the Averton head coach who had also clearly seen the result of the play, "Do you really want to win that way coach?" The target of her comment pretended not to hear the honest fan and clapped his hands celebrating the result. Tempest again said, "How can you let that call go unchallenged?" As the coach was trying to hide under a rock, Caleb, who by then was standing next to Coach Hayes waiting to bring a new play to the huddle, reached towards the frozen adult's belt and threw the scarlet red challenge flag onto the field. He looked at the coach and said, "We don't want to win that way."

The Averton fans, who had not witnessed the entire scene unfold were outraged. They rained a verbal deluge from the stands when they saw the flag hit the grass. They could not comprehend why Coach Hayes would dispute a result that favored Averton? When the officials completed their review the pass was correctly deemed to be incomplete. It was fourth down and three yards to go on the opponent's thirty yard line. There were four minutes left. The coach had to make a decision and he looked at Tempest, who he knew to be the daughter of Mark Arrck, the man he had played with the last time Averton won the county title. Tempest looked back at the coach and said in the surprising silence of the moment, "Now, go win this game honestly."

Once the crowd realized the coach was going for the fourth down the remaining shouts turned to cheers. He called a running play off left tackle. One in which Caleb would handle the ball. The opponents anticipated the less than creative choice and the defensive end of the Birchwood team had his arms on Caleb before he could leave the backfield. Caleb struggled mightily to break the tackle and freed himself. Once out of the grip of the rather large lineman he scampered for the final thirty yards, ending the play in a touchdown.

The Averton team held on to win due to a last minute interception of the Birchwood quarterback by one of the many Blount brothers who were on the roster. Some deserved credit was given to Butchy Wagner for rushing the quarterback. Caleb was honored as the star of the game. Both he and the coach knew that the real star was Tempest. Her need for precision and honesty allowed them to truly savor an earned victory.

The ranks of the knowledgeable of what really happened that day would have remained in the single digits had it not been for the reporter from the local newspaper who witnessed the entire event. She wrote an article titled, "This is no Tempest in a Teapot." The article began, "A funny thing happened at the Averton – Birchwood title game the other day, someone told the truth." The Averton coach did not take credit for the burst of honesty that led to the flag being thrown. He was happy he took this position once the article hit the newsstands. Tempest became even more of a legend in the community. Although both Mark Arrck and Diane Arrck were incredibly proud of their daughter's character, the additional scrutiny was not something Diane could take the time to truly appreciate.

The instant success brought with it a flurry of well-wishers who were interested in thanking the two young people for being honest and setting an example for the community. You could be honest and still win. The teens were surprised at what they learned from the poignant stories shared by those impacted by their courage and what their example had meant to others. There was one admirer in particular who had a most surprising message for the young couple. A message that they chose to remain a secret that they would keep solely between them. It could wait to be revealed sometime in the future, maybe the very distant future, maybe never. Perhaps telling the truth was becoming contagious in the now slightly larger than average sized small town of Averton.

Chapter Thirty One: My Test Tube Baby

The fame that the newspaper article brought with it faded into the background as the rest of the school year was slipping by without any additional reason for the spotlight to shine on the sixteen-year-old high school junior. That is until Tempest was named as a finalist for selection to the Averton Math and Science team. The team would represent the school in regional matches with the regional winners moving on to state level competition. Tempest did not qualify based solely on grades. Her reputation as a math geek made her a "Principal's Choice" to join the team. The principal was none other than Mr. Harold Zurck. One year earlier he had decided to leave his front line teaching position and try his hand as High School Administrator. The students liked his style and he was well-received by the parents. Mr. Zurck loved his new role and was suited for the job.

When Tempest was asked to join the team she found it an honor to be placed with the legendary minds that had previously only been names to her. With the exception of Kelly Ackerly, Tempest did not know any of the other contestants. But they all knew her. There were seven students competing for the three spots on the traveling team. Kelly and Tempest were the only two juniors and the only two girls. The senior boys didn't treat the girls with disrespect, they just didn't want to talk with them. For the most part they were all bookworms who may never have even had a conversation with a non-related member of the opposite sex. Given the fact that both Kelly and Tempest had become well-known for their appearance and accomplishments the boys may have even been afraid of them. But the girls were also afraid of the accomplished boys, so it was all even on that score.

Because of his desire to stay close to the students and since he lobbied the school board for the extra money for the program, Mr. Zurck was named the faculty advisor. He would also be responsible for selecting the three top students to represent Averton. Harold was a pretty tuned in person. He decided the best way to select the ideal candidates was to hold a series of mock competitions where the seven students would rotate between groupings in order for him to determine the brightest students and gauge the chemistry between team members. Tempest was average in science and actually average in math but was able to nail the most difficult questions when her team needed someone to deliver. She didn't always know the formula or what was considered the proper method, but she could think her way through problems and come up with solutions others would miss.

When Zurck's iterative process had come to an end he was left making the difficult decision as to which students would make the team and which would not. In an effort to deal with contingencies he added an alternate position to the roster in case any one of the top three choices needed to be replaced. The top selections in no specific order were Kelly Ackerly,

Daniel Blount and Bobby Sharp, who was Arlene's other brother. Tempest Arrck was named as the alternate. No one begrudged Mr. Zurck his selections. The group agreed he had made the right choices. The seven students had come to know and like each other during the process. It was a growth opportunity for the boys. The five young men now had female acquaintances. They hadn't suffered negatively from the experience. All seven were focused on the success of their colleagues and a positive representation of the school.

The team would travel on consecutive Saturdays to participate in a single elimination style game show like tournament. The first weekend there would be two matches for each team. This would bring the number of schools competing rapidly down to eight survivors. Then the next weekend, the eight would become four and in the final weekend two semi-final and one final contest would be held. The final three match showdown would be aired on a regional television station. For the math community this was a big deal.

The Averton team won both of their opening matches with relative ease against much larger schools. Zurck's model worked like a charm. At least one Averton student usually knew the answer. In the case of the other schools, generally all three contestants were knowledgeable or no one knew the right answer. The other schools might have had some smarter kids but Averton had the best team. When the students arrived back at school on Monday the principal, who had a vested interest in the outcome, announced the results over the public address system. The news brought with it a surprisingly raucous cheer from every homeroom. The entire school was behind the team and it felt good for the bookworms.

The next weekend the Averton Ratio Rangers, a name coined by Butchy Wagner's younger brother, were scheduled to go up against a team from a school nearly five times the size of Averton. It was a true David and Goliath match. When the producers of the event realized that the contest that was shaping up to be the most interesting was occurring in an early round and beyond the television cameras, they orchestrated a back room deal that Harold objected to mightily. He found no way however, to stop the reformatting of the brackets that would lead to an Averton verses Wallburg showdown in the finals if both teams progressed. Harold had to explain the change to his team without making the process look like a sham. Mr. Zurck needed his players to stay focused on their performance and not the sideshow that was playing out amongst the adults. Tempest found the move totally ridiculous but not unexpected given the potential advertising money involved.

The weekend of eight teams arrived and Averton just crushed their opponent, as did Wallburg and the two schools were among the four teams to make it to the final matches. The contestants were now in opposite brackets and a win by both would set up the much anticipated definitive duel. The fact that Averton had a girl representative was also something that made the sponsors lick their chops. When the Averton team took the stage for the first of the semi-final matches the team was a little camera shy and got off to a rocky start. The live studio audience that included mostly students and family members was also a little unnerving for the kids from the slightly above average sized small town. At the first commercial break Harold and Tempest settled the team down. The Avertonians got their answering legs under them, making a twelve consecutive correct answer dash to the finish. The even dozen string of accurate responses set a record. The strength of Averton's teamwork was once again in evidence as they cruised to the next round.

Wallburg was next on the stage. They would be taking on the outfit that won the prize the prior year. That school was only returning one member from the previous team. They had lost one player to graduation and one to corporate relocation. The boy who was left from the prior year was a real dynamo. He nearly single handedly carried his colleagues down to the last question, leaving either team in a position to win the contest. The final question was generally a more complex problem that required the team members to work together to derive a common answer. There was a time limit for the teams to prepare a written response. The answer to this question would often determine the winner.

Many on the scene thought Wallburg did not get their final answer written down in time. In fact those who had devices able to replay the event confirmed the tardy response. The live call made by the judges, counted Wallburg's answer as official. In the end Wallburg won by ten points. The result was a real squeaker in Math and Science Tournament circles. The dream final had been set. Tiny Averton was slated to go up against mighty Wallburg, in a televised event, broadcast in near prime time at seven o'clock that evening.

Mr. Zurck wanted to keep his team together. Rather than having them scatter to eat dinner they all went across the street to a restaurant and ate as a group. While they ate, family and well-wishers stopped to congratulate the team members and to cheer them on. One of the parents remarked that the hopes of the Averton High School academic image rested on their performance. During the course of the meal, the entire situation became a little too real for Daniel Blount and with a rather pale look about him told Mr. Zurck he wasn't feeling well. He ran from the table and into the restroom to get sick. Mr. Zurck was hoping Daniel would recover in time but he was not able to answer the bell. At seven o'clock the alternate player from Averton filled the third seat at the table.

Although Tempest was an alternate, Mark, Diane and Clark were in the audience. So was Mr. Baxter, Caleb and Edward. Noah and Joan were glued to the television at home, as were ninety percent of the residents of Averton. Marley was watching along with Joan and Noah. When the team was announced, people were surprised to see Tempest on the panel. In introducing Averton's newest contestant the moderator decided to have a little fun with her name.

The host named Dee Farber said to the alternate, 'Tempest, now that is a name you don't hear very often. What is it like to have such an unusual name?" The redhead maintained her composure saying, "Well, everyone in town knows who you are." This brought a chuckle from the crowd. Then to the much older Mr. Farber's surprise she countered by saying, "What is it like being called Dee? Does everyone wonder what happened to the rest of your name?" The audience exploded in laughter. The now crimson faced man moved on, deciding that poking fun at the girl was not a good strategy. Tempest just being Tempest was off to a great start.

The game began and both teams were holding their own. Averton would have probably crushed Wallburg if Daniel had not gotten sick, but with Tempest on the team they were neck and neck with the much larger adversary. At the commercial break the score was tied at two hundred points per team. The sponsors could not have been more delighted. When Dee welcomed everyone back, the fans, both in the live audience and in living rooms throughout the region were ready for a barn burner finish. The academic setting also raised the excitement level. The students were arrayed on either side of a lab room with the tools of math and science clearly visible as they readied themselves for the final stretch.

The remaining set of questions was playing out like a tennis match. One school would correctly answer and the other would respond correctly to the next inquiry. It went on like this as the excitement built. When time ran out in the second round Wallburg answered the last question correctly and had a ten point edge. The score was four hundred to three hundred and ninety. As Dee Farber pointed out, it was already the most combined points ever accumulated in a single contest. There was still the twenty five point bonus question remaining. It would decide the champion. The team with the most precise answer would be awarded the twenty five points, assuring them victory.

After a short commercial break, Dee Farber welcomed back the audience and then theatrically unsealed the final question. He directed the contestants to take a look at the monitor. On the monitor was a picture of a test tube. There were measurements written on the test tube. He laid out the question, "In two minutes, without the aid of a calculator, tell us what is fifty percent of the volume of this test tube? The closest to the accurate measurement wins." The cylindrical shape and the round tip of the test tube required the incalculable constant pi be used in order to arrive at an accurate answer. The students from Wallburg all started writing down formulas that included the constant pi. Kelly and Bobby also started scribbling feverishly.

Tempest thought for a moment and then got up. None of the other contestants saw her but the audience was enthralled as she made her way to the rear of the set. Grabbing a test tube of the same size in the question and two very finely delineated beakers she placed them in full view on a lab table. There was no beaker of this model available to accurately measure the liquid from the entire test tube. She filled the test tube with water. Then she poured what she estimated was half of the water into the first beaker. She then poured the rest into the second and compared the readings. The math geek then averaged the two numbers to get half of the volume. Because there was some residual water in the test tube she performed the task again and calculated the average of the two observations. She then returned to her seat.

When Dee called out fifteen seconds Tempest said to her colleagues, "Unless you have a better number than this write it down." She showed the other two students her answer. Both of her teammates were horribly lost in the equations and happily took the number from Tempest. The Wallburg students were probably late again but they too entered a number and Dee accepted their answer. After all, there would be no excitement if the Wallburg team was disqualified. The question called for an answer nearest to the right number. With both teams responding someone would be deemed correct.

Since Wallburg was in the lead, Dee went to them first. The team captain showed the answer and said, "thirteen milliliters." Dee then turned to the Averton team, "We need your response. Did you use the math or did you rely on your colleague's physical observation?" Kelly Ackerly, who had been designated captain said, "We went with the physical observation. It has to be close as or probably even closer than our calculations." She revealed the teams answer as fourteen and one half milliliters. Dee Farber smiling into the camera then said, "We have the two answers. We will crown our champion right after these messages."

The contestants were on knife's edge and the tense crowd was ready to explode. There was debate all over the region as to whether Tempest's inconceivable method was legitimate. But it was well within the rules. Tempest had done the less complex supporting math properly and knew her overall calculation was correct. When the show returned, Dee had the audience in the palm of his hand. He raised the tension by asking, "Who will be right?" He then repeated the previously given answers. With the background drum roll from a canned tape he proclaimed, "The correct answer is fourteen and one half milliliters. Averton is the winner!"

Her teammates went crazy and the crowd on both sides of the camera went nuts. Paul Baxter, who was barely hanging on to his wits these days screamed out, "That's my Baby!" Diane Arrck nearly hit the ceiling but thankfully no one knew what he meant and those who actually knew Paul realized that just about anything might come from his mouth these days. The fact of the matter is it was probably the most cogent remark he had made in the prior two months. Mr. Zurck who recalled his alternate's obsession with the fact pi could be measured physically but not mathematically just shook his head slowly and smiled at the outcome. Knocking her off of that horse in the future would now prove to be nearly impossible.

Chapter Thirty Two: Junior Prom

Edward had been in college for nearly a year. With his studies and long daily commute, he became insulated in his own life and lost track of the goings on at Averton High School. The end of the school year brought with it prom season. In his senior year of high school, young Mr. Jacobs concocted a complex scheme to invite the then tenth grader Tempest to his senior prom, only to have it all go up in smoke before he pulled the trigger on his offer. Just prior to Edward setting the wheels in motion to ask his potential date, she offhandedly shared with him that Anne Nubbler had been asked to the prom and was going. Mr. and Mrs. Arrck however, had told the target of his affections that she was too young to attend any prom. If anyone asked she would need to decline. Being more beautiful than ever and rather popular, in a friends with everyone way, she was asked multiple times to both the junior and senior event. Tempest did not object to the restriction since formal dances were not a primary concern for her. Junior prom was somewhat of a tradition for juniors however, and the next year her parents relaxed the restriction, particularly when Caleb asked their daughter and she accepted.

A few days before the prom Caleb needed to get fitted for his rented tuxedo. He selected a brown tuxedo and accompanying accessories. He chose brown for two reasons. First, someone told him it was neutral and would go with anything his date was wearing. Second, his best shoes were brown and of the type that could be worn with formal attire. The thrifty young man would avoid the extra rental fee and potential for transmitted foot disease that he had long ago been alerted to by Mr. Arrck. Mark Arrck knew a great deal about contagious foot ailments and if anyone ever got him started on the perils of rented bowling alley footwear he could go on for hours.

The arrangement for the tuxedo rental was the first indication that Edward was given that prom season had returned to Averton. The second was the night of the prom. Edward was in the kitchen finishing some dessert when Caleb descended the stairs in formal attire. His aunt and his father were waiting outside. Two chairs were now regularly stationed on the front porch. Paul would spend quiet hours watching the traffic pass in front of the Baxter house. He was often joined by Marley, Caleb or Tempest. He would be on his own this evening as Marley would be driving the attendees to the event and then take on the role as one of the official chaperones.

The young man came into the kitchen for a glass of water. He cut a dashing appearance with his athletic build and boyish good looks. When Edward saw his cousin he was struck by the young man's appearance. There was no getting around the fact that he was a good looking kid. But the elder boy seethed with jealousy over the fact that Caleb was attending the prom with the girl who at this point wanted little to do with him. He said to Caleb, "Have fun and don't do anything I wouldn't do." From Caleb's viewpoint that left his options pretty wide open.

Tempest planned to wear a pale green flowing gown. With the help of her father she had selected icy emerald sling back shoes. He had purchased the pair months earlier and had them hidden at the store. He opened "Two by Two Shoes" especially for his daughter two Sundays earlier. When he was showing her the potential selections he had placed the lovely pair among the choices for her to consider. Upon seeing the glimmer and near glow of the green marvels she wanted none other. Mark was on cloud nine. Shoe guys don't often get the adrenalin rush you might find in other occupations but he felt as though he had just climbed Mount Everest.

When the appointed time arrived, Caleb made the familiar walk to the Arrck residence. It was a walk he had made more times than he could remember but tonight was different. He chose not to cut across the lawn but strode up his walkway, across the sidewalk and down the other walkway to arrive at Tempest's front door with clean shoes. Only in winter, when avoiding the snow, would he ever follow this route. He held a corsage, a light green orchid that Marley had helped him pick out. His finger hit the doorbell and Diane Arrck answered.

There stood Caleb, her son. Diane Arrck was shocked to realize how much the boy looked like his father. She was hoping no one else made a similar observation. Diane welcomed Caleb with a hug. The young man then stood waiting in the living room where he had stood thousands of times before but for some reason this evening he was sweating.

A couple of long minutes later Caleb, Diane and Mark could hear the sound of Tempest's ice green high heels on the upstairs hardwood floor. Joan had been helping her sister with final preparations as Tempest planned to do the following week when Joan attended the Senior Prom as the date of Bobby Sharp. The sixteen-year-old descended the stairs and when she appeared midway down the flight and saw Caleb she stopped. With her elegant green dress, glimmering emerald shoes and flowing red hair, she was to Caleb what could only be described as a jaw dropping vision. Joan had nicely applied a hint of mascara and a very light lipstick. If her date thought he had been sweating previously, he was now in full gusher mode.

Tempest was equally impressed with Caleb. She had seen him in everything from his underwear, when he ran through their yards at age three, to ratty old jeans, to his Sunday best. But she never saw him like this. It would have been a "Goody, goody time for phonics" moment if any words would have come to her mind. After taking the measured pause, that most Hollywood Director's would have salivated over, she then did what any schooled debutant would do and continued gracefully down the stairs. Arriving in the living room, she silently put out her wrist for a very tense Caleb to present the corsage that he had narrowly avoided crushing in his distracted hands.

The two prom goers were somewhat nervous which was odd for a pair who knew each other so well. After enough pictures had been taken they gave the Arrcks a fond farewell with Clark Arrck hugging his sister before she made it out the door. Diane and Mark watched as the two proceeded towards Marley's waiting car. Marley was standing with Paul Baxter on the front porch, looking quite ravishing herself, as she said good-bye to her brother. Edward did what he did best, peeking from the window at Tempest. Maybe you could give him a pass, there would be more than a few people staring at the young woman this evening. As the three prom goers entered the car Paul shouted out, "There goes my baby." In this case he was right on a couple of counts.

Arriving at the big event was quite a production as the students and organizers had gone with an Oscar's theme and that meant walking the red carpet. Caleb and Tempest looked as though they had just wandered off the silver screen as they prepared to enter the high school gymnasium which had been decorated quite nicely with the help of the good people at The Parker Boutique. There at the door was Mr. Zurck. As principal he would also serve as one of the chaperones. Seeing Marley walking alone up the red carpet, he made an inquiring gesture to ask if she would prefer to be escorted. She nodded in a very stylish way and the two older participants followed the two younger attendees into the event. Anyone who had paid special attention to Tempest and Marley would have thought they were watching a time lapse clip from a science movie. The flower had matured from budding to full bloom right before their very eyes.

When the young couple reached the midpoint of the walkway, they were greeted by the King and the Queen of the prom. Wilma Nubbler, who had slimmed down noticeably and now grown completely into her "Nubbler face", was attending the event with Elston Blount. Elston was the fifth member of the math team. In the process of trying out he had become friendly with both Kelly Ackerly and Tempest. Taking advantage of the opportunity, the bright young lad learned how to converse with young women. He put his new found knowledge to good use. As Wilma would say, "She loved her man for his mind."

With yet another intertwining of the Blount and Nubbler family trees there had been the requisite gossip surrounding their dating. Aunt Hazel Blount, the Blount family genealogist, had convinced them both however, that there was nothing to be worried about if the relationship evolved into something more. Her work was considered suspect. Often when attending a Nubbler-Blount family event, one would have the uneasy sense of staring into a common gene pool.

At the end of the red carpet the two young prom goers grabbed a glass of non-alcoholic punch and drifted over to see their friends. Mr. Zurck, the confirmed bachelor, who had enjoyed the stroll with Marley, an entrance that also turned a few heads, made the comment, "I am hoping we have the opportunity to share a dance later." Marley responded, "I would have been terribly disappointed if you didn't ask," and as they parted she said, "Until later Archie." Marley used Harold's obscure nickname from when he attended Averton as a student. Although he had been a couple of years behind her, the age disparity made little difference at this point in their lives.

Caleb's arrival was welcomed by the rest of the young men. It was appreciated even more by the young women. His familiarity and comfort with the girls made him the perfect catalyst for the breaking up of the boy's unisex huddle, prompting them to venture across the gym to rejoin their dates. As the night progressed the gym was really rocking. Some liquor had to be confiscated from Butchy Wagner but other than that there were no serious code violations. Harold was expecting Butchy's outlawed behavior and was waiting at the door with his hand out when the lawless student arrived. It was more of a game of cat and mouse between the two with no hard feelings. Harold would have bet on the current trajectory of Butchy's lawlessness long ago based on his now famous "tent card indictor". Harold was undoubtedly a math geek through and through.

When the band finally settled into the music most of the young men wanted to hear, Caleb and Tempest found each other in a marginally awkward embrace, slow dancing in the corner of the gym at the edge of the mass of partygoers. They had been friends for so long the position felt a bit strange to Caleb. The young man was having an internal intellectual battle, trying to convince himself he was not dancing with his sister. Tempest was more comfortable and harbored no thoughts that Caleb was her sibling. She readily held the young man who she had always loved. She recalled the spontaneous kiss she gave him years earlier and realized that it would be hiding her true feelings to consider Caleb as anything else than the logical choice to be her boyfriend and maybe much more.

Almost as though Tempest was reading her partner's mind the astute young girl said, "You know Caleb, I am not your sister. It is alright for you to hold me tighter." Caleb increased the intensity of his embrace. While staring into her placid eyes, which he realized for the first time were the deepest shade of green, he said, "How is that, close enough?" Tempest, looking back into his warm blue eyes, smiled and thought to herself, "It is never close enough."

A magical evening unfolded for the young couple. On three separate occasions an unsuspecting suitor attempted to cut in. On three occasions neither Caleb nor Tempest noticed. They also didn't notice the four or five dances that Marley and Harold shared. They were probably the only ones in the gym that didn't. Harold was quite a versatile dancer. A talent he had acquired at a dance studio in Barretown. When he was in his twenties, he would utilize the venue as his own personal meeting place for slightly older women. The fact that Marley was nearly three years his senior was right up Harold's alley. It also didn't seem to bother Marley.

When the dance was breaking up, Anne Nubbler approached Tempest and asked her if she and Caleb wanted to join a group of friends who were going to a nearby lake to extend the party. Tempest pointed to Marley, who was saying her good-byes to Harold and replied, "We already have a ride and the lake is probably not in her plans." If Marley had been alone the lake might have been in her plans but Tempest had properly read the situation in declining the offer. In addition it was already nearly one o'clock and her mother had once told her, "Only bad things happen after two o'clock," and she was in no hurry to test the premise.

The threesome, having all enjoyed their evening immensely, made the short drive home. Marley went inside and Caleb walked Tempest to her house. When they arrived at the front door, Caleb stopped her from entering and said, "I had a great time tonight." She turned to him and raised her arms to put them around his neck and said, "So did I," and she kissed him on the lips. Once finished he kissed her back and they held it for a few seconds. Then Tempest said, "Let's try this," and she put her lips on his and let her tongue slowly come out of her mouth to caress his lips. Caleb asked his companion defensively, "Where did you learn that?" She replied in a sly way, "Just a little something Anne Nubbler mentioned to me at lunch."

Caleb knew the word on Anne Nubbler was that she was a little forward. He also knew Tempest was anything but. He repeated the maneuver on his partner tasting her sweet lips for the first time. With the validation of a lifetime of inevitability, the release of a deluge of pent up emotions collided with a surge of teenage hormones and produced a runaway chain reaction of incalculable proportions. The young couple lost themselves, heatedly making out on the front porch. Edward was having a tough time watching these first moments of true romance as the light from the streetlamp was partially blocked by the now much larger "Nubbler bush". He was given the full show however, when an awakened Clark Arrck went downstairs in search of his sister. The newly lit porchlight exposed two unhindered teens ensnarled in a fiery impassioned embrace. A hold you might expect to be seen between two more experienced lovers.

In the Baxter house there were four people who had a lot to think about when the lights finally went out that night. Marley was left wondering whether she had just kicked off what would become a torrid affair with Harold Zurck. Edward had to make a decision whether he would make a last ditch play for his beautiful neighbor or stand aside, allowing Caleb to fulfill the role that was considered by some to be destiny. Caleb smiled when he put his head on the pillow realizing that he could love Tempest as something more than a sister. Paul Baxter was having one of his few remaining lucid moments and realized he needed to finally do something to better conceal the letter that documented the dirty little secret.

In the Arrck house there were only two people who had not already long ago fallen into dreamland. Tempest had just completed the most wonderful night of her life and knew in her heart that Caleb was the boy for her. She recognized that their relationship would still need to progress carefully as it had for nearly seventeen years. Starting tomorrow however things would be different. Diane Arrck also gazed at the ceiling of her room. She had seen the way her son and her daughter had looked upon one another. Maybe it was realistic to think the dirty little secret would find a way to wash itself clean. Paul would have the son his wife so desperately desired for him and his grandkids would still have the "Baxter nose".

Chapter Thirty Three: A Working Girl

Tempest was a practical girl. She knew that with two Arrck children already in college, in a year from the upcoming fall she would need to provide some financial support of her own in order to extend her education. She would make every effort to earn scholarships but was not counting on the additional funding as she began to develop her plan. The focused young woman needed to find a job for the summer. Preferably employment that might also extend beyond the summer if time devoted to work would allow for the continued pursuit of her studies. During the final week of school she by chance raised the issue of working with Anne Nubbler. It could not have been a more timely discussion.

Tempest was gazing out of the cafeteria window while chewing her sandwich. Anne, knowing her friend said, "Hey, what is on your mind? If I didn't know better, I'd say it looks like smoke is about to start pouring out of your ears." Tempest replied, "I need to get a summer job and was thinking about what would be the best kind of work." Anne responded, "My uncle Cameron owns Mennetti's, you know the bar and pizza restaurant in town. He is always looking for good help. The women who work there make great tips and I would venture to guess with your looks, after a few beers by the patrons you will do very well." Tempest was excited by the prospect. She said to Anne, "But I am not eighteen yet. Can I work in a place that serves alcohol?" Anne replied, "Well technically no, you can't. But my uncle can keep you on what they call the pizza side of the restaurant. Then it is legal. I work there sometimes when he is busy. It is legit for me to work the entire restaurant because I am family. By the way, with all the inbreeding in this town, you wouldn't have to scratch the surface too hard to find that we are probably somehow related." Tempest was interested in moving forward and asked what she should do next. Anne replied that she would talk with her uncle and find out more. Tempest then asked, "Why is it called Mennetti's?" Anne gave a look saying, "Do you think anyone would go to Nubbler's for pizza?"

Tempest broke the job plan to Joan on the walk home. This would be one of the last times they would be walking together from school as Joan would be graduating from Averton High School in a few days. She was going to attend the local community college in the fall. Her goal was to accumulate credits and transfer to another school where she could pursue a degree in international studies. The exposure to Asian cultures she had gained through her martial arts and the cramped setting of her small town conspired to trigger the wandering spirit in the young woman. Joan had been raised to be more grounded than to just slap on a backpack and see the world. She wanted a better plan than that.

Joan thought the waitressing role at the pizza place was a great idea but cautioned her sister that she was going to get a lot of unwarranted attention. Joan volunteered to show Tempest a few less obvious defensive moves that she might find helpful in the event some of the partially inebriated customers decided to get a little handy. Once considering the benefits, Joan could not figure out why she hadn't offered her sister this assistance previously.

Diane was working late at the library that night. The end of the school year always brought with it the final collection of books. Some of the more delinquent students needed to be tracked down. Often if you didn't locate the books before summer break they were never returned. Butchy Wagner was the target of the most recent pursuit. Her final task was signing the form letter that would be sent to his home quantifying the assessment the Wagner's would receive if seven currently overdue books were not returned. It was an annual ritual with the Wagner's sending a check to the school for the books that Butchy lost during the course of the year. It always surprised Diane that he could even find the library.

Tempest had no sooner put her texts on the dining room table and was half way to the kitchen when the phone rang in the Arrck house. Joan answered the phone. There was a polite male voice on the other end. One with a strange Italian accent asking, "Is this the Arrck residence?" Joan replied, "Who may I say is asking?" The voice went on to say, "This is Cameron Nubbler. I am looking to see if Tempest Arrck is available to come to the phone." Joan put the phone to her side and told her sister that it was Cameron Nubbler. Tempest asked excitedly for the receiver. She answered, "Yes Mr. Nubbler, this is Tempest. What can I do for you?"

Anne's Uncle replied, "My niece tells me you might be interested in a waitressing position for the summer. It so happens I have an opening but you have to be ready to start this week. Have you ever waitressed before?" Tempest responded that she thought she would be available but had not discussed it with her parents yet. She added that she had never waitressed but she could learn quickly. Cameron replied, "You ought to be able to pick it up. I have good people here to help you learn. Look, you need to let me know by noon time tomorrow or I can't hold the job for you." Cameron Nubbler was thrilled when Anne mentioned that Tempest Arrck might be interested in waitressing at his establishment. Her reputation in the community and list of friends would be very helpful in driving additional traffic into the restaurant.

Tempest shared the content of the call with her sister. Joan was very happy for her. Anne had come through with flying colors. Now she needed to run it past her parents. They trusted their kids' decisions but Mark was also protective of his youngest daughter. He had long ago realized there was less reason for shielding Joan. The man gained that insight while attending a martial arts tournament, when at the age of fourteen, Joan brought a two hundred pound grown man to his knees just by turning his hand in a certain way. Joan exhibited her wisdom once again when saying to Tempest, "Trust me, Dad will feel a lot better about you working if we get dressed and go down to the basement for a couple hours so I can show you some very subtle moves."

The Arrck girls were in the basement when Diane arrived home. She saw Clark at the kitchen table and asked where his sisters were. The youngest Arrck pointed towards the open basement door. Diane looked at her son and said, "Cat got your tongue?" He nearly choked on the milk that he had in his mouth as his mother's comment struck him very funny for some reason. "What are they doing down there?" she asked. "Joan is showing Tempest some moves to fend off drunk guys at the bar." Diane thought to herself, "Bar, what bar" and called down the stairs, requesting that the girls come up.

When they emerged Diane looked at the two of them. Joan was fresh and neat, Tempest was sweaty and untidy. Diane asked, "Do you mind keeping your mother informed about what is going on?" After Tempest excitedly explained the opportunity her mother mulled over the pro and cons of the situation and said, "I trust your judgment Tempest. Let me talk it over with your father." Diane had spent many a night at Mennetti's and knew it to be for the most part a family place. It was only four or five blocks from the Arrck's house. A little real work might be a good perspective builder for her maturing daughter.

Caleb was out of town with the baseball team. The Averton squad had made their way into the State round robin competition and would be staying over that Friday night to play Saturday whether they had won or lost that first evening. Caleb's being away from home was practice for his going away to college. Not being able to speak with him directly was uncomfortable for Tempest. She planned on attending the game the next day with Harold and Marley. They had become much more familiar with each other since the night of the prom. The three of them were leaving at two o'clock, to make the three hour drive and catch the twilight start.

When Mark Arrck came home that evening he was welcomed by his family with the news of Tempest's potential employment. While he ate his dinner with Diane, Joan, Clark and Tempest he considered the implications of his girl waitressing at the local pizza joint. He knew she needed to work and he knew she needed to learn how to deal with people but did not jump right to an affirmative answer. It was only when Joan indicated that she had been teaching her sister some of the more subtle martial arts holds, especially his favorite hand hold, that he consented to the request. He laid down some rules regarding her walk back and forth from the establishment and then hugged his daughter who was now truly growing up. It was always tough on Mark having such an attractive child. It would especially rankle him when he would see grown men take an interest in her appearance. But he knew he couldn't protect her forever.

Her father's dinner had been over for about an hour and Tempest already returned to her room to finish studying for a final exam she had the following Monday. It was her trigonometry test, the last of her junior year. She wanted to review a few items. If she was still having any difficulty she could ask the always willing Harold Zurck for some pointers on the ride to the game. The still dyed-in-the-wool math geek put the book on her lap and was focusing intensely on a topic when the phone rang. She remembered immediately that Caleb was supposed to call her from the hotel where the team was staying.

No one called the Arrcks this late. She knew it had to be her boyfriend. Clark answered the phone and sure enough it was Caleb. He was excited to report that Averton had won the game and his hit in the midst of a last inning rally helped the team secure the victory. Two more wins and they would be in the finals. He said he had already spoken to Marley and Harold and they were planning on staying over on Saturday just in case the team was still alive for the Sunday afternoon semi-final game.

Tempest was thrilled for Caleb and the team and what they had accomplished. Averton was by far the smallest school left in the competition and once again in the role of David to the larger Goliath's of the New York State public and private school system. She said she would find out from her parents if she could stay but was pretty sure it would be Ok. She then decided to deliver the news about her potential employment.

In retrospect, she probably should have waited to break the news when they were in person. Although he was not averse to Tempest working, his initial reaction was less than enthusiastic. Knowing her partner she could feel the emotions he was not verbalizing from nearly two hundred miles away. Caleb made an effort to sound supportive but she knew better. Tempest wasn't sure why he had some unspoken objection but was unwilling to consider he was jealous to share her with other people in this way. If you asked Caleb he couldn't tell you what bothered him either, but was not willing to take any root cause off of the table.

The next day Tempest confirmed with her parents that she would call to advise Cameron Nubbler, the proprietor of Mennetti's Restaurant and Pizzeria, that she would take the job. She was not ready for what happened next. Once she gave her consent to fill the position the proprietor said to her, "Good, now I really need you to start today. Can you be available at five o'clock this evening?" She was caught flat footed and did not know what to say. She wanted the job but had committed to Caleb. She kicked herself for not seeing this coming. She did what she considered the responsible thing and answered that she would be available for work. Cameron asked her if she needed anyone to call her about the specifics of the job. The newly employed server indicated that it would be helpful. The restaurateur replied that his wife would be contacting her around noon.

When the new hire hung up the phone she realized that committing to work would reduce her flexibility to do other things in her life. It was a limitation with which every working person on the planet was familiar. But it was the first time in a long working career that it would affect Tempest Arrck. After she hung up the phone, she told her mother what happened and Diane Arrck replied, "This is what you wanted isn't it?" Her daughter's response was, "But I told Caleb I would come to his game." Her mother answered, "Welcome to the working world my lovely daughter. These are decisions and choices you will need to make for the rest of your life. Your father and I make them every day. If you want my opinion, I think you made the right decision. Caleb will understand." Tempest hoped he would but harbored a gnawing concern that he might not appreciate the choice. After getting dressed she went over to the Baxter home and Marley answered the door. She advised Marley that she would not be able to make the trip to the game. When Marley asked her why the change in plan, Tempest said for the first time, "I have to work."

There was no way for the newly minted restaurant worker to contact Caleb. Her boyfriend would find out when she was noticeably absent. She hoped it would not affect his performance. When the phone rang around noon there was a woman with a weird Italian accent in Tempest's ear. She knew it must be Mrs. Nubbler. She was correct. The call was from Samantha "Pudgy" Nubbler, who gave Tempest the full and complete run down on her employment at Mennetti's.

Marley and Harold set out to the game around two o'clock. When Edward heard Tempest was not making the trip he had a muted sense of joy. Perhaps there was an opportunity for a rift in the legendary relationship. Edward still entertained hopes that he would one day have a shot with the girl who had stolen his heart. He could jump in and sweep Tempest off of her feet. There was about as much chance of this happening as a pig flying but Edward was not seeing very straight given his tunnel vision yearning for her hand.

Chapter Thirty Four: First Night

Tempest arrived at Mennetti's at ten minutes before five and found "Pudgy" Nubbler knee deep in pizza orders, directing the staff to various tables and acting as field general for the Mennetti's employee body. When Tempest walked in the door the ranking officer said, "Good I am glad you are here. Take that pitcher. Keep it filled with ice water and make sure everyone's glass is always full." With that Tempest began her waitressing career at Mennetti's.

By the time the evening was finished she had graduated to delivering bread and setting tables. Pudgy found her to be a quick study. She also found the tables with men tended to hang around a little longer than her mental clock had experienced in her years running the restaurant's operations. The checks were bigger by the average price of an additional drink and there was a longer wait for seating. They also ran dangerously low on ice for the first time since the August 1994 heat wave. Tempest had made a good first impression on her colleagues and completed a strong first showing that would only improve during her tenure at the restaurant.

Caleb was having a much less productive day. When Marley and Harold pulled into the site of the baseball tournament, heavy rain had already been falling for over an hour. The field was covered with puddles. An unpredicted line of strong thunderstorms had sprung up and stalled, as they had a tendency to do in June in upstate New York. The game before the Averton High School team was to take the field had been cancelled and the umpires were minutes away from deciding the fate of the Averton game. When Marley and Harold approached Caleb in the adjacent hotel lobby his first question was, "Where's Tempest?" Marley said, "She had to work but wanted us to give this to you." Marley handed Caleb a note. It explained the reason for her absence.

After he read the message he folded the note and put it in his pocket. He then thanked Marley and Harold for coming, just as the official word of cancellation was being received. The Averton squad was scheduled to take the field the next day at eleven. Harold and Marley retired to their hotel room. Although he wouldn't admit it if asked, Harold was quite happy that Tempest had found employment.

Mennetti's was closed on Sundays. It was a tradition. Pudgy had told her husband he was losing boatloads of money by doing so but as he said in his weird Italian accent, "What do we have if we don't have tradition?" Tempest was free to attend Sunday's game and convinced Noah to drive her, sharing a cut of the tip money she herself had received a cut of the night before. The tips were good the prior night. It was the first time Pudgy could recall tables specifically designating gratuities for what patrons called, "the water girl".

Tempest's arrival at the ballpark was going to be a surprise as she had not spoken to Caleb but had called the recorded message set up for fans interested in the updated game schedule. Three hours after leaving home, brother and sister pulled into the confines of the baseball stadium to find the Averton team on the field taking batting practice. Caleb was in the batting cage when Tempest and Noah climbed into the stands. Caleb saw his girlfriend and was happy that she had the chance to make the trip. After finishing his turn at bat, he circled past the stands to let Tempest know he was glad she could make it. Due to weather delays the tournament had now been shifted to a single elimination style win or go home model. If Averton won the early game they might be asked to play again later, time permitting. According to tournament rules a game could not begin after seven thirty in the evening.

Caleb was the catcher for the Averton squad. His accurate throwing arm and leadership made him the clear choice for the position. He managed the young Averton hurlers on the field actions and the combined battery of two right handed and one left handed starter had nailed down a stingy two point five earned run average for the season. They would be called upon to do their utmost today to hold a team that hailed from just south of the state capital. They were scoring an average of eight runs per game and rolled up a twelve run tally in their last outing.

Averton was chosen to be the home team and whether the squad from the smaller school would be effective on the mound would be found out quickly. The lead-off man for the South Albany team lined the first pitch into left field for a base hit. It looked as though it might be a long day. But Caleb had a plan to pitch the opposing power hitters way inside, challenging them to pull the ball. Which they did. But they pulled nearly all of them into foul territory rather than over the fence. Averton squeaked out a four to two win in a game that went on for nearly four hours due to the number of extra strikes that needed to be chased down lest the umpires ran out of balls. The next game for Averton would be the following Wednesday. School would be over for Tempest. She just wasn't sure whether she would have to work.

Caleb drove home with Noah and Tempest. Her older brother was treated to the conversation that took place between boyfriend and girlfriend regarding the new job. Caleb was happy but was clearly apprehensive about the behavior of some of the customers at the establishment. He wanted Tempest to know she didn't need to take any crap from the men who had a few too many and that he would step in if necessary. The damsel thanked him for his gallantry but let him know she could take care of herself and showed him one of Joan's martial arts moves. Caleb immediately felt the pressure and asked Tempest to stop, which she did before causing the young baseball star any serious injury that might have affected his ability to play in the coming game.

When they arrived home Tempest thanked her brother for the lift and the young couple then reenacted their moment of passion on the porch. They spent a few glorious minutes before Tempest said it was getting late. She reminded Caleb that they both had a final exam the next day. The seasoned student was ready for it but would have liked a little more preparation than the weekend schedule had allowed.

The next morning the two teens walked together to school. The State Regents trigonometry test was being administered in the gymnasium. It would be taken concurrently with the rest of the junior class. Tempest said to Caleb, "Don't forget the trick for remembering the three main trig functions. Sine, saddle Our Horses, Opposite, over Hypotenuse. Cosine, canter Away Happily, Adjacent, over Hypotenuse. Tangent, towards Other Adventures, Opposite, over Adjacent. Caleb replied, "Saddle our horses, canter away happily, towards other adventures. That I recall but only time will tell if I remember everything else."

Tempest found the exam to be rather easy and was even able to make a well-educated guess on the three out of seventy questions where she did not definitely know the answer. Once she was done she waited for Caleb in the hallway. He was the last student to finish. When he exited the gym Tempest asked whether he had trouble with the questions. He answered that he struggled with a couple but was confident in passing with room to spare. When the final scores were posted a few days later Tempest had scored a ninety two and Caleb a seventy nine. He had passed with a somewhat above average grade but Tempest knew her boyfriend could do much better.

The day after the test Tempest received a call from Pudgy. Her boss was hoping that Tempest could work Wednesday, promising that the following week she would be on the schedule and not subject to last minute calls. Tempest had no way to get to the ballgame and agreed to work. If Averton won she would make every effort to be at the final game that Saturday but was not looking forward to again choosing between her boyfriend and new employer. As it turned out there was no need for Tempest to make the difficult decision as the locals were defeated by a team from just north of New York City by a five to four score. Caleb had the chance to knock in the winning run but was robbed when he hit a line drive right back at the pitcher. The opposing hurler stabbed the shot for the last out of the game. He couldn't feel too bad for the effort. It was less an issue of Averton losing than the other team finding a way to win.

Tempest learned of the defeat while at work. The Barretown radio station broadcast the news and word circulated through the pizzeria. Tempest was sad for Caleb and the team. They had worked hard to get to this position and they should be proud of the result. She felt a huge weight come off of her shoulders however, realizing that on the following Saturday she did not have to choose between work and loyalty to her boyfriend. She wasn't happy that the team had lost. She was just happy she didn't have to be in two places at the same time. The rain had bailed her out once. The chance of that happening again was pretty slim. Just as her mind wandered towards thinking of how Caleb was feeling, her head was invaded by Pudgy's penetrating command. "More bread on three." Tempest was off in a flash.

Chapter Thirty Five: Read Any Good Books Lately?

Paul Baxter's condition continued to worsen that summer and by the beginning of the next school year he was in serious decline. In addition to his father's health, Caleb, now a high school senior who walked to school holding hands with his girlfriend, was also in the midst of considering his future as college was beckoning. He had already distinguished himself in three sports and with a solid senior year would be expecting numerous scholarship offers from four year universities across the land. His slightly better than above average grades made him a most sought after candidate. Tempest considered her future as well but when it came to college she was more occupied with its impact on their relationship than her educational choices. She was also a slightly above average student however, most of the areas where Tempest excelled were not being sought after by college recruiters.

Edward was in his second year of college. Once again he would focus on his studies as a distraction from the lack of attention given him by Tempest and the constant reminder of his uncle's looming demise. His commute also kept him occupied an additional two hours a day. Just how difficult it was to layer a long commute on top of the pursuit of a degree was a distressing reminder for Caleb. He also needed to add participation in a college level sports program to the demands placed on his time. It was the unwavering elephant in the room, when either of the romantic teens tried considering any other reality than Caleb becoming a resident student at some potentially distant college. If he were to live on a remote college campus it would be the first time they were totally apart since they had been in their respective mother's wombs.

The day that Paul drew his last breath finally came. It was on a Monday. Anticipating the inevitable, Caleb skipped football practice and was with the man he called "father" on that final afternoon. Tempest had asked for the evening off and had someone else cover the four hour shift she worked at Mennetti's three times during the school week. In his final moments, Marley and Caleb along with Tempest looked to provide whatever comfort they could give Paul.

The man who had sometime earlier lost his ability to distinguish between his loved ones and the paid caregivers brought in to tend to his daily needs passed very quietly. His floating in and out of any rational understanding of the important aspects of his life had ended on the prior junior prom night. He would never again think of the hidden letter that documented the dirty little secret. As a result it remained in the Bible for anyone to discover.

With Paul's death the Baxter family closed ranks with help from the Arrcks, who had grown even closer as their teenager children became even better friends. During the arranging of the funeral Marley, Caleb and Edward visited the church that Mr. Baxter had attended for years. It was the same church the

Arrcks called their own. It was a very solemn meeting and during the conversation Father Blakely asked if they were in possession of the family Bible. Edward said, "I know where my uncle kept his Bible and will be able to make it available for the proceedings."

Edward went home after the meeting with the priest and found the Bible in the rear of his uncle's bed stand right where he had seen it resting a few years earlier. He carried it downstairs and placed it on the table near the back door so it would not be forgotten the next time he or another family member ventured to the church or funeral home. After he put the holy book down he opened the front cover and an inscription read, "A Gift from the Jesuit Priests on the Occasion of Your Wedding." The label was filled out in impeccable script, Names: Paul Caleb Michael Baxter and Ruth Ellen Mary Baxter, the next entry read, Married: March Fourteenth 1978.

The grieving family made arrangements for the wake with the help of the local funeral director. The current generation of morticians ably represented the business that the Baxter family had used for many years. The company was a pillar in the community and had buried generations from various families across Averton. It would be a traditional burial. The plan was for a wake of the standard two day duration. There would be a final mass at the church and then Paul would be buried next to Ruth in the Catholic cemetery.

Although Paul was a veteran and could be buried in a military cemetery, he wanted to be where the rest of the Baxters and his wife were laid to rest. It was the same place his parents and their parents before them had been interred. As part of the final celebration of Paul's life, the family Bible that had been presented to him and Ruth would be used to read scripture by those participating in the mass. Caleb would be reading a verse as would Edward.

After two days of viewing the day of the funeral mass arrived. As expected the wake had brought out many of Averton's finest as the Baxter family had gone back in town history as far as anyone could remember. The Baxter name would live on with Caleb. Whether the Baxter genes would live on through Caleb was still an unknown but after junior prom night it was a higher probability bet than before. To her knowledge, Diane Arrck was now the only living keeper of the dirty little secret. She should have been relieved but would have been much more at ease had she known where Paul had secreted his copy of the letter. It was an anxious pang that she had always hoped to confront by asking Paul, but avoidance was her greatest defense mechanism and now it was too late. If she knew how poorly hidden the evidence was she would have been exponentially more concerned.

It was Caleb's job to bring the Bible to the church. It was Edward's job to remember to take it from the lectern and carry the good book to the graveside where once again it would be used to read a few meaningful passages. As Caleb took the book off of the table in the kitchen, the letter slipped slightly from its longtime hiding place and he instinctively pushed it back inside the cover returning it to its previous home. Following his cousin, he carried the good book by his side on his way to the car and placed it in his lap for the drive to the church. Once they arrived at the church the teen took the Bible to the lectern and opened it to the proper page. He then took his seat on the end of the first row with Tempest at his side. Edward sat at the end of the first row on the opposite side of the aisle.

When Edward finished the reading he brought the Bible with him back to his seat. In the process of placing it in the book holder in the back of the pew the folded letter fell onto the floor. He did not notice it at first but one of the Blount brothers seated in the pew directly behind him saw the letter land on the church floorboards. He tapped Edward on the shoulder and pointed to the fallen correspondence. Paul Baxter's nephew picked up the letter, thanked the man for pointing it out and put the recorded reminder of the dirty little secret into his jacket pocket without checking its contents. His attention returned to the ceremony where Marley was delivering a eulogy for her deceased older brother.

Upon completion of the mass six pall bearers from the local funeral home took Paul's casket and placed it in the hearse. Harold Zurck drove Marley, Caleb and Tempest to the burial site in procession with the rest of the Averton mourners. Edward drove himself and at the last minute asked Joan if she could use a ride as the Arrck car was brimming with passengers, given that Noah's vehicle had failed to start that morning. Joan accepted Edward's invitation and together they drove behind the car operated by Harold Zurck and in front of the vehicle holding the balance of the Arrck family.

About midway through the slow drive, Edward asked Joan if she would check his jacket pocket for a letter that had fallen out of the Bible. Initially he asked her if she would just replace it in the rear of the good book. Then apparently realizing that there was no one else who would be interested or had a stake in its contents, changed his mind and asked Joan if she wouldn't mind reading it. It might be personal, or it might just help provide the grieving nephew with some additional insight into the lives of his now deceased aunt and uncle. But he didn't see the harm in checking out the contents.

Joan turned and found Edward's jacket on the back seat. She took the jacket and checking the right side pocket discovered the letter. When she unfolded the correspondence she immediately recognized her mother's handwriting. The fact that the document was in her mother's hand instantly put her on guard and while saying nothing she began to read the letter silently. An agitated Edward asked repeatedly, "What does it say?" The letter was not that long. Without a great deal of fanfare it described the situation and how it was arrived at. It left no question as to where the real blame needed to be placed. Joan was shocked, but she channeled her martial arts training in an effort to avoid tempting Edward's interest by giving him any indication of the explosive nature of the document's contents. Joan's mind was racing to create a false narrative regarding the letter's subject.

To her good fortune Edward was distracted by a rapid braking of Mr. Zurck's vehicle. This gave her an additional instant of reprieve but the best she could concoct in the development of her own deception was to report to Edward that the letter was just a note written by his uncle to his bride the day before their wedding. She suggested that out of respect for the dead it might best be left private. If the oldest Arrck girl had a better appreciation of her neighbor's penchant for voyeurism, she might have said it was a grocery list that was misplaced. But when Edward thought the letter might provide some titillation he excitedly again asked Joan to read it out loud. Her reluctance to do so just made him even more adamant.

The newly informed young woman maintained her reluctance to share the contents of the letter suggesting that his insistence was a little creepy. Edward being somewhat sensitive to being considered creepy, outwardly backed down. Inside however he was burning with desire to see the contents if for no other reason than Joan would not let him know what it said. They were at a standoff when the car began its entrance into the cemetery where Paul would be rejoining Ruth in her final resting place. Little did the two deceased Baxters know the huge loose end left behind them would be playing out at this last poignant moment in Paul's lifetime journey. Little did they imagine that their neighbor's daughter would be the last rational sentry to guard against the world becoming aware of their sinful act. A secret that once revealed would change their legacy without hope of ever recovering their honor.

As the car rolled through the narrow cemetery path on route
to the open grave site the couple past head stones reading
Nubbler, Blount, Mann and Wagner. In fitting fashion the
Arrck and Baxter headstones were located in close proximity.
In a final rebuff of Edward, Joan said, "Look Edward, we can
discuss this later. For now let's try and focus on what is
happening here today and maintain some level of deference
and respect to the newly deceased. He was, after all your
uncle. His deepest personal thoughts about the woman he
loved are not the substance of gossip." She stopped herself
when the word scandal nearly escaped her mouth and thanked
some unseen force for blocking her tongue from forming the
word and speaking it. Maybe Ruth's unrested spirit had put
her hand over Joan's mouth before she could utter the
unrepeatable.

The assembled mourners stood by the graveside as the priest
completed the rituals that attend the occasion of such a
gathering. As the service was nearing its end a more than
moderate rain began to fall. It had threatened the proceedings
from the start but held off the entire day. The humid heavy air
now could become no more humid. Since only the most
prepared were equipped with umbrellas, the mourners stood
in the grasp of a late summer rain. Out of reverence for all
those who occupied the sacred grounds on which they stood,
they maintained their respect for the proceedings as hearty
citizens of Averton had always done in years past.

As the rain began to take on a more soaking nature Joan
removed the letter from her pocket and exposed it to the

elements. The water smeared the words from the fountain pen that her mother had used to write the contract, turning them into an indecipherable mess. The dirty little secret had survived its greatest challenge since the day it was written. Although the number of those knowledgeable had just been restored to the day before Paul Baxter died, the written record had now been reduced to a single copy.

When the ceremony ended the soaked participants returned to their cars. Edward encouraged Joan to return to his vehicle with him but she said she would be riding home with Mr. Zurck. Before leaving she said, "Oh, you wanted the letter from the Bible?" Edward was thrilled that he would finally learn the secret and replied, "Yes, I would love to read what my uncle wrote." Joan handed him a handful of what was now nothing more than an unreadable ball of paper mush and smeared ink saying, "Here you go. Knock yourself out."

Chapter Thirty Six: The News Gets Out

The tropical storm tracking up the Atlantic coast centered far enough out in the ocean that it generated a warm moist gusty breeze. The rain had ceased and it was a balmy yet pleasant night. The windows were open in nearly every residence in Averton and a quarter of the drapes were spending a good deal of time dancing playfully from the west side windows. Another twenty five percent billowed in a ghostly manner into various rooms from the east. The Arrck house was no exception and Edward was enjoying the wider than normal view from Marley's studio when the drapes sailed into Diane Arrck's bedroom. The view was exciting but not the optimum exposure. To take advantage of a once in a lifetime climatic convergence, the morally deficient boy went outside hoping to improve his chances at spying on what might be his partially clad adult neighbor.

Arriving near enough to the house to see and hear the television in the downstairs living room, Edward also caught the sound of voices coming from the upper floor. The conversation he overheard was unmistakably an exchange between two women. The vocals were raised in order to emphasize their opinions but not so loud that anyone inside the house could hear them. He moved closer and from his strategic placement spied the upper half of Diane and Joan

Arrck under the ceiling light behind Diane's closed bedroom door. Edward strained mightily to eavesdrop on his neighbors. The strong wind was swirling through the trees. The sound of the leaves overpowered the voices. During a fateful pause in the heavy gusts the infiltrator plainly heard Joan ask her mother, "So when on earth were you ever going to tell Tempest that Paul Baxter was her father? We buried him today. She won't even be able to grieve properly when she finds out."

Edward was stunned but instead of being sad for Tempest, he coldly processed the stand alone information. Paul Baxter was her father. He then improperly calculated the implications. Paul plus Diane equaled Tempest, one plus one equaled one. His math was nowhere close enough. He concluded that the information must have been recorded in the now destroyed letter. That is why she had the "Baxter nose". It meant that Caleb and Tempest were brother and sister. This striking news would split them up forever. He chose not to fuss over the detail that the discovery meant that he and Tempest were first cousins. Even in Averton this was generally recognized as a show stopper for two young people with amorous intentions.

Edward labored to hear more but he missed most of the continuing discussion, catching only a random word and occasional phrase. He was not exposed to the entire truth. Realizing there was little else for him to accomplish, he returned indoors. He didn't hear it all but he had heard enough and now he needed to decide how to disclose the information when it would provide the greatest advantage.

There was a good deal of dialogue that Edward couldn't hear. After Diane made a sincere apology to her daughter, she nervously launched into a series of questions. Her first anxious inquiries were, "Where did you see the letter and who else knows of its existence?" Joan explained how Edward had told her that the letter fell out of the Baxter's Bible in church. He did not have a chance to read it. Joan was the first person to see the secret correspondence and recognizing her mother's penmanship decided to read in silence. Edward was driving and could not intervene.

Diane then asked, "So Edward has no idea what is in the letter?" Joan replied that he did not. Before Diane could relax she asked, "Where is the letter now?" Joan answered that the unreadable remnants were returned to Edward as a wet ball of paper and indecipherable blotches of runny fountain pen ink. After successfully enlisting Joan as a somewhat reluctant co-conspirator, a now less stressed Diane took a deep breath and shared with her daughter that there was one more copy created for her safekeeping. It was intended to keep anyone from ever being able to question her loyalty to Mark Arrck. Unknown to Diane that letter would soon be prepared to be used for the very purpose it was created.

Chapter Thirty Seven: Senior Year Begins

Senior year was the culmination of the numerous scenes from an orderly staged twelve act play. Having witnessed family members and older students pass through this permeable milestone, the players had a pretty good idea what to expect from their final performance. They also knew it was a once in a lifetime experience. For some class members however, there were unexpected wrinkles not initially envisioned. Tempest for instance, was balancing work and school and was quite busy at Mennetti's where she had distinguished herself as a capable worker. Pudgy became so confident in Tempest's abilities when it came to numbers, that occasionally she even requested that the waitress complete the evening register close. Prior to the redhead's arrival this trusted task was reserved for Cameron, herself or a few select family members.

Tempest's love of math and ongoing battle with pi influenced her into making a few meaningful suggestions regarding pizza production. The ideas added positively to the character of the eatery. She was first and foremost a notorious stickler for anything other than a perfectly circular pizza. The constant challenge to any of the pizza chefs was that the pizza had to be round. There were times she would refuse to serve a pizza because of its shape. Her rants became legend among customers. They observed pizza creation as intently as one

275

would follow a jousting match at the equivalent of a Middle Ages themed dining establishment. The pies also had to be perfectly divided into twelve equal slices. Cameron made a template to put over the pizzas to ensure proper sizing. Her ideas became the basis of a successful marketing campaign that included sixty nine cent slices. If your piece wasn't the perfect size, you got it for free. With the input from the newest server the restaurant was just printing money. Her coworkers could not have been happier. The ideas became so popular they wiped out every other pizza joint within five miles.

For the young waitress the money was good, the work was actually fun but her schedule was packed. She was also regularly reminded of that incalculable mathematical constant that was still the cause of too much unnecessary angst. Tempest would get especially cranky when there was a measurable bulge or dent in the pizza crust. One quiet Wednesday just prior to the dinner rush, when she was particularly upset about the misshaped effort put forth by one of the newer chefs, a new patron quietly entered the restaurant and pizzeria. He was a familiar face from a long time ago. With the confluence of math and work it was rather fitting that the first time customer was none other than Charles Farley.

She had not seen Charlie in years but his former student recognized him immediately. Owing a delay in recognition to context and years of maturation, Charles did not recognize his soon to be server at first glance. When the college professor came forward to secure seating Tempest was waiting and said, "Ok Charlie Farley, where would you like to rest your weary bones?" It was fair to say the young man was very pleasantly surprised.

Charles Farley became a regular at Mennetti's. Every Friday night come rain, shine or maelstrom Charles Farley would be in attendance. Before he left, he would always check the next week's schedule with Pudgy to ensure that his usual waitress's schedule had not changed. The owner's wife liked having Charles Farley as a customer. Her calculated eye had determined a marked increase in the eligible female population on the nights when Charles would come to the bistro. The young women would go out of their way to gain the professor's attention. He had grown up to be quite a handsome man, with a very athletic build, topped off with an accent that would melt women yearning to be the object of his affection.

Although he would not readily admit it to himself, Charles was not coming to Mennetti's solely for the good fare. He enjoyed the proximity to his former student. He would have considered it merely an intellectual attraction and comfort with her familiarity. He further justified his actions by an overall enjoyment of the setting and his observation that the restaurant was a remarkable locale for scoring dates with Averton's loveliest women.

Caleb was following a different path through his senior year. He was the star of the football team, the apple of many a girl's eye and a hit with the teachers. He could have been a big man around school if he leaned towards that sort of thing, but he wanted none of the attention. The young man's goals were to perform for his team, be a good boyfriend, have adequate grades in order to be accepted into any school he desired and help his aunt around the Baxter home, where she now found herself head of household. He was meeting three out of four of his targets. The demands of sports had already dented his academic standing and the time he spent as team captain and with recruiters was putting an additional strain on his grades.

He had hoped to attend a University in the Finger Lakes Region of New York. It was the nearest tier one sports school to Averton. With the grades he was posting this dream was rapidly going up in smoke. Had he been able to land the college in the center of the state, Tempest might be able to make an occasional trip to see him mid-semester. This fiction would be used to ally many of their fears of being apart. But on a daily basis it was looking like a lost cause. He began focusing his attention on western New York, an additional ninety minute drive from Averton. If he ended up any further away, he might as well have been going to the moon.

Caleb had grown comfortable with Tempest's employment, although it did constrain some of their activities. She wasn't able to attend the football team's Saturday away games. She did go to the home contests but generally had to leave at halftime. The waitress was apprised of the outcome by patrons streaming into the restaurant after the game. To the extent possible, the young man altered his schedule to provide support for his girlfriend. He found opportunities to carve out time to be with her. On the three week nights when Tempest was working, Caleb would show up at Mennetti's a few minutes before eight with a text book in his hand. Pudgy would give him a slice of pizza and set him up in the office where he would study until Tempest finished her shift. Sometimes the shift would end later than others but Caleb's desire to make sure his favorite Avertonian made it home safely did not affect his grades.

On a normal evening, when the establishment calmed down, Tempest would complete a few assigned tasks, then settle up on tips with the other waitresses and the busboy. Her final act was to take off her red and white checkered apron, stand in the doorway of the office and announce to her patient boyfriend that she was ready. Some nights he would have his face planted in a book. On quieter evenings, he would be in discussion with Cameron, who would slip into the office to talk sports with his favorite local star. People in town liked Caleb. In fact, he and his girlfriend packed a mighty one, two punch in the community. All of Averton wanted them to do well.

Caleb was aware that Charles Farley was a regular at Tempest's place of employment. The young man was not one to partake in jealous behavior. He did find it a little uncomfortable in an unthreatening way that Charles had decided to become one of his partner's regular customers. He realized when you work in the public domain you can't avoid people who chose to associate with you. He did not think Tempest was encouraging the behavior and was not obsessed with the professor's intentions. The recognition of a competitor's existence was just a rational defensive response for the young man to have regarding anyone as important in his life as the girl next door. Tempest had learned long ago that it was unnecessary to remind Caleb that Charles had visited the restaurant on his usual night.

Despite all the distractions, Caleb and Tempest had fallen deeply in love. They were convinced that unless something unforeseen happened they were meant to be together. As their senior year progressed both of them knew however, that the trajectory of their lives would conspire to separate the pair. There would likely be many consecutive months spent apart. This was a difficult realization for a couple who could count on their hands the number of days separated since birth.

For the twosome from Lincoln Avenue, senior year was settling into one of comfortable reliability as they continued to become more than just friends. At least one of Tempest's other acquaintances had a much more tumultuous start to her final year of high school. Anne Nubbler had found herself in a love triangle between a college boy and his fiancée. Anne had always been a little ahead of the rest of the pack. The fiancée had become so distraught that she actually tried to run Anne down with her car but mistakenly took her anger out on her near identical twin Wilma.

Wilma barely avoided the oncoming late model sedan and became a bit of a local hero, appearing on television news programs to tell her story. She was later asked to star in a commercial for a woman's skin product. The "Nubbler face" apparently had national appeal. Anne for her part, split company with her college sweetheart in an effort to distance herself from his crazed fiancée. It did little good and only after Anne was advised by Aunt Hazel Blount that she might actually be related to the young man did he back off from seeing the thinner Nubbler twin.

The scrape with misfortune and the subsequent discovery motivated Anne to take on a new cause. She sought out the help of Aunt Hazel Blount, the local self-proclaimed genealogist and decided she was going to initiate a project to map the genes of the founding families of Averton. The goal was to identify any hidden blood ties that might later in life become issues leading to birth defects or other weakening of the Averton community stock. With the advent of Averton becoming a more tony and upbeat venue and a magnet for new arrivals, there were new genes in the pool but in Anne's opinion, there was still a huge historical base that needed sorting out.

Anne began her quest by seeking assistance in circulating a questionnaire that asked students to best describe their family trees. Anne knew Ms. Carter. In her current role as schoolboard member, the former principal could influence approval of the project. Tempest's friend surmised that even by this very simple exercise a number of intertwined branches would be discovered. If more detailed information was needed to investigate previously unknown linkages, there were other means at her disposal, including records from the town hall or even paternity tests if necessary.

That night was a Thursday and as Tempest sat at an Arrck dinner table that included Mark Arrck, her mother became a little nervous as her daughter explained what Anne had planned. Ms. Carter had not given approval yet but Anne had provided a copy of the form. Tempest suggested that it might be fun for the Arrcks to try and fill out the information together. First Tempest put the current generation on the template, identifying the four Arrck children. Then she wrote her parents and their siblings on the paper. This was a fairly simple exercise and Tempest completed it without error. The next level of linking her parent's siblings, their spouses and spouse's parents was where the fun started. The Arrck side of the family was pretty straightforward but the Mann side became squirrelly from the word go. There were so many Manns in and around Averton, that when the first one crossed with a Nubbler or Blount all hell broke loose. The sheet started to look like a maze of lines and names.

With over an hour invested in the effort, the family thought they had finished the connections in the first three generations. There weren't many blank spaces left on the sheet of paper which was loaded with lines, arrows and circled groups of people. A scan of the document led those at the table to conclude that this exercise might have been something that should have been done years ago. Noah rose from the table saying, "Thank God my girlfriend comes from Albany." Tempest made the comment, "Well, at least it doesn't look like we have any direct linkages with the Baxters." There was someone next door however, that was spending some time with the same sheet Caleb had brought home from school. He had drawn one additional line that did not appear on the Arrck's version.

Anne received the bad news that Ms. Carter was not able to secure approval from her fellow schoolboard members to use the school as a mechanism to circulate her work. Apparently they did not want to be in the middle of what would likely shed unwanted light on many relationship imperfections that people didn't want to be revealed. Ms. Carter did encourage Anne to continue the project saying she would help in any way possible without directly involving her office. In the former principal's mind getting this all on paper was worth the effort.

Luckily for Anne's cause, Carla Blount had also taken a copy of the form home and shared it with her mother. The older Blount was so enthralled by the possibilities, that after making three copies of the document, she laid them on her kitchen table and began to try and fill them out. It was amazing the complexity of the outcome. The Blount family touched nearly every household in Averton. When she showed the results to her husband, who was running for Town Supervisor that fall, he immediately made it a key platform of his campaign. The support and emphasis that the effort needed to flourish would come from within Anne's close sphere of friends. The fallout from the ongoing study would cause many an Averton family to circle the wagons. The result of the exercise although expected by some, would come as unwelcome news to many.

283

Chapter Thirty Eight: Good News and Bad News

Anne Nubbler's project was the talk of the town and once Eldred Blount unexpectedly won in a landslide, with the undertaking firmly front and center in his campaign platform, the work effort received a solid shot in the arm. The newcomers to Averton watched with interest as the founding families worked tirelessly to once and for all untangle the web of inter bloodline relationships that had developed throughout the years. Many of the connections identified were a surprise. Some were downright shocking. In the end the conclusion from the study was twofold. The first and most useful output was a documented roadmap of who was related to who and how direct or distant those associations happened to be. The second conclusion of the study was that the scrambled gene pool in Averton left little hope that any additional level of scrutiny regarding ancestry would yield more solid information. Expanding the analysis to include DNA tests would be a waste of time and money. All agreed that what was now known would be the gospel going forward. The town praised Anne for finally bringing the issue to a head, even though certain members of the community wished she never had the idea in the first place.

The Arrcks and the Baxters came through the ancestral study relatively unscathed. The most affected was Diane and the

Arrck children. Mann genes were found to be well distributed across the general population of the now larger than average upstate New York town. Her children would need to be particularly mindful when choosing a spouse. Noah and his Albany girlfriend felt safe. Tempest and Caleb were deemed to be a nontoxic pairing, despite the rogue Mann gene or two that might be coursing through his biology. The Nubbler genes carried from Ruth Baxter were also a little more than a passing concern but not deemed to be worthy of additional action. Many people did marvel that the likeness of Tempest and Marley did not yield more common genetic links between the two than was determined by the study. Rounding out the Arrck family situation; Joan still had not found anyone she was serious with and Clark couldn't really care less. Edward Jacobs had to be considerate of the complex genetic construct of his mother. The Jacobs' boy was also secretly reminded that the apple of his eye was his first cousin.

The actionable results of the study were that ten currently married couples decided they would be best served to limit their current family size, unless expansion came via adoption. Two remarkably onerous unions were annulled. Five current engagements were dissolved. Any number of ongoing high school and college relationships were terminated. Dreams of various unknown secret admirers were prematurely concluded. When all was said and done it was agreed that the town was a better place because of the realignment. It was a major effort but in the end the result was considered by most to be good news. Despite the conclusion that additional testing would not be appropriate, around this same time a test was requested at a Barretown medical facility by one E. Jacobs. He quietly ordered a paternity analysis on one T. Baxter.

With the election, the ancestry study and a disappointing football season in the rear view mirror, one late November evening Caleb Baxter made his usual walk to the restaurant and pizzeria to pick up the love of his life. The afternoon had been bright and warm for that time of year but when night came the winter wind began to blow and the temperature had dropped by twenty degrees. Knowing Tempest had only taken a light coat, he wore a heavy sweater under his jacket anticipating that he would share his outwear to save her from the elements. It was a chore he looked forward to with pleasure. He would do anything for the girl he treasured since birth. Upon arrival at Mennetti's the place was really rocking. Pudgy welcomed him, told him to grab a slice and get comfortable, her star waitress might be a little later than usual.

Caleb retired to the office and opened his senior year physics book. He found physics to be interesting. He was drawn to the Newtonian laws, especially the concept that every action had an equal and opposite reaction. He observed the rules were very applicable to the contact sports he played. The flight of a batted baseball was also governed by Newton's principals. A half hour later while engrossed in his studies, Tempest swept in, kissed him on the cheek and said, "A half hour more. There is a big party that is getting ready to leave and I need to help get them out the door." Then she blew back out of the office. Caleb watched as her whirling form cleared the exit and returned to the controlled mayhem of the dining room. The young woman was the master of her domain. Any thought of age related limiting of Tempest's duties had long ago gone by the boards.

True to her estimate, nearly a half hour later the tired waitress returned to the office. She had already removed her checkered apron, donned the light jacket and was ready to walk home with her escort. Caleb suggested that she take his coat as she had no idea how cold it had gotten outside. Tempest replied that having a table near the door made her very aware of the weather, especially when the front door of the establishment repeatedly opened and closed in response to the brisk take out trade that evening. Gratefully, she took his coat. He was well prepared with the heavy ski sweater. They said their good-byes for the evening and left on their five block walk.

It was very cold and Tempest being without gloves buried her hands deep in the pockets of her borrowed overcoat. In the process of warming her hands she encountered an obstruction in the right hand coat pocket. Out of curiosity she pulled out what felt like a brochure. When she read the cover of what turned out to be more of a pamphlet it said, "Welcome to Southern Wisconsin State College, We build future leaders." Although Tempest knew Caleb had been communicating with many college recruiters, she had thought he was trying to stay as close to Averton as possible.

Her first reaction to seeing the material was, "When did you have a meeting with people from Wisconsin? That's an awful long way from Averton." Caleb replied that he had just met them that afternoon. He was going to review the material while he waited but physics took over. She then said a little more aggressively, "Are you seriously considering them? What kind of offer are they making you?"

The young man had hoped to be able to have this conversation with Tempest in a more controlled setting. Walking down the street, with her already on full guard, was the worst possible scenario. The fact was that although he had initially given little credence to a potential offer from the mid-western institution, the package they were proposing was far and away the best he had yet received. The only problem was that the school was far and away. If he went to as distant a location as Wisconsin, the only time he would see Tempest would be on major holidays. If he was playing football, which is where the institution's interest centered, he might not see her from late August until February or maybe even April. Before he had a chance to respond to her first two questions she asked, "When were you going to tell me about this?"

Caleb was not thrilled with the inquisition that was underway and could have been more patient with his very upset sweetheart. He would have certainly liked to put the words back into his mouth but said, "I met with these people because they wanted to discuss a serious offer. I shouldn't have to get your permission when it comes to managing my future. If you really were sure of our relationship you wouldn't be so hung up on us being apart." No sooner had he said the words than he realized it was not what he wanted to say. He was also troubled with the idea of being apart from the girl he loved. Before he could recover, his very hurt neighbor stopped, looked at him and said, "I can't believe you would say such a terrible thing. Don't you know how sick I am about the fact that we will need to be apart from one another? Apparently I love you a hell of a lot more than you love me." Different words would have also been chosen, if given more thought.

The two young people were remarkably mature. Rather than the discussion turning into a screaming match right there on the street, they both held their words and walked the rest of the way to the Arrck house. Caleb walked Tempest to her door where she took off his coat and she kissed him saying, "We have a lot to talk about. Let's find the time tomorrow before this becomes a bigger problem." She kissed him again and went inside. Caleb walked home and found Edward sitting in the living room watching television. He could see his cousin was distressed and asked somewhat gleefully, "Trouble in paradise?" Caleb replied, "No, just a few bumps in the road."

Edward who still harbored an unrequited love for his neighbor took any potential pothole as a possible opening to sweep Tempest off her feet. Rather than trying to comfort his kin he withdrew into his own little fantasy world. Caleb commented to Edward, "Thanks for asking," but received no response. The troubled young man then hung up the coat that still smelled like the girl he may have just lost. He slowly climbed the stairs to his room. The dreadful scene could be considered nothing but the harbinger of bad news.

Chapter Thirty Nine: The Unthinkable

Tempest slept very poorly that evening. Caleb had an even worse night. Neither one could even begin to think about what their world would be like without the other. The young woman from the Arrck house and the young man from the Baxter house had from the very beginning been on a collision course for a life together. Now Tempest was thinking what it would be like to be away from Caleb for months on end. She did not think he would become interested in another woman, she was just going to miss his touch and his voice.

Caleb pondered the legions of losers that would try to hit on his girlfriend with him out of the picture. There was little concern that she would decide to replace him. He would just miss the smell of her hair and the warmth of her company. But he could not believe the amazing offer the Southern Wisconsin State people had made. A complete four year ride, without any guarantee he remained healthy enough to even play football. He just needed to maintain a two point five grade point average and his college would be fully paid. Given the non-public state of financial affairs in the Baxter house this was music to Caleb's ears.

The next morning the couple left their homes as they always did and walked together to school. It would be the last school day of the week as Thanksgiving was only two days away.

Caleb said, "I had a terrible night. I love you Tempest and can't stand the thought of being away from you. But the offer these people have made is totally unbelievable. They will pay for one hundred percent of my four years of school." This was not what Caleb had decided that he was going to say the night before. What he was going to say was, "Let's not get ourselves overly concerned until we have the time to discuss this properly. Thursday is Thanksgiving. We have all day to be with each other. Let's discuss it then."

Based on Tempest's response he would have been better off sticking with the plan. She responded in a way that was also not contemplated the night before, "Sounds like your mind is already made up. Sorry we didn't have more of a chance to talk about it." With the exception of footsteps, that was all he heard the rest of the walk. First work, now college, for the second time in five months a third party, with different plans for their futures, had intervened in the trajectory of the two young person's lives.

Caleb decided that he would take his lunch in a different venue than the usual table, choosing instead to hang out at the gym. He would make this decision from time to time and it did not raise red flags with anyone other than Tempest. She knew why her boyfriend was in avoidance mode. This also turned out to be one of the few days in the recent past that their paths did not cross between classes, something the redhead noticed and the young man had orchestrated. Caleb didn't know what to say and did not want to be forced, once again, into saying something wrong. He was worried that the third time might mean the death knell for their relationship.

When the bell rang to signify the end of the day most students were happy that they would be starting a five day Thanksgiving holiday. The young man, who now had the weight of the world on his shoulders, wished the school day would have gone on much longer. As he approached their usual meeting spot his anxious lifelong companion was waiting for him.

Sensing her partner's uneasy state the young woman demonstrating wisdom beyond her tender age said, "Let's just walk home. We don't have to talk about anything if you prefer not to." Caleb wanted to make it all go away but knew he was not equipped to meet that challenge at this point. He silently assented by gently taking his walking companion's hand. They made the stroll home without saying a word. There were no discussions about what they might do that evening. There were no words shared about what they might do the next day. They parted company at the top of the Baxter's walkway and both went into their respective homes.

Each knew they needed to resolve the issue and clear the air. Neither accepted the only plausible solution available to unravel the Gordian knot they were both struggling to solve. Caleb needed to take the best offer he could find regarding his college career. Tempest needed to prepare herself for a four year interruption in their relationship. Together they needed to make allowances to survive the storm. The simplest solution was the most obvious but it was also the most painful. Tempest railed within at the idea that she could not alter the incalculable trauma and find a better way to solve it.

The two mature combatants could have gone to their neutral corners for the entire long weekend. That might have been the best solution for the time being. The Thanksgiving dinner plans of the Arrcks and Baxters would not allow for that course of action. Diane Arrck had invited Marley, the two boys and Harold Zurck to join them for a holiday meal. It had been a tough few years for the Baxters. Losing the family patriarch was difficult on Caleb and Marley. The close neighbors could use some extended family time.

When three thirty on Wednesday afternoon rolled around, Clark Arrck asked his sister if she was going to the center of town. If so, he would walk with her and Caleb in the service of dropping her off at the diner to fulfill her evening waitressing duties. Clark wanted to continue on to the sporting goods store to check out a new hockey stick he was hoping to get for Christmas. When three forty five came and there was no movement from the house next door Tempest said to her younger brother, "Come on Clark, we need to go. It looks like Caleb is not going to make it today." Clark, who was now old enough to walk to town by himself and Tempest, who had walked to work alone on many an occasion, left home and began the short trek. As they moved away a solitary drape shifted in an upstairs window of the Baxter house.

The eatery was busy for the night before the holiday. Clear roads and a warmer than usual evening brought out the patrons who were ready to let off a little steam and enjoy the company of other hale and hearty Avertonians. The register was ringing and the tips were flowing and the employees of the establishment, that was now a part of Tempest's life, were enjoying the evening right along with the guests. Although there was a nagging thought in the rear of her mind, it was hard for her not to get into the spirit of the evening.

Sometime near eight o'clock the door swung open and Charles Farley appeared in the entry. This was not his usual night or the usual time for his arrival and he appeared to be particularly festive. At the same moment a few blocks away Diane Arrck rinsed and dried off her hands and lifted the receiver of her phone to call the Baxter home. She intended to ask her true son if he was going to pick up her adopted daughter that night, if not she would drive the few blocks to retrieve her.

Mrs. Arrck's child, who might have actually received as much love and attention from Diane as any other son, answered the phone. He was happy to hear a friendly voice and told his real mom that he would be happy to meet Tempest and fibbed that he was just getting ready to walk to Mennetti's when she called. Diane thanked Caleb, told him he was a good boy and went back to work preparing the trimmings for the upcoming holiday meal.

When Charles Farley entered the very busy dining room he had one purpose in mind. He wanted to let his former pupil know that he was going back to England to visit his mum for the holiday. Charles had made many female acquaintances. There were many who would have wished he had taken the time to single them out for a farewell but he felt the need to let Tempest know of his absence in case she might miss him on his usual night.

When Charlie Farley was finally able to get his target to slow down enough to deliver the message, being filled with the spirit of the evening and out of pure happiness for her teacher, she gave him a big hug and a kiss on the cheek and wished him a safe journey. She always had strong feelings for Charlie, he was a kindred math geek and a loyal friend but nothing more. Caleb who had just walked through the door when her lips were on the Brit's cheek was now struggling for an additional reason. He would have been much less disturbed if he was more aware of his girlfriend's true feelings for Charles.

The now veteran server was in her element bouncing from table to table like a ball bearing ricocheting around in a metal box car. When she raised her head to look towards the side door she saw Caleb waiting there and she stopped and smiled at him. He was considering a retreat back out to the street but remembered he had committed to Diane that he would see Tempest safely home. The trip started about a half hour later. It began with the identical silence that had dominated their prior two walks.

As they made the last turn onto Lincoln Avenue, in a final and complete surrender to the life she would be forced to live for the next four years, Tempest said, "Caleb, our relationship is strong enough to survive whatever distance the world can throw at us. It won't be easy but you need to do what is best for both of us. Someday we will look back at this and realize the stress just made us stronger." Caleb was listening to Tempest but all he could do was replay the kiss she laid on the cheek near the lips of Charles Farley. In words he would have given anything to put back into his mouth, the stressed teenager said, "Sure Tempest, that makes a world of sense. Who knows, with me out of the picture it might even give you the chance to get to know some of the other men in your life a little better." And with those words, the storybook closed.

Chapter Forty: A Frosty Thanksgiving

Two o'clock on Thursday found Caleb sitting in a chair in the Baxter living room watching a college football game. Edward was deep into some science fiction novel. He had been waiting for months for it to arrive at the local bookstore. Harold Zurck was reviewing the school budget trying to find money for new wrestling mats and Marley was putting the finishing touches on two apple pies that would be taken across to the Arrck's house. The smell of the pies filled the kitchen and reminded Caleb of the days when his mother would prepare desserts for the Baxter Thanksgiving feast. This was the first time that he would be having his turkey dinner anywhere besides the table in the Baxter family dining room. Since Ruth passed away, the recent celebrations were much less joyous affairs. Paul, even in his worsening state, always tried to make Thanksgiving a special time. He always held the belief that his family arrived in the New World around the same time as the Pilgrims. The recent ancestry study revealed many Averton family histories and supported this assertion. Had Paul still been alive, he would have been thrilled that there was evidence to corroborate the case that many assumed was mere bluster on his part.

Marley left the kitchen and while she was taking off her baking wear said to the boys, "I am going upstairs to get ready. It won't take long. We told the Arrcks we would be there by two thirty so let's be good guests and be ready to go when I come down." She then ascended the stairs to put on her holiday clothes. Caleb would always look forward to seeing Tempest and even more so on special occasions. Today he was not looking forward to their encounter in such a public setting. The families were not aware of the current tensions that existed between them and it would be hard to hide the friction from those who knew the couple better than anyone.

A half hour later Marley descended the stairs as promised. She was radiant and Harold could not take his eyes off of the woman he now called his fiancée. The boys grabbed the pies and other items they were bringing across to the neighbors. With a deep laboring breath Caleb walked out of the front door towards the Arrck house as he had done countless times before in much less trying circumstances.

The Baxters did not have to ring the doorbell. As they strolled up the walkway Joan opened the front door in welcome and the two families came together as one in the living room. Caleb did not seek out Tempest as most would have expected. She was busy in the kitchen and when he took a seat between Mark and Noah in front of the television no one took notice of his lack of attention. Tempest popped her head out of the kitchen, maybe just to check that he had arrived. She then rejoined the rest of the women at her post, helping to put the finishing touches on the meal.

The two families mingled without incident for the next hour. When Diane announced dinner to the men, who were all huddled around the television prior to the start of a traditional Thanksgiving football game, there was a mixed reaction of delight and disappointment. Luckily none of the males were imprudent enough to make the dissatisfaction known to the busy cooks.

The table was set with the family members interspersed amongst one another. Tempest and Caleb were sitting together near one of the ends of the table. Marley and Mark sat at the heads as the symbolic leaders of their respective households. Diane thanked everyone for coming, led a short prayer of grace and then asked who would like to make the toast. There was a brief silence before Caleb volunteered to offer the sentiment that would set the tone for the rest of the day. He raised his glass and in words that were only truly fully captured by one other person at the table said, "Let's be thankful for what we all have today. You never really know how certain even the most predictable things in life can be."

It was a rather dour outlook and not as celebratory as the guests had hoped but for most a grim reminder of what had befallen the young man a few short months previously. To Tempest however the toast meant something much more. It was a confirmation that their relationship was over. The difficult words were a dagger to her heart, yet she maintained her composure, lest the entire table be made aware of Caleb's true meaning.

Dinner progressed, although there was a noticeable chill between the two previously inseparable devotees. Three people at the table took notice. Diane had a bird's eye view from her angle at the end of the table and could watch the couple unnoticed from afar. Joan sat at mid-table across from them and could tell by her sister's lack of attention towards Caleb that something was amiss. Edward sat directly across and only after the redhead had continued to attempt conversation with him, instead of her usual fixation on his cousin, did he realize something had changed. Maybe he still had a chance with his fiery haired neighbor. Based on the events unfolding in front of Edward's eyes, he truly had a lot to be thankful about.

The college man was even more thrilled when Tempest accidently dropped the entire bowl of turnips in Caleb's lap. His joy was short-lived. The attention she managed to shower on her former boyfriend was reminiscent of her past affection, including running upstairs to get a replacement sweater from Noah's dresser. She placed the soiled garment in the wash and said it would be returned once it was cleaned.

When dinner was over the men retired to the living room to catch the final quarter of the football game. Caleb could not get away from the table quickly enough and this behavior, leaving Tempest unaided, sealed Diane Arrck's suspicion that something was terribly wrong in their paradise. After the table was cleared, the kitchen was cleaned and all of the leftovers were appropriately apportioned between households the evening broke up and the Baxters started to make their way across the lawn to their home. Caleb wanted to be the first to escape but Diane said she had a question for him and asked the boy if he could stay. Her son returned to the living room. He kept himself occupied watching the postgame show that focused on a particularly boneheaded play by one of the combatant's defensive stars that ended up costing his team the game. The young sports standout thought to himself, "What an idiot. You need to get the job done and not be worried about hot-dogging it in front of the fans. Never be the guy who loses sight of the real prize." When everyone had cleared the scene it was Diane and Caleb and she asked him to join her in the kitchen.

Diane had always treated the boy as her son. She felt they had a special bond. Caleb could feel it too and always treated Mrs. Arrck as more than just a neighbor. Diane sat down and said to the young man, "Caleb, I am not going to try to get tricky with you. It is clear to me that something is going on between you and Tempest. If she was going to confide in me she has had ample chances to do so and she has not. But it is clear she is hurting as well. Tell me if there is anything I can do to help resolve what is going on between you two." Diane would never admit it but her motivation was more than a little driven by the secret. How nicely everything would be tied up in a bow if Caleb and Tempest married and had children. Their genetic fusion would erase any biological inaccuracies. Her desire to protect that projected outcome may have pushed her too far in taking allowances with her true son.

Caleb was caught off guard and became overly defensive of what felt like a double team being applied by the Arrck women. He did not respond immediately and in the interim silence Tempest happened to enter the kitchen. She was visibly surprised to see mother and son in the room alone and asked, "Mom, what are you and Caleb talking about?" Caleb decided it was finally time for him to speak. Rather putting his foot in his mouth, which he had done the last three times he had opened it in front of his former girlfriend, he simply said, "Your mother is worried and is trying to figure out why we broke up." Then looking at Mrs. Arrck he said, "I appreciate your concern, but you are not my mother. Maybe you should be asking Tempest why we can no longer be together."

It was another dagger into another heart. This time the sword ran deeper than the young man could have ever imagined. He then excused himself from the table and left the Arrck residence. Diane was left in tears with Tempest holding her hand. Joan had been on the opposite side of the kitchen door and had heard the entire exchange. She came into the kitchen with an insight shared by no one else in the world. Joan sat down at the table and took her mother's other hand and said, "It is Ok mom, everything is going to be Ok."

Chapter Forty One: Everything is Not Ok

The days after Thanksgiving brought with them a new paradigm. Tempest walked alone to and from school. There was an empty seat at the lunch table and she did not have to wait to meet anyone at the doors of the school at the end of the day. The word that Caleb and Tempest had broken up spread through the school like wildfire on a parched prairie. There were any number of young men thrilled at the prospect of enjoying the company of the now unattached young woman. The giddiest about the entire affair was Edward. The inability to hide his pent up glee nearly cost him a knuckle sandwich, delivered personally by his clearly distraught cousin.

The girls were also flocking over Caleb, prompting Tempest to remark, "You really know who your friends are when something like this happens." She had always held out hope that the separation would be a passing circumstance and the couple would find a way to pull it all back together. It was a hope she held out until the following August, when a Wisconsin bound freshman was loading his bags into Harold Zurck's car, in preparation for a drive to the airport.

The disillusioned young woman watched as the boy she once and still loved more than anything in the world moved suitcase after suitcase to the car in the driveway. One of those suitcases contained Tempest's picture, which Caleb had sadly included during his packing. One included a broken Christmas ornament. Harold was going to drive the college bound young man to the regional airport in Albany, where he would catch a connecting flight to Cleveland, then onward for the rest of the trip to Wisconsin. Caleb had never flown before. It would be an entirely new experience.

Tempest had never been without her partner before and this would be new for her as well. Over the past months she had become a bit of a recluse. She would still attend school and speak with her friends, although graduation held much less joy than expected. She skipped the senior prom as did Caleb. She still waitressed, although with much less gusto than previously. Her studies would now shift to the community college for the coming semester. She would see Charles Farley on a near daily basis. A situation which Caleb was painfully aware.

When the packing was finished Caleb returned to the Baxter house for the last time and emerged with Harold. Marley monitored events from the back porch. Diane Arrck watched through her kitchen window. Tempest had been observing restlessly for the past two hours and could finally stand it no longer. Ripped from any pretense of safety she bolted down the stairs, out the front door and bounded off the porch, past the "Nubbler bush". Yielding to the power of the least common denominator she ran to Caleb stopping inches before him. With a vulnerability spawned by the failure to calculate an alternative solution she said, "I can't believe it all came to this. I love you and will always love you. I know you need to go but please come back. I will be waiting for you."

Caleb's emotional base being harmonized with his soulmate, took Tempest into his arms and like a star from a Hollywood movie caressed the now gorgeous woman saying, "I love you too Tempest. If I didn't have to do this I would stay here and be with you forever. I belong in your arms. We will be together again someday." He gave her a deep passionate kiss and said with a conviction confirming the sentence life had passed upon them, "I need to go now." She released her grip and stepped back dutifully, resigned to the future they now faced. He methodically entered the car and Mr. Zurck slowly backed down the driveway, setting Caleb on the first steps to a new life.

The climactic farewell hung in the hearts of the Lincoln Avenue residents like a dangling participle on a poorly crafted sentence. What would happen next? Were they back together? What was the protocol that they would follow while Caleb was away? All of these questions were running through Tempest's head. No matter what the answer to any of them, in her judgment the situation was far better for what she had done in these final moments. She cursed herself for letting it get so far out of hand. The reconciled girl took some solace in the fact that the clock that needed to run its course had now finally begun ticking. There was only so much time that needed to elapse before this nightmare would be over. With four years ahead of her however, the inevitability of time's passage provided little comfort. She walked back to her house alone with her thoughts and prepared to make her way to Mennetti's for her usual afternoon shift.

Chapter Forty Two: Life without Caleb

Since the devastating fallout from the prior Thanksgiving, Tempest had learned to live her life without Caleb as the daily centerpiece. He had been her one calculable constant. Although for months his activities had become shrouded from her, she always knew her former boyfriend was just across the yard if she chose to try and make amends. Now to some extent, amends had been made but he was gone. Her life had also changed in other ways. Tempest was now a college student. Her academic schedule still allowed for work at Mennetti's. She did not get as many scheduled hours and to maintain the income that she had begun to rely on the working student needed to be more flexible to jump in and cover other waitresses' shifts if the opportunity arose.

Making matters more complicated was the fact that she did not have her own vehicle. The first year college student was constantly juggling ways to get back and forth to school. Joan now had her own car and between Noah, her sister and Edward she was managing to be in many places at nearly the same time. Edward was always willing to assist and left a standing invitation for the target of his desire. The offer would only be accepted as a last resort. Tempest would much rather take the bus than lead the young man on by even remotely suggesting that she had any amorous feelings towards him.

The one positive outcome of the frenetic pace of life was that it gave little time to think about the focus of her fractured love now hundreds of miles away. When she did think about Caleb, her thoughts most often turned to the morning of his exit and not all the other good times that they shared. She tried to understand what had exploded in her heart that made her run to him. In retrospect it was almost like an out of body moment but one she was terribly glad to have experienced. In their period of self-imposed separation she knew she still loved her friend and now she was nearly certain he shared the same feelings.

Seeing that their estrangement was no longer self-imposed, the big question for Tempest was how to go forward? What was the formula they would follow? Had they not split for the nine months prior to his exit, she would probably be sobbing nightly, spending long hours writing letters and waiting for the phone to ring. Now she was much less despondent but still waiting for something. She just had no idea what that something might be.

The answer to the troubled young woman's question appeared in the mail three weeks to the day from Caleb's exit. A letter postmarked Ardsley, Wisconsin, arrived and before identifying the sender by the postmark she had already recognized her friend's handwriting. Diane had taken the mail from the box and placed it on the kitchen table and was also aware of the letter. She was cautious to bring it to her daughter's attention and waited until Tempest found it, then played more of an observer role. The addressee took the envelope and retired to her room. It was better to be alone in order to allow for the full range of emotions that the message might elicit.

The nearly eighteen-year-old closed the door behind her, sat down at her small desk and stared at the flat white correspondence. Whatever it said would change her life forever. She paused and then opened it slowly, using a small metal ruler in an effort to preserve what might be the second most important letter in her life. The first was still a mystery to her. Inside were two sheets of paper. She was not sure if this was good or bad. If he ever wanted to say good-bye to her it would not be easy and might take many words to accomplish. But then again, Caleb was not a rambler and generally went right to the point. Maybe he was describing the life he was living so she could share it with him. Rather than speculate further the letter was in her hands. She began to read it.

My Dearest Tempest:

Here we both are, in a place where we feared we would one day be, separated by many miles. Whether we spent our last few months together or not, this is how it would be at this very moment in time. It has to get easier, because writing to you from faraway can't be any tougher.

Since being here I have had little time to think of anything else but you. This is not the best situation because it is important that I also take the necessary time to stay current with my studies and learn a pretty hefty playbook. Running a quarter of a mile in full pads every time you miss an assignment can get very old, really fast. What I have thought of most is how much I miss you. If there was a way to see you by just walking across the lawn my feet would be on the grass right now. But we both know there isn't.

One of the freshmen already bailed out because he couldn't stand to be away from his girlfriend. He was from Arkansas, about the same distance apart as we are but in a different direction. At first listening to him talk was like hearing my own words coming out of someone else's mouth. But when I listened closer it became very clear to me that his relationship was not as strong as ours. In fact, Tempest, I am convinced that no one's bond is as strong as ours. If you had not come to me the morning of my departure, I had already decided that I was going to go to you. My message was going to be the same as yours. It is the only message that matters. We will be together. I hope you believe that as completely as I do.

When you get this letter it is my hope that I have not misread your thoughts. Going through life knowing that you are not physically by my side would cause me to rethink my very existence. Don't think I would jump off a cliff or anything like that, but realize my life would be much less meaningful without you there with me.

I realize this is heavy stuff for me to write but it took me two weeks and half a pad of paper to get it right. I will write to you once every two weeks and hope you do the same. My address is on the envelope. The telephone number for the dorm is written under my signature. It would be great to hear your voice if you care to speak with me. The university is installing ISDN internet access to the library and some of the dorms. Soon I will be able to email you. Maybe we can communicate directly between your college computer network and here. You will still be faraway but anything would be an improvement.

On most nights after eight o'clock I am in my room studying and remember we are on central time. The best thing about this place is central time. I can watch the end of sporting events on TV without staying up too late.

My studies are not that difficult. Averton prepared me well for college. Being in college yourself you probably realize that. The football team is rebuilding. I am being used as a third down back, mostly catching passes out of the backfield, although there are a couple running plays they have me practicing. It looks like I might even get into a game or two. As a freshman that is more than I expected.

Tempest, let me close by just saying I love you, I have always loved you and I always will love you. No matter what, we will be together again.....Caleb

414-555-3147

She kissed the letter, folded it and put his words back into the envelope. She laid her head on the top of her desk and rested. With a solitary tear hanging on her cheek she drifted off to sleep.

Chapter Forty Three: A New Start

Tempest was gently woken by her mother reminding her of the shift she had to work that night. When the sleepy girl saw the time she flew into action and was out the door in nothing flat. The letter remained on the desk. When Diane Arrck saw the note, she wrestled between the curiosity of knowing what her son had written and respect for Tempest's privacy. Realizing that she had played with the direction of Tempest's life on one too many occasions, she opted for privacy and closed her daughter's door prior to proceeding downstairs to prepare the evening meal.

It was Saturday but Mark Arrck would be home for dinner. The nightly table was a lot less populated these days. Noah and Joan had carved out lives of their own and Clark participated in Averton High School sports. He was a chip off the old Arrck block and used his own bounding skills on the basketball court and to mimic the actions of his older brother during the daily dismounting from the family porch. Given the kid's busy schedules there were even days when Diane was alone for dinner. On those occasions she might join her daughter on the walk to Mennetti's and grab a bite there. Then she would walk over to meet Mark. After locking the door of "Two by Two Shoes" they would occasionally share some hanky panky in the stockroom.

Tonight for the first time in memory Diane Arrck and Mark Arrck would be dining at home alone. The lady of the house took advantage of the opportunity. Recalling the very first meal she had prepared for her then boyfriend, the former Diane Mann went to work seasoning a nice steak, prepared a large baked potato and had found some sweet corn at the local market that somehow survived uneaten from the prior summer. The corn appeared to be juicy but Diane had some reservations. The theme of the meal called for corn however, and she was willing to take a chance on its freshness. Dessert was a homemade cherry pie that she had just popped in the oven. When Mark Arrck came home that night his wife was dressed in a provocative yet presentable manner. She never knew when one of the kids might come barging through the door.

The parents shared what began as a romantic dinner. Diane used the still tempting aspects of her well-maintained "Mann body" to ensure that Mark made the connection between this Saturday evening and that first night in the kitchen of her family's residence. Luckily for Mark, he connected the dots between this evening's fare and Diane's first attempt at a homemade meal. His recollection made it worth the effort for his spouse. After a stimulating discussion, interspersed with references to their youth and memories of their courting, it was time for dessert. When the pie was served, for some reason the two turned back into parents and the subject shifted to their children. For months Mark had been worried about the well-being of his youngest daughter. He thought the world of the boy she loved and considered him almost to be his son. If only he knew the reason for his feeling that way.

Returning to that night when they were young reminded the mother of four of the days when her life was not burdened by the secret. She longed for that freedom and the moment just felt right. It was the perfect opportunity for Diane to come clean with her husband after all the years of hiding the truth. She started to recalculate the harm of bringing him in on the dirty little secret. Then, before saying the words she longed to say, she stopped herself and thought better.

Instead of shattering his reality she offered her husband more pie. Mark took her up on the suggestion and while cutting a piece she mentioned that Tempest had received a letter from Caleb. Mark responded, "Why didn't you tell me that sooner? That is huge news. You really buried the lead on that one. I hope it was the message she was waiting to hear." Diane said, "Of course I respected her privacy, but she read the letter and fell soundly to sleep. I am thinking that is a good sign. She didn't say much of anything. She was nearly late for work and ran out the door once I woke her." "Did she look as though she had been crying?" was Mark's reply. Diane answered, "It didn't appear so." Mark figured that had to be good news because a "Dear Tempest" letter would have likely set off the waterworks, even for his unshakable girl.

The truth was that Tempest was very happy to hear from her boyfriend. Pudgy was thrilled that she had her former crowd pleaser back. The red haired waitress was her old self that evening and she had the tips to prove it. Charlie Farley was a patron that night and commented to his former student that she seemed to have the weight of the world lifted off of her shoulders. She replied, "Some good news came in the mail today. In fact, the best news anyone could ever imagine." Charlie was happy as he had not only seen her struggling here at the restaurant but had noticed a good deal of moping around on the community college campus. He had considered approaching her to find out what was wrong but thought better of making an advance of that nature. Charles always held a fondness for Tempest. That fondness did not extend beyond warm feelings. At eighteen she was now old enough for him to begin to have a different level of interest but he could not consider it given their previous relationship.

That night when eight o'clock rolled around, Mark Arrck entered the door of the restaurant. Mrs. Nubbler said, "Well, well look who's here. Are you craving some late night pizza?" Mark was one of the few people who even remembered Pudgy's real name and said, "No thanks Sam, I am full, big dinner. I am here to pick up my daughter." Samantha replied, "She has a table over there to finish up and should be ready in fifteen minutes." She then showed him to Caleb's usual waiting spot in the office.

When Tempest finished her work she came into the office ready to go. She said, "This is a first. How did you get stuck walking me home?" Mark replied, "Stuck, what do you mean stuck? I have been waiting for the day when it would be my turn to walk with you." Father and daughter walked from the diner. The autumn weather had begun to take hold and there was a chill in the air. The air was fresh and the slate was clean and as they walked Mark said, "Your mother tells me you received a letter from Caleb. She saw it on your desk when she woke you for work." Tempest smiled and said, "Yes, I was beginning to wonder if I was ever going to hear from him. He loves me dad and he misses me." Mark said, "Well since when is that news? That boy has been crazy for you his entire life."

They continued to walk and she said, "You know dad, we always knew that being apart would be hard. We never were going to be prepared for it. Losing nine months of time together was really stupid but in some ways it better prepared us for what we are going through now." Mark who had lots of time for philosophical thoughts while looking at customers' feet said, "Let me say this sweetheart, sometimes you just know when two things belong together. Take it from a person who knows a perfect couple when he sees one. You two, are without a doubt the most perfect pair I have ever seen." She would have much preferred to have been walking with Caleb but when hugging her father there was a feeling of warmth and happiness. When she arrived home she took the letter off of her table and read it to her mother.

Chapter Forty Four: The Revelation

Tempest's mood had improved measurably for a time. She and Caleb were managing their long distance relationship like they had been at it for years. The sad truth was as Thanksgiving approached they had only burned through seven point two percent of the three and half year separation that life had thrust upon them. She thought having the right attitude would make time go faster but although it might have helped, the time apart was just very hard for the young woman. The calendar was also working against her. When she had been asked to work the Wednesday before Thanksgiving it reminded her of the anniversary of the fight. Refreshing those negative feelings caused her demeanor to take a gloomy turn that brought on some restored broodiness.

The fact that Caleb would not be home for the holiday was the icing on the long distance relationship cake. To make matters even worse a prominent old chestnut had reentered the scene with a vengeance. By early November her loathing of oblong pizzas had returned. The chefs had been given a much appreciated reprieve in the past couple months but lately she was on them like tomato sauce on a meatball. She also rekindled her general distaste for anything "close enough" with her old nemesis pi once again squarely in the cross hairs.

Charles Farley had enjoyed the ups that Tempest had experienced and even from afar was able to witness the downs. During his usual Friday journey to Mennetti's he had a ringside seat to view her attitude swings. Her demeanor had clearly taken a turn for the worst. The recollection of the trip he had taken to England to see his mum the year earlier was cause for Charles to have his own depressed mood. He would not be going home this year and the idea of being alone for the holiday made him quite blue. When exiting the restaurant six days before Thanksgiving, he made little effort to catch his favorite waitress's eye.

The next week was truly a wild one for Tempest. She needed to study for late mid-terms, fill in at Mennetti's due to vacationing coworkers and chip in helping her mother around the kitchen in preparation for the holiday meal. Marley and Harold were still together and yet to set a date for their wedding. They would be leaving the Wednesday before Thanksgiving for a long weekend in the Bahamas. Edward would be home alone and was invited to the Arrcks to share their feast. He graciously accepted the dining invitation and the opportunity to brighten his forlorn neighbor.

Tempest was sitting in the living room of the Arrck residence on Monday evening, reading a social sciences text and half listening to the television. Her ears perked when the evening news anchor mentioned Wisconsin. There were videos of an enormous snowfall hitting the state as a Canadian storm had dropped from the artic and was working its way across the country. The weatherman warned that the system from the west might meet up with low pressure moving up the East Coast. If it did, Wednesday night could bring with it a blizzard of monumental proportions. On the other hand, there could just be light flurries. It would all play out over the next day and was difficult to forecast. The mention of her boyfriend's new home had piqued her interest more than the news of the weather. The potential for meteorological hell to break loose did sink in, but did not make that big of an impression.

Late morning on Wednesday Tempest was at school getting ready to drive home with Joan. Her shift would be starting at one o'clock. A small crew would man the store as the day before Thanksgiving was never busy. The staff would consist of two waitresses, who would bus their own tables, and one pizza chef. If there was a surge, Pudgy or Cameron could always swing over and help out.

Tempest made the lonely walk to the eatery by herself that day. There were some flurries sailing through the air. Her thoughts turned to the holidays and the heavy snow Caleb must be trudging through. When she arrived at the store she found Pudgy putting on her coat. The owner told Tempest she had to leave and that Anna Belle had called in sick. She would be on her own with Mario the pizza chef. After wishing her favorite waitress a Happy Thanksgiving, Pudgy left the store. Tempest was glad, she liked Mario, he rarely made a less than perfect pie.

It was very quiet and the two employees had a lot of free time. Tempest could not understand the reason it was so dead until she peered outside and saw that the street and sidewalk in front of the restaurant and pizzeria were covered with at least four inches of snow. Between the time of day and the ominous clouds, it was already dark.

It did not look like there would be too much traffic coming their way. Tempest left the drapes open to be able to monitor the snowfall with help from the nearby street light. She called Pudgy for instructions. Her boss's response was that it was a tradition to stay open until eight on the day before Thanksgiving. In deference to Cameron's sentimental leanings towards the importance of tradition, she wanted the two employees to keep the restaurant open.

With the absence of customers, Mario and Tempest were both trying to entertain themselves. The cook was in the office watching television. Any news was mostly about the storm. The bored young woman was just staring at a couple of uneaten pizzas. She was lost in thought. There was an entire cheese pizza and three equal slices of a pepperoni pie sitting under a warm orange light, resting on the steel plates that they rode into the hot oven during baking. She was not getting much satisfaction from the pies and she raised her head and took another look outside. Now there had to be just short of a foot of the white stuff and it was still flying. Although she only lived a few blocks away, getting home might start to get to be an issue.

After reacquainting herself with the volume of snow her thoughts returned to the two pizzas. There was something bothering her. Then as she thought deeper, a light went off in her head. She grabbed for a napkin and took the pen from behind her ear and began to write down some numbers. The first thing she wrote down was the equation, circumference equals pi times two, times the radius. She then put the number four under the symbol for pi. She deduced that the revised equation would accurately calculate the length of the partial circumference remaining from the quarter of the pepperoni pizza. She then checked her math.

The math genius confirmed what she already knew. Any one of the three elements in the multiplication could be divided by four to achieve the proper result. If the radius was eight, the number two could be exchanged. Instead of two times the radius, a quarter of two or one half could be used. The same would be true for the constant, where one quarter of the incalculable number could be substituted.

She paused, then ran through some figures. Zero divided by four equals zero. One divided by four equals point two five. Two divided by four equals point five. She went all the way up to nine and calculated nine divided by four is two point two five. She assigned the variable, K, to the final number in the result. No matter what the last random number of pi, if there was a last number, if you divided it by four the resultant fraction would never be a non-repeating decimal. It would always end in a whole number. A number she now defined as K. She realized that this wasn't the complete breakthrough she had been seeking but she was on to something.

Tempest wasn't the only one who realized she was in the midst of a brainstorm. Standing alone in a foot of snow peering at the worthy mathematician through the frosty window of the pizzeria was Professor Charles Farley. Friday night was his usual night to come to Mennetti's but being alone for the holiday he needed company. His longing for companionship and a desire to be near the redheaded girl pulled him like a magnet to Mennetti's. He opened the door and snow flew into the dining room. Tempest looked up in surprise and said elatedly, "Charlie Farley, you have to be nuts to be out on a night like this." Then realizing how fortunate she was that her former tutor had arrived, she continued, "You are never going to believe what I may have just figured out." Watching her from the other side of the window he knew she was up to something big, but after she sprang across the room, gave him an over-sized hug and helped dust off the snow, he knew it must be gigantic.

Tempest sat Charlie down on a barstool directly behind the two pizzas that rested on the counter and said, "Ok Charlie, what you see?" Charles thought maybe she had gone a little stir crazy because of the weather and said, "It looks like two pizzas. One is complete and one has a quarter of the pieces uneaten." The waitress said, "Yes, that is right. But what else do you see?" She knew he would not make the same leap she had made and after giving him a fair chance said, "In order to use the formula two times pi times the radius to calculate the remaining curved segment of the quarter pizza what do you have to do?" The professor said, "You would have to divide the result by four." Tempest answered, "Very good professor. Now, which element of the equation do you want to divide by four?" Charlie replied, "It doesn't matter." She answered, "That is again correct. Now, did you ever think of what happens if you divide pi by four?"

Charlie focused on the question. Then after considering her inquiry said, "It doesn't matter what the final digit of pi is. It will end in a whole number." Tempest stood up and raised her hands and said, "Right again Charlie Farley! Now I am not sure what that tells you. It tells me that something is definitely amiss. Why is it you can't calculate pi to a whole number for a full circle but for a quarter of the circumference the calculation ends in either a one, two or five? Seven out of nine times it ends in five. But either way, it is a whole number that can be calculated."

Charlie looked at the napkin and asked, "What is the letter K for?" The waitress replied, "That is just the variable I assigned to keep track of that nth or final digit of pi. It cleans up the way I think about it." He raised his head to look at his former pupil and said, "You are really on to something. I am just not sure what it is. One thing I do know however, you need to stop referring to the quarter circumference as a curved segment. It should be labeled an arc. In this case it should rightfully be referred to as Tempest's arc."

The tenacious student had not been seeking fame or fortune. She was just looking for precision and to do her part in ending the mediocrity of a "close enough" world. Although she still hadn't found the total solution, she was more certain than ever that pi was a paradox, a contradiction and a clue to something bigger. Attempting to prove her belief had just taken a huge leap forward. By stepping back and concentrating on the exact nature of the partial circle she peeled away part of the mystery, revealing more of the incalculable secret. With its enigmatic nature exposed, it could no longer completely hide from the truth. Her focus on less had revealed much more.

Mario had now taken an interest. Having been lured away from the television, with crossed arms he shook his head up and down saying, "Tempest's arc, Yes, I like it." Tempest liked it too but realized that the discovery was going to require even more analysis and deep thinking. She thought about a single thread pulled from a wool sweater. Once you started pulling the thread it never seems to stop. She wasn't sure she was up to the challenge to pursue the breakthrough further but she had opened the door. It was now up to the waitress slash mathematician to walk through it.

There was a new energy in the bistro but it had nothing to do with customers and everything to do with pizza. As the two men were congratulating Tempest the phone rang. The well-trained waitress assumed it was a hungry customer looking to order a pizza, but instead it was Diane Arrck. The concerned mother was on the line asking, "Tempest when you are getting out of there? Do you have any way of getting home? I can send Noah but he will be walking. The cars are going nowhere." Tempest looked at the clock. It was already half past eight. They could have left thirty minutes ago. She replied to her mother, "Let me get the place ready and I will call you back." With that, she hung up.

Charles asked his accomplished friend, "Who was that calling? There is no way someone wants to pick up a pizza at this hour." She responded, "It was my mom. She wanted to tell me that my brother was prepared to come and get me." Charlie said, "Nonsense, I can walk you home. Tell your mother I will be glad to get you there. My car is somewhere in that direction and I have to go find it anyway." The three occupants of the restaurant departed together and the still excited young woman locked the door behind them. The snow had grown to well over a foot and in some places over two. With shared wishes for a Happy Thanksgiving, Mario went in one direction and Tempest and Charlie trudged off in the other.

The walk was taking much longer than usual. Halfway home Tempest remembered she had not advised her mother that Charlie would be her escort. As a result, they soon ran into Noah. After greeting the snow covered couple Noah said, "I can take her from here." Charlie agreed, but the threesome quickly concluded that there was no chance the professor was going anywhere, even if he was lucky enough to find his car. Tempest decided, "Come home with us Charlie Farley. We can either put you up at our house or over at the Baxter's."

When they finally made it to the Arrck residence the snow on the front porch was so high they had to walk around the house and come in the back door. Diane was waiting with two hot chocolates. When she saw Charles Farley she was surprised but without skipping a beat said, "You are going to need a hot chocolate." Diane had always liked Charles Farley. She appreciated his character, recalling the days when her daughter wrestled with getting "the cough" to run its course. A lot had changed since then but rather than reminiscing Diane helped the three get their snowy outer wear off and tried to make them more comfortable.

After sipping their piping hot drinks to the halfway mark Tempest said, "Let me call Edward to see if Charlie can stay in Caleb's room tonight." When she dialed the Baxter house Mr. Zurck answered. Tempest said, "Hey, I thought you would be in the Bahamas by now?" Harold replied, "We made it as far as the Thruway and had to come back. There is no way we could get close to the airport and even if we did all the flights were cancelled." Tempest put the receiver by her side and said, "Looks like we are having a bigger group for Thanksgiving."

Chapter Forty Five: A Measured Start

The craziness of the prior night served to accomplish one thing. Time had flown by. Tempest was not dwelling on the fact that her boyfriend was having Thanksgiving a third of the way across the country. He was with teammates but not family. The Arrcks would be with family and friends and acquaintances, who they could now also count as friends. The Thanksgiving Day sun was shining on the deepest snowfall recorded since the mid-seventeen hundreds. That storm had been chronicled by one of Paul Baxter's kin. The record was kept in the town hall. Ezekiel Baxter was considered to have been embellishing when he documented the accumulated blizzard to have neared the shoulder of his horse. The disparaging reference to "Zeek the exaggerator" would henceforth be expunged from the town's historical archive.

No one was going anywhere. The plows were not moving. Bulldozers and backhoes were needed to get the regular snow removal equipment freed. Luck would be needed to free the bulldozers. When Charles Farley woke in Caleb Baxter's bedroom the town was silent. The only sound came from the hot water circulating through the heating pipes protecting the four occupants from the outdoor cold. Charles was happy to have been given shelter from the storm and now began to think about his plan to return to the comfort of his own apartment near the college. He waited in bed until he had confirmed stirring from the Baxter family. After hearing the perking of a coffee pot, he made his way downstairs. Marley was in the kitchen wearing her robe and slippers. Whether recently awoken or fully adorned she was a sight to behold. With the light streaming from the window through her long red hair, Charles could not get over how much she looked like a time-shifted version of Tempest.

Having forgotten about his arrival the prior evening, Marley was a little surprised with Charles's presence. She invited him to join her and offered him coffee or tea and the Englander accepted the latter. The topic of the day was the weather. It might have been the polite topic to turn to in any event but today it more than made sense. The rear door of the Baxter house was completely covered in snow and despite her ancestral capability to accurately measure the accumulated flakes, Marley would not even venture a guess to how much had fallen. Edward was next to join. He commented that he could not even see his car in the snow covered backyard. He poured a cup of coffee and sitting next to the refugee said, "Happy Thanksgiving governor." Charles raised his tea cup cheerily in recognition of the sentiment.

The last to arrive on the scene was Harold Zurck. The Principal was already dressed for the outdoors saying it would be a long day of moving snow. He was ready to create an outlet so the marooned denizens could safely gain access to the rest of the world. After he looked out the window he realized the rest of the world was in the same snowbound shape. He poured himself coffee, took off his hat and joined the imprisoned threesome at the breakfast table. Harold was trying to gauge the damage and asked Charles, "How much snow was on the ground when you arrived last night?" Charles replied, "It was well over my knees and up to Tempest's thigh. Good thing it was powdery because we would not have been able to walk otherwise." Harold's first thought was if it had not been powdery there would be much less. Then his mind turned to the slopes and the great skiing for anyone lucky enough to already be on the mountains. Had they not planned to go to a warmer climate, they would have been knee deep in this luscious powder for the entire weekend.

Charles felt compelled to explain how it came to be that he was escorting their neighbor home from the restaurant. He was about to report her mathematical discovery to Harold when the phone rang. When the lady of the house answered it there was another redhead on the other end. "Good morning Marley, looks like we have a snow day." Marley replied, "Looks more like a snow week. Is everyone in your family accounted for?" Tempest said in return, "Yes, we are all here, getting ready for Thanksgiving. Since you hadn't expected to be in Averton, we want to invite you to join us for dinner." Marley was preparing a response that they couldn't impose as the Arrcks had not planned for the expanded roster when Tempest added, "We would love to have you. We have more than enough food. Please let Charlie Farley know he is also invited to join."

When Marley hung up the phone she was laughing to herself regarding Tempest's playful reference to the professor as Charlie Farley. She was not fully aware of the circumstances of the first time they had met. She immediately began checking her cabinets for the fixings to make a couple of pies. In the process she advised her companions that they had been invited for Thanksgiving dinner at the Arrcks. Charles said, "That won't work for me. I have to get back to the college." Marley replied, "Tempest asked for you specifically. That is if you are Charlie Farley." His faced turned a bright shade of red as he began to explain the genesis of the nickname. Edward's face also turned slightly red because he just discovered another potential rival.

The four shut-ins were still in the kitchen when the phone rang again. This time when Marley answered her nephew was on the line. He called to wish everyone a Happy Thanksgiving. The college man said he would brag about the amount of snow they had in Wisconsin but that he had just gotten off the phone with his girlfriend and she said Averton was totally socked in. In the course of the conversation, Marley mentioned to Caleb that Charles had walked Tempest home from work the prior evening and had stayed in his room. He would also be staying for Thanksgiving at the Arrck's. Although Caleb knew that the professor was something on the order of ten to fifteen plus years his girlfriend's senior, he still felt a little uncomfortable with the news. Edward was not the only Baxter whose face had a slight reddish hue to it. When Caleb hung up the phone to return to his dorm room in order to prepare for the game his team would be trying to play that day, he wished he was back in Averton.

With the call from Caleb complete, Marley rested the receiver on the hook. Charles had already begun to explain to Harold the idea that the math-centric waitress had clarified in her mind the previous evening. Harold shared with Charles the degree to which Tempest had desired to explore the very essence of pi, including the creation of her hypothesis. Charles filled in some blanks of his own related to the hypothesis, then commented on the repeating decimal conundrum and her less than favorable response to the term "close enough". He mentioned that he predicted that the girl, who was revealing herself to be something of a math whiz, would have issues when it came to an incalculable constant.

Edward chimed in, relating the story of how she once threw a pizza and the metal baking dish clear across the kitchen at Mennetti's because the pie was so warped it couldn't be considered to be a circle. Charles said, "We ought to have a very rousing discussion about this topic at dinner." Having been made aware by Caleb of Tempest's penchant for stubbornness when it came to this subject, the lone female in the room rolled her eyes and thought that rousing must be one of those words that means something very different when used in jolly old England.

Chapter Forty Six: Same Day Different Year

Marley rummaged through the cabinets and discovered enough spare ingredients to make two pies. When the men finally came in from the cold, having only cleared half of the driveway, the house smelled like a fine bake shop. Harold stood by the front to the stove to warm up and was sternly warned by his fiancée to be sure he didn't open the door. He responded that he would not even think of it and thanked his lucky stars for having closed it moments earlier. He really loved the woman who he had now been with for nearly two years. He had planned on setting a wedding date when they were in the Bahamas and thought he would take the step that evening after dinner. The following Easter would be at the end of March. Caleb would finally be home from college on spring break. It would be the right time to seal the deal with the woman he loved.

Edward and Charles stumbled in from the snowy driveway. The younger man opened the stove before Harold had a chance to provide adequate warning. An angry Marley just about ripped his head off. Her son might have gone into an immature pout had it not been for the presence of Charles. Instead he said he was sorry, made a joke about not being able to resist her legendary cooking and went off to his room. The smell of the baking pies reminded the Brit of his mum's kitchen and he commented that he missed England during the holidays. That morning was Marley's first occasion to better know the professor. He had been at her brother's funeral but they did not get a chance to talk. She found him to be more than a little interesting. Thinking to herself, if he happened to be five to ten years older, she might find him worth more than a second thought.

Standing in the kitchen, Harold knew he still needed to clear a path to the Arrck's house. After a short break the two educators returned to the elements to open a single passage up the walk, across the sidewalk and towards the "Nubbler bush". Mark, Clark and Noah were busy shoveling. They started from the garage and worked out towards the road. When a snowplow's initial pass down Lincoln Avenue left an enormous pile of snow at the end of the driveway, they gave thanks for starting where they did.

The huge plow tossed enough snow that it also refilled the path that Harold and Charles had just created. They would have to shovel their way back home. Although disappointed in the setback, they decided to first complete the initial task. When they finally arrived at the Arrck's front door, Tempest opened it up and handed them both a hot chocolate. She thanked them for the snow removal effort. She also gave a bag to Charles. It contained some fresh clothes. He thanked the young woman. The two then shoveled their way back towards the original starting point, knowing full well this would likely not be the last time performing the task. The big loser in the entire affair was the "Nubbler bush". Covered in snow by the storm, it was now being packed down with newly directed shovel loads, bending it nearly in half.

At two o'clock the four residents of the Baxter house hiked to the Arrck's for Thanksgiving dinner. The Arrck's driveway was totally open. It was one of the few in town to be in that condition. Most of the roads had not even been cleared. Upon arriving at the front door Noah answered it and invited the four of them in. When Charles entered the house Joan recognized the clothes he was wearing. The sweater belonged to Caleb. It was the one her sister had dropped the turnips on the prior Thanksgiving. Maybe Tempest just thought Charles and Caleb were of similar builds and the sweater would be the right choice. She did not consider that it might be a Freudian indication of something more.

Diane also recognized the sweater and found it more worrisome than did Joan. She knew Caleb and Tempest had set their ship back to an even keel, although they were trying to steer it from long distance. Diane had never considered Charles to be anything more than a teacher to Tempest. Now she was a little angry at herself from creating an opportunity for the attractive man to have additional exposure to her daughter. Creating any whirlpools that could interrupt Caleb and Tempest's arrival at a final safe harbor was not her intent.

When dinner was over Clark, Edward and Noah went to watch the football game. Tempest asked them to keep an eye out for the South Wisconsin State score. The team from the Midwest would not garner any national television coverage but was significant enough to warrant the score being posted at halftime of the televised game. Harold, Charles and Tempest found themselves at the dining room table along with Mark Arrck. Harold decided it was a good time to hear from his former student and asked, "So Tempest, Charles tells me you had a bit of a breakthrough last night." What followed was a lively dissertation from the waitressing mathematician regarding her concept and the implications for the existence of another way of considering our entire numbering system. She said, "This makes me even more certain that pi being immeasurable is a huge clue to turn over more rocks." Mark was proud that his daughter was not willing to readily accept the status quo. Although he did not fully understand all of his daughter's assertions, the man she called father counted her as more than an equal to the two older men.

After well over an hour of lively debate Harold said, "Kelly Ackerly has mentioned to me that she has contacts at the International Math Federation (IMF). They are always looking for new ideas and opinions that run against current beliefs. The organization recognizes that just because an idea is embraced by everyone, doesn't mean it is right. They cite the earth being the center of the universe and the world being flat as two prime examples. Maybe they might also be interested in learning more about the theory behind Tempest's arc."

Charles suggested that he work with Tempest to put her proposal into better order and prepare something that could be formally presented. She agreed one hundred percent. Edward, who had joined the group midway through the conversation, saw this as nothing more than Charles Farley trying to make an overt play for Tempest's attentions. Marley, who had entered sometime before Edward, had become more impressed with Charles's intellectual capabilities and was hoping this meant more opportunities to see the interesting young European. As the conversation wrapped up, seeming to have finally run its course, Clark came into the room looking for more dessert and made the announcement, "Caleb's team won and it looks like he may have even scored a touchdown." At that moment, her boyfriend seemed further away than he had ever felt in Tempest's lifetime.

The occupants of the Baxter residence returned home, gingerly navigating the sidewalk that had been revisited by the plow's multiple trips up Lincoln Avenue. Harold and Marley found themselves alone in the kitchen. Charles would be staying one more night and settled in Caleb's room. Edward had returned to his room realizing that he was now no better than number three on Tempest's list of suitors. Harold asked Marley to have a seat and said, "If we had made it to the Bahamas I had a surprise for you. Seeing that we won't be wading in the Caribbean any time soon it seemed that now would be a good time to bring it up." Marley was not ready for Harold when he said, "Let's get married the week before Easter, Saturday March twenty third. The weather will most likely be nice and Caleb will be home for spring break. What could be better than that?"

Marley was surprised. They had been engaged so long she had grown accustomed to the situation. The barely middle-aged woman had not pressed her future spouse for a set timetable and as a result was less enthusiastic than the anxious man had anticipated. Marley was not averse to the idea, just not burning to tie the knot again. She wondered whether the surprising feeling for Charles Farley was influencing her opinion or if it had just been a long day and she had eaten too much turkey.

The proposal had somewhat of a time released effect. Upon further consideration Marley did muster the interest to agree with the plan and after a few minutes more she seemed thrilled that Zurck had finally set a date. There was little time however, for Champagne corks or other revelry. The shoveling of snow and consumption of turkey conspired to cause Harold to already be sound asleep when Marley finally made it to bed. She laid there quietly while thoughts of the young professor sleeping a mere twenty feet away crept into her head. In a trance of thoughtless excitement, she rose from the bed and slowly walked into the hallway.

Edward's door was closed but she could still hear him sleeping and knew her son was gone to the world. Charles' door was slightly ajar and although he was asleep, would certainly not mind being awakened by the mother bursting with the age defying elements of her shapely body and of course the "Baxter nose". She toyed with the idea that he had left the door slightly open as an invitation for her to join him. Marley found herself being drawn by an unseen force. The unrelenting power of magnetism was once again being demonstrated by the now unknowing professor.

Moments before succumbing to the thrilling titillation and pushing the door further open she stopped, catching herself in a more coherent frame of mind. Finding sensual pleasure with the young man while mere feet away from her fiancé and son made little rational sense. It could only lead to very negative consequences. The rendezvous with self-destructive behavior would need to wait. For the time being at least, Charles would remain forbidden fruit for the older woman.

The unsatisfied female slowly returned to her room. When finally placing her head on the pillow next to her soon to be husband she realized the right decision had been made. Tonight the younger man may be a more exciting target for the temptress but if there was any real strength in a long term relationship with Charles, on the day of their nuptials, she would have to deal with the fact that her name would be Marley Farley. She chuckled inwardly thinking of the introduction at the reception. Ladies and gentlemen, let me be the first to introduce Mrs. Marley Farley and her husband Charlie Farley. Mark and Diane Arrck would have had the only two straight faces in the crowd.

Chapter Forty Seven: A Surprise Visit

The Thanksgiving holiday was barely over when Tempest and Charles went to work perfecting her theory and positioning the assertion in a more credible manner. Harold had touched base with Kelly Ackerly and now understood the process for getting an audience with the highly selective IMF. Tempest honed her idea to razor-like precision, stating succinctly the position that the inability to calculate pi was a glaring indication of a greater flaw in the entire numbering methodology used since the founding of mathematics itself. As Harold Zurck was heard to comment, "There is nothing quite like aiming high, is there?"

The forms for application were rather tedious and the two submitters worked day and night to get the documents to the IMF. The first hurdle was being selected to be heard by a regional committee. The cutoff for submissions to the annual review process was approaching. They made the deadline by barely one hour, postmarking the letter and accompanying documents by December second. They would receive an answer by December tenth and if accepted be invited to make their case the week between Christmas and December thirty first. Given the number of approved submissions, the time for their presentation could be any one of three days in a "yet to be determined" location.

Unknown to Tempest at the time was that Caleb's schedule was also becoming less certain. The coaches at South Wisconsin State had been so sure that a seven win season qualified them for post season play that they had already penciled in a bowl game between Christmas and New Year's Day. The Thanksgiving Day win however, had only put them on the bubble for selection. The additional contest was not a given, as the team had stiff competition and was at the mercy of various bowl committees as to whether or not they would get invited to play again. Caleb had been aware of the potential for being able to come home at Christmas for at least a few weeks but had kept the news from Tempest in both their written correspondence and phone calls. He desired to avoid raising their collective hopes only to have them come crashing down. For her part, Tempest had found so much to keep her occupied she still missed the long distance target of her attention but was not pining for him.

The response from the IMF arrived at the Arrck residence on December tenth. When Diane Arrck brought it from the mailbox and set the envelope on the kitchen table, she knew the message contained inside would have an incalculable impact on the future of her daughter. There was only one other letter that could mean more to her and the girl would never be seeing that one. Being that it was a work day, the waitress in waiting flew into the rear door of the Arrck residence to prepare for her walk to Mennetti's. She was three quarters of the way through the kitchen when she saw the envelope on the table.

Judging by its size the message was short and sweet. Charlie had suggested the bigger the return mail the better. They would likely be asked to fill out more forms associated with her presentation. Tempest hoped he was wrong and held her breath while reading the verdict. On a very official looking letterhead the message said only; We appreciate your submission for our consideration. Your proposal has been accepted. Please be prepared to present your theory, findings and any research on Sunday December 22nd at ten a.m., at the Grand Hotel, DuPont Circle, Washington D.C. It gave a contact number in case there were any questions. The title of your paper has been logged as, "Tempest's Arc and the Illusion of Pi." The event had been moved to the week of Christmas due to scheduling conflicts. What had been a short fuse was now made even shorter. The presenter didn't care. She was finally about to have a chance to make her case to the world.

Tempest read the letter over and over and could not believe her eyes. She then ran to the phone to call Charlie Farley but he was teaching a class and she left a message. The excited girl took the letter upstairs, running all the way and hurriedly prepared for work. Any Arrck within ten miles knew the answer she had received. There was no need for her to spell it out. She was going to Washington and that incalculable constant pi was going down.

The elated young woman was enjoying her shift. Her smile and upbeat demeanor were just the right recipe to drive tips into the stratosphere. It didn't hurt that the restaurant was really rocking for a Tuesday night. When Charles Farley arrived on his not so normal night, wearing an exceptionally broad grin across his very British face, Tempest knew he had received the message. She ran to him as he came through the door. He hugged her and twirled her around for the entire restaurant to see. It brought cheers from the crowd. When the patrons were advised what the celebration was about most of the regulars, who had witnessed legions of rejected pizzas, knew exactly what the opportunity meant. To the newcomers, there was an underlying sense of importance to their public display but a lack of clarity as to the true meaning. To Edward, who had been sitting in a booth by himself enjoying his angel hair pasta, the celebration meant a call to Caleb.

Edward arrived back at the Baxter house around eight o'clock, seven o'clock central time. He would wait fifteen minutes and try to reach Caleb in his dorm. When he called the Freshman Sportsmen's Dormitory the phone rang ten times before being answered. The soccer team members were in residence but there were no football players. The team had all been asked to attend an unscheduled meeting. The players were about to learn that despite what the coaches had prepared them for the entire year, there would be no bowl game. The seniors would be crushed because they had played their last game and didn't even realize it. Caleb was also crushed but at the same time thrilled. There was a window for him to go back to Averton and see his girlfriend. He considered how he would break the news and settled on making his arrival a surprise.

Edward was told that the players were at a meeting and he should try back later. Before he had the chance to make his call however, Tempest called her boyfriend as soon as she arrived home from work. Caleb had just returned from the meeting. She gave Caleb the great news of her acceptance by the IMF. He was excited knowing what this meant to the girl who had lifted her mighty sword against the inexcusable pi many years earlier. Now the case would be made in front of experts who could seriously consider her position.

After the call with his sweetheart, Caleb immediately called Edward and enlisted his help in pulling off the surprise. He had a troubling feeling that asking his cousin to assist in this effort was risky. After all, Master Jacobs was a bona fide loose cannon and known to do some pretty ridiculous and selfish things. But the freshman relied on the fact that Edward would help given the importance that Tempest had in his cousin's life. Unfortunately for Caleb, his trust would not have been more misplaced had he asked for help from the devil himself.

Edward was tasked with getting all of the travel details regarding the presentation. He approached the assignment cheerfully. Being asked to participate in the scheme was just the break he needed. Caleb's goal was to surprise Tempest at the hotel. They could be together on the most important night of her then young life. A less emotional assessment of the pros and cons of Caleb's decision might suggest that he had taken too many big hits in the head during football season. But to the young man it was a surefire way to ensure that the woman he had known since birth would be in the perfect frame of mind for her big day.

Edward was just as conniving as he was intelligent. He came to the conclusion that by playing his cards right he could eliminate both men that appeared ahead of him on the list of those vying for Tempest's affection. The first move was to keep Caleb's arrival a secret, even though his cousin had asked that his aunt be informed. Edward concluded that if Marley knew Harold would be advised and the former teacher would counsel Caleb that surprising Tempest the day before the presentation was not a great idea.

In his investigation of travel details, Edward discovered that Tempest and Charles would drive together to Washington, arriving the day before the presentation. They would leave two days later. Tempest had mentioned to Edward there are often follow-up questions. Being available to respond in person secured the best result. They had booked two rooms at the Grand Hotel on DuPont Circle. That is until Edward, impersonating Charles Farley, cancelled one of the rooms and changed the remaining room from twin beds to a king size bed for two adults. Edward then called back immediately and booked the just cancelled room for himself as the hotel was full. The shameful plotter then arranged for Caleb's air ticket, paying with his own money to keep the arrival hush-hush.

The day before Caleb was scheduled to travel he called the Baxter house. Edward counted himself lucky that he grabbed the upstairs phone before Marley had a chance to answer. The man in Wisconsin asked if everything was in place. Edward confirmed that Caleb would be ringing the bell of Tempest's hotel room three hours after her scheduled arrival and in plenty of time to take her to dinner. Caleb was so delighted he even shared with Edward that he intended to propose marriage to his lifetime sweetheart. Even Marley's unstable son had pangs of regret for what he was about to do to his cousin but he could not bring himself to step back at this point. He cared very little for the immeasurable damage he was about to create, so long as he was advantaged by the con. The malicious depths of his deception were as unfathomable as pi itself but he still found a way to sleep well that night. He awoke refreshed and ready to travel to Washington. It would be a big day.

The plan called for Edward to meet Caleb at the airport and ferry him to the hotel. The plot was nearly spoiled when the fraudster almost walked straight into Harold Zurck as he exited the men's room at a rest stop on interstate highway ninety five, just after entering Delaware. He could not believe Zurck didn't see him. He settled in a bathroom stall for twenty minutes, while enduring the heckling from the urgently waiting patrons, in order to ensure that his mother's fiancé had left the building. The schemer had not counted on the fact that Harold would also be in Washington, a detail he should have been able to figure out. His mind raced as he sped down the highway in order to make up the time he had lost while perched on the toilet, all the while wary of Harold's vehicle.

As the conniver neared Washington Dulles Airport, he decided to stay the course with the origin plan. Zurck's presence would be factored out of his calculations. In his warped logic the rest of the plan was airtight. Luckily Caleb's plane was on time. After Edward waited impatiently for the bag that his cousin checked, they were on their way to the hotel. In Edward's devious dream Tempest and Charles would already be in their room together. Maybe the professor would even answer the door partially naked. The best case scenario would be for a fight to break out. In his underhanded hallucination, he would step in and save the day, thus elevating himself to hero status.

The vehicle was left in the carpark as they walked to the front desk. Edward checked-in while Caleb asked politely for Tempest's room number. Despite the hotel policy, the desk clerk readily provided the restricted information to the well-groomed, polite young man. Edward convinced Caleb to first place their bags in his room. They would seek out Tempest together. He wanted to be front and center when the door opened to see Caleb's expression and of course to rescue the fair maiden.

Five minutes later an excited Caleb was knocking on the door of room three fourteen. Edward was absolutely gleeful that it was taking some time for the door to be answered. Maybe they had really caught the passionate pair in the optimal position. When the door finally opened Caleb and Edward were both surprised because the occupant was Harold Zurck. The older man nearly fell over when he saw Caleb, although he was a little less surprised to see Edward. As he was inviting them into the room, a British accent was heard from around the corner asking, 'Who is it Harold?"

The hotel was indeed fully booked. In an effort to put the room situation into proper balance, Harold and Charles decided to bunk together and allow Tempest to be by herself in the room with the king size bed. The only question Caleb had for Harold was, "What room is Tempest in?" Harold said five thirty two and Caleb was off like a shot. When he knocked on the door of five thirty two it took a full thirty seconds for the door to be answered. When finally looking out of the peephole and seeing it was Caleb, Tempest nearly pulled the door off of its hinges. There was a joyous reunion on the fifth floor and a significant inquisition of Edward on the third floor but all five were together in the lobby at six o'clock, ready to make their way to the restaurant.

Chapter Forty Eight: The Day in the Spotlight

The original intent of the dinner was to review the package for the presentation. The meal now took on additional meaning. It was a chance for Tempest and Caleb to reacquaint. It was also an opportunity for the wise girl to explain her theory to someone who was hearing it for the first time. This would make a huge difference and pay dividends the next day, as one of the four IMF panelist she would face was purposely a non-math oriented reviewer. Balancing her explanation between geeky math and layman's terms so Caleb understood, took the edge off of the material, making it more understandable to the average or slightly above average person. Based on the discussion, a few small changes were made in the presentation and after eating the five retired to the hotel.

It was an interesting dynamic when the group returned to the lobby. Charles and Harold were proceeding to room three fourteen, Tempest to five thirty two and Edward to his room. Where Caleb would go was the elephant in the lobby. There was some hesitation as the players began to move in their chosen directions. Tempest cut through the tension like a hot knife through butter by saying, "Caleb will be coming with me for now. We have a lot to talk about. Don't worry, I won't let the late hour cause any issues that will affect my delivery tomorrow." With that the two young people walked away, holding hands and laughing like Tempest hadn't laughed in over a year. Back in her room there was more talking. The only physical contact was Tempest putting her head on Caleb's shoulder as they lay together in bed. It had been a long day for the young man, which made it easy to be an early night, allowing her to keep the promise made to the team. They slept together for the first time. Caleb dreamt while still wearing his socks and blue jeans.

The next morning at eight o'clock the alarm went off. The hotel wakeup call came moments later. The careful girl was not risking anything. To make it even more of a certainty, the phone rang a second time. It was Diane Arrck calling as requested. Tempest had already run into the bathroom leaving Caleb to answer the phone. Before Tempest could say, "Don't answer that!" he had picked up the receiver. Diane's first reaction was to say, "Sorry, the front desk must have directed me to the wrong room." Then, like a mother seal in a crowded rookery, recognizing her son's voice she corrected herself asking, "Caleb is that you?" He replied, "Yes, it is me Mrs. Arrck. I surprised Tempest last night by coming home for Christmas. We had dinner with Mr. Zurck, Charles and Edward. It was great. She has really done well for herself. Right now she is in the shower. Can I give her a message for you?"

Diane's head was spinning. She didn't know what to say except, "Good to hear from you Caleb. Nice to know you will be home for Christmas. Let Tempest know I called as she requested. We will see you when you get back." Then in a bit of a fog she hung up the phone. When Tempest exited the bathroom, wearing nothing but her bath towel, she was advised that her mother had called. She looked at Caleb and asked, "Did she leave a message?"

When the Averton team of five arrived at the prescribed location the previous presenter was just finishing up. They waited outside in the hallway. You could hear a spirited debate underway inside the room. Apparently they had moved into the question and answer portion. When the door opened a young man emerged with a stack of papers under his arm. He was accompanied by a much older gentleman. The younger of the two was crying. A well-dressed woman then emerged and upon seeing Tempest and the four men said in a serious tone, "You must be Tempest Arrck. Please come in and begin your presentation."

The hotel conference room, where the presenters were to deliver their proposals, was quite unimpressive. It was rather small. There was a single table, which the four members of the assessment team sat behind. The furnishing had a white cloth draped over it. There were paper name cards identifying the esteemed members of the committee.

Tempest walked directly to the podium, deposited her notes and then circled back to the table introducing herself to each member of the committee. The four men in her company found chairs in the rear of the room. Once Tempest returned to the lectern another man entered and stood in the corner near the door. After a brief shuffling of papers, Tempest began. She had no sooner opened her mouth than the grey haired man on the left end of the table, a Professor Abler, who had a long list of accreditations said, "Forgive me for interrupting, but are you seriously going to come before this group to tell us why the constant pi is an error?" The room fell silent. Tempest appeared to freeze ever so slightly. Then sizing up the man, like she had any over imbibed male patron at Mennetti's, said with all the confidence in the world, "That is exactly what I am going to tell you." Charlie Farley got goose bumps.

Tempest began her assault on the constant by attacking the physical nature of a circle. She stood next to an easel. On it was drawn a circle. A loop of blue yarn was glued lightly over the round figure. The formula C equals two pi times R was written inside the circle. She slowly pulled the yarn from the easel, revealing slightly more than four feet of material. Tempest then took the yarn and cut it in half. After cutting the fiber she drew a line through the number two in the equation. The presenter then announced that the radius of the circle was eight inches. Taking the wool and folding it over she cut it in half, then repeated this two more times. The young woman then went over to the board and put a line through the letter R. She returned to the podium with a single short piece of yarn in her hands. It was one half of one eight of the original piece. Tempest raised it in front of her and said, "How can this length of yarn be incalculable?" The three math oriented listeners shifted in their seats while the non-math observer was firmly planted on the edge of his.

She then turned the page on her easel and said, "Let's look at this issue in a different way." She had one large circle drawn next to one quarter of a circle. Inside the larger circle was written the familiar formula. Next to the arc of the quarter circle was written the formula, except being a quarter circle, there was a four underneath the symbol for pi. She pulled a blank page off of a second easel. On the new page were the numbers ranging from one through nine vertically displayed, each was shown to be divided by four. All the calculations ended in a whole number. Pointing at the second equation she posited the argument. "Whatever the final digit of pi, the result that is derived in this alternate formula will end in the whole number one, two or five. Seven out of nine times the factor, defined here as K, is five. By the way, for an eighth of a circle, eight out of nine times K is five." The geeks shifted again and the non-math officiant became even more interested.

What Tempest's team had not been aware of was that Professor Abler had predicted to his colleagues that he would, "Blow the next presenter out of the water." At this point however, he was the one flopping around on the beach. The well-decorated mathematician on the end of the table then said. "Wait a minute. You are assuming pi is calculated over time and that the last number changes like an odometer as the calculation is being made. In that case you are assuming the factor of time. Pi is not determined like the spinning of an odometer being calculated over a moving period. The constant is just what it is, constant, immutable and incalculable."

Tempest thought for a moment. Charles and Harold now shifted in their chairs. They had not even thought to consider the variable of time or to incorporate the notion into her thinking. This wrinkle was taking the discussion to a whole new intellectual level.

Unfazed by the additional concept, the bright young woman held her ground and replied, "If you do not assume the ubiquity of time in calculating the constant then pi and the entire discussion for that matter is merely an abstraction." She held up the piece of yarn and said, "I can assure you professor, this piece of yarn is anything but abstract." Then to the complete surprise of her companions and the committee, thinking back to all the imperfect pizzas and the not so round snowman she and Clark had constructed, she made the following observation. "How infinitesimal a dent would need to be made in a circle or a sphere to have the circumference divided by two R yield something other than pi? Is gravity a factor that needs to be considered?" The female member of the IMF team made the comment, "Given that there are known variations of gravitational force in the universe maybe we can refer to these as no pi zones." The room full of math wizards let out a tension reducing laugh.

The belligerent professor was still animated but had no response for the points Tempest had just made. The other three IMF associates were mumbling amongst themselves. The frustrated member of the panel finally said, "So what is the point? Why would you attack pi in the first place?" Then the girl from the above average sized small town delivered the blow that would rattle the math community for years to come. "You sir, have found the proper question that I have been trying to get people interested in. The question is why! Why is it that the key component to the most simple and fundamental shape in the universe is a number that given our current state of mathematics can't be calculated? Doesn't that make you wonder what we might be missing?"

The room fell silent. What had long ago been hidden in plain sight had just been exposed. The four committee members turned to the man in the corner of the room. He raised from his chair and began to slowly clap as he walked towards Tempest. He said, "Bravo, you have done something that hasn't been done around here for a number of years, maybe a number of decades. You have come to us with a simple idea that shakes the very foundations of our belief system. It may be just what we need to get to the next step in developing technologies that have been up until now beyond our grasp. You must tell me though, why did you come to think about this in such a thought provoking way?"

Tempest was still guarding the podium. The question of why was now directed towards her. Pausing in an effort to refocus, she readied to reveal more than she had anticipated she ever might. "When I first learned of the existence of pi, I knew immediately that we had something in common. We share a parallel path. Certainly there are many times when I too have been considered irrational. Often when alone in my room, I silently ponder the equation for the area of a circle. Area (A) equals R-squared (RR) times the constant pi (C). Then I thought, by assigning the designation (K) and assuming there was an nth or final numeric digit to pi, it all might somehow become rational. The random rolling numbers that could at some point define that ultimate integer, passed through my mind. To me they were like the consecutive series of episodes that define my life. It seemed that it was more than a coincidence that when I took the variables and the constants from the equation and put them all together, A-R-R-C-K, it spells my name. That is why I need to get to the truth." A comforting stillness permeated the room. No one expected such a rational answer. To the assembled group it now all made sense.

Although she did not solve a problem, she answered many questions in the minds of those who thought they knew her best. Additionally, she had resurrected an important discussion that was deemed worthy of an invitation to Switzerland to present her work. The committee made the judgment on the spot and then invited Tempest and her entourage to join them for lunch, which was about to be served in the adjoining conference room. Five additional places were set. Harold Zurck and Charles Farley were thrilled to be in the company of such accomplished math minds but were mostly just brimming with pride to be associated with Tempest. Edward was happy for Tempest but disappointed that his plan had failed. Tempest sat between Professor Abler, who would become her friendly tormentor and most ardent supporter, on the one side. Caleb, without a doubt her most devoted fan, was on the other. The world had now heard from the girl from Averton and would have to face up to the fact that close enough would never again be remotely considered to be a good answer.

Chapter Forty Nine: Popping Something

After lunch was completed, Tempest was asked to meet with one of the coordinators for the Switzerland conference. The gathering was to be held in February, the venue Geneva. The committee would provide two tickets, one for her and one for her support team. The purpose of the event was not to judge the participants but to provide an opportunity for the members of the IMF to ponder the implications of their ideas and use the information to push the boundaries of math knowledge. This was rarified air for the girl from upstate New York and when she was done meeting with the committee coordinator she calmly said to Caleb, "I better call my mother to let her know I will be needing a passport."

Diane Arrck was tickled by the news and the notion that her daughter had turned the math world on its ear. Leave it to Tempest to make a huge impression. She could hardly wait for their return. Given the closure that they received, the five decided they did not need to remain in Washington the extra days. To the relief of the severely overbooked hotel, they journeyed north early to avoid another forecasted winter storm. Harold figured that the meteorological community was just a little sensitive about not nailing the last Nor'easter and that the storm was not likely to be as massive as the prior snow dump. He relied on his firm belief in mean reversion to support his theory. He agreed to leave immediately however, thinking if the next storm was anything like the last one they wouldn't be making it home until June.

Caleb joined Tempest and Charles for the five hour drive. They used the time to discuss the approach to the presentation in Switzerland. Tempest had a decision to make regarding her support team. She knew that Charles was the right choice for the conference but was not sure of his schedule or how others might perceive her traveling abroad with the handsome gentleman. She didn't let the thought dampen her spirits however, and was riding high when her former tutor pulled into the driveway of the Arrck residence. Diane, Joan and Noah all came out the back door to meet them. After Diane gave Tempest a hug, she hugged Caleb and welcomed him home saying that she missed him. Joan thought Charles was being left out and decided to give him a hug and he reciprocated.

They all went back into the house and found that Joan had baked a chocolate cake just for the occasion. Most had cake and coffee; of course Charles had tea. Harold and Eddie pulled in separately about thirty minutes later and were redirected by Noah to come to the Arrck kitchen. When Marley returned from delivering a couple of new art pieces to the bustling Parker Boutique, she saw the cars and the crowd and joined the party.

Mark Arrck arrived home after cutting Sunday holiday store hours short. He carried four pizzas from Mennetti's. Cameron had finally caved, agreeing to open on the holiday Sunday. On top was a note from Pudgy congratulating Tempest and letting the math star know that if she wanted to work the next day the restaurant could use the help. When they opened the pizza boxes they found perfectly round pies and a note from Mario that read, "The perfect pies for questioning pi, good job, your friend Mario."

Tempest realized that if she had not been pondering the perfectly round pizzas that Mario always produced, the thought that popped into her head may never have seen the light of day. She knew there were a lot of people to thank and hit her fork on the side of a glass to quiet the group saying, "Thanks to all of you for supporting me. As painful as it sometimes was, giving me the chance to get my thoughts out of my system brought us to this day. You all are to be thanked and I appreciate everything you have done." Charles gave out a mighty "here, here," and raised his tea cup. The rest of the crowd followed with a toast. Too bad Mrs. Grady and "Tomato Head" weren't there to share in the celebration.

As the pizza was being bisected, Clark Arrck came through the door with snowflakes on his woolen ski cap. He was returning from a pick-up basketball game at the school gym. The youngest Arrck announced to the unknowing crowd that they ought to be mindful of the weather, "It looks like we are in for another storm." Not wanting to get trapped again, Charles made his exit after advising Tempest that he would be in touch. Giving the remaining revelers a hearty wave he was off. Harold said he needed to check the weather. There might be a decision required regarding the fate of the upcoming school day. The students had already lost the Monday and Tuesday after Thanksgiving because the parking lot was not properly cleared. He preferred not to miss more time before the Christmas break and needed to consider asking the town to move the plows early to get a jump on the storm. Marley and Edward left with Harold.

Caleb stayed with the Arrcks and the discussion shifted to life in Wisconsin. Diane and the swapped children talked until late into the night. Tempest had already decided to skip class the next day. She had expected to still be in Washington. She had one last test that would be rescheduled until sometime during the Christmas break, thanks to some intervention by her professor friend Charles. Caleb had already begun his vacation with final exams being completed for the semester. Tempest was thrilled to have Caleb home for Christmas and could not keep her mind from gyrating when she thought of all the fun they would have over the holiday.

By the next morning there was only a little more than a dusting of snow. Harold's mean reversion theory had been correct. The students of the Averton Central Schools would have one and a half more days before they would be enjoying Christmas break. Harold, being so proud of the lofty accomplishments of an Averton graduate, made an announcement over the public address system that morning before the school day began. All those who knew their former colleague were thrilled for her. Many of the younger students knew her only as the hot waitress from Mennetti's.

When the newly ordained math wizard opened her eyes that day she laid in bed and thought about how good her life had become. The best part was that Caleb would be home for Christmas. She then startled herself thinking, "Christmas!", she had been so wrapped up in her presentation she had forgotten to get her boyfriend a present. The second thing on her list, after applying for a passport, was to decide on the perfect gift for Caleb.

The young scholar took her time getting started that morning. She had earned a little lazy time and when finally leaving her room the house was empty. She picked up the phone to call her neighbor. The only current denizen of the Baxter house answered. Tempest suggested that he come over so that they could have breakfast together. The phone had barely been hung up when there was a knock on the Arrck's back door.

Standing on the cold back porch, wearing his slippers and sleep wear, holding a bag of day old doughnuts, stood Caleb. She opened the door and said to her companion, "What are you nuts? What if someone saw you run across the backyard dressed like that?" Caleb was more interested in seeing his girlfriend and less worried with the impression he might have on the other neighbors. Raising the bag he said, "Want a doughnut?" She shook her head and said, "I'll give you a doughnut you idiot, come in." Then she disappeared through the kitchen door into the dining room.

Caleb was standing in the kitchen. He had never been in the Arrck kitchen with just his pajamas on and had surmised that with the exception of Tempest the house must be empty. As he opened the bag of pastries the phone rang. More out of reflex than anything else he answered it. Diane Arrck was calling to see if her daughter was awake and to let her know what was available for breakfast. Upon hearing her son's voice she said, "Caleb is that you? What are you doing there? You and Tempest shouldn't be alone in the house together." The truth was her daughter and her son had been in their home alone together on many occasions. What she really wanted to say was, "You two should not be left in a position where you might do something that could jeopardize your young lives." It was the second time in as many days that she had been surprised in this way by her son. This time, she was better prepared.

Diane began to suggest what she was thinking and the young man, being quicker on the uptake than the average college student said, "Don't worry, I am going to ask Tempest to marry me this Christmas. But don't tell her. It's a surprise." When he turned away from the windows toward the kitchen door he found Tempest standing in the doorway with nothing but a large bath towel covering the shapely form of her Mann-like body. Caleb said into the phone, "I think I have to go now. I might have just spoiled the surprise." Before Diane Arrck could respond, the call was ended. Caleb walked over to the door and embraced the cotton clad beauty asking, "Did you hear what I said to your mother?" As Tempest returned the embrace, her hands were working their way down his back and she replied, "The answer to both questions is yes."

361

Chapter Fifty: Home for Christmas

Knowing her mother as well as she did, Tempest expected either the phone to ring again or Diane Arrck to get into her car and make the two minute ride home from the library. Caleb was painfully aware of this as well and said to the target of his desire, "We are kidding ourselves if we think your mother is going to leave us alone." The response was another ring from the phone. Still under the cover of her towel Tempest walked across the kitchen and raised the receiver. It was Joan. Joan had a short message for her sister, "Mom just called me. She is on her way home. She said something about you and Caleb alone together. She is coming now, so you better be ready!"

No sooner had Joan finished her sentence than Diane Arrck's car tore into the driveway. Tempest said to her sister, "Got to go," and hung up. She ran back out of the kitchen while shouting at Caleb, "Make yourself decent!" When Diane Arrck came crashing into the kitchen, Caleb was at the table trying his best to look casual and said, "Hi Mrs. Arrck, what are you doing home so early?" His partner came through the door moments later in her sweatpants and a floppy t-shirt and while yawning said, "Hi Mom, didn't expect you back so soon."

The slightly flustered mother said, "Don't think I wasn't eighteen once myself. I know what can go on at your age. It is just that it occurred to me that neither of you would be prepared for the situation you just found yourselves in. This could become a very memorable morning for you and whoever else might come along nine months from now." Diane managed to maintain a mature posture while at the same time reacting to her fear of unplanned carnal activities between the two teens. Her caution was well-placed. Young Caleb had brought nothing across with him from the Baxter house than his passion and a bag of doughnuts. It was a documented fact that glazed pastries did not make for very good contraception.

Once Mrs. Arrck thought that the situation had been placed on a more stable footing, she needed to return to work. She did not even have the chance to take her coat off. When turning to leave Caleb asked, "So what do you think of me becoming your son?" A shock ran down the spine of the woman who had been hiding the dirty little secret for the previous fifteen years. When she remembered the boy's comment about asking Tempest to wed, Diane's heart began to beat again.

It had always been her hope that this would eventually happen. At eighteen, they were still a little young to be considering marriage, although she knew they were meant to be together. In as nonchalant a manner as she could muster she answered, "I was ready to print the invitations when you two were six. Just be sure you have a plan so that both of you can finish college. Long engagements are just fine." Looking at the couple sitting at the table she then said more directly,

"And please, promise me that you both won't go crawling into bed the minute I walk out of here." The pair promised Mrs. Arrck that they would control themselves for some time longer and they kept their word. Soon after Diane left for the library the phone rang again. The woman with the weird Italian accent said, "We heard you were back in town. We could really use your help tonight."

Rather than just hanging around doing nothing the entire Christmas break, Caleb landed a job at The Parker Boutique. The shop was one of the busiest at what had become known as The Averton Town Square. Not only was Caleb occupied moving boxes and stocking shelves, he was also busy filling his late father's car with his aunt's new creations and bringing them to the store as soon as she was able to get them finished. The Baxter house was the warmest in town as the massive old kiln, which Marley had assisted the movers with getting into the basement, was running nearly twenty four hours a day to keep up with demand.

Under the category of other interests, Edward appeared to finally get the message that he and Tempest were not an item. He narrowly avoided the most intense scrutiny that would have come his way regarding the foiled plot in Washington. If anyone had been interested in doing a little investigatory work, they might have asked how he was able to get a room in the fully booked hotel. There was so much going on that he escaped without paying any other price for his bad behavior than an additional room fee for a late cancellation.

Edward decided that moving on with his love life meant finally asking Beth Anderson out on a first date. He had flirted with Beth for the two and a half years that they both attended college but the attraction was left to lie fallow given Edward's infatuation with the Arrck girl. It was now time to move on and he asked Beth if she would like to attend a movie with him. She also lived in Averton, a member of one of the newer families in town. Edward did not need to consult Anne Nubbler's genealogical data prior to beginning what he hoped would be a successful romance.

Christmas fell on a Wednesday that year. This meant that Tempest would be off for both the holiday and its eve as it was still a tradition that the restaurant be closed on Christmas Day. Having been tapped by Pudgy her final work day was that Monday. It just so happened that this was the same day that Edward had chosen to ask Beth out to the movies. Given his date's attraction to the dashing good looks that Edward had acquired from his father and mother, they shared a few kisses in his car before deciding where to have a late bite to eat. Beth had only been to Mennetti's on a couple of occasions as her family's taste did not lean towards Italian food. She loved pizza and since she was deprived of the delicacy she asked Edward if they could go to the restaurant and pizzeria. It would not have been the twenty-year-old's first choice. He was making a real effort to distance himself from his neighbor but thought that there was an even chance that Tempest would not be working that night. He reluctantly agreed to the dining venue.

When the couple arrived at the eatery the place was packed. Movie goers and shoppers alike were making a final stop at the end of their busy days. Much to Edward's chagrin, his former heartthrob was right in the thick of the action. He made an effort to ignore Tempest and hoped they would not be seated in her portion of the dining area. After a ten minute wait they retired to a booth at the edge of her section. Tempest's workmate had just been saddled with a table for eight; when she saw Edward and his date take the booth on the edge of her colleague's section she told her now harried coworker that she would cover her flank. No sooner had Beth and Edward taken a seat when the redhead arrived with menus and two glasses of water saying, "Hi Eddie, what can we get you this evening?"

Edward introduced Beth to Tempest. He then advised Beth that Tempest was his neighbor and the girlfriend of his cousin Caleb. Beth was very friendly towards the waitress and said she was pleased to make her acquaintance. They ordered a pizza and some drinks. Tempest said, "It will be about twenty minutes for the pizza. Would you like to have an appetizer to get you started?" Edward asked Beth. Having been denied Italian food for so long she suggested they get some mozzarella sticks. Edward agreed and Tempest said they would be out in five minutes. True to her word, she brought their drinks and the appetizer on her next swing past the booth. Edward and Beth were in a deep conversation and barely noticed her.

The place was very busy and Pudgy delivered the pizza to booth number eight. Beth commented on how perfectly round it was, causing Edward to begin an explanation that included the exploits of the now well-known resident of Averton. Shortly after he began describing the event in Washington, Beth said, "Oh, she is the girl who is going to Switzerland to make the presentation to the IMF. I never would have pegged her for a math genius." Edward was startled by the remark and asked, "Why would you say that?" Beth replied, "Face it Edward, she looks more like a pageant contestant than a math geek." Edward should have left it at that but inquired, "Don't you think someone can be beautiful and smart at the same time?" Beth countered with, "I didn't say she was beautiful, those are really your words but it is a rare combination to find someone who stands out so prominently in two categories. It is just the math Edward nothing else." The disgusted young man thought to himself, "Just the math, Just the math," it always seemed to be just something that came up to bite him in the butt. First it was Caleb, then Charles Farley and now Tempest herself. He was wondering whether he would ever get a break.

Later, once exhausting their ability to finish the pie, Tempest arrived at the table and asked, "Would you like to take the rest home with you?" Edward said, "Sure, let's wrap it up." Then he asked Beth, "Would she like to split the last four pieces?" She replied, "Certainly, I can take two home and have them for lunch tomorrow." The mention prompted Tempest to say, "Lunch or even breakfast, this pizza is good anytime." Beth then replied, "Well if it is good for breakfast maybe you can just leave the four slices together."

Edward was a little surprised by her remark. He was not sure what she meant by it. He found out while driving her home that Beth's parents had gone to Norway for the holidays to visit family. She had the entire house to herself. She asked Edward if he didn't mind having cold pizza for breakfast. Beth had quietly calculated that she needed to raise her game if she was going to compete with the likes of Edward's neighbor.

The holiday schedule at the pizzeria caused Tempest to work much later than her normal hours. At ten minutes after ten o'clock, Caleb came walking into the diner. He had made the short drive from the boutique after closing. When he arrived his girlfriend was still bringing the final round of food to her tables. He retired to the office to watch television with an exhausted Cameron. Nearly an hour later Tempest entered, taking off her apron. She didn't say a word. Communication consisted of waving to Cameron and gesturing to Caleb that it was time to go. It had been a long night and she was beat.

On the way to the car she said to her secret fiancé, "Edward came in tonight with a girl named Beth Anderson. She seemed nice but a little sheltered when it came to Italian food. Do you know where she lives?" Caleb replied, "Edward said they bought Mrs. Grady's old place not far from the elementary school. Why do you ask?" Tempest answered, "Let's swing past on the way home. I have a feeling that your cousin won't be home for the night. Marley shouldn't have to worry about his whereabouts."

When they turned into the block just up from the elementary school sure enough they saw Edward's car parked in the driveway of what was once Mrs. Grady's house. Not only had she taken enough crap from her students but when her ancestry was called into question during Anne Nubbler's study, the aging former teacher decided it was time to leave town. There were no lights on in the house but the glow of a candle could be seen through the shades of an upstairs room. Tempest made the observation, "Their relationship seems to be moving along rather quickly." Caleb replied, "I guess they all don't take eighteen years to get to that point. By the way, when we tell everyone on Christmas that we are engaged, do you think we should have a date in mind?"

A date for the wedding was one of the furthest things from her mind. She was in the long engagement camp but agreed it made sense to consider a time frame. Feeling out her partner she said, "Are we looking to set a far in the future date or a let's get this done, we really ought to be together date?" Caleb had his eyes on the road as he considered her question. He turned his head and said, 'Why wait until the last minute, we know we belong together. How about we get married at Easter time?" His partner looked over at him and said, "Spring is a lovely time to get married but which Easter time, certainly not this Easter?" Caleb had actually considered a wedding at the same time as his aunt but when Tempest seemed to balk he said, "Actually there are a few wrinkles we would need to iron out before this March. Maybe we can just announce our intentions without providing any additional details." The couple realized that this seemed like the best outcome and the discussion made a turn back to Edward and his date.

Soon they were at the Baxter house. There was an empty spot in the rear of the driveway for Caleb to park. Their pledge to Mrs. Arrck was not meant to extend beyond that morning and in the absence of any similar assurance, on that warm evening for December, in the back of Paul Baxter's old sedan, their relationship rose to the next level.

When Tempest laid her head on her pillow that evening she committed that the introduction of a new intimacy would not change the lifelong bond between the two neighbors. They would continue to go about their lives. Tempest had to schedule her final test. She also carved out time to be with Charles Farley in order to strategize how to present the paper in Switzerland. February would arrive quickly, leaving no time to waste. She decided that asking Charlie to join her would be the best choice but had not shared her conclusion with anyone else at this point. There were some other stakeholders she needed to manage before making that announcement.

The next day the young woman who had proven herself in the field of math and the ways of love had a second day in a week to languish in bed prior to rising. It was Christmas Eve and there were a number of Arrcks taking advantage of a little extra sleep. There would not be a spontaneous inviting of

Caleb for a little alone time today. Tempest was resting but her mind was turning trying to determine the ideal gift for her fiancé to be. Time was running out. She had banked a significant amount of money from her waitressing and had been frugal in not spending a great deal frivolously on herself. Most of the outflows had gone towards education. When her mind wandered to Geneva, she realized that a wonderful gift would be a plane ticket for Caleb to join her in Switzerland. Since February was in the middle of the next school semester, their time together would be limited, but a couple extra days alone after the conference might be just perfect.

She spent the afternoon calling a few local travel agents to get pricing and availability. Caleb would be flying from Wisconsin and his best route was a short connecting flight from Chicago direct to Geneva. She was surprised however, that if she routed him through Paris, then on to Geneva, the fare was cut in half. She then checked to see if the same would apply to the ticket she had already booked for Geneva. It was also the case. Rather than having two extra nights in Geneva, she would arrange that she and Caleb would layover in Paris after the event and spend two days together in France.

Prior to announcing the plan she realized the need to check with her parents. Being in Europe alone with Caleb would require parental approval. Given her mother's recent intervention in the couple's morning rendezvous it seemed her greatest issue was adequate planning and not potential intimacy. Tempest anticipated that a green light was all but assured.

Chapter Fifty One: Christmas Present

It was a beautiful Christmas Eve night in Averton. The weather had cooperated and the stores were crammed with last minute shoppers. Given the incalculable number of times Caleb had picked up Tempest at the end of her shift, she thought it only appropriate to join him for the walk home at the end of his day. Caleb had left the car at home, seeing that Marley had exhausted her stock of new items for delivery and because the day was just as beautiful as anyone could expect for that time of year. When his girlfriend walked into the teeming boutique a few minutes before eight he was pleasantly surprised.

In testament to the volume of shopping that had occurred over the prior month, the shelves of the store were rather bare. It had been a good year for retailers and an exceptionally good year for Parker's. When Caleb proceeded out the door at the end of the day he was given an envelope by the store manager. She said while handing it to the young man, who had been there for a mere two days, "Thanks for all your help. We never could have pulled off the final push without you." Tempest inquired to her boyfriend, "What was that all about?" In response he referenced fixing a broken cash register the day before. It was not in his job description but calling upon his engineering studies, the boy's agile mind quickly surmised what was causing the problem. He was considered a bit of a handyman and when he was able to figure out why the safe wouldn't open earlier that day, he was elevated to wizard status. It seemed her boyfriend was also endowed with some unusual talents.

As they walked home that night, for the last official time as simply boyfriend and girlfriend, Tempest needed to do a little fishing as to Caleb's availability for the end of February. If he couldn't make the trip her gift would not have the desired impact. She positioned the discussion to describe the time she would need to spend in Europe while attending the conference. She said it would be a total of four, maybe even five days and she would lose a good deal of class time. She then cleverly said, "Wouldn't you find that a five day gap in your attendance at school would impact your performance?" Caleb reminded her that she would be in Europe on what would be a lifetime adventure. He said, "You can miss five days. I remember when you missed five days with "the cough" and it didn't set you back." She recalled that she had Charlie Farley to help her at that time and was reminded that she had yet to break the news about her tutor's likely attendance at the event. Realizing how much easier it would be for her to invite Charles if her fiancé was there, Tempest decided that Caleb was going to get plane tickets for Christmas. If there were problems with the gift she would deal with it later.

Caleb dropped Tempest off and then went home to clean himself up. He would come back over to the Arrcks when he was done. Mark Arrck had closed the shoe store early and he and Diane were in the kitchen with Joan when Tempest entered. After waiting for them to finish their conversation, Tempest made her pitch for her boyfriend's gift. Tempest explained her plan, which included her and Caleb being alone in Europe together. Mark Arrck was a more conservative force than Diane and although not dismissing the request out of hand, was not accepting the inquiry warmly. He said, "Let me understand this. You and Caleb will be in Europe alone together for five nights?" Tempest replied, "No, for two of the nights Charles Farley will be with us in Geneva." The additional information did little to soothe her father's concerns. Mark wanted to support his daughter but also had his principals to uphold.

Tempest was not beyond begging but before she had to resort to that Joan jumped in and said, "You were also eighteen once weren't you? Do you remember what that was like? Do you remember what you were like? Whether it is in a car behind the high school or a hotel in Europe, what's the difference? My sister has demonstrated a level of maturity far beyond what anyone might expect from someone her age. She and Caleb are perfect together. Why would you stand in the way?" Diane looked at Mark and said, "He is going to ask her to marry him tomorrow." Tempest jumped in stating, "And I am going to say yes!" The man whose last pivotal decision regarding his daughter's love life had been the color of her prom shoes, acquiesced given the ferocity of the onslaught. Joan the ninja, had once again played an important role in her sister's life. The Arrcks had given the all clear for takeoff.

Caleb was not one to stick to protocol. When he arrived to spend Christmas Eve with Tempest he was prepared to present the gift he had already revealed. The warm weather pattern continued late into the evening and the boy asked his girlfriend if she wanted to take a walk. She thought that it was a marvelous idea and together they exited the house and turned left, walking towards the elementary school as they had on any number of mornings so many years ago. There were a few wet spots to navigate as some snow that had fallen the week before was still in the process of melting. Whenever they encountered a puddle, Caleb would lift Tempest and carry her over it.

When they arrived at the school, the parking lot had emptied earlier that day and the streetlight left a solitary halo of illumination on the yellow lines and black pavement. Caleb was walking slightly behind Tempest and dropped to one knee while at the same time calling her name. The young woman turned to see the man with whom she had shared a maternity ward kneeling before her holding a ring. She walked back to stand before him as he said, "Tempest Arrck, will you do me the honor of being my wife." She dropped to one knee herself and looked at her equal saying, "Only if you will do me the honor of being my husband." They both rose and hugged romantically beneath the streetlight.

A few cars passed while they were in the embrace and most honked their horns. When Caleb went to place the ring on her finger she could see it was his mother's engagement ring. She had left it for him to someday present to his betrothed. When

375

Ruth gave it to Caleb in her final moments, having never recovered from "the cough", she said, "Someday you can give it to Tempest." Today was someday. He knew in his heart that this act was wholly consistent with Ruth Baxter's final wish that he take care of her daughter.

Tempest had seen the ring on Caleb's mother's finger as long ago as she could remember. Now it found a home on hers. It was a beautiful diamond solitaire. Paul had hocked just about everything he had to purchase it at a time when he had very little money. The proprietor of Blount's jewelers said it would be a great investment and he could not have been more correct. The ring was now paying greater dividends than Paul would ever have imagined. Although he had been deceased for over two years he was about to get his daughter back.

The newly engaged woman thought to tell Caleb of her gift but did not want to do anything to take away from the moment. They walked back home arm in arm and despite having been made aware of his intentions days before, the whole thing was still a surprise. She was on a cloud. A cloud that she shared with the only person she would ever dream of sharing it with.

When they returned to the Arrck house, Tempest found her parents, Joan, Noah and Clark and asked that they join her and Caleb in the living room. Once the Arrcks were assembled Tempest said, "Wait a second." She picked up the phone and called Marley. Ms. Baxter and Harold were together on the couch reading Charles Dickens' holiday classic, "A Christmas

Carol." Tempest asked Marley if she and Harold would be able to come over. They had an announcement to make. Fortunately Edward was off with Beth, probably eating more Italian food. Although he may have been nibbling on a little Norwegian.

When the collective families were in the living room, Tempest took her hand from behind her back and they both announced that they were engaged. Joan flew across the room to hug her sister and her brother. Noah wore a huge smile. Mark could not have been more pleased and Clark Arrck was glad that the inevitable had finally occurred. Marley was very happy for the couple. She had stood by as the boy put both of his parents into their graves. The young man needed love and stability in his life and she knew he had found it.

The most relieved person in the room was Diane Arrck. The dirty little secret had come full circle. Ruth Baxter's husband's ancestry had found a way to live on and now his genes would even carry the Baxter name. The "Baxter nose" would hopefully be seen on many a Baxter face whether it had the Nubbler traits or the recessive hair. Two children, born minutes apart and clandestinely switched at birth, were now engaged to be wed.

When Edward Jacobs arrived home the next morning he was not aware that the major announcement had taken place the prior evening. He enjoyed Christmas Eve with Beth Anderson, whose family continued an extended vacation in Norway. Edward was glad he could provide companionship for his new girlfriend. Over the time they sparred and flirted he had become quite fond of her. But the embers in his heart still burned for Tempest.

The now engaged young man came down to breakfast as Edward read the morning paper. Caleb asked playfully, "Is there anything in there about our big news from last night?" Edward responded, "It says here there were a couple of car wrecks and some ass wipe stole toys from a kid's charity but no other big news. What should I be looking for?" Caleb replied, "It is probably a little too early for the announcement. Tempest and I are engaged to be married."

Even on Christmas morning Edward was overcome with unvarnished jealousy. The candy cane he was holding snapped, sending red, green and white shards across the kitchen floor. The announcement spiked a renewed passion for his neighbor. If he couldn't have her, neither would Caleb. The devious conniver pondered the use of the nuclear option. The paternity test was always available as a last choice to split them up. Although it would also end his chances with the redheaded woman, he couldn't bear a lifetime of seeing Tempest in the arms of his cousin. Patience would be his ally and time would be on his side. He now plotted, waiting to drop the genetic bombshell at a time and a place, where it would prove to be the most devastating.

Chapter Fifty Two: A Trip to Europe

The remaining days of Christmas came and went with less fanfare than had been experienced on the eve of the holiday. There were some changes required in the European travel plan. The IMF seemed to have a pretty fluid schedule and moved the event to the first week in February. By mid-January Tempest had already rearranged the tickets and the lodging. She wasn't able to change Charles Farley's schedule. The day of the event now coincided with his mother's seventieth birthday. Farleys from both sides of the Atlantic were going to meet just outside of London to celebrate the milestone. Charles was still a major contributor to the effort and did not skimp on his input but Harold had volunteered to substitute in order that Tempest have a friendly face to accompany her at the gathering. Mr. Zurck was very keen on going. The event was a rock concert for math geeks and it would have certainly been on his wish list if he ever entertained the dream of having the opportunity to attend.

The week prior to the trip the presenter was putting the finishing touches on her production. The simple content that set the committee on its ear in Washington would still represent the thrust of the performance. She had made some changes in delivery and positioning of the questions in order to generate a more dramatic effect. The fact was, that since she had stimulated the thinking regarding the illusive nature of pi, other scholars had advanced her ideas and were running headlong down many paths to get to the bottom of what had become a broader pursuit. This is just what the Avertonian had hoped would happen. Tempest did not mind being a catalyst for the renewed effort. She knew she was not equipped to solve the entire conundrum but had always demonstrated the persistence to get other people interested.

The day that the three travelers were set to begin their voyages to Europe a major storm threatened the continent. It had the potential to bring countries from England to Greece and everything in between to a grinding halt. The latest word prior to flying east was that the IMF would still be holding the event. Harold boarded a plane for Geneva. Tempest and Caleb boarded separate planes for Paris. The engaged couple would meet at Charles De Gaulle airport and fly together to Geneva.

When Tempest arrived at the gate in Paris she found Caleb waiting for her. They had not seen one another in just over a month and shared a warm embrace. Caleb then broke the news that her flight was the last one coming in that morning. Nothing was going out. They were stuck in France. The determined young woman said, "Can we rent a car?" Caleb said, "They need an international driver's license to complete the transaction. Besides the roads are impassible. Right now we are stuck. I was able to book a room at the airport hotel. At least we have a home base for the time being."

After walking through the terminal to the hotel, Tempest called home. It was just before one in the morning Eastern Standard Time but Diane was waiting for their call. After making sure her daughter and her son were safe, she advised Tempest that the IMF event had not yet been cancelled and that Harold was already in Geneva. He was asking if he could make the presentation if she couldn't get there. Tempest was more than happy to have her former teacher make the case. Zurck knew the presentation as well as she. With eight hours to go, there was still a chance that they could get to Geneva by three o'clock. But it wasn't looking great. Since the couple was jet lagged and tired they agreed the best thing to do was to try and get a few hours of sleep. They went to bed.

The two woke around ten o'clock in the morning. The departure schedule displayed on the television in their room listed page after page of flights that were either cancelled or delayed. There was still nothing going out of the airport. The first flight scheduled to leave the facility was at noon that day. Since the hotel was connected to the airport, they decided they would walk down to the terminal to see if there was a more current update. The place was organized but the line to get any information was about twenty people deep. There was a coffee shop not far from the information counter and they decided to relax there. After waiting for ten minutes, they were lucky enough to get seats.

The departure boards in the terminal displayed the same information as the television in the room and given the number of frustrated passengers who appeared to be hovering around the closed gates the message was the same. No one was going anywhere until at least noon. After finishing their coffee and a mind clearing walk around the terminal they returned to the room. Tempest had the telephone number for the hotel in Geneva and decided to try to call Harold. Once she figured out the dialing pattern, the phone made a funny ring and after a few repetitions of the signal it was answered, "Bon Jour." Tempest replied, "Bon Jour", and asked if the person spoke English, which they did. She asked to speak with Harold Zurck. The operator replied, "One moment please." There was a series of double rings and Mr. Zurck answered the phone. Tempest called out, "Mr. Zurck, this is Tempest with Caleb. We are stuck in Paris. How are you doing?"

Harold had been awake since arriving in Geneva. His jet lag was not that bad since he managed to sleep on the plane. Her teacher asked Tempest, if she couldn't make it on time, would she mind if he delivered the presentation. Tempest replied, "Mind, I would be honored for you to take my place. Do you have everything you need?" Harold responded, "Yes I do. In fact, I was just speaking with Charles. He just made it to London before they closed those airports. It seems as though Europe is blanketed."

The team was intact but scattered. The good news is there was a key member in position to deliver the message. It was the best they could ask for given the circumstances. When Tempest found out later that the original plane that Caleb was scheduled to fly directly to Geneva had skidded off of the runway and that there had been injuries, she felt bad for the people on the plane, but was more comfortable with the decision to redirect her fiancé.

With little else to do, Caleb and Tempest laid down together. They were happy to once again be in each other's arms. After a short period of time resting they fell asleep. When they awoke they saw that the flight information on the television had been updated. It was now three in the afternoon local time. The presentation should just be beginning. There were now no aircraft leaving until six. Caleb suggested that they just proceed to the hotel they had booked in Paris and start their vacation early. To Tempest it sounded like a wonderful idea.

Before they left the airport lodging, Tempest called the hotel located just off the banks of the Seine. The staff was glad to hear that they would still be making it. The place was nearly empty and they would certainly be welcome a day early. Before relinquishing the room, Caleb checked outside the terminal and spoke to a taxi driver who said the main roads were clear and the roads in the city were passable. The Parisian committed to get them to their destination. With reliable transportation secured the two checked out.

The taxi driver made good on his promise and they arrived at the Paris accommodation in no time since the roads were nearly devoid of traffic. The concierge, who doubled as the reception clerk for the small boutique lodging, helped them with their luggage. After leaving their bags in the room, they returned downstairs where the two on-duty staff members arranged for a lovely late lunch with pastries and finely prepared eggs. Once the concierge learned the couple were newly engaged and making their first trip to Paris, he went all out to treat them special. The hotelier prepared drinks of fresh orange juice and Champagne. Tempest toasted Harold Zurck and the IMF. Caleb made his toast to the snow.

After a wonderful meal they both took a shower in the very tiny bathroom and prepared to venture out into the snow covered city. As darkness was falling, the dramatic scenes of the snow hanging off of the Eiffel Tower were incredible. As were the white-lined streets of the French capital. When the bells at Notre Dame struck six all Tempest could think of was Harold and wondered how the presentation had gone. She was happy for Harold but sad for not having the chance to deliver the message herself. She knew the team was in good hands.

Later that night, when she had the chance to speak with her former teacher, he said the presentation could not have gone better. The entire committee wanted to meet Tempest and they would arrange to do so in the future. Lastly, one of the members had invited him to go skiing the next day on Mont Blanc, just outside of the city. Once the young woman knew the basic mission had been accomplished, she relaxed and the two young lovers enjoyed the next three days alone in the city of light. She swore that they would return once they were married. Paris would always be in their hearts.

On the final day of the trip, the two were resting comfortably. Tempest was lying in bed considering the potential that modern day nobility was shamelessly flaunting the twenty two sevenths related to pi with the 2.2 and .6 conversion ratios associated with the metric measures of weight and distance when there was a tap on the door. The concierge had been trying to ring the room but apparently they had accidentally knocked the receiver off of the hook. He had a note for Tempest to call home as soon as possible.

Tempest realized this was not a good sign and immediately tried to dial the phone but needed the concierge's help. When the phone rang it was Joan who answered. Tempest said, "Joan, I was asked to call home immediately. Is everything ok?" Joan replied, "No it isn't. Mr. Zurck went skiing after the heavy snows and there was an avalanche. He and the people he was with have been lost for over a day. There is little hope that they will make it out alive and more than likely they won't even be found until spring."

When Tempest put the receiver back, Caleb could tell something terrible had happened. He thought maybe there was bad news about her father or another family member. The stricken woman sat in a momentary state of shock and said simply, "Mr. Zurck is gone."

Chapter Fifty Three: Change in Plans

The good news was that it didn't take until spring to find the body of Harold Zurck and his skiing companions. The bad news was that it appeared he had been buried alive for some time and had suffered a horrific fate. Two days after being declared lost, the Swiss rescue team recovered the frozen bodies. Caleb and Tempest were in transit on the way back to Averton when Marley received the news. His aunt had the Arrcks, Edward and her friends to console her. Even though Caleb knew he had to get back to Wisconsin, there was an overwhelming desire to stay and comfort Marley in her time of need.

When Caleb and Tempest arrived back on Lincoln Avenue they immediately went to the Baxter house. They found Marley and Holly Dane at the kitchen table. Along the way, in the midst of their competition to provide artwork to a number of The Parker Boutiques, they had become good friends. Before Holly was properly introduced she said, "I didn't realize you had a daughter." Marley, being used to the error by now said, "No this is my nephew and his fiancée. Although you are not the first person to make the mistake." Holly with an artist's eye made the comment, "The resemblance is uncanny," but dropped her line of thought as Caleb offered his condolences to his aunt. Tempest held her neighbor and said, "We are going to miss Mr. Zurck. He was a good man and a good friend."

Marley thanked them both for their thoughts. She mentioned that the wake would be in two or three days depending on when the Swiss released the body. She told Caleb, "I don't want you or expect you to stay around for the funeral. You need to get back to school because you are missing too much time." Tempest was torn with the idea that Caleb was leaving her again, but knew that the woman who shared her features was correct in the assessment.

After Holly left, the three relatives and soon to be relatives, remained at the kitchen table. The next time the doorbell rang the person on the other side was Charles Farley. He was devastated because he was supposed to be in Geneva, not Harold. He apologized to Marley, trying to help alleviate the pain both of them were feeling. She was very appreciative of the sentiment. They all sat quietly pondering the unlikely events leading up to Harold's demise, each having a new found respect for the tenuous and fickle nature of life. A life that all four still had time to live. For Harold, his time had come and gone.

The Baxter-Zurck nuptials were just over a month away and most of the planning was complete. Now there would be no wedding. In an effort to dramatically alter the mood Marley said to Caleb, "You know we have a wedding all planned. The invitations haven't gone out yet. They can be changed to

Tempest and Caleb. I know Harold would be honored for you to take our place." The words she used hit Tempest like a freight train. They were the same words she had used with Harold Zurck days before. Caleb looked at Tempest and she nodded back at him gently. Caleb then replied, "We would be honored to take your place."

The change in plan made it even more important that Caleb return to Wisconsin to catch up on the time he had lost on the trip to Europe. The day before he left, Tempest received a wire of condolence from the IMF. The message included the news that she had been awarded a four year scholarship to the college of her choice. The communique was bittersweet. She shared the condolences with Marley. She shared the rest of the news for the time being with Caleb and her family.

The day of Caleb's departure he and Tempest were driven to the regional airport by Noah. Edward watched as his cousin and his soon to be wife drove off. The rat knew that he still held the key to splitting them up for good. He had convinced himself that not only was he doing himself a favor but he was saving the two of them from the anguish that might occur if the facts of their ancestry were discovered long after the wedding. There could be children involved. The warped young man actually fancied himself to be a savior.

With Caleb back in Wisconsin, life needed to go on and Tempest maintained her current schedule with school and work. She had a decision to make about transferring to a different college next year but had not decided where to attend. A mid-western venue seemed like a logical choice. Over the next few weeks, in addition to her rather hectic regular duties, she had to keep the wedding plan on course. Marley was a great help safeguarding a smooth transition, but there were certain aspects that would need the bride's touch. Marley made sure she steered clear of any decisions that belonged to Tempest.

The patrons at Mennetti's, as well as the rest of the townspeople, had all become familiar with the story of the girl who went to Europe and the man who lost his life in the Alps. Everyone was pulling for both families to find peace and closure. It was three weeks after the shocking news that Tempest finally noticed her usual customers were putting the tragedy behind them. For a time, some were grieving more than she was. But she was finally instilled with a sense of normalcy when Charlie Farley made the decision that he could once again feel comfortable eating at the restaurant.

It was a fateful night when he came through the door. Tempest had not seen him since the funeral. He had not gotten over the loss of Harold at that time. It took him until now to begin to feel normal. Tempest dropped her tray and ran to the professor, who now looked a little more middle-aged than he really was. She hugged him, welcomed him and showed him to his regular booth.

Life has a funny way of working out and shortly after Charles Farley settled into his seat and began perusing the new menu, which included the Sunday hours, Marley Baxter entered the restaurant. She was there for take-out, having ordered two pizzas to go. She was planning on taking them home to share with Edward and the ravenous pizza eater he still called his girlfriend. When Marley saw Charles, she joined him for what she thought would be a quick stop.

Marley always had an attraction to the good looking man. Now she had another reason to seek his company. Tempest watched as she and Charles were starting what would become a very long conversation. When Tempest saw the intense nature of the discussion, the waitress brought over one of the pizzas and a pitcher of root beer, Charlie's favorite, and said, "It's on the house." Marley objected mildly saying, "I was supposed to bring this home to Edward." Tempest said, "Leave it to me." When she left the table she called Edward saying, "If you still want your two pizzas let me know. Your mother is busy. You will have to pick them up yourself."

Edward told his neighbor that he would come by to take one but that both pies would be excessive for just the two of them. Edward had taken a bit of a shine to Beth and was trying to cut down on her caloric intake. When they arrived at the store to pick up the pizzas, Edward saw that his mother was deep in dialog with Charles Farley. The vision conjured up thoughts of his position on the pecking order for Tempest. If Marley and Charles became an item and Caleb was taken out of the picture, Edward could still take the prize. In an effort to show Tempest what a caring boyfriend he could be, when Beth caterwauled for garlic knots he gladly added them to the order. He then decided that it made sense for them to repose at the

Anderson house for dinner. Leaving the Baxter domicile vacant would provide a venue for wherever his mother's discussion might lead. The actions were entirely consistent with the sociopath's end game.

Charles and Marley tied up booth number three all evening and Tempest made one of her tables available to her colleague to ensure he was not disadvantaged by the long stay couple. Tempest dropped by every so often to check on the pair but applied a very light touch so not to disrupt the conversation. She thought the world of Charles and had grown to have an enormous appreciation for her neighbor. If they had a chance together it would be a blessing. In Tempest's assessment, Harold would approve.

When the restaurant was getting ready to close Tempest had to fight with both of her friends and not allow them to pay the bill. When she said it was on her, she meant it. They thanked Tempest and left the eatery. As luck would have it, their cars were parked in the same direction and they walked together down the street into the darkness. They reached Marley's car first and Charles being the perfect gentleman opened and held the door for her. She stopped before entering the vehicle, looked into his eyes and said, "I really don't want to be alone tonight," and kissed him on the lips. After a long second kiss, Charles walked a few vehicles further, entered his car and followed Marley to the Baxter residence.

Clark walked Tempest home that evening. When they arrived, the waitress noticed Charlie Farley's car parked at the curb a few doors down. Charles knew that any one of the Arrcks would recognize his vehicle. In an effort to be discreet with his new found companion he took steps to maintain their privacy. Marley may have been a recent interest for Charles but Charles had been on Marley's radar for years. The older woman wrestled with the fact that she had strong feelings for him while Harold was still alive. But tonight, rather than wrestling with her feelings, she decided it was much better to be wrestling with her new found British gentleman.

Chapter Fifty Four: The Days Before

Marley and Charles became something of an item and although out of respect for Harold she wanted to keep the matter as discreet as possible, the news did trickle into the Arrck household. In recognition of the relationship, Tempest wanted the couple to be seated side by side at the reception's head table. Anyone who was not aware of the affair that had sprung up so rapidly would simply think they were paired because of their standing with the bride and groom. Marley and Charles would be happy to be together, making the event even more of a special occasion. Caleb and Tempest saw it as a win-win. Once again, it took Joan's persuasive powers to convince Diane Arrck that the idea made sense.

As the final days before the ceremony approached everything seemed to be lining up. Averton was buzzing with what Ashley Parker had spun as the wedding of the year in upstate New York. The once separated brainy beauty, is reunited with her star athlete. They were coming together after eighteen years as friends, to join forever in matrimony. The town could not have been celebrating a more fitting storyline. Holly Dane had created permanently linked circles as the wedding giveaway that was just right for the occasion. The only pothole in the fairytale road could come courtesy of Edward Jacobs. He had the results of the paternity test that indicated Tempest

Arrck was the daughter of Paul Baxter. He was ready to crater the festivities at the most decisive moment of the big day. As Saturday March twenty third approached, he could hardly contain his perverse enthusiasm.

The Thursday prior to the wedding, Noah and Tempest drove to the airport to meet Caleb. He would get married and be home for the Easter break. Then a week later, the attached man would travel back to Wisconsin. He would leave his wife and put their honeymoon on hold. This is the plan they signed up to and they were very happy with the present situation. When Caleb arrived he found Charles in the kitchen. Marley had not told Caleb about their relationship but Tempest had, thus making for a smooth transition. There was no need to tempt fate with any kind of blowup. Besides, the two men liked each other and for some reason Caleb liked Charles even more now that he was seeing his aunt.

When it came to executing their wedding plan there was no time to spare. Caleb had to proceed without delay to get the final fitting for his tuxedo. His best man would be Noah Arrck. Clark Arrck would be his groomsman. In deference to a request from his aunt, Edward would also join Caleb at the altar. The truth of the matter was, his best man was Tempest but she already had a role. Tempest's maid of honor would be her sister Joan. Her bridesmaids were Arlene Sharp, Carla Blount and Anne Nubbler. With two bridesmaids, Clark was double teamed. He was not at all complaining and was looking forward to escorting both Carla and Anne.

Friday at six o'clock, the wedding party and close family were directed to the church. Father Blakely would take the principals through a dry run of the proceedings. The rehearsal wouldn't take long. After the practice, a reception would be held for the wedding party. Tonight however, the guest list would be secretly expanded. Pudgy and Cameron Nubbler had organized an invitation only evening at the restaurant. The list was compiled by Joan, Arlene and Marley, without the knowledge of the bride and groom. Tempest and Caleb thought they were heading to a rehearsal dinner at the nearby country club. When Noah unexpectedly stopped his car in front of the restaurant he said, "Come on in, Cameron and Pudgy want to see you the night before the wedding." Five hours after seventy three close friends shouted, "SURPRISE!" the bride and groom were being driven home to prepare for their big day.

When Tempest laid her head on the pillow of the bed in the room she had slept in since she was a little girl, she knew it would be the last time she would do so as Tempest Arrck. Tomorrow she would be Tempest Baxter. But she had always been Tempest Baxter. Up the hallway, Diane Arrck sat in her dark bedroom holding the only remaining letter that contained the truth about what happened the morning of Tempest's and Caleb's birth. She would bring it the next day, in hopes that it would not have to see the light of day. Her motherly instinct told her that tomorrow would hold the highest probability for it ever to be put to use in defense of her honor and to protect her husband and the children from public ridicule. Once beyond this danger zone, the risk of the secret being revealed would be greatly diminished. But they all had to pass through the eye of one last storm. With undertakings the likes of Anne Nubbler's genetic inquiry in the rear view mirror, the chances of future discovery, once this day was over, were practically nil. She stood on the precipice of once and for all being delivered from the shame of the dirty little secret.

She carefully folded the envelope and placed it into the purse she would be carrying to the church. There was no chance on earth she would forget it, but its placement the night before gave her comfort that it was there. Her neighbor in the next house on Lincoln Avenue was also holding an envelope. He folded it and placed it in the inside pocket of his tuxedo jacket. The placement of the report offered him similar comfort.

Chapter Fifty Five: A Lifetime of Regret

At half past twelve the next day, all the key players packed into their cars in preparation for the one o'clock start. Marley and Charles were traveling together and responsible to get Caleb to the church on time. They took special care that he did not see his bride before the wedding. His best man would meet him at the house of worship after driving the bride's parents to the venue. Tempest and her bridesmaids, along with Clark, would be taking the limosine that Harold and Marley had arranged to carry them to and from their previously planned ceremony. Edward would be arriving at the church with Beth, who was now carrying an additional ten pounds. It looked good on her. She had been carb deficient for years and now with regular exposure to pasta and other Italian treats she had a healthy glow. Many men around town were beginning to take notice of her, much to the distress of Edward. It was now or never to make his final ill-conceived play for Tempest. The day of reckoning had come.

The central cast made their way to the church. The bride arrived and was promptly whisked to a room in the rear of the building. There she was attended to by her best friends and her sister. When Caleb arrived, he went into the other side of the structure. With the aid of the groomsmen, the attendees began filing into the church. It could easily be said that when the music began for the bridesmaid's procession that the place was packed. Caleb stood at the altar anxiously awaiting the arrival of his bride. The individual bridesmaids, in deliberate procession, approached the front of the church. Anne Nubbler looked especially delightful, prompting Noah to reconsider why he had bounded off of the porch for so many years. It was only fitting that there be a Blount represented in the wedding party. There was rarely a wedding held in town without at least one. There were more than a few times when both bride and groom were Blounts. When Joan made her way to the altar, it became clear that the only reason people had not been more considerate of her appearance was the woman in white, who still remained in the vestibule with her father.

When the organ shifted from light church music to the sounds of the familiar tune, everyone was waiting as Mark Arrck stood side by side with his daughter and they took their first step up the aisle. Every eye in the house was on the redheaded beauty. Everyone was thinking of what a lovely bride she made. Everyone that is except Edward, who tapped his breast pocket to be sure he had the report that was about to be made public.

Diane Arrck watched as her husband handed her daughter to Caleb. He gave her a light kiss in the process. The mother of the bride had a tear running down her cheek. Whether it was for more traditional reasons or just out of relief that this day had finally come was difficult to determine. Tempest then joined Caleb. She took a good long look at her groom as they stood before Father Blakely, who welcomed everyone to the ceremony.

The center of attention had always been a stickler for precision. She had often wondered why during some weddings the obligatory question as to whether anyone had good reason for the couple not to be married was asked after some of the preliminaries had already been completed. In her organized and orderly mind this formality should be cared for at the very start. When the priest welcomed the good people of Averton to the church that day, the first question he asked was, "If there is any man or woman who has good reason that this couple should not be joined together in holy matrimony, speak now or forever hold your peace."

When Anne Nubbler heard the words she thought of all the relationships that her study had affected. For many of the impacted couples that information came well after this routine question was asked and went unanswered. She figured the, "forever holding your peace language", was intended to be merely ceremonial in nature. Anne, along with everyone else in the church, was shocked however, when Edward stepped forward and said, "I have good reason, Father."

If you could have caught the expression on almost anyone's face it would have been the picture of surprise. There were at least five people with a different facial expression. Caleb had the look of anger. He could have strangled his cousin given half a chance. Tempest had the look of resigned expectation.

In her math-oriented mind, she always knew someday there would be an interruption in a wedding. Having been to so many uninterrupted ceremonies, she knew the odds were growing and the math just worked against her. Joan Arrck had a questioning look. The maid of honor knew this was a danger zone but had no idea how Edward would have come into any knowledge that might embolden him to speak. Mark Arrck was more puzzled than surprised. Diane Arrck most assuredly had the look of pain and of being found out. She opened her purse to be sure the letter containing the dirty little secret was close at hand.

Noah had to restrain Caleb as the priest, who thought there was a first time for everything, calmly looked at Edward and said to the protestor, "What say you young man?" Under his breath he added, "It had better be good." Edward calmly pulled the report from his breast pocket announcing that he had conclusive evidence that Tempest Arrck was the daughter of Paul Baxter.

An audible gasp came from the collective audience. Diane's heart beat faster and her mind began to spin. Edward had only half of the information. It implicated her in the infidelity that she had hoped to protect herself from with her letter. The priest looked over the report and announced to the audience, "This document does say that Tempest Arrck and Paul Baxter share the same DNA." He looked over at Edward and said, "Son, why didn't you bring this information to my attention sooner?" Caleb, still being restrained by Noah and Clark shouted, "Because he's a moron!"

Diane was nervously fumbling through her purse to retrieve the letter that would now see the light through stained glass windows. The unwilling conspirator had feared this moment for the previous fifteen years. She kicked herself for choosing the path of secrecy, only to have the lie surface at this worst possible moment. Diane knew she was prepared to deal with the most devastating fallout. Her only questions now were, how far under the bus would she have to throw Ruth Baxter and what would it mean to Caleb? If she had been a deceased party to the letter, how would the living depict her involvement? She cursed herself for not considering and preparing for all the options that might have presented themselves at this critical time. The priest looked at Caleb and asked him, "Why would you say that son? Your cousin is just trying to clear his conscience. Granted, he did not have to do it in such a theatrical style." Caleb began to speak but before he could say the words, a rather small, older, plainly dressed woman, standing in the aisle of the church said in a very loud voice, "I will tell you why!"

It was odd in this town where everyone knew just about everyone else that the person standing in the aisle was not immediately recognized by most of the gathered crowd. The woman slowly approached the altar. Stopping a few feet away, she began her confession. The admission was her reason for leaving Averton in shame many years before. "Eighteen years ago, I helped that girl's father and mother do a terrible thing." She paused, then continued, "He wanted a son and his wife couldn't deliver him one, so they plotted to increase the odds of having a boy by giving birth on the very same day as their neighbor. They figured at least one of the families would be having a boy. The Arrcks did have a boy and the Baxters had a little girl."

The people in the church were now hanging on the woman's every word. "I was working in the delivery room that day. Mr. Baxter came into the ward and first he tried to convince me that I had made a mistake and that the Baxter baby was a boy. But I would not make a mistake like that and told him so. He then offered me money, saying Mrs. Arrck was not aware of the sex of her child, since she had been heavily sedated at the time of the birth. He said no one would know the truth." Then as she fell to her knees breaking down in front of the entire church she cried, "And I took the money. God forgive me, I took the money!"

Caleb, who by that time had been released by Noah, then rushed to the woman's side. He stood by her as she kneeled on the floor and said, "But wait there is much more." Tempest came down from the altar and stood next to her husband to be saying, "Yes, there is so much more." Diane, who was now more of a spectator than a contributor, watched as the scene played out before the spellbound crowd.

Tempest lowered her hand to raise the nurse to her feet, helping her straighten the dress that had become wrinkled in the process. The crowd was silent as Tempest announced, "When we were sixteen, this woman came to us one afternoon while we were walking home from school. She told us there was something important we needed to know and the two of us were now old enough to understand. Although initially cautious, she was so intent on delivering her message we listened to her. She said based on our actions we had clearly demonstrated to her the maturity to handle the information." Tempest paused, then went on. "This woman explained how important legacy and ancestry was and why some people were willing to do terrible things to maintain their blood line. She told us that we had been switched at birth by my parents, Ruth and Paul Baxter. They wanted a son and I wasn't a boy. They took Caleb as their own and raised this fine young man that I am marrying here today." Tempest glanced at Caleb and continued, "My mother, Diane Arrck, knew this when I was three." Another gasp ran through the crowd as Diane nearly fainted. "She decided to protect us from the scrutiny that would certainly follow. She would keep silent and allow the secret to continue, carrying with her a lifetime of burden. She knew Caleb was her son and even though she truly loved me, my mother was aware I was not her natural daughter."

The bride continued, "Today, is an even more joyous event than anyone could ever have imagine. With most weddings the parents of the bride and groom are blessed by adding a son or a daughter based on the law. Today, Diane and Mark Arrck get their son back and Paul and Ruth Baxter can rest knowing that their daughter has been returned." With Tempest's conciliatory words ringing through the church, the dirty little secret had been vanquished and no one had to be thrown under the bus. Edward did decide it made sense for him to leave the altar and took up a defensive posture in the rear of the building. Tempest knew he was in possession of some kind of report. Arlene Sharp's Mom had a relative who worked at the lab. She tipped Tempest off to the request years earlier. Tempest just wasn't sure of the diagnostic scope, the result or where it would emerge. She was surprised but not shocked that he would choose to drop this hammer at the wedding. Later when reflecting on Edward's past indiscretions, she figured it was par for the course, although it demonstrated incalculable disregard for his cousin.

Caleb helped the nurse back to her seat with the assistance of Butchy Wagner. As the bride and groom walked back up to the altar, Tempest stopped at the first pew where Diane and Mark Arrck were standing. She had pulled her mother from the darkness of the dirty little secret. Diane's eyes were red with tears. Tempest leaned over and hugged her mother and said, "Thank you Mom for protecting us." She said to her father, "Sorry Dad for keeping this from you." Mark Arrck although due an apology, was likely the least fazed by the announcement. In his mind, which thought in terms of pairs that belonged together, he had always thought of his daughter and son as one.

Once she had addressed the man and woman who raised her, Tempest returned to Caleb's side and walked up to the altar. When the wedding participants, sans Edward, had returned to their places and the crowd had settled down, Father Blakely, who had been a fixture in Averton over the past thirty years and had been known to be a bit of showman, then raised his voice and said, "Anyone else?" The entire church burst into laughter. It was the most appropriate comment anyone could have made at the time. The truly joyous celebration, for the first time without any unknown variables hanging over their young lives, was about to begin.

Chapter Fifty Six: Words from Beyond

The ceremony was back on track and moving along in standard fashion until Father Blakely came to the point where the bride and groom were asked to commit their lives to one another. The priest started, "Do you Tempest", and then hesitated saying, "Baxter, take this man to be your lawfully wedded husband? To have and to hold from this day forward, in sickness and in health, until death do you part?" The response to the first and only question in the life of Tempest Baxter was answered in a most precise fashion, "I do." The same question went to Caleb Arrck and he also replied precisely in the affirmative. The officiant of the wedding then said, "I now pronounce you husband and wife, you may kiss the bride." The crowd let out a huge cheer. While the rest were reveling, Edward skulked out of the door. He would wait outside for Beth.

With the most incalculable of odds, Tempest Arrck had entered the church, been married and re-emerged as the immutable Tempest Arrck. Her inevitable marriage to Caleb was not the elusive nth digit and last episode that would secure her rationality. Although she loved him and they were destined to be together, their union was not the final chapter that would bring her closure. Just as Dr. Abler had theorized, similar to her longtime nemesis pi, there was no nth episode.

Her closure came through clarifying her true identity. She could finally be, who she really was. The prior evening was not the last night she would lay her head on the pillow as Tempest Arrck. The well above average, unshakable woman from the now slightly larger than above average town, would always be Tempest Arrck.

The reception that evening was held at a fancy restaurant just outside of Averton. There was more than enough for everyone to talk about at the party. A common theme amongst most was that they suspected something was amiss given the resemblance of Tempest and Marley. It was very clear to longtime Avertonians, that the bride and her neighbor shared the "Baxter nose". The fact that they were the only two redheads in town, might have also been a clue to those suffering from sub-par deductive powers. Caleb Arrck's sports ability now also made perfect sense as Mark Arrck had been the last man in Averton to achieve the lofty levels of achievement that his son had accomplished. There was such a buzz from the enormous twist that had occurred during the ceremony that nobody really paid much attention to the fact that Marley and Charles were treating each other more as a caring couple, than as two people randomly paired by the whim of a wedding planner.

Edward had convinced Beth that his actions were pivotal in ensuring the newest Arrck couple began their life together on the most solid of foundations. She accepted that premise but was sharp enough to realize that the outcome was not what he intended. Rather than making a scene and missing out on the carb-filled wedding fare, she waited until the following week to dump the conniving rat.

When the time came for the coordinator of the event to announce the arrival of the bride and groom, there was enormous anticipation in the room. The bridesmaids and groomsmen were first to be introduced. Anne Nubbler was noticeably absent when her name was called, providing the genesis for a murmur from the audience. The mystery was solved when Noah was announced and she came into the room on his arm to the cheers of the crowd. The happiest spectator was Wilma Nubbler, who would no longer have to listen to her sister go on and on about Noah, on those many lonely nights they shared out in "the sticks".

Joan Arrck was the last in the wedding party to be introduced. Realizing that Tempest was now officially off the market, the single young men in the audience would now turn their attention towards her. Her wisdom, martial arts chiseled body and combination of fine ancestral attributes made her a worthy target for those looking to land the perfect mate.

The drummer began the anticipatory drumroll that would welcome the newlyweds into the room. It was a special moment and an anticlimactic one at the same time. Anyone who had not attended the ceremony and had not spoken to a soul at the reception might have been totally perplexed when the announcement was made, "Ladies and gentlemen, let me have the honor to be the first to announce the arrival of Mr. Caleb Arrck and Mrs. Tempest Arrck.

When the newlyweds entered the room, the crowd stood and applauded for the young couple that everyone always knew would be together. The most remarkable aspect of the Avertonians prophecy was that the town was so certain of their futures and yet no one even knew who they actually were. There were many times when their inquiring minds threatened to expose the secret, but they had never quite come close enough. In the final analysis it was a happy ending. A result that was certainly worth at least one more recollection of the phrase, "Goody, goody time for phonics".

Later that evening, when the party became much more relaxed, Diane had a private moment with her daughter, who was now her daughter-in-law. The older woman looked at the young lady she had raised as her own and was proud of what she had become. Tempest knew there was one question that she was going to have to face before the end of the night. She had long been ready for the inquiry that was on its way.

Diane Arrck stood before her daughter and looking into the green eyes she had gazed into for the previous eighteen years asked, "Why didn't you tell me that you knew?" After a long pause, the girl who had a way of seeing things differently than everyone else said simply, "Since I was sure you had to know, I wanted to protect you. Just like you were protecting us."

For years Tempest had been ready to provide this very simple answer. But had she chosen instead to share her true rationale for not confronting the secret, it would closely match the words Paul Baxter used to support the deception fifteen years earlier. "Mom, before telling anyone I knew, even you, I realized that my life fell further out of my control once I did. My search for the truth was determined by the path you chose for all of us." Diane's gut wrenching choice to let the dirty little secret stand was at the root of what drove the behaviors that shaped Tempest into the woman she had become today.

Her obsession with math was a way of striking out against anything else in her world that didn't quite add up. The confrontation with the nature of pi was an outlet to bring rationality to an otherwise irrational existence. Her life bred a textbook storm. One that looked to lash out against any imprecision and detest the close enough. She and Caleb were close enough but the fact that they were in the wrong houses, with the wrong families, was a constant source of incalculable tension in her young mind. She could not resolve that condition and as a result, created other conflicts she could immerse herself in with hopes of finding alternate truths.

Tempest had been piecing together the puzzle for years. The visit from the nurse provided insight regarding motive but the main message was not news to the astute woman. She had already figured out she wasn't the natural daughter of Diane and Mark Arrck. She recognized the contradictions in her life at a very young age. The evolving Baxter feature, that was as plain as the nose on her face, was an early indicator and a constant reminder to support her hypothesis. The germ that triggered "the cough", exploiting the common denominator in Ruth's and Tempest's genetic design, was growing evidence of her true hereditary roadmap. If she hadn't been all but certain before Marley's arrival, the appearance of her more mature look-alike, with the fiery red hair, confirmed her lifelong suspicion. She deduced the swap given that she and Caleb were born on the same day, at the same time, in the same hospital. Caleb's sports ability and his head down unassuming approach to life, mirroring that of Mark Arrck, was just one more indication of their true origins.

Rather than sharing these thoughts with Diane, the now accurately designated woman let her simple concise answer stand on its own. She was completely satisfied that less was indeed more.

The newest Mrs. Arrck hugged Mrs. Diane Arrck. She hoped that the woman who raised her would come to understand the immeasurable positive impact she had on her life. In return, the girl she loved, carried Diane and her unknowing husband through uncertain times. She shielded them against the irrational nature of public opinion. She protected all three conspirators from the shame of being found out that they had orchestrated an unforgivable lie. Then today, similar to the red flag at the football game and the solution at the quiz show, through some inconceivable method, without the assistance of some established formula, the calculating young woman orchestrated the improbable solution that finally delivered everyone involved to complete safety. Bringing the ultimate relief that Diane Arrck was so desperately seeking.

When the party began to wind down. Marley, who had already done so much for her look-alike niece, approached the newlyweds who were standing with Joan and Charles. She had been absent for a few moments. When she returned there was redness in her eyes. She was holding an envelope. Marley stopped in front of Tempest and said, "I wasn't sure whether I was going to give this to you. It was in his desk. He sat down and wrote it after we came home on Christmas Eve, the night you and Caleb were engaged. He was laughing the entire time. Harold would have wanted you to have it." Marley handed the letter to Tempest. On the envelope in Harold Zurck's hand was written, "To be presented to my friend Tempest Arrck on the day of her wedding." She repeated the words on the envelope aloud, then opened the letter and began reading the contents for the group.

"Tempest, you are a most amazing person. Your desire to find the truth in everything is an attribute that we all should hold dearly. You have taught me more than I could have ever taught you."

"Most people realize it is a risky proposition to set your mind on a new math adventure. Hopefully, I am far away when you read this and begin to ponder its implications. It is my gift to you for being such a strong and positive influence on me and all of those around you. Now that you have helped the mathematics community turn its sights on understanding the mystery of pi, here is a very famous riddle with roots dating back centuries. It should keep your mind busy for a while."

Tempest paused and looked up. Charles said, "Go on sweetheart, I can't wait to hear what he had in mind for you."

She continued, "Here is the riddle. On a cold snowy night, three men enter a hotel together. They try to book separate rooms but are advised by the hotel clerk that the inn is nearly full and that there is only one room available. The men need a place to stay. They agree to share the room. When asked the price, the clerk quotes thirty dollars. Each man pays ten dollars and begins up the stairs. The manager overhears the transaction and she asks the clerk, "How much did you charge for the room?" The clerk replies, "Thirty dollars." The manager advises the clerk, "That is a twenty five dollar room. We owe those men five dollars.""

Tempest turned the paper over but it was blank. She then flipped the page back but she had not missed any of the text. Harold had not finished the riddle. Marley had sealed the contents, thinking he had completed the brainteaser. Tempest was already deep in thought and muttering, "What was the challenge? What was the rest of the puzzle? What am I missing?" Joan looked at Charles and said, "Ok friends, here we go again."

The riddle was not complete. Harold's only oversight had not been the failure to complete the puzzle. It was his stated desire to be far away from her when she read it. He could not have been closer to his former student if he tried. Because as she read the message, the fond memory of Harold Zurck was gently resting deep within in her heart.

Chapter Fifty Seven: Where Did the Dollar Go?

The following fall Tempest decided that her education would best be pursued in the Midwest. She enrolled in a small college near where Caleb studied. Husband and wife were within range to be considered close enough for the three remaining years of their undergraduate education. Tempest earned her degree in theoretical mathematics and Caleb fought through four years to become a chemical engineer. Getting his left knee wrapped around his head while returning a punt, during the opening game of his junior season, left more time to study than he might have otherwise expected. The couple came to love the Midwest and after earning multiple graduate degrees, lived in that part of the country where they both distinguished themselves in their fields.

When the couple decided it was time to start a family, they could think of no better place to do so than Averton. Upon making the announcement that they were moving back home, Diane and Mark Arrck as well as their neighbors Charles and Marley Farley could not have been happier. Anne Arrck, who now had a little girl showing signs of sporting her own "Nubbler face", was also thrilled her friend would be returning. So was her husband. On the day Noah proposed, as a symbol of his love, he replaced the "Nubbler bush" that died in the aftermath of the "Great Thanksgiving Snowfall".

Not long after the Arrcks returned to Averton, the couple found themselves, as planned, in a delivery room at Averton hospital. Tempest had just given birth to twins. Tempest did not want to know the sexes of the two children prior to their birth and as a result the names to be given were still undecided. There was a great deal of anticipation given to name selection. As most were aware, strong naming traditions had always carried immense significance for the Arrcks.

Once the deliveries were complete and the mother was resting comfortably, the new father stepped out of his wife's room and was saying a silent prayer, thanking God that the children were both healthy. One was a redheaded boy, the other a girl with green eyes and bald as a cue ball. As Caleb finished giving thanks he heard Tempest saying in a raised voice, "Where did the dollar go? Where did the dollar go?" Caleb didn't know what was going on with his wife and he rushed back, stopping dead in the center of the room. His heart was pounding. Tempest looked at him with a gleam in her eye and said, "Listen to this."

She began, "The hotel manager says they need to give the five dollars back to the three men or they will be overcharged. She tells the bellhop to take the money to the men in their room. On the way the bellhop thinks, they can't split five dollars evenly among three, so he will take two for myself. He puts the two dollars in his pocket. After all, the guests weren't expecting anything and returning three dollars would make them just as happy as five." Caleb stood spellbound as he watched his wife's mind cranking out the scenario she had been thinking about quietly for years. As she rattled off the riddle, the drugs that had been administered were beginning to retake their toll. "When the bellhop gets to the room he gives each of the men a dollar. Now the men each paid nine dollars. That is a total of twenty seven. The bell hop has two. That makes it twenty nine." Then almost as though she was hit by a brick, her eyes closed and she went fast to sleep.

Caleb was mildly shocked and said to himself, "Wow, it would appear she just figured out the rest of Harold's riddle." If his wife, who had just given birth to twins and delivered a math riddle of equally difficult proportions, had still been awake she would have said, "I haven't solved anything. All I did was figure out the problem." Caleb shook his head as he gazed at the spent woman and said under his breathe, repeating Joan's prophetic comment, "Ok, here we go again." Later that evening she finally awoke. She attributed the insight to spiked cognitive ability coincident with the intensity of the incalculable pain associated with childbirth.

It was indeed a "here we go again" moment and maybe even cause for "Goody, goody time for phonics" in more ways than one. The Arrcks were beginning a new family in Averton, which was now a much more than slightly above average sized town. When names were finally decided, they determined that their son would be named Baxter Arrck. There was too much debate over the middle name of Paul, Mark or Harold and that decision was deferred for a future date. The young girl would be named Ruth Diane Arrck. If they had another girl they considered giving her the middle name Marley but her first name would be Tempest.

Paul and Ruth Baxter would have both been pleased that the family name had lived on, although as a given name and not a surname. There was no getting around the fact that Paul's lineage did carry forward in the two newly arrived Arrck children. In fact, the first observation made by recently elected mayor Carla Blount, who owed her victory to some very inside information about many of the long-term Averton residents was, "Oh look Tempest, your parents would have been so very happy. Both Ruth and Baxter are already showing clear signs of the "Baxter nose"."

The sound alike, double labelling of Baxter Arrck, with the "Baxter nose" might lead to uncalculated consequences that could affect the young man's upbringing. It was at that point that Tempest and Caleb realized they needed to make a definitive decision to figuratively bury another Baxter. With the middle name Harold officially in place, his true identity would become obscure but nowhere near what anyone could describe as a secret, no less a dirty little one. From that point onward, around Averton and the loosely defined area still known by many as upstate New York, the boy would be named B. Harold Arrck. He would come to be called by friends and family as simply Harry. Tempest Arrck's first son would be Harry Arrck. He and his twin sister Ruth Arrck, would one day have three younger siblings named Barry, Larry and Tempest.

417

Young Tempest was herself a handful and a bit of a corker. Amongst her various quirks was a struggle to pronounce her older brother's name. As a toddler, she usually called him Baba. Musical talent apparently skips a generation and when the children grew to become teens, for a short time, the five Arrck's formed a band. The name was Baba and the BLTs. Ruth's name was purposely left out of the title in order to avoid flirting with trademark infringement. It was however, blended into the bass drum logo, in the form of a small tooth-like figure, courtesy of the good people at The Parker Boutique. Given Ruth's well-documented obsession with pi, and young Tempest's not so surprising fixation with all things round it was only fitting that their favorite group was "The Bangles". Their favorite cover song, "Walk like an Egyptian".

Recorded on this fifteenth hour of March fourteen, Two Thousand and Fifty Five.

In loving memory of my best friend Tempest Arrck. May she forever find the precise answers she is looking for.

Former United States Agriculture and Nutrition Secretary, Wilma Anne Nubbler-Blount.

At 5555 Averton Way, Room K, Arrckville, New York, USA.

A Pi/4 Nth Digit recording.

About the Author

I dream one day to be sitting with my wife Novita in an airport waiting area and hearing a mother say to her young daughter, "Tempest, don't go too far, the plane will be boarding soon." I look forward to the opportunity to ask her, "Tempest, what a lovely name. How did you get that name?" In my musing the young girl would look at me and say, "My mother found it in a book. She really loves the book and read the parts to me that I am old enough to understand." My next question for Tempest would then be, "What did you think of the book?" If I continued without being awakened she would reply, "I really loved it. In fact, it's my favorite and I can't wait to be old enough to read it all." Finally, if our conversation continued uninterrupted, when asked why it was her favorite she would answer, "Because it taught me to really love math. It is my favorite subject. When my class gets to that subject I always say, Goody, goody time for math!"

ADDITIONAL TITLES BY JOHN LACK

THE OTHER SIDE OF THE KNEELER

SCARCITY BITES

HEIDING FORTUNES, FEINDING TRUTHS